SILAS

MORLOCK

Mark Cantrell

Inspired Quill Publishing

Published by Inspired Quill: October 2013

First Edition

Silas Morlock © 2013 by Mark Cantrell
Contact the author through their website:
www.markcantrell.co.uk

Chief Editor: Peter Stewart
Cover Design by: Lucy Lindsell

Paperback ISBN: 978-1-908600-14-1
eBook ISBN: 978-1-908600-15-8
Print Edition

Printed in the United Kingdom
1 2 3 4 5 6 7 8 9 10

Inspired Quill Publishing, UK
Business Reg. No. 7592847
http://www.inspired-quill.com

Acknowledgements

Quite a few years have passed since I first became acquainted with Silas Morlock in a Bradford drinking den. Pint in hand, he caught me unawares, and the seeds of the story slipped down my neck with the last dregs of my drink. Ever since, he's always been there, in the background, urging the novel towards completion.

Sanity sometimes beckoned, but friends were on hand to ensure the occasional dousing of common sense didn't quite dampen my spirits. Over the years there have been many. So, without further ado, here's the roll of honour.

Thanks must go everyone at Interchange (Bradford Writers' Network): they know who they are, but I think special mention should go to Joe, Phil, Ruth, Bruce, Sheila, Howard, and Kevin for their attentive support and encouragement during read-rounds at the group.

Special mention must surely also go the bar staff at The Priestley Centre for Arts (as it was then known) for keeping us supplied with beer and good humour at our weekly sessions.

On a similar note, let me pay thanks to everyone at the Love Apple Cafe, Bradford, (one of my regular writing dens of old, now sadly closed), where I thrashed out a huge chunk of the novel. In this case it wasn't the beer, but the coffee, that kept my creative engine revving furiously at the keyboard.

To Ann M go special thanks for her enthusiastic support and encouragement, and the critical eye she cast over my drafts to ensure I never took the easy option.

Lastly, a big thank you to the crew at Inspired Quill: Sara, the indomitable master and commander of the venture, for giving Silas Morlock its moment in the limelight, and Peter and Austin for their excellent and insightful work editing the manuscript into shape.

None of this would have been possible without your efforts, guys, so this author is much obliged.

"The Mind is not a vessel to be filled, but a fire to be kindled."
Plutarch

"I am the Alpha and Omega, the Beginning and the End; what is, what was, and what is to come."
The Essene Book of Revelations

"If you gaze for long into an abyss, the abyss gazes also into you."
Friedrich Nietzsche

"We are a way for the cosmos to know itself."
Carl Sagan

Prologue

From A Shade
Primordial

MY name is Elzevir. That's not my real name of course. You don't need to know who I was; that's not important, only what I have become since they started burning matters now.

Madness, it is. Utter madness, but you cannot reason with true believers, especially when they are backed by the powerful. And people have come to believe so hard that our works are the source of the sickness.

The HazMat teams have been busy, scouring and torching our precious legacy; it's all become so indiscriminate. The police are mobilised against us, too: hard to know who to trust these days.

Still, there are a few of us now; we're beginning to get organised. We've found places where we can hide, gather, build a safe haven to survive for better times. We're taking what we can underground; there's a warren of tunnels and forgotten structures beneath London. We can hold out down there; we must hold out.

Let the politicians get into bed with this MorTek Corporation, this 'Conqueror of Silicon Valley' as they're calling it. Why not, they might think, as its rapacious appetite acquires so many of the battered corporates that managed to survive the war's calamity, but what else—who else—does it seek to conquer away from the public gaze?

From their perspective, this emergent superpower must seem a Godsend to help stitch our world back together, but it will be a dark and sterile place without the precious seeds of our growing knowledge of what we now seek to save.

So, let them build their new city. Let them regenerate the shattered skyline with MorTek's bio-engineered towers and sweet promises. Yes, those towers already maturing are breath-taking to behold; maybe as they multiply they will cleanse our air and harness the sun's power, as we are told, to heal the Earth's hurts and deliver us to salvation. Maybe they'll do all that, but to my mind there is something about them that is not quite... right.

No matter. We head into exile. We will build our own citadel beneath their feet and wait for the promise to fail. As it will, I am sure, and allow us to someday return humanity's birthright back into the light of day.

My guess—no, my hope—is you're reading this long after I am gone (of old age preferably). You're living in the better times we're holding out for, and curious about these strange days.

Good. So let me share this with you. It was given to me by a man who claimed to have salvaged it from the ruins of the British Library, a few pages of an otherwise lost typescript, as seemingly crazy as the man who delivered them into my care.

On first reading it, I confess, I considered it meta-physical mumbo-jumbo, but he seemed to believe it important to our cause. Since then, it's come to haunt my thoughts. The more I read it, the more I wonder if he wasn't right. Perhaps I too am becoming a believer...

"SOME say that the Universe will end in eternal darkness. Not this universe of quarks and neutrinos and photons and all the other cosmic components that curdled into stars and planets and living things, but the other universe: the one that knows itself.

"So it shall. Some day. And so it began. With a darkness that had nothing to do with a deficiency of photons, with a shade unknown and unknowable until something emerged to divine its creation.

"Such a time arrived late in the 'pre-history' of the Universe, when a strange bipedal creature covered in matted hair shivered under a star-filled night.

"This organism knew nothing, then, of the minor world it occupied, of its place in a mediocre galaxy orbiting an insignificant star, but here in this stellar backwater it was about to do something profound.

"It struck two flints together.

"The sparks ignited a fire. Not merely the kind that consumes kindling, but the kind that unravels reality. For in those sparks, <u>Mind</u> was born. And with it, crawling from the primordial shade emerged <u>Soul</u>. The Universe awoke and became aware of its existence.

"Something else, however, was born with that primeval spark. The antithesis of Mind. The equal and opposing force. The 'Siamese Sentience' forever bound to its twin by the umbilical cord of the Soul.

"It stirred in the heart of darkness and was drawn to its coruscating sibling. Yet it could never breach the physical and metaphysical event horizon that was the mental light.

"So it watched from the shadows.

"Watched. And waited.

"Patience eternal.

"That is when the Dark came alive in the primordial ocean of potential: when Evil, as some call it, was born to existence.

"So Mankind took to the fireside, for warmth, to cook, for the light to see, for protection from predators. Yes, they took to the hearth for all the mundane treasures of fire, but also for so much more.

"Flame danced as the physical metaphor for another firelight shared around the hearths: the flickering tongues of human stories. The fires of spiritual awareness, bright against the dark skies of death, grew the brighter for every re-telling, to repel the lurking shade of evil.

"Yet even the brightest flames perish when left untended..."

FIRE, as we know to our cost, burns to destruction; the flames can also illuminate. The choice is ours. But for those few of us who seek haven underground, Humanity has chosen the fire that burns, and so our story nears its end.

Unless... unless the madness ends first, but I cannot see tomorrow, only rue the present and hope hindsight offers you the understanding that evades me today. Until then, we can only do what we must to survive.

My name is Elzevir, and I am a dead man, as are all those who illuminated the path before, but as I head into the valley of the shadow of death, I shall fear no evil, only embrace the light.

It really doesn't matter who I was—only that I carried the torch. Yes, I believe.

The First Folio

And In The Darkness, Find Them

CAXTON was late.

Only, Caxton was *never* late.

Still, there was always a first time. Adam tried to stay calm amidst the maelstrom of anxiety. Anything might have upset the man's punctuality. This was *Terapolis*, after all. He just didn't need this shit. Not here. Not now. Not *ever*. Not with the *hunger* making macramé out of his guts.

The brutal music pummelled his skull. He took another shot of cheap vodka and tried to look casual, just another patron smouldering at the sight of feminine meat writhing to the rhythm. On any other night, for sure; the sybaritic display of lithe bodies was one of the few genuine attractions to the place, but tonight he wasn't up to that game. Not even sexual frenzy held any favours.

He needed another release; one only the *Man* could provide. Desperate was not the word. Still worse was the paranoia chaser: the Constabulary might be here already. Mingled with the crowd. Watching. Waiting for the moment.

The bastards liked to draw it out, he knew. Hit on the junkie just as the pain really started to maul.

He shivered. Took another hit of booze. The glass was nearly empty now. He didn't relish the thought of squeezing to the bar for another, so he decided to nurse it and lurk in the shadows, just like he was taught.

The place was dark and loud: the way Caxton liked it. But there were still too many eyes for Adam's liking. Any of them might belong to the Cons or their informants.

"*Relax*." Caxton's voice was strangely soothing, even as a memory. "Always do business in a crowd. The herd is a good hiding place. Among the *Gestalt[1]* fodder nobody cares. I could gut you here and nobody would flick an eyebrow. That's the beauty of this place."

Beauty. Not the word he'd use. The place was a basement bar somewhere off the edge of *Locus Prime[2]* in a pocket of Old City that somehow managed to survive beneath the towers of *Terapolis*. Hundreds like it existed in *L-Prime* alone, but this one just happened to be Caxton's. Not that he owned the place; it was just one of his regular haunts. A place for business. Nothing more.

Adam found it easy to imagine nobody owned this place. The people turned up, the booze materialised from the shadows and the bouncers coalesced from the garbage in

---

[1] The Miracle of *MorTek*, Morlock's Gift, this esoteric technology has been called many things since its inception, but its fundamental nature has ever remained a mystery. That it grants release from worldly woes is beyond doubt, proven by its position at the heart of human fulfilment. In time, it promises to unleash humanity's deepest, most cherished desire. For some, that is believed to be eternal nirvana; for others, the ascendance of the species to a god-like existence beyond the physical plane.

[2] An administrative district in *Terapolis* is called a 'Locus'. The primary district, *Locus Prime*, is commonly shortened to 'L-Prime'.

the alley. If the bar had a name then nobody bothered to remember. The place was nothing but raucous amnesia. A place for the unknown and the lonely, the silent wanderers lost in the shade of the night, a haven of chemical cocktails, noise and sex. Here's where the friendless and alone gathered to silence the pleading voices of self-perception, the *Gestalt*-exiles unable to afford a night's trip in a G-Spot.[3] They came to lose themselves in the only way left.

So what did that make him? No different. Except what he craved was better than anything he might know in the *Gestalt*. Far better. But he needed Caxton for its deliverance. Sometime, like *now*.

He scanned the place for any sign of the man. That's how his roving eyes located the woman. She was sat on a stool by the bar, where her alien calm in the midst of this meat maelstrom captivated his vision. The breath caught in his throat. Her allure stroked his cravings into temporary submission; she was the mongoose, mesmerising his snake until it raised its cowled head to the rhythm of the mood. Adam let his eyes linger. A hormone-chaser to let his mind idle off the smouldering ember of addiction and – who knows – one score to follow the other just to complete the night. She was certainly worth it. Her dark hair, cut in a razor bob, framed a slim face that glowed pale milk in the shadows of the bar. Then she smiled and completed the vision. A flash of moonlight silver gleamed an invitation from her opal teeth.

---

[3] In *Terapolitan* street parlance, this refers to a *Gestalt* Node, a facility for accessing the *Gestalt*.

A large man with a beard appeared from the herd and began to mock his fantasy. The intruder slipped an arm around her waist and leaned in to suck on the nape of her neck. The other hand reached to grope her breasts while his crotch rubbed against her hip. More meat.

Adam turned away. His interest sagged; the cravings peaked to offer no solace. The vodka burned in his belly like disappointment, and left an oily taste in the back of his throat. The sweat on his forehead no longer had anything to do with the heat and perspiration of crowded lechery. He gritted his teeth and cursed. The roller-coaster ride of addiction burned towards another peak of pain.

"Come *on*!" Tight-lipped. Face ache.

His insides writhed like a nest of angry snakes. Each bombastic thud of the bass was a grenade making war inside his skull. The high-pitched caterwauls were strummed from his taut nerves. He needed his fix fast. Caxton or the *Gestalt*. One or the other, if he was to get on with living in this cauldron's brew of a city.

The woman at the bar again. She stared with the tight beam focus of an accomplished sexual predator. He felt himself stripped naked to his very soul. Something about her was familiar, something that provoked a nagging unease. He'd seen her around, a face in the crowds, seen in too many places for coincidence. Or was that just paranoia? She knew him. She *knew* what he was. What he *needed*. Exposed, he couldn't move. She had him and all he could do was wait for her to spill his shame.

Then she giggled. Her head fell against her consort's shoulder. The dread connection snapped as her companion's hand groped. The woman's mouth opened with a silent shriek of pleasure.

So normal, until *things* tumbled from her gaping mouth. Maggots. Rotten, *disgusting* maggots. Adam blinked, felt his stomach flip. He swallowed the nausea even as the maggots were regurgitated down the man's back. They wriggled and bounced over the floor, over and under people's feet to be trodden into sticky mulch.

Revolted, he looked away. Shock and fright pummelled his cravings into acquiescence, but the phantasms of pain and paranoia hadn't finished. Not by a long way. *They* were back. Death-heads grinned at him from the dance floor, from the nooks and crannies, the tables and seats, from the crowds filling the empty spaces. Flashing in stop motion in the strobes, the dead watched – and laughed at his unfulfilled cravings.

"*Join... usss! Joooiiinnn... uuusss! Beee... onnne... wiiith... usssss!*"

The words – rasping, laboured – made a dreadful chorus of whispers audible over the musical tempest. He was losing it. He had to be *fucking* losing it. The chant filled his ears; the dead writhed and danced and pointed and laughed until his head began to spin.

The glass cracked like a gunshot when he slammed it down. He groaned and put his face in his hands. The room started to spin. He was definitely losing it. Too much alcohol shit and the taught *need* raging berserk in his brain.

"CAXTON! Where the *fuck* are YOU?"

He hadn't realised he'd shouted. He looked up in alarm. A couple of dead-eyed glances from nearer patrons, but that was all. He was still background. Flesh in a flesh bar, nothing more. No laughing damned. No corpses. Except those of a chemical kind. A trickle of sweat tickled his upper lip and he wiped it away.

"Keep your fucking voice down!"

Shock. Pleasure. Relief. They washed through his nervous system like a purgative. Caxton squeezed his large frame into the seat across, briefcase quickly slipped out of sight beneath the table. Adam felt so relieved he actually reached out and grasped the big man's hands, but Caxton brushed him off.

"Cax! Man! Where have you been? I'm *hurting* here."

The big man stared past him and into the mirror on the wall behind, milking it for detail like some kind of surveillance camera. His eyes, bright orbs glaring from a dark face, drank up the bar and its sordid milieu. The man's dreads were flecked with rather more grey than Adam remembered from their last meeting, and a few lines had settled into the skin around his eyes, but whether these indicated age catching up with the old dealer, or the rigours of his mysterious trade, it all meant little right now. All he wanted was the man's goods; blessed release from the *Gestalt*'s haunting cry.

"Been doing the rounds," Caxton said. He fumbled in a pocket and withdrew a tobacco pouch and papers, finally looking away from the mirror to roll a cigarette.

Caxton was a powerful man with a deep, resonant voice. This he seldom raised; he rarely needed to. His words conveyed strength and authority. Even in the decibel hell of this skin saloon, he could hear every word the man said. Caxton was that kind of guy; he'd make himself heard even at the end of the world.

Adam looked down at the table and clasped his damp hands together, contrite now for his impatience and lack of faith. The old dealer's presence was like a soothing balm, calming his nerves, settling his fears. Safe, now the man was here, safe and protected from the necrotic visions.

"Things are bad." Caxton glanced up from his half-rolled cigarette. "You been shouting your mouth off?"

"No! *No!*"

"You'd better not have."

"Have you got it? I *need* it!"

"Keep your voice down."

"I don't care about them. I *need* it, Cax, real bad."

Caxton stared hard, as though really seeing him for the first time. Adam flinched under the gaze, not used to the scrutiny. "You look like shit. You've been Gacking.[4] I told you about that."

"I know. *I know.* Have you got it?"

With a deep sigh, Caxton reached under the table and a few moments later a package was tapped against Adam's leg. He reached underneath and they completed the transaction. As discreetly as his trembling hand allowed, he slipped his fix into a deep pocket of his jacket.

"Thanks, Cax," he said, the relief tangible.

"You got a double hit there. Don't rush it, okay?"

"Double?"

"You won't be seeing me for a while."

"But —"

"Don't worry, I'll find you when the time is right. Just go easy on that stuff. Pace yourself. Savour it. And stay off

---

[4] Accessing the *Gestalt*, or any subordinate technology used as a temporary substitute.

the *Gestalt*, it fucks with your sense of reality. I mean it; it's not my shit that's tearing you up right now – it's the *Gestalt*. They don't mix."

"Sure, yeah, but why are you –"

"They've been following me, but I can play the game better. They've been following you, but you're not so good. You brought them here."

Adam started with fresh fright. He scanned the crowd for staring eyes. "What? Who? Cax… I'm *sorry*…"

"Forget it," he said, rolling his tobacco tube into shape. Then he flicked his head to indicate, the gesture so minimal, as usual. He licked the cigarette complete and placed it between his lips. A flare of dazzling flame, then the tip glowed red and smoke funnelled through Caxton's nostrils. Through the coiling haze Adam glanced in the direction of the nod. The woman and her consort.

"Cons?" He almost choked on the word.

"Try again."

"Then who?"

"Bad couple. Marla Caine and Otto Schencke. *Morlock's* people."

Morlock.

The name pummelled his mind with fear's hammer, though he couldn't say why the name filled him with so much dread. Silas Morlock. Master of *MorTek*, the world's largest company, creator of the *Gestalt*, the keeper of humanity's every desire and dream.

Except one.

"What are we going to do?"

"Lie low for a while. Make some new arrangements. That's why you got a double dose."

"But why... what do they want?"

"Right now? To keep tabs on us. That's why I'm not worried. If I was, you'd still be playing solitaire. I've been playing this game with them for a *long* time, but I haven't seen this level of interest for years. Something big is going down. We can't take them for granted any more. And you – you gotta get *smart*!"

"They followed *me*?"

"Probably. They might have found this place themselves. That doesn't matter. We just gotta deal with them."

"But what do they want with us?"

Another inhale, followed by a plume of smoke. His eyes glared infernal through the tainted haze.

"*MorTek* owns the *Gestalt*. Every human dream, every craving, every want and desire, is either controlled or influenced by Morlock. Except for my organisation. We push the most powerful drug ever used by Mankind. He doesn't like that."

Caxton wasn't always this talkative. When he was, the words were fascinating. Adam waltzed on the sense of trust and confidence they conveyed in him, *him*, a mere contact, a mere body to relish his goods. But what he said now, scared him. Now he wished he'd gone for a night in the nearest G-Spot.

"What am I going to do?"

"Remember what I told you. Don't go straight home. Take the long way, hide in the herd, stick to crowded places – but don't do anything to draw attention to yourself. *Be the herd*. It's me they really want. With any luck they'll follow me when I leave. I'll let them. You just get home, get yourself sorted. And remember go easy on that stuff. *You got to make it last.*"

He nodded, dumb.

"Good," Caxton growled slowly, finishing his cigarette and stubbing it. "Now go. Don't come looking for me. I'll find you, when the time's right."

*   *   *

JUST like that, Caxton switched him off. Adam rose reluctantly and struggled out from under the table. The lights dazzled. The alcohol weighed heavy in his arms and legs, making him stumble as he clambered out. He stopped to steady himself, to say something to Cax, to prolong the haven, but the man was already constructing another roll up and paid him no attention.

Adam felt stupid, standing there. The fix shifted in his pocket, spurring him to move. The children of the night howled and babbled in his ears. The herd. The hiding place. He plunged into the flow of *Gestalt*-fodder and tried not to think about the dead things mingled with them; they were just a stress-addled vision from a precocious imagination. That's all. Nothing more – *right?*

Living or dead, drunk or stoned, sober, or just lost, he squeezed through the density of flesh and tried to look normal. The dazzling lights, the swirling thick fog, the shadows that moved with a life of their own. Bodies crowded and shuffled and moved in a cocktail of claustrophobia. They made him dizzy; they moved him where he didn't want to go.

Slowly, he migrated towards the exit. The sign flickered briefly overhead, a beguiling mirage of promise. He stopped and turned, managed to squeeze through. Then he found a space leading by the bar and towards his source of freedom. He rushed into the vacuum.

Only to find *her* waiting.

Marla Caine turned in her seat and presented herself full on. She leaned back against the bar like she was taking aim with her jutting tits. Then she smiled, as if she'd just heard the thought. The dance light glowed on her face, playing through the rainbow. A face both young and old, he saw. Artificially rejuvenated and almost convincing, but attached to a body still capable of quickening a man's pulse. Adam felt his accelerate now, but not with any erotic appreciation. Not now he knew *what* she was.

He swallowed, before he drooled, and tried to overcome the rigour those eyes cast in his limbs. Marla crossed one elegant thigh over the other and raised her arm to inhale a breath of smoke. She breathed the plume across the distance and Adam felt the aromatic haze caress his face. He felt sick; not from the nicotine smog, but from the knowledge he'd just been marked.

Slowly, without averting her gaze, Marla moved to flick ash from her cigarette. Not one of Caxton's asymmetric roll ups, but an elegant tube, finished by the contrast of the ebony holder. One slender digit rose to tap and the cluster of burned tobacco seemed to fall forever.

"Be seeing you, *Darling*," she mouthed. Then she blew him a tantalising kiss.

The ash hit the floor and crumpled. Adam felt released. He turned in panic and felt his shoulder slam into solid flesh. The blow wrenched his spine, and almost spun him to the ground. He looked up into another personal fright. The face was bearded and grim.

A curt nod of the head and the man – Otto Schencke – stood aside.

Adam felt both sets of eyes stare as he scurried for the exit and the freedom of obscurity. Only then did he remember to breathe.

NOT that way, he silently urged.

Too late.

Marla had him.

The lad froze like a sailor caught in the siren cry, and all Caxton could do was sit and stare at the scene in the mottled mirror. The observation caught in his throat and tightened his chest; the rising tickle, the gurgling of deep-seated phlegm was combining to overthrow his impassive exterior. The condition was growing worse, stealing his precious time, but he must not succumb.

Not here. Not now.

Iron will just managed to surf the pneumatic wave. The embryo death rattle remained only a gurgle, the itch surrendered to a harsh clearing of his throat. The throttling embrace of his chest muscles eased. A little. The turmoil in his mind refused to let up as he watched the glass sheet that formed the eyes in the back of his head. The tableaux painted a sorry story: the lad might hang them all yet.

Outwardly, he managed to remain steadfast as a rock. Had to; there was no other way to survive in this town, but the emotional stress still played out its physical manifestation. A tiny tic beneath his right eye, a faint ripple in the flesh of his arm was the only outwards sign of the internal turbulence. The ripple dislodged ash from the tip of his cigarette. Anger crushed the ember tip in the ashtray.

Caxton watched. There was no sign of Otto. It almost revived the morbid raptures gathering strength in his body, but he held firm to his composure. He let his eyes scan the image, taking in Marla and her captivated prey, the seething crowd, the frenzied dancers oblivious to this feud taking place in their midst. Ghosts belched from the smog machines and writhed in the barbaric light show, but no sign of Marla's accomplice.

Left to their own devices, his fingers reached for the tobacco pouch and began to assemble another ticket to the grave.

Don't just stand there. *Move.* He didn't enjoy the feeling of the helpless observer, but in this encounter the boy was on his own. This was no time for liabilities, he knew this too well. Better prospects had already been cut loose to face a harsh fate. Many had failed to survive. That was an unfortunate drawback of the business; get a man hooked, then cut him loose without further supply. It put him on a par with a snowflake on a hotplate. Little chance for the lad, then, if the worst came to the worst.

Events hadn't reached that desperate phase yet. There was still a chance for him to measure up. Always a chance. Adam broke free of Marla's audience and scurried for the exit. A couple of heartbeats and he vanished from reflection. Otto calmed Caxton's mind further when he appeared from the crowd and engaged Marla in conversation.

The tension faded from his rib cage. Now the play was back on script, he could linger and give the boy some time.

Time to reach safe ground, or safe as possible in *this* city that is. He watched his old adversaries. The façade of the decadent *Terapolitan* fell away as they presumably talked shop. Lips moved in mime. Marla listened, head cocked, a smile on her face. Caxton hadn't moved throughout the drama since his fingers completed their unbidden task. Now he relented with a silent curse at addiction's drive and ignited the patient tip. Smoke billowed like a tiny fog machine as he drew on the intoxicant material, but he took care not to inhale. Not so soon after an episode. Instead, he took his nicotine the cigar-smoker's way.

When the fog of exhalation cleared, he resumed watching, patiently permitting the seconds to carry Adam further away from this dangerous game. Marla and Otto remained locked in conversation. No interest in the little fish, he mused. That was something. He flicked ash again and watched as Marla's eyes suddenly swivelled to meet his gaze in the mirror. He felt the connection crackle live between them with the energy of too many unburied ghosts. He held the reflection's gaze, his own face stern.

Marla raised her glass in mock salute. No good pretending he hadn't seen. A curt nod of the head acknowledged the gesture. She held his eyes a moment longer, then returned to her mimed conspiracy.

OUTSIDE, a passerby would never know there was a bar lurking in the shadows. Sure, the music throbbed underfoot, but the sound lacked any specific point of origin, or even the strength to drown the spattering noise of Adam's retching stomach.

The thin trickle of resurrected vodka washed over the ground while the stale alcohol smell flooded his nostrils. The half-hearted but insistent flow went on and on until his stomach creased in pain, but it voided none of his fear. From the shadows behind, a muttered comment and sniggered barb pricked his pride.

Once the spasms subsided, he stood up, unsteady, sucking air into his lungs to cleanse the stench. The air smelled of the city: of oil, garbage, ozone and the ever-present emanation of mould, but it was virgin fresh compared to the smoke and perspiration that passed for air inside.

Heat tickled the back of his neck. He turned to where memory told him the entrance to the club lurked. Fear expected to encounter Marla Caine's malevolent stare, but only weak light glowed from the entrance. Just enough to reveal the bouncers as spectral figures, their eyes gleaming points of suspicion in the weak glow, faces nothing but a luminous sheen in the shade. Fear subsided. His heart slowed. Adam shrugged his jacket into a more comfortable fit, and turned up the collar against the cold.

"*Fuck. You,*" he said, but not too loud in case the words carried. Then he turned and began the winding walk through the alleys.

Broken glass scraped beneath his feet. Scraps of rain-sodden paper and food packaging squelched. A soft breeze rustled over-flowing bags of garbage, mouldering far from the redemption of a *necrolyser*[5] belly. Adam walked through

---

[5] Located in the sub-terrestrial entrails of the city's towers and buildings, *necrolysers* are giant stomachs – part of the structure's organic infrastructure – that digest and recycle waste material and refuse. Commonly, in a city as crowded as *Terapolis*, they are also used

the mildewed remains of the Old World like one of its ghosts, proud of himself for blending in, until his foot caught an empty beer bottle. It clattered with a heart-stopping sound, then surrendered its existence against a wall with a crash. His heart mugged his throat. He turned to scan the shadows, fearful of potential predators lurking beyond sight.

At least here the darkness was honest. A straightforward lack of light rather than the neon-haloed shadows of *Terapolis* that seemed to have a life – no, a *presence* – of their own.

Only the rats scurried around. This relic was their city after all, and he was the alien intruder, but they reminded him so much of the denizens of the bar; flesh eking out a torrid existence in the detritus of urban squalor.

At the end of the day that's all life was; humanity built its monolithic spires of hopes and dreams and tried to believe that the whole sordid mess actually meant some-thing. Life meant nothing, never had. Until the *Gestalt* came along to show humanity the real way to meaning. And even that faded, compared to the wondrous existence hidden in his pocket. No wonder Morlock hated it.

Caxton's 'shit' was something far more glorious and fulfilling than anything gained from *MorTek*'s wares. And that's why he had to cling to the shadows to hide, or merge with the flow of humanity in the streets: 'hide in the herd' as the dealer put it, pretending to be something he wasn't. At least not completely.

---

to process the remains of the dead. The digested material provides nourishment for the living architecture, as well as basic nutritional material for the habitat residents, via nutrient glands.

Meaning. Yes. Only his package held that. The only meaning he had ever found in this sombre city. Otherwise, there was none. None at all, except perhaps for his companion rats. For them the city meant food and warmth and dark places to scurry and hide. But they didn't thank humanity for any of it. They didn't erect effigies and monuments to their ignorant benefactors. They just ate and shit and fucked and bred and got on with living.

Just like people, really. Rats of a larger breed, but cursed with an overblown sense of what they might aspire to be. *Gestalt*-fodder. Or Caxton's. That's all they were. Why else did he crave the shit in his pocket? Why else did he surrender to those cravings, even though it was dangerous and singled him out against the herd?

As if he really needed an answer. It softened the *Gestalt's* urgent pleading that beguiled to the seat of his soul. That's why. It offered him something this world couldn't give, something he never truly found inside the *Gestalt* or the other escapes he used to squander life. No, this was something beyond all that. It made him larger than life, greater than the cosmos, brighter than the most apocalyptic supernova, more angelic than the angels, and more devilish than the devils of the Old World. It uplifted him from the gutter of baseline[6] existence and took him to meet the stars. It was love and life and creation, and it made this drab existence in *Terapolis* bearable.

For that, Caxton's gear was worth all the risk. It had to be. He felt it move in his pocket to nudge him home. He

[6] Ground level.

almost heard its urgent voice on the breeze: "Hurry. Hurry. I *need* you."

He obeyed the command, eager to be *needed*.

CAXTON stepped into the cool night and nodded to the bouncers as he passed. He paused a moment to re-ignite the remains of a dwindling roll-up and then turned to walk up the alley.

Moments later Marla Caine and Otto Schencke emerged from the club's lurking entrance. They watched Caxton's retreating silhouette, then moved apart and sloughed away the signs of apparent inebriation.

"Always watching, Darling. When will it *ever* end?"

"Be patient, Marla. You've waited all these years. The time will come."

She nodded, only slightly mollified. "Caxton's *mine*. You take the whelp."

Otto looked stern in the weak light. "Better I follow him, Marla. He's better at this game than you."

She frowned and turned to him. Her elegant face moved close to his bearded one as though to kiss, but her teeth playfully nipped his lips. He winced, and she pulled away with a girlish giggle.

"There's no time to argue, Otto, Darling. He *is* mine."

She turned and stalked up the alley. Otto shook his head.

"Marla. My dear, vicious Marla … when will you ever learn?"

He watched her vanish into the night, and then turned to trace the boy's steps. Inexperienced. This one never varied his routine. So, there was no need to hurry. Once they hit the crowded streets of *Locus Prime*, then he could close in and observe.

"Too easy," he complained to the shadows.

The bouncers watched him leave, their eyes filled with bored incomprehension and a longing for the *Gestalt*.

AN *aquavein*[7] had burst somewhere overhead while he waited for the old dealer. Now the water cascaded in a liquid curtain that gleamed with an iridescent rainbow of distant neon.

He walked into the waterfall, letting the heavy drops batter his cap and his shoulders. For a moment, he paused to remove his cap and raise his face skywards. The water was cool and cleansing. It felt good against his skin. The pattering impacts massaged his tired muscles. There was something irresistibly clean and pure about the flowing cascade, so long as you ignored its source of ruptured flesh.

When he replaced the cap and stepped through to the other side of the veil, it took him from one world to the next; the shimmering liquid some kind of event horizon separating two distinct realms. Behind him, the dark alleys of Old City. On this side, the glistening hive of *Terapolis*.

The water spattered behind him and sluiced over the *pedederm*[8], washing grime and detritus on its way. More of the spillage dribbled down the base of the towers that forever

---

[7] A tough network of tubes that use muscular contractions to shunt clean water around the city.

[8] A thick integument of keratin and chitin enriched tissue, generated from the underlying dermal fabric of the city. The growth provides pedestrian traction for the inhabitants of *Terapolis*. It is similar in nature to the archidermis. Frequently shortened to *derm*.

imprisoned the world he had just left behind. The liquid skin adhered to the city's living integument like heavy sweat.

The water splashed underfoot as he followed the rills and puddles down the incline of the street. On the skin of the towers and the *derm*, thousands of lipless mouths mimed 'O' at his passage. Roughly child-sized, they sucked water into the flesh of the city, but not enough to stop the flow coursing down the street. Eventually the water pooled in the gutters where it gurgled into the sucking mouths of the drains.

Terapolis was claustrophobic in a way unlike the old alleys. They were narrow, tight-packed. Here, the architecture vaulted high overhead. A sense of vast space and flowing air, but it still enclosed him like a subterranean cavern. A place that was gloomy and lightless but for the bio-luminescent lamps and neon signs glowing from the heart of *L-Prime*.

Far above his head, if he guessed the time right, the sun was still a brilliant fire in the sky, diving headlong towards true night. The almost-mythical dusk was hidden from his eyes, here at *Terapolitan* baseline, for the towers were too tall for its light to flood the ground. Barely a trickle penetrated this deep into the urban enclaves, where it was overwhelmed by the city's inner luminescence.

He looked up to the starscape of illuminated windows glittering like constellations; the nebulous shimmer of bio-luminescent street lamps, the phosphorescent aura of neon signs. An Earthbound Cosmos glittering against the city's dark hide and clinging shadows.

There was a haunting hum of mingled sound emerging from the heart of the urban organism, a miasma of many human voices rumbling at once. Even the rush and whine of traffic on the causeway, suspended overhead, did nothing to drown the babble of human appetites.

As Adam trudged up the street, he felt a deeper rumble vibrate through his feet. He looked up. The web-work of roads and utility shafts and suspended plazas seemed to tremble from a heat haze. He was just able to make out the distant transit tubule. It gaped like a gagging mouth poised to vomit over the streets far below.

A shriek, still ear-piercing despite the distance, a sonic boom and the tubeworm[9] leapt into the urban void. They were terrifying in their power. Still, a sight to behold. Red neon gleamed from the carrypods[10] embedded in the tubeworm's muscular carriage: each jammed with passengers hurtling towards their destiny. The worm-like chassis undulated and writhed in suspended space, then located the junction pod and dived into the required tubule. Even from the distance, Adam saw the plume of compressed air and filth blast from the tube mouth. Moments later, sound caught up with light and his ears were bombarded again. The rumble died as the tubeworm vanished into the orifice and continued on.

Adam continued his pedestrian journey, but the sight of the tubeworm had set his mind to work. He wanted *home*. He wanted to hide away with his package and relax. Ten minutes to the south there was a tubeway opening. Not long at all. West was central *L-Prime*, where Caxton told him to

---

[9] The city's mass transit system.

[10] Literally a 'pod' for carrying items. Ranges in size from those for carrying personal items to larger varieties capable of conveying people.

lose himself in a circuitous route. He felt the subversive pull of home, and started to look into the shadows for the welcoming maw of the desired intersection.

Keep it together. Don't expose us. Hide in the herd. Be the herd. It's me they want. Keep it safe and make it last. Caxton's voice haunted him with its desperate disappointment.

Damn this fucked up addiction.

Damn this fucked up life.

Damn Caxton.

But he was right. As always.

Adam almost wept as he thought of the maelstrom of *L-Prime*. Far worse than the bar. He just wasn't in any state to cope. Here, he was exposed and vulnerable. But there, the long route, he could hide among the surging waves of flesh. Again, there was no choice in his life. He abandoned the tube, and walked onwards to the place he least wished to be.

Suddenly, he yearned to see the city silhouetted against the sky, a true cityscape. Something that might reassure him there was more to the world than all this. Not the occasional haunting glimpse of something that *might* be a patch of cloud.

There existed only a few places where a *derm*-dwelling *Terapolitan* might actually see a little sky. In every corner of *Terapolis*, the monoliths of *MorTek* provided that unique insight. Each *MorTek* spire formed an axis in a city without an orbit, without a centre. Each pinnacle stood within its own clearing in the forest of soaring monoliths. These served to create a light well deep into the base of the city. Only there was the sky blue, only there was the sun a burning brilliance, only there were the clouds revealed as graceful sculptures drifting aloof far beyond human concerns.

This detachment was something the clouds shared with *MorTek*. Alone in its plaza, *MorTek Prime,* or any of its daughters across the globe, stood detached from the city and its denizens. It was the calm eye around which the maelstrom of *Terapolis* whirled.

From there, the tower stood as a symbol and a living testament to the ascent of Man into the glorious mysteries of the *Gestalt*. In the *MorTek* Plaza, even the sun, from its rise in the East to its descent into Western slumber, orbited *MorTek*. That was a lesson learned early.

Maybe someday he'd take a pilgrimage to *MorTek* Plaza and revisit the lost sky. But not this day. Not with the precious gift hiding in his pocket and begging him for salvation.

TERAPOLIS was home to billions. But for all that the city's spread had globalised its urban embrace; the inhabitants had grown insular and parochial. Adam knew he was much the same, and it rankled; he wanted to belong, yet at the same time he wanted to be himself, something *more* than himself, but all he knew was this darksome pocket of a city beyond his comprehension.

Many of its denizens knew nothing else but the enclosing towers and sullen streets of their own *Locus*, cared less for what went on beyond. In any case, there was little to see in a city that had subsumed and smothered the diversity of a dead world, even less to captivate the curiosity of a race long-since absorbed in the allure of the *Gestalt*.

The older generation had known of other places, of course, but in the unified world of the *Gestalt* the memories they carried were dim. Maybe they had good reason to forget the past, to let torments fade into forgetfulness; bad things belong buried. Maybe it was something about their new reality that was Adam's tired normality; it didn't encourage memory to stick around.

Even Caxton, who seemed to hold some familiarity with the ghosts of history, kept his recollections concealed; just enough let loose here and there to stir a desire for more, much like the contraband he pushed. Well, though he had gleaned only precious little, still Adam had learned enough to be utterly bewildered by the alien world that had gone before, to wonder how it all came to this netherworld beneath the shadows of *Terapolis*.

"They were beautiful once, the towers, when they were few and far between," Caxton had said, his tones now a memory replayed to the background noise of the urban milieu. "*MorTek* offered us a miracle of bio-engineering – that's what they were called – that'd save us from ourselves, and we were always such suckers for the latest technological wonder. Yeah, we were suckered in and here we are. The towers spread, *Terapolis* grew. It absorbed the cities of history, swallowed entire nations, embalmed continents, and somewhere along the line we stopped noticing; we had the *Gestalt* by then – and Morlock had us all. Well, not quite all... Hey! You listening to what I'm saying?"

Adam smiled and nodded. No, he hadn't been listening, not really. Then he woke up to where he was and what he had to endure before he found the sanctity of Caxton's goods. The tension returned, tightening his shoulder muscles, clenching his bowels, as he recalled he was no longer quite a part of the *Terapolitan* herd; that the old dealer had pulled him into the fringes of a world that set him apart, that singled him out, that made him a memory of a bygone world he did not comprehend.

Suddenly, he wished he'd paid more attention to Caxton all those times, but it was far too late for any of that now. He was still a long way from home.

THERE was no turning back now. This was the torrential storm of human existence crashing through the streets and byways of central *L-Prime*. Adam struggled against the tide of pushing, jostling bodies. He sweated with the effort, bewildered and dizzy by the sensory flood of faces and bodies and smells and sounds.

Millions of people coagulated into writhing, fragmenting, condensing knots of flesh. Waves crashed against the base of the mighty towers, sluicing and splashing down the avenues and streets, erupting from vestibules and foyers in a frenzy of activity. Human magma, boiling white-hot, gushing through vents and fissures in the canyons of corruption.

And somehow he was supposed to keep his cool in the midst of this frenzied ecology of raw vice. Caxton had to be *fucking* crazy. He winced at the disrespect, but it *was* easy for Caxton to say. In truth, Adam was scared. He felt naked.

Nobody paid him any attention; just another burden to shift aside. An obstacle in the pursuit of the cherished goal of pleasure and release. He was alone. As utterly isolated and alienated as only a being can be when washed away amongst the sea of strangers.

All those faces, bland masks of skin that blurred and flickered in his vision. Dark faces, pale faces, young and old, man and woman, boy and girl and those somewhere in between. Dressed in the height of fashion, or the street attire of the youth tribes and the *G-Tek*[11] junkies. The neon made all appear the same.

He scanned the ashen crowds with eyes that darted like a cornered mammal beneath the gaze of its predator. The herd paid little heed, but something was out there. It battered its way into his senses; an aura of dread that even managed to crush the addictive need.

Somebody was *following* him.

Somebody was *watching* him.

He gritted his teeth against the urge to hide. Swallowed the tide of nausea rising in his belly. This was no place for that weakness. Caxton relied on him; he had no option but to get through this.

A sudden sound above his head made him look sky-wards. It wasn't the thud of bass music from some club or bar. It wasn't the roar of a million vehicles racing on their circular route to nowhere. It wasn't the combined animal bellow of the multitudes marching towards their empty tomorrow.

No. The sound that cut through all this was a leathery creak. A slithering sibilance emerging far overhead, in the deep shadows that clotted out the distant roof of the world.

Adam felt cold, despite the heat of so much sweating flesh. He struggled to move faster through the cloying bodies of his own kind. Followers of *G-Tek*. The minions of *MorTek*. Barred by momentary circumstance and fortune from the *Gestalt*. All of them searching for *their* next hit; in

---

[11] 'Geist-Tek' refers to any technology relating to and including the *Gestalt*.

the bars, the clubs, the arcades, the brothels, the opium dens, whatever fancy offered the chance to drown the self and stifle the haunting lure of what they craved most of all.

Through all of that, still something watched him.

He had to get away. Had to get out. He was suffocating. Drowning in sweat and heat and liquefying faces. His feet picked up the pace. He felt the beginning of panic override sense. *Keep it together.* He tried. Really he did, but he was feeling himself beginning to unravel. He gritted his teeth and pushed his way through, until he found the brooding shadow of some musty alley. Hardly Old World, but clear of people. To Hell with being part of the herd...

He lunged into the maw of shadow and mildewed mist. The voice of the *Terapolitan* maelstrom faded into a bluebottle buzz. Feet picked up the pace and matched his own hurried footfalls, surely the proof his paranoia needed to shout down sanity's suggestions they were only echoes. Far overhead in the deeps of utter black, the leather thing shuffled and slithered. The unseen menace kept pace, enveloping him in some unfathomable aura of observation that made the sixth sense squirm. What could possibly rationalise *that*?

A sharp whine of terror burst from his throat. The package danced macabre in his pocket. Adam ran through the dark, as if his heart might stop if he didn't run harder, faster. His precious package shrieked its own urgings from the womb in his jacket.

Help me! Help me!

Adam tried. He ran, until there were no shadows left. Just the sickly lights of home, and the swirling blobs of colour oozing across his exhausted vision. He panted and coughed like a terminal consumptive. The light washed away the lingering murk of the city, but not all of his trailing apprehension.

Sweating hard, and trembling, he glanced back at the dark alley and tried to peer into its depths. There was something there, he was sure, but his eyes detected nothing. The package whispered seduction. He forgot about the moments of terror, staggered into the orifice of Otranto Towers, and hoped that today the lifts were operational. After this awful night, he must be due some kind of break, however small. Tonight, he might get lucky. There was always a first time.

THE shadows were old friends but they lacked the capacity to mask the panting exertion. The unexpected break from routine was a welcome exhilaration, even if it reminded of encroaching age.

Now he lurked in the shadows of a disused commercial doorway and watched his quarry pause outside the habitentiary's[12] foyer. The boy was staring hard into the shadows, but he clearly detected no hint of his presence. Not this time. Perhaps not at any time during their little game of *follow my lead*.

So, what prompted the boy's hurried flight? A propensity to panic was not a sound survival trait in this city, but it was a question that was not his to ponder. Just complete the observation, and return to make his report. The old game. He shook his head at a flurry of uncommon feeling.

---

[12] Otherwise known as an apartment block.

"I pity you, boy," he breathed, "this game will be the death of you."

The target staggered into the habitentiary and passed beyond further consideration. Otto Schencke remained a component of shadow for a few moments more, then slipped away. Behind him, the darkness swirled as if it were smoke.

THE stairs got steeper every time, he was sure, but now he was back home. Safe and secure in his private universe, where he didn't need to worry about who – or what – was watching.

The door slammed shut and he leaned against it, taking in deep breaths and letting his heartbeat return to normal. The darkness enclosed him like a secure womb. A hiding place, far better than any claustrophobic crowd.

He straightened, ready to take his fix into the living room where they might become better acquainted. Then something slithered in the darkness and bunched his heart into a fist.

HE led. Marla followed.

Caxton took her first through the maze of Old City, then into the quieter streets around it. Now he was moving inexorably towards central *Locus Prime*, ready to leave his tail chasing amorphous shadows and might-have-beens.

They'd played this old game many times on and off over the years. Marla was getting better. Clearly, Otto tailed the boy. Well, there was nothing to be done about that. Adam was on his own. Consider it part of the learning curve. He frowned. Lessons didn't adhere if the student was dead. But no, this was an observation mission. Follow and report. Nothing more. Otherwise, by now, Marla's deadly intention would be clear of its holster.

He paused outside a restaurant lit up like an oasis in this desert of shade. He peered at the menu on the window. His mind ignored the human banality inside. Instead, he let his eyes focus on the reflections in the glass. He stared long and hard, building a mental map of the glimmering beacons of street lamps and shops and the gloomy pools of night between.

Where was she?

Ah! There. She lurked in the shadows by the street corner he had so recently vacated. She was not in deep enough, he noted. The light of a street lamp caught her pale face and made it glow like a ghost's visage. An opponent's errors were always a blessing, but it was dangerous to take them for granted. Especially when the opponent was Marla Caine. What she lacked in skill, she made up for in murderous intent. She had been schooled harshly.

A sombre thought. It created a cascade of memory from the back of his mind. Memories long buried. For a moment they shouted loud enough to reach the seat of conscience.

"Ah! Marla," he sighed. "It should have been so different. You will never forgive me. I can never forgive myself. But perhaps I can atone yet."

No time for regrets. He slammed the door on the thoughts before they could crack his composure. Soon it would be time to lose Marla. He turned away from the menu, glanced at his watch for effect, then tightened his grip on his briefcase and its precious contents as he paced towards the centre of *Locus Prime*.

AFTER the death-rattled gurgle, a shimmering iridescent light invaded the murk. Adam stared at the *simulacomm*[13] as its fluid molecules began to sculpt the recorded message. The esoteric substance slurred into shape, like a bubbling glob of gleaming mucus lit from within.

A face emerged. He recognised Claire as the colour swarmed across her features. The eyes snapped open. A recording it might be, but the eyes still glared contempt from the re-animated effigy.

"Hey shit head! I don't like being stood up!" Gobs of 'mucus' wobbled across her features, as the device tried to stabilise the animate. *"They warned me at work about you. Well, I've had better pricks than you, pal, so if that's what you wanted to show me just forget it!"*

The head glared a moment longer, lips drawn tight to underline her anger. Then the dimensioned-recording dribbled back into the plinth.

Adam breathed again. *"Shit!"* Clean forgot. Some date.

There was nothing to be done about it now. He pushed himself off the door and wondered whether to 'comm her back. This was no time for smarm or charm. Even less a tongue-lashing. Best leave her to sweat. The package nudged him as he leaned over the *simulacomm*. "Forget her," it might have said, "let me do that *special* thing…"

The voice dripped with honey and guile.

Adam responded. Excitement charged him up. He took it out and weighed the package in his hand. His mouth watered in anticipation. The excitement was a tingle in his

---

[13] A by-product of *Geist-Tek* research, a communications device that utilises an esoteric non-atomic material.

chest. He stumbled through the dark towards the living room, all else forgotten.

Light flickered into frail existence as a sluggish presence sensor detected his existence. The insipid glow vaporised the shadows, revealing the worn out furniture, the peeling wallpaper and the seedy carpet. Probably the place had never been done up since its origin as an Old World apartment. Now it was just another relic consumed into the living substance of *Terapolis*. The backdrop to the mess of his living. None of it mattered right now.

He reverently placed the package on the coffee table and shuffled out of his jacket.

Hurried now, sweating with anticipation, he sat down and reached out for the package. He ripped off the wrapping. The smaller packages within slid out onto the table. Caxton had promised him a double dose. And he wasn't joking. One was a fat promise, bursting with gratification. He reached for the slimmer dose first. Told himself to take it steady. He had to ration himself. Keep it together. Control. Keep control. But the addiction was no longer prepared to be patient.

He raised his salvation to his nose and savoured the scent. Already, his own small world and the wider world beyond collapsed into the singularity of a forgotten thought. Now his universe consisted only of this frayed armchair, the light, and the contraband he held.

This was his world, and in his world there was no such thing as forbidden pleasure. There was only the moment and the momentous joys that lay beyond this portal. A very

Gestalt sentiment, but he was beyond caring now, beyond anything but the need his fix possessed for him.

He opened its battered cover and settled back to read; with that first precious sentence, the words transported him to a place where he was truly free.

The Second Folio

On The Eighth Day,
MorTek Made... Utopia

SILAS Morlock gazed through the window of his office and watched the bristling towers of *Terapolis* become bathed in fluid fire.

The dazzling sun was descending behind the Earth's bulk, where it appeared to ignite the dust and smog to create the display of atmospheric pyrotechnics. An ocean of golden clouds and nebulae of red-hued dust cast smouldering auroras on the ember silhouettes of *his* city.

It was... *beatific.*

Of course, the sun never truly set upon *Terapolis*, a city voracious in its appetite for such raw energy, but here in this portion of the globe at least, the ancient star was retiring for the night. As always, nature's light show reminded him that he was not the Master of all he surveyed, only a portion, and even then only as a servant of something far more profound.

Human Fulfilment. Human Transcendence. Human Destiny.

These formed the Trinity of his purpose. To their end, he had sown the seeds of *Terapolis* and he had granted

Humanity the *Gestalt*. Together, they made the old dream of *Utopia* a reality. *Terapolis* was the gateway to that realm, and the culmination of his mission was so perilously close now that the impatience to reach the final goal of Completion was *maddening*.

Morlock buried the thought with a sigh. The future arrived in its own time; that much the passing orbits had taught him. He leaned on his ebony cane and stared down into the city's murky depths. Nearby, Bill sat reposed on his pedestal, where he hummed a soft melody. Normally, Morlock found his companion's wordless croon soothing, but now the mournful hum was a distraction from a different kind of tone: a note that itched the nodes of curiosity and compelled him to look upon the spectacle of human existence.

The note was down there, its physical root, in the geography of the city, and also out *there*, in that esoteric realm of the human soulscape. The discordant euphony was maddening, distracting, yet alluring in a way. As he listened, he pondered the avenues of memory in search of a clue. He had sensed this manifestation once before, long ago in another time and another place.

He closed his eyes for want of better concentration. Dark was so much better for thought, he always found. So shrouded, he strained to locate the note's tiny reverberations within the rest of the muted human chorus. If only…

"Oh, *do* shut up, Bill."

The melody died. The discordant note was clearer now, a beacon amidst the synchronised frequencies of humanity's mental energies pulsing to the *Gestalt*'s harmony. The creature he sought was a regular conjoiner too, as was right and proper, but its spirit was conflicted; torn between the *Gestalt* and… *something* else… this soul throbbed to a broken beat.

Morlock frowned. The *something* that frayed this sentient's hold on transcendence went beyond matters of idle curiosity. It demanded investigation, the expenditure of precious reserves of energy he needed to bring his purpose to its final fruition. Such are the demands of existence, he knew. He sighed and allowed his essence to unfurl from his physical shell, outwards into the ethereal realm from which mundane matter coagulates into being.

In that astral plane of energy, Morlock found himself awash in the radiance of humanity's mental aura, a plasma field of intense illumination emitted by each human sentience to create, in effect, the soul of the species. The days of its ancestral vitality were long since past, but still the brightness stung his perception; even the eyes of the physical shell anchoring his spirit watered in sympathy.

For a moment, he stared into the eye of the *Gestalt*, letting it soothe his sensibilities, and then he veered away. As he migrated further into the emanations of sentience, he saw the *Gestalt* revealed: in appearance, a spiral galaxy, not of stars but of individual human essences, its hub a restless vortex where these sundered spirits gushed towards fulfilment.

Morlock moved on, locating the object of his investigation by the ripples left in the wake of its migration. Of course, he found the being in the vicinity of the *Gestalt*, fighting its pull, even as so many of the creature's fellows flocked to its calling. This spirit was brighter than most. Closer inspection revealed the tight balls of light – false *souls*

– bound to its essence, feeding the wayward creature's light, almost shielding its presence, but for the saving grace of the *Gestalt's* tug.

This was a danger unlooked for; a rare folly, but perhaps also a timely discovery, this itinerant lost to the herd. Morlock closed in, carefully – so carefully – encircling the wanderer. As they converged, he began to perceive an impression of the physical world. Here, in this realm, matter was intangible; ghost-like wisps of substance, as ephemeral as flesh in ancient x-ray images. They provided a tenuous reminder that this sentience was rooted in the geography of space-time; drawing closer, he began to discern snatches of sound, the smells of flesh and city, an impression of close-packed bustling streets – an emotional surge of fear and distress.

Somehow, though the core of its aura was bound up in the flesh of its neural root structure, this sentience detected his scrutiny. *Interesting.* Once again, Morlock lamented that he could only detect minds, not read them. Still, it was better than no sense at all.

He moved closer, bracing himself against the stinging presence of those false souls, trying to divine greater clarity. This spirit was familiar; he had sensed something of its essence before, long ago. Closer now, refusing to flinch, seeking the trigger of recollection; he almost had it…

"They are ready for you, Master."

Concentration collapsed. Mundane reality rushed in to fill the void. The connection with the ethereal realm sundered as he was pulled back into the restrictions of the flesh. There remained a fleeting hallucination of an opaque bundle of illegible thoughts and feelings crawling forth like an ephemeral amoeba. Soon it was gone, subsumed into the denser regions of Humanity's mental glow. With a sigh, he turned towards the source of the interruption.

Belial bowed, as always perfect deference.

"Indeed," Morlock said. "Then we had better not keep them waiting, had we?"

Morlock smoothed some ruffles from his sombre frock coat. He paid no heed to his patient assistant, until the man stepped towards the pedestal with outstretched hands. The cane lashed out. The silver tip rapped a reproach to his wrist.

"How many times must I tell you, Belial: Bill does not like to be handled by anyone but me."

"Of course, Master."

Belial stepped away from the skull with a small bow. Morlock retrieved the skull from its perch, placing his faithful companion carefully within the crook of his arm, before he followed Belial out into the corridor.

"I trust this presentation will be worth it."

"I am assured that it will, Master. They would not disturb your contemplation for nothing."

"No. But Creek is new, fresh, and he has so much to learn."

"Even so, Master," Belial said.

Morlock smiled at the skull's silent remark. "That is unkind, Bill. The poor boy has not yet warmed the shoes of his predecessor, yet already you compose his eulogy. You may be right, of course, but his sanity is expendable. His talent invaluable. I have every confidence in Mr Creek."

To that, the skull had no answer. Bill knew the goal was paramount. "You will find this interesting, Bill, I can promise you that. Technology has moved on at a great pace since your day, and young Creek is said to be quite the *Necrofycer* even by today's standards."

Morlock nodded at the response.

"You are so right, Bill. Now, let us see what Mr Creek has in store for us. Destiny awaits – and she is *hungry*."

THIS is back story. I make no apologies, for it is my task to make you understand something of what befell us and how it came to be...

Caxton paused, fingers poised over the typewriter's well-used keys. The mechanical beast waited, patient, for him to gather his thoughts. Ever faithful, he'd long since overcome the urge to requisition a laptop; few and far between and difficult to maintain nowadays, they were far too precious for this indulgent pursuit.

No, it wasn't entirely an indulgence. There was method, even if the whole thing was madness. Nobody would ever – should ever – read this composition. If he succeeded, there would be no need to share these sombre recollections; if he failed, then what he had to say here might provide humanity's only shot at redemption.

The evening's *follow-my-lead* with Marla rose to mind unbidden. Some things can never be redeemed; some secrets must remain unspoken to the grave. The bitter truth, he knew too much; he knew too little, and that might damn them all or save them – but it would never expunge the guilt. Nothing ever could. He felt his jaw tighten at the ache in his chest, and he lashed out at the keys...

Stories seldom start at their true beginning; so it is with the story of our times. The road to Terapolis and the Gestalt has been long and winding.

But it was in a world far removed from such archaic origins that the story of the Incunabula is rooted; a mere blink of an eye in terms of historical recollection, a thousand centuries ago in the reckoning of G-Tek induced amnesia.

In a world broken, our time was seeded. By our own foolish hand did we condemn ourselves. In war did we lay the foundations of Terapolis—and open the way to the Gestalt.

War, of course, is an age-old companion of Man, but in those later days we had fitted and armed the First Horseman with all the sophistication that our knowledge of science commanded. We invoked the Horseman and thought we might control him: here, there, everywhere in the service of our goals. For many long years, so it was— he was a leashed hound gnashing our foes at our whim.

Until he turned on his deluded master, this demonic Horseman, and called forth His brethren. Together, they consumed a proud and powerful but terribly lost world.

So ended what we've come to call the Old World.

The civilisation that crawled bleeding and broken from that cataclysm of violent global indulgence was not too different from the proud and wilful one that conjured forth the demon horde.

Corporations still wrestled for the bottom line. Politicians still chanted their cant and schemed for power. Priests still bickered like thieves for possession of the human Soul. Nations still sparred and jostled for position, but there was something missing. The world went through the motions of living and healing, but it had become an empty vessel.

People struggled with the hardships of austerity, economic calamity, ecological distress, social disloca- tion. Life was hard, the future bleak, as this once proud civilisation puzzled over its fall from grace.

The first towers that would become Terapolis germi- nated in the bomb-blasted ruins of the most blighted cities. They provided a herald of what was to come; a promise of salvation, a healing for the world's hurts. MorTek began to emerge from the shadows of anonymity to succour a populace bewildered and lost.

Even before the devastation, the world had turned ever more from books. Lives were too busy; we rushed from place to place, life was but a blur of fast paced moments.

Technology dazzled our befuddled senses, bewitched us, then bored us, and we moved onwards.

We had taken our mighty leap into the hinterlands of Terapolis. It brooded on the horizon, ready to welcome us into its embrace. It could not have arrived at a worse moment in human history; it could not have arrived at a more fortuitous moment in the history of the hitherto little-known MorTek.

For there we were, vulnerable, wounded, bewildered, already forgetful of the magic of the Word, mesmerised then desensitised by decades of short-lived technological wonder, until here was something new and fresh and vibrant. So we were captivated like an awe-struck child, and even once sober commentators fell to their knees before the altar of the Gestalt to babble adulation.

And so, lost in the twilight of Terapolis and embraced by the Gestalt, we lost track of time and history. The pages of our story turned, until there were no pages left, for the books burned, the periodicals ceased, and the digital webs unravelled as electronic information systems were left to corrode.

Terapolis engulfed the world, and the fledgling Incunabula fled to the safety of yesterday...

GHOSTS often gathered in the cathedral void of the Conference Hall, where they would whisper in huddled groups of unseen conspirators. Morlock walked through their assemblies unperturbed, as always, to send them scattering like startled butterflies.

To the newcomer, the susurrations first seemed like piped recordings of the wind blowing through summer trees, or waves crashing against distant beaches.

Morlock found the voices soothing. His servants found in them a healthy fear: not that they understood the true nature of the murmuring exiles. Both were good reasons to let the lost ones whisper in the halls of *MorTek Prime*.

A few more steps and he entered the combined corona of his servants' emotions. He tasted and appreciated the complex bouquet they effervesced. Impatience, fear, desire, lust, envy, greed; a complex cocktail that fuelled their utility. Now they sat with heads bowed, hands rested flat on the surface of the horseshoe table. They appeared almost a congregation at prayer. More apt, perhaps, to say participants of some archaic séance. Neither mattered to the world any more, but both considerations amused Morlock.

"Good evening, ladies and gentlemen."

They glanced up and chorused their polite incantation: "Good evening, Sir."

Morlock placed Bill at his seat, a twin of the velvet pedestal in his office, and then took his place at the head of the table. Belial took up post behind.

Morlock smiled. He looked slowly round the gathering. None held his gaze for long; their brazen self-confidence melted like wax in the blowtorch presence of their Master. They all wore the *MorTek* logo somewhere about their person. Displayed bold, or discreet, it mattered not, for it was the brand indelibly etched upon their souls. Each of them belonged to *MorTek* more than they would ever care to admit.

He savoured the faces, the emotional turbulence each one masked. On the right, sat Lorelei, the ever-youthful head of Marketing. An ironic position, for *G-Tek* so often sold itself. She gave him a warm and affectionate smile, as genuine as a serial killer's.

To his left sat Bayle, head of Finance. A man as desiccated by his occupation as any ancient beneficiary of the embalmer's trade. Trailing along the table on both sides were their hand-picked acolytes. Comet trails of fragmented personalities along for the ride, but ever vigilant for the opportunity to supplant a chief and fulfil ambition. Morlock so knew this institutional ritual; many orbits old, but still a source of amusement. He scanned the acolytes one by one. The enthusiastic, the cynical, the manipulative, the arrogant and the over-burdened. Not one worth committing to memory. Another batch for the slaughter. They will learn in time. Perhaps in this batch, the one who might finally supplant a chief. No, he decided, as he completed his sweep. Lorelei and Bayle were still the secure incumbents.

Finally, Morlock turned his attention to the far side of his flock, where Boris Creek and his team of technicians waited at the pincer's edge. Creek was the new boy, and scared. The *Necrofycer's* trade is a lonely one, Morlock knew, but he felt no pity. Creek must be made or broken. And there was no better time than the present.

"Let us proceed," he said. "What do you have for me, Mr Creek?"

The man was a hand wringer and sweated profusely. Clearly, he did not relish being the centre of attention. Today, all would discover if *MorTek's* new division chief was worthy of the trust and responsibility so recently conferred. Morlock rested his hands on his cane and leaned forward, intent.

"Sir… er… colleagues. As you are all no doubt aware, we have long struggled to open up the young demographic to the benefits of our work. You will also know, I am sure, that this has presented certain… erm… *difficulties* to the fulfilment of our mission."

Creek paused, perhaps for effect or simply to settle his nerves.

"Do go on," Morlock encouraged.

"Up to now, Sir, er... the pre-teen through adolescent demographies have had to make do with conventional technology. *Geist-Tek[14]* is – simply – unsuitable for their nascent biology. The early developmental stages, the hormonal chaos of puberty and the formation of adult neuronal structures has rendered *G-Tek* connectivity dysfunctional at best, and has led in the past to some long-term developmental... er, *issues*... within the host."

"This is common knowledge, Creek. Is there a point to this history lesson?"

"No. Sir. I mean yes, Sir. Precisely that. As of today it is a history lesson. I mean..."

Creek's face sagged as the combined glare of his audience glitched his own neuronal structures. Perhaps it was a bubbling of his hormones, as the poor boy absorbed the full heat of Lorelei's projected sexuality. As always, she was so precocious in her duties, if a little inattentive of appropriate timing.

A few smiles fluttered through the congregation. Creek glanced round them, searching for a sympathetic face and finding none. A pace, a glance back at the mysterious equipment and the veiled pedestal placed centre stage. Underneath that veil, Creek found some inner steel to resist Lorelei's proclivities.

"Today those problems are history! We have forged the revolution in *G-Tek* that finally permits us to penetrate this neglected demographic and realise –"

"A hitherto unrealised revenue stream."

---

[14] Any technology relating to and including the *Gestalt*. Commonly shortened to 'G-Tek'.

The dry interlude came from Bayle. He leaned forward, his briefing pad gripped in his left hand. The right index finger tapped and danced over the *simulacomm*-based screen. He stared at Morlock for daring moments, then looked over towards his adversary in marketing. Creek looked on, bewildered and abandoned.

"Sir, I must add that we can enjoy significantly better returns with a higher unit price than the one pencilled in by my colleague across the board. We are not running a charity here."

Lorelei's eyes flashed. The two were old sparring part-ners. Office rumour occasionally reached Morlock's ears. It suggested this endless duel arose out of his marketing chief's refusal to sleep with his chief accountant, which made him a rare functionary indeed. Mere matters of the flesh were more suited to ordinary *Terapolitans*, but he did find a certain fascination to observe the complexities of his people's behaviour. The hindrances and distractions inherent in primate biology.

"Retail indices are subject to change, as you know," Lorelei said. "I don't understand, nor do I care about the technical aspects, but I do know that we need to develop this sector quickly. The retail figures we have projected will permit our rapid penetration."

"Even so —"

"We get the little bastards hooked now and then we have them forever. That's when we up the price."

Lorelei relaxed her posture and took hold of her own briefing pad. She glanced around the table, finally looked to beseech her master. Morlock gently nodded his head.

"Our work to promote young people's interests in educational facilities, day care centres and kindergartens clearly demonstrated how our target demographic has long envied its older peers. Now we can absorb them into the future of *Terapolis*. How can any parent resist this: we are talking about a device that readies and enables our youngsters for the *Gestalt*. We can incorporate educational facilities that will help our young ones learn. Better education means better prospects, better prospects mean better employment, better employment means more disposable income – that means more *Gestalt*. We win every way."

"Even so, Lorelei, we can win *more* if we up the price. I must protest at this, Sir."

"Money is not the only consideration here, Mr Bayle. We must serve humanity's needs. It is why we exist."

"Yes, Sir, but we all know that the c'roaches[15] *live* for our products. There is *nothing* they will not do to achieve the *Gestalt* state. Nothing! Set against that, how can we suffer by imposing higher exchange values? C'roaches will even sell their souls to gain what we have!"

Morlock was unable to help the smile. Bayle had scored a point over poor Lorelei. *Sotto voce* he admitted: "They frequently do."

Lorelei scowled. Morlock sighed. It was time to end the ritual of debate.

---

[15] The term is a contemptuous reference and a colloquial shortening of the word 'cockroach'.

"Suffer not the little children," he said. "We must not leave our young ones abandoned a moment longer than necessary."

Across the table, Lorelei and Bayle glared. Then their heads bowed. Almost as one, their forgotten people did the same. Morlock let the moment stretch, looking round the table. Let none forget that the mission of Completion is paramount.

"We have neglected poor Mr Creek," he chided. "Now, perhaps we should let him finish his moment in the limelight."

Creek stepped back into awareness. Hesitant. Caught between gratitude and dismay.

"Before we move on, Sir, I think I should point out a couple of added benefits that we have achieved. These will work for us across the board of our demographics."

"My dear boy, there is no end to your enlightenment."

"Er... yes, thank you, Sir. Firstly, given the nature of the technical breakthrough that I shall present today, we can soon ditch the conventional implant. Furthermore, once certain infrastructural prerequisites are put into place, we can significantly raise the throughput of *Gestalt* visitation. As you know, at any one time there are hundreds of millions translinked to the *Gestalt* throughout the city, but we've long-since hit a bottleneck in what we can provide. Until now. We are on the verge of a major expansion of what we can offer. Soon, we can trans-link *billions*. And beyond that, well, with this new product it becomes theoretically possible to trans-link the entire planetary population."

Lorelei stifled a yawn, and turned her chemically brightened eyes towards the young *Necrofycer*. "Yes, Boris. We have perceptualised the abstracts you offered, but when are we actually going to *see* the infernal machine?"

Boris stammered, then went red. "Erm, well…"

"Lorelei is correct, Mr Creek. It is time to behold our children's future."

"Yes, Sir. Of course. May I then present to you the *Succub-I* – the first portable and fully *Gestalt*-capable interface unit."

With a proud flourish he pulled away the cover sheet and stepped aside to reveal a small glass case. Everyone stared. Fascinated, Morlock leaned forward to watch the thing inside twitch into life.

SOME might have likened him to a lost soul, back in the days when such things mattered; nowadays there were few to care and that suited him just fine. After all, they'd never taken him seriously, even when he'd tried to warn them of the darkness rising; he was just the crazy man.

Now the darkness was all around, and he was the crazy *old* man, but he'd made his peace with the shadows. More or less. People were another matter, especially the *man's* people, but he'd long-since dropped from *his* radar. There were ways and means. He shrugged the heavy haversack into a better position on his back. The weight inside shifted, glass clinked.

"Keep things fuzzy," he muttered, taking a swig of liquor from the bottle in his hand. "Can't find a man wi' a fuzzed 'ed! Oh no!"

Crazy he might be, but he *was* the world's greatest living author. Since nobody else knew this – or even cared – he kept it to himself. In any case, even as he swigged on the bottle of cheap booze, the kind that had rotted senses and sensibility, a few fizzing brain cells acknowledged that with the world the way it was, this was doubtless for the best.

So the Author kept his precious writings to himself, secure in the old haversack slung on his back. Besides the booze, and the few works he had deemed worthy of salvation all those years ago, it contained his most prized possessions. The only original manuscripts to still wander free in the heartland of *Terapolis*. All his. The works of his hand and brain. A sacred trust, but they were a part of him, and he carried the heavy burden alone.

In some vague way, he was aware that he wasn't quite the last author living. Long ago one or two had even invited him into their midst, but that wasn't for him, no, for he had long shunned the company of others, even before the gestation of *Terapolis*. Even so, it was the fool's way, this fraternity of bibliophiles they'd created.

"Fuck 'em," he spat. "Sittin' targets, the lot of 'em. Keep on the move, tha's the way..."

So he shunned the *Incunabula* and was lost to them, not that he was the only bibliophile to have become lost along the way. Others survived in isolated obscurity, long since worn down to pale shadows, forgetful even of the books they kept hidden in closets, or abandoned to some long lost hideaway. Many more captured, some simply died, as is the way of things.

"Fuck 'em," he grumbled to nobody in particular. Perhaps the shadows listened, and egged him on. Maybe.

As he emerged from the deep shade of the labyrinthine alleys that backed onto each *Terapolitan* tower, the bio-luminescence from the nearby thoroughfare stung his eyes. On the whole, he didn't realise they were such vast monoliths. They were too tall for his blurred vision to comprehend. As ever, he cast his eyes downwards. Ever down to his feet, and the *pedederm*, or the bins, where some morsel of leftover food might be found discarded.

"Fuck th' lot of 'em. Folio Plagues[16] m' arse. Conspiracy. Burned 'em instea'. But not 'em all. Got some, did'n I? Saved some."

A rumble of phlegm that sounded thick as tar. Laughter, or what was left of it.

"Fuck 'em…" he began again. Then he swigged the clear booze and spilled some down his filthy beard and coat. "Saw 'im comin'. Tried to warn 'em. Almost d'd. Said 'e was out there. Didn't listen. Said it was fiction. Ha! Locked me up! Bastards! T'was all in t' book. He burn't it. But not all. Not all…"

The alley was quiet, except for the guttural ramblings of a mind dimmed to near dark. The sounds of the city echoed indifferent from afar. Voices. Traffic. The rumble of visceral music and mass transit. The Author cursed it all, this world that rejected him and all his works; that ignored and then burned all he tried to be.

Neon brighter now, it bounced off the damp ground to strain his ancient eyes. "Oh poor me, p… p… poor me."

No name, other than the one he chose for himself. To remember his birth name, he'd have to open the haversack and peer at the stained and faded manuscripts inside. Not

---

[16] The name given to a syndrome of contagious agents discovered to be lurking in stockpiled books and journals. Contemporary sources believed the agents to be a legacy of the war, although conspiracy theories abounded to say otherwise. The resulting epidemics so sourced to paper quickly resulted in the medium's timely obsolescence in favour of digital delivery systems. However, with the advent of the forerunner of the *Gestalt* all but a tiny minority had abandoned the concept of books and related material.

that light would have allowed such recollection. It hurt too much for eyes so used to the dark hideaways of the world. The Author would do; it proclaimed him for what he was, gave shape to his purpose.

A deeper shadow lurked to the right. A sullen red glow from distant lamps, kind to his old eyes. He staggered closer. Something nudged his foot and he blinked down over the bottom of the bottle.

A rat's dark eyes stared back. Its whiskers twitched, then it scampered away. The Author giggled, even as the solitary rat became a river of furry bodies. They flowed over and around his rag-wrapped feet. Startling in their silence. Flurries of motion, they scampered into the shadows behind. Like his memories, they faded and were gone.

"Be like the rats," he muttered, taking another swig. "*He* don't care about 'em. To dim f'r '*im*.'"

He turned towards the city light and spread his arms wide in declaration. Glass tinkled and fluid spattered. Head held high, he cackled and yelled: "*He's* not coming any more! *He's* already here! He'll drink your *Souls*!"

The moment passed with another gurgle of mirth. He raised the bottle, unconcerned that the denizens of the city beyond or behind paid no heed. Then he noticed the shards that once held the liquid secure.

"Fuck." He let the disembodied neck slip from limp fingers.

The coolness of the shadows beckoned. Somewhere quiet to sleep off the liquor. Plenty more to be had tomorrow. Begging had always been risky, no more so in *Terapolis* than other times and places, but its rewards satisfied the broken. The shadows closed in, welcome around him.

The alley was narrow and filled with an acrid vapour. The Author coughed, and waved his hand through the dancing tendrils of mist. Red light lit the smoke, making it look eerie. He wasn't bothered by such things; he lived in an eerie city and the light was kind to his eyes.

A few paces and the alley opened up into what looked like a courtyard, enclosed on one side by honest brick walls, the stained remnants of an older city. The tower to the other side loomed organic and lustrous in appearance. More vapour whispered from unseen exhalation ducts.

The Author staggered forward, peering into the gloom for somewhere to curl up. Ducts and utility shafts ran overhead, clung to walls to build an industrial-organic sculpture. Another shaft ran across his path at knee height. He staggered over it, one hand resting against it as he balanced himself for the clamber. It felt yielding like a muscular limb.

On the other side, he saw the piles of refuse bundled up against the lee of the tower, like flaccid boulders in a scree deposit. Some spilled across the courtyard. Beyond the mounds and huddled outliers of refuse, there was a deep shade that beckoned to another alley.

Not every synapse was pickled by the cheap booze. A threadbare sixth sense still operated, even in these latter days of his scavenging existence. A thought that bordered on instinct nudged him through the courtyard, away from the vapours and conduits, to that place of blessed darkness.

A shadow moved to the extreme left of his vision. A few refuse bags tumbled from the mound. For a moment he swore that the ground rippled. The greasy hackles on his neck tried to unstick and stand to attention.

"Fuck 'em," he muttered, but this time his heart wasn't in it. "S'Bloody rats."

He had to climb over the bottom of the mound to reach that tantalising portal. The rubbish shifted beneath his already unsteady feet. He stumbled to his knees, and his hands sank between the bags. He swore incoherently and pulled himself upright. A bag tumbled and hit him in the side. Something swished out of the darkness. A gurgling noise came from behind.

Somehow he turned and peered into the red light. Steam gushed up from gaps between the bags. The ground was falling inwards, the edge rising like a lipless mouth. He grunted, then managed to scream. Bags began to tumble towards the hole as it spread to ellipse the refuse. He was on the wrong side.

Orifice. The word entered his head unbidden, the way they did in the days of his composition. He tried to crawl over the rubbish towards the next alley. The air stank of mould and something that made him think of vomit.

Almost to the other side. No more than an outstretched arm's length from blessed safety. That's when rubbish leapt into the air. Writhing tentacles erupted from the walls of the tower and from deep within the mound. One caught the side of his head and sent him sprawling.

Lucidity returned from its long retreat and he understood everything he saw.

"God!" A long forgotten plea. "Help me!"

Tentacles as thick as a man plucked up the bags and swallowed them down. Others scooped the refuse and moved them into the toothless mouth.

There was a tug on his shoulder. The haversack's ancient strap broke. The burden of years was torn from him. He turned and saw the repository of his life's work swinging in the grip of a thin tentacle. He leapt and grabbed hold of the bag. The tentacle proved too weak to take both his weight and that of the haversack. It sagged. His feet mercifully touched ground and he pulled with a rejuvenated strength.

"My manuscripts!"

Something else wrapped around his legs and pulled him off his feet. Still, he refused to let go. His efforts failed with the old canvas. The fabric ripped and came apart. The pages streamed out, scattering and billowing across the courtyard. Books tumbled, fluttering into the noxious maw below.

The Author screamed as his pages scattered over the refuse and spilled unhindered into the tower's yawning gullet.

"Not my words!"

The tentacle discarded the bag and gripped the Author. In a tug of war they worked until he came apart. Blood spurted to stain vanishing paper and rotting bags. Offal slopped to join the refuse. Then the Author vanished – still screaming – into the noisome abyss.

The last of the refuse was consumed. The courtyard slowly returned to normal. A single solitary page remained to drift across the false ground, forlorn and lost, like a dog missing its owner. Wherever it brushed the surface, a faint ripple spasmed, the *pedederm* discoloured, and the tower itself shivered.

Far away in their hiding holes, only the rats heard the harmonic rumble of a living tower's distress.

WITHOUT the finished exterior, the *Succub-I* looked like a forced mating of a spider, a crab and a standard model *Geistmasque*.[17] The bony claspers scraped impatiently against the glass as though the eyeless body sensed the audience beyond.

Morlock leaned forward, fascinated. "Yes, Bill, it is *beautiful*."

"This is the latest in *Geist-Tek*," Boris declared. "Never before have we been able to present *Gestalt* capabilities in such a small mobile package. And the breakthroughs we have made in interface technology will benefit everyone who uses our products. Ultimately – we can dispense with the conventional implant."

Morlock rose stiffly and walked round the table. As he passed Bill, he noted his companion's expression of awe. Poor Bill was speechless. It was good to see his friend so moved by such innovation.

He turned to Creek. "It looks good, but a thing must be more than well-packaged to succeed."

"Yes, Sir. I know, Sir. I have prepared a demonstration. Natalie has volunteered to test the *Succub-I*."

"Natalie?"

"My niece, Sir."

Morlock gently nodded his head. A moment later a little girl – perhaps eight or nine orbits old – was escorted into the room. She walked nervously and appeared so small between her two escorts. Her eyes scanned the room until it

---

[17] A device worn on the face to blanket the primary senses, but also to safely couple the active components with the client's sub-cranial implant.

found her Uncle. Her face was suddenly illuminated by a bright smile.

"*Uncle Boris!*"

She ran towards him. A teddy bear swung wildly beneath her arm. From the way it moved to maintain a grip, it was clearly an antique; an obsolete 'pet-mech' made by a long-since subsumed rival. Creek picked her up and swung her round, for a moment forgetting where he was. Then he remembered. He placed the girl back on her feet and turned with a red face.

"I'm sorry, Sir." He coughed nervously. "My niece will demonstrate the device for us. I think you – and she – will be impressed."

Natalie hugged her old teddy close. The toy's dark eyes turned this way and that, scanning the faces around the table. The girl looked up at him then, her face wide-eyed.

He could read the emotions flitting through her young mind. Fear of all the adults, but a joy at being the centre of attention. Another layer peeled away and there it was: the greed at the prospect of a new toy. *Delicious.*

"This is Mr Morlock, Honey."

The girl's eyes widened further and her mouth opened in an awe-inspired 'o'.

"The guy looks like a *fucking* undertaker!"

The room went quiet. Lorelei and Bayle looked hastily at their briefing pads. Creek looked horrified.

"Hush, Ted." The girl frowned. "That's Mr Morlock and he's going to let us play with a new *toy*."

Yes. The greed. Delicious. Savour the little children, for they are the key to the future.

"I still say he looks like a *fucking* undertaker."

"You shouldn't speak like that!"

"Hey, *Babe*, you taught me everything I know."

"Bad Teddy. You're embarrassing Uncle Boris – and Mummy too!"

She twisted the bear's neck. There was a sharp crack and a quiet 'gurk'. Then she dropped the creature to the floor and turned her greedy eyes onto the latest *MorTek* machine.

"Is that for me?"

"Yes, my dear, we'd like you to be the first to try it."

"You broke my neck! *Fickle slut!*"

Morlock had to suppress a rare urge to laugh out loud. Children. So entertaining. So precious and full of life. He walked towards the girl, smiling like a grandfather. His stick clapped his pace. He paused at the stricken bear. It struggled on all fours, trying to crawl away with its head back to front. As his shadow fell across its furry face it glanced up.

"Ohshit."

Morlock raised his cane and pressed the silver tip into the bear's right eye. It squawked and its arms and legs writhed. The unblemished eye widened and rolled in its socket. There was a faint pop as the cane entered followed by the crunch of expensive – but now obsolete – photonics. Then a squidge of something organic, more felt than heard. Purple gore spattered onto the floor and stained its fur. The bear stiffened and twitched, then flopped still. With a brief flick, Morlock sent the thing slithering across the floor.

The girl watched unfazed as he approached and placed a hand gently on her shoulder. Creek trembled at her side.

"We are so pleased that you have volunteered to help us, my dear," he said calmly. The little girl smiled and then turned towards the case. Her eyes gleamed.

Digitals scrambled frantically as the thing in the case sensed the girl's presence. The motion at once suggested a puppy pleased to see its mistress... or of a parasite sensing its host. Morlock suppressed a brief frown, and made a mental note to have Creek adjust the device accordingly.

"It's a bit excited, Sir. The idea is rather similar to the, er... *late* bear. Pet and Tek in one module. It encourages nurturing, which causes the *Succub-I* to generate more synaptic enhancers. It's been pre-nurtured and we programmed it to imprint on Natalie's neuro-electric aura. That's a security feature. It imprints on its owner and can then only be reset at one of our approved service outlets."

"A synaptic enhancer? On one so young?"

"It's another of our developments that made the *Succub-I* possible. It is similar to our standard product, but suitable for juvenile neuron fabrics. It is *chemically* non-addictive."

Morlock nodded and rested his hands on his cane. Creek gestured to Natalie to come closer and then carefully reached into the cage. The thing went still as he caressed its back, but it was a stillness filled with stored power. He lifted the thing. Its legs automatically furled beneath its body.

Natalie gasped in combined fear and lust as Creek placed it in her outstretched hands. It sat there, buzzing almost like a purring cat. She looked up. "What do I do, Unc —"

Her words collapsed into a shriek as the thing became a blur of motion. It clambered up the girl's body and clung to her face. Legs gripped, tentacles coiled, some merely holding the body in place, others sought out points of invasion. They probed, discovered, inserted. Pulsed. Small beads of white glistened on her skin around where the interface connectors had merged into the flesh behind her ear.

The girl gave a muffled sigh and reached up to caress the pulsating mask.

"As you see, the interface coils find their entry points and burrow inside, then they inject the synaptic enhancers and extrude micro-tendrils that create the neural interface. Since she has only used it for the first time, it will take a few minutes to achieve full connectivity."

"How do you achieve the interface?"

"It is similar to our high-end products and the standard implant, in that it injects the enhancer into the blood stream through tiny needles in the suckers on the main coil. Interfacing is achieved in a similar vein, but as I said, we have dispensed with the implant. Micro-fibril nano-tubes burrow into the skin. They are so small that they cause no tissue damage. They extrude through the brain to shadow the synaptic connections. Completely harmless, immuno-neutral, and enzyme-degradable by the body."

Morlock nodded and watched the girl. In truth, there wasn't much to see. Then she went rigid, her tiny head raised, arms outstretched to her side. Then she fell backwards and hung suspended in the air, hair flowing as though statically charged.

"Hmm. I take it she has now acquired full connectivity. And where have you sent her?"

"A simple manifestation for this demonstration, Sir. She is taking a flight over *Terapolis*. I'm sure she'll appreciate seeing the city in its true glory. I'm almost jealous…"

It sounded promising; nevertheless he felt a nagging doubt. "We cannot rely on the subjectivity of a child, Creek."

"There is a recording device attached, Sir, and an array of perceptualisers. We can analyse the device's performance as well as Natalie's experiences and responses."

"Good. But we will need more than that. We will need a full range of tests. Including a post-mortem."

"A post... *mortem*? Sir? She is my *niece.*"

Morlock lifted his cane and twisted the head. Then he pushed it down. There was a click and something popped out into his hand, like a cartridge ejected from a shotgun. It was a vial of golden liquid. For a moment, the contents glowed with a light of its own and then turned an opaque amber. Everybody in the room glared at the vial with greedy eyes. Morlock merely stared at Creek.

Creek stared at the vial and licked his lips. The boy had yet to experience the invigoration of *The Vytez*, but he had clearly heard of it.

"A post-mortem... Yes, Sir. Right away, Sir."

Morlock smiled as he placed *The Vytez* in Creek's trembling hands. "I am impressed, Mr Creek – and quite pleased. This is a perk of working for *MorTek*, and I am glad to confirm your position as head of technology. Well done. You will find the work most... *rewarding.*"

They left the table now and surrounded Creek. The ritual greeting. They patted the bewildered *Necrofycer* on the back, shook his hand. Bayle, a stiff "Welcome," then he was replaced by Lorelei's warmer more intimate style. She slipped her hand around him and stroked his ample belly; her lips pressed and lingered on his cheek. Creek flushed.

Morlock smiled; already Lorelei was at work. She would mould him into shape, make him truly part of the brood. Morlock watched, and was satisfied.

Then the greetings were done and the departments filed out. Alone again, Creek stuttered to speak. "I... I'll make the arrangements for Nat... for the *subject*... right away."

"No need, Mr Creek. We have special facilities for that. Belial can make all the arrangements. You go and celebrate, my boy. You have earned it."

Creek stared greedily at *The Vytez* still held in his sweaty palm. When he looked up, Morlock noted with satisfaction that there was a little less life in his eyes. The boy had much to learn, but clearly he would find his place in the *MorTek* corpus.

Sooner or later they all did.

One way, or another.

The Third Folio

For The Book Is The Life

INSIPID light managed to peer in through the blinds like a peeping Tom taking advantage of the gap, but Adam was only half-aware of the feeble rays trying to tickle his eyes. It was midday when the distant light source was directly overhead and its rays managed to infiltrate some of their force into *Terapolis*. It was as good as it ever got, but after a night's book surfing it was like the hopeful welcome of an imagined spring morning.

Adam stretched and yawned and slowly sat up in the chair where he had fallen asleep with the book on his chest. It rested on the floor now, open – he hoped – at the point when his tired eyes shut down for the night. No matter if it wasn't; he'd find his place.

He leaned forward to reach for the book and winced as a cramp pulsed through his side. Slowly the pain subsided and he finally managed to retrieve the item and place it carefully on the coffee table. That's when he noticed how thin was the stack of pages still left to cruise.

The shock was like another attack of cramp. He remembered Caxton's warning. The fix was limited. He had to ration it. And he had guzzled on the pages like a glutton. He cursed his lack of self-control, but he had been hurting bad this time. There were still some pages left to read. That was some comfort. And there was the other book still waiting on the coffee table. Untouched. Unread. And satisfyingly fat. He could take his time with that one. He relaxed a little and let his gaze fall on the first book.

Fahrenheit 451.

Sat half open on the coffee table, it looked as though it was resting. He savoured the title in bold print. The grubby cover was cracked and lined with age, but the cover art was still visible. Bold and vibrant once, faded now, but it still showed a fiery image. His imagination brought those flickering flames to life in their original glory.

He might have damn near burned it out at one sitting, but he knew that at need he could dive into it again. That was the strength, the attraction. He might read it again and again, each time finding something new, a fresh insight, a subtlety to its texture. It still pulled him. Even now. He felt the urge to surf the pages.

Touch *me*. Read *me*.

The voice was a whisper in his mind. Beguiling. Alluring. Seductive. He reached out and picked up the battered volume, felt the texture of the paper and savoured the organic quality of the sounds the pages made as he flicked through. Then, he placed it to his face and breathed deep of its musty scent.

Caxton was telling him something with this one. He had hinted at the secret world and society that he lived in and which Adam could only guess at.

In Bradbury's world, as in his own, the book had been condemned to die, and not for entirely dissimilar reasons, he gathered from Caxton's half-remembered talk. But there was more, much more to the death of books in this reality. As ever Caxton had only hinted at the depths of knowledge he contained. Perhaps with this book, Caxton was letting him know that the cloak of mystery was about to be slowly unveiled?

In that universe, the world of Montag and Faber and the Salamanders, the preservationists remembered the book. Word for word, they committed each precious volume into the fickle database of solitary human memory.

They had no choice. To keep the book alive, they needed to retain each one as a neurological will 'o the wisp. In this reality, in the world of the *Gestalt*, he knew that the book must be preserved in its physical form. The fight was to retain its tangible qualities, its three-dimensionality. Trust not to fickle memory, he knew, for they lived in a world of sensual gratification and instant experience where memory struggled to stay alive.

Yes, Caxton was telling him something. He was hinting that Adam was no longer the junkie, scoring paper fixes in basement bars. He was an acolyte, an initiate to a secret society that existed to keep the light alive. He'd been entrusted with something more than a book; he had been granted a mission and a purpose in life. At long last.

"We're all living in the gutter," Caxton's voice whispered unbidden, "but some of us are looking up at the stars."

He remembered the phrase, a sudden interruption in Caxton's chain of thought, as though the man had just thought of it. He'd asked, if only for the sake of conversation, "Who said that?"

"Oscar Wilde. He was a writer. You should read some of his stuff sometime."

"What's a writer?"

The big man laughed at that. His booming mirth turned too many heads for Adam's liking. When he regained control Caxton said: "Where do you think these things came from? They weren't grown in a vat like that *MorTek* shit you Gack. Somebody had to *write* them. Somebody had to *print* them."

Funny, what stuck in the mind to reappear later. He couldn't even remember when or where the conversation took place. He shrugged the memory away and let his thoughts return to the book. Not to the world it depicted, but to the thing itself. It was such a simple thing. Simple, yet beautiful. And he was to be one of the Keepers. He was to be groomed. He would join the *Incunabula*, where he would nurture and preserve an endangered species on its fight back into life. He would no longer be the misfit and the outcast, the lonely *derm-rat*[18] wandering the streets of *Terapolis*. He would have purpose and a place to belong.

---

[18] A colloquial expression for residents of the city's lower levels. Typically, it refers to youth gangs and other itinerant wanderers through the city's night life, though its usage is fairly loose in its application.

"You are the torchbearer," Caxton's deep voice added in his mind. "Not to burn but to illuminate the page."

He nodded. He remembered the conversation. Caxton unusually talkative. There had been more, but he had only caught snatches against the backdrop of the music and his impatience for a fix.

There was a warning accompanying the signal. That with this trust came a danger. A danger he couldn't quite fathom, but he sensed it involved more than police and courts and prison sentences for dealing with contraband and hazardous material. Something worse. And clearly, it involved *MorTek*.

He shuddered at the memory of Marla Caine and Otto Schencke, but he felt the book calling him again as though to soothe the uncomfortable recollection. Or was that just the latency of the cravings? It didn't matter. Not really. He thought about work. Checked the time and was elated to find there were moments to spare. He reached for the book and settled down to read some more.

Only a little, he told himself. A few pages. A few minutes. He could put the book down any time. He was in control; he knew when to say no.

"AND where did the books go when the world turned against them? When the flames of wrath blackened their pages and erased the words, they fled to find solace and redemption in the dark places of the world.

"They were exiled into darkness so their own light might one day return to illuminate the world. They went underground, literally and metaphorically, so that their haven became the hidden places far beneath the feet of their persecutors.

"Thus was born the Incunabula: it was forged by fire and persecution, to preserve and protect until the book might rise, Phoenix-like, from the ashes of demise."

So wrote my old friend and mentor, Elzevir, in the days when duty and health still left him the time and the luxury to lift a pen. And all these years later, underground we remain, but we endure in hope...

CAXTON glanced up from his typescript and looked around this cathedral of literature they'd constructed long ago. No longer was the great library the dark and damp place of his youth; more warehouse-come-cavern in those days. Now it looked like the real deal; a glimpse of the past brought lovingly back to life. Not as nostalgia, not as heritage – not entirely – but as a living entity: a seed bank for the preservation of humanity's mimetic diversity.

Around him were the desks and benches of the central reading 'room'. Beyond those was the labyrinth of shelving, with its precious hoard of paper: the books and periodicals of ages past, the plays and movie scripts, scientific papers and more.

Further still into their little citadel, store rooms held the artefacts of a neglected culture; photographic archives and a myriad of artworks; old film stock, salvaged from half-remembered collections; music, in sheet form and antique vinyl, tape and compact disk, digital players and – he swore – even a box or two of ancient wax cylinders. Then there were computer games too, gathering dust in wait for the revival of technologies sidelined to obsolescence by the advent of the *Gestalt*; but it was books, ever books, that bore the brunt of Morlock's malice.

This was their little world, the tunnels and corridors, meeting rooms and chambers restored from ruin that led on to the warrens of an older time and the metropolis buried beneath *Terapolis*; just one of many arks adrift in time.

For a few moments, Caxton indulged himself, taking it all in. He watched the people sit in their private pools of lamp light as they absorbed the thoughts of dead minds, or the browsers who walked the shelves. Here was another time replayed before his eyes; here they kept the light burning against the growing shadows of the present.

If arts and music, precious gifts in themselves, were akin to memory, literature was the self-knowing of the species; the human mind accumulated, a manifest of wisdom and knowledge, self-doubt and awareness, folly and foible, all transmitted through the generations. Books amplified the light of mind, reinforced the soul; everything that *Terapolis* was not.

"What an astonishing thing a book is," he mumbled, memory invoking a mind long dead. *"One glance at it and you're inside the mind of another person, maybe somebody dead for thousands of years. Across the millennia, an author is speaking clearly and silently inside your head, directly to you. Writing is perhaps the greatest of human inventions, binding together people who never knew each other, citizens of distant epochs. Books break the shackles of time. A book is proof that humans are capable of working magic."*[19]

Yes, magic; he smiled. Then his mood turned sombre. Across the way a team of scribes copied out works by hand. Next to them, even more patient in their laborious task, men and women worked their precious laptops; obsolete machines made by long-dead tech firms, they were carefully maintained from scavenged parts and luck. Now these 'techheads' from a bygone age tested old memory sticks and

[19] Carl Sagan.

storage devices, searching for the gems of digital texts and cultural artefacts that might yet be recovered.

Caxton sighed. He knew from long experience how fruitless the task too often proved. The promise of a dead future; the curse of the digital dark age. Still they would keep such media in the hope that some day, in better days, they might re-engineer the combination of code and tech to unlock the past, and turn those fossilised accretions of binary data back into human-readable sense.

Until then they held such artefacts in trust, and hoped they contained more than the tax returns of extinct dotcoms.

Meanwhile, theirs was an age of analogue, the vulnerability of paper and ink proved their last redoubt. A precarious position, and a burdensome irony; of that there was no doubt. He sighed, and returned to the document in hand...

ELZEVIR is one of few now. The few who remember directly those sombre days, when the sum total of human life was deleted, when the book burners raised ascendant, and cast Humanity into the Abyss of this, our Dark Age of the Gestalt.

Of course, in those first days of burning, there was no such organisation. There were only isolated people acting alone. Such was Elzevir, but he worked tirelessly and fearlessly to bring together those of like mind.

It was only chance—or fate—that enough came forward to stand against the darkness. On the wings of the storm, they gathered what they could and scurried to safety. In those desperate days, books were hidden in warehouses, garages, attics and basements, and even in small piles hidden amidst the dust beneath the bed. The sanctuaries were as varied as those who flocked together. People came from all walks of life, bound to the writing by a common calling.

As they found one another slowly and cautiously, so they also learned that not all bibliophiles were what they seemed. For some were but the agents of Morlock, and those too trusting or incautious saw their precious collections added to the pyres of the Hazamat.

So as the flames scorched away human memory, those unlikely few who survived nurtured the seeds of what was to become the Incunabula.

The word is old beyond our reckoning, but it is a fitting appellation for our organisation. In naming ourselves we looked to the past. The word derives from ancient Latin and means 'cradle book'. We, however, cannibalised it from the history of the European printed word, when it referred to books printed before the year 1501 of the old Anno Domini system.

So today, the Incunabula is the cradle that preserves and protects the book.

This is not all we learned from those many volumes we stored and preserved. We learned the lessons of 19th and 20th century (old calendar) radicals and revolutionaries. We took their advice on forming our organisation. So we are nebulous, lacking a defined centre. We exist as cells—free and independent Chapters, dislocated from the others, so that if one falls, the others go on. Few of us know more than one or two of these safe havens—and none know them all.

Against all the odds, against all of Morlock's malice, we still exist. It must be said that as the years piled up, our persecutors helped us. For the intensity of persecution faded and we settled into a long 'cold war'. Morlock and his agents turned their hands to other things, thinking that we were dead or dying or too weakened to ever become a threat. And so we gained a breathing space to build, to grow, to plan.

But we can never think that this will remain the case forever. One day, Morlock's malice will return. And make no mistake, my reader, that Morlock knows the importance of the book far better than many of us today.

For we push the most powerful drug ever used by Mankind. We are a distraction and, ultimately, a poison to the Gestalt. We are human living and awareness, diametrically opposed to its amnesiac release.

When books were destroyed, the memory of humanity was destroyed with it. That is in part what Morlock planned:

to eradicate the collective consciousness that bound us to the past and gave us a stepping-stone to our future.

Such is human living today: an existence with no memory. A life of no direction, other than to satisfy mere cravings and gratification through the medium of the Gestalt. There is no tomorrow, only the pleasures of the immediate. Life has become solitary and disconnected moments scattered across the floor like a broken string of pearls, and we must prostrate ourselves before _him_ to gather them up.

But the Incunabula threatens this, it promises memory over forgetting, it binds us together and severs us from Morlock, indeed it takes him away from the centre of our existence.

So, we must not lose faith.

Yet, many have despaired over the years.

That is understandable, but we must never give in to such feelings, for that is Morlock's way. At times our cause does indeed seem hopeless, but we must succour our hope, because our enemy has a weakness that is our greatest strength.

For the written word _still_ lives. Though illiteracy today runs high, ours is not yet a post-literate society. Look around you.

The words are there for eyes to see. They shout their defiance in the only places where they might currently live free of persecution. Look at that which you most take for granted. There you will find the hiding places of the written word, under the very noses of our persecutors.

In shop signs, menus, corporate reports, instruction manuals, memos and more, the written word clings to existence. It can be no other way. Even Morlock cannot make it otherwise without destroying the mechanisms of his existence.

For Morlock it must be a sad and terrible irony. While these forms of the written word are functional, cold and uninspired—the desiccated 'Newspeak' of our times—they are a doorjamb keeping the way open, if only by a crack.

Yes, that door is open my friends, and even Morlock cannot close it. That door is heavily guarded, but even the most vigilant sentinels grow weary. The day will come when we can usher Mankind back into the light.

For now we must wander the tunnels of darkness, but we of the Incunabula are the torchbearers: not to burn the page, but to illuminate it and keep its own light intact.

We nurture the candle flames that show the way ahead. We are guerrillas of the word, unsung heroes breathing softly on the embers of the human mind, so that they might re-ignite the hearths around which we once found safe haven.

The book is the <u>Light</u> and the <u>Life</u>. Morlock can never defeat us, so long as we hold to that.

YES, so long as we hold to that and stay the course, but Caxton knew just one mistake would cause it all to become ash.

As if to emphasise the point, Caxton tapped his manuscript on the table, tidying the bundle's edge. Then he flicked through slowly, his eyes scanning the lines of imprecise type. A long-anticipated moment approached, for the years of labour were almost complete.

Satisfied, he placed it on the desk before him. Then he reached into a pocket for his tobacco pouch and papers and began to roll himself a cigarette.

"I trust you *won't* smoke that in here."

He paused with the incomplete cigarette halfway to his lips and glanced up at the speaker. Despite the stern intonation, the man's face smiled. Caxton smiled back, then he licked the paper and sealed the tobacco tube.

"For later," he said and slipped it behind an ear.

"Those things will be the death of you," Elzevir said.

Caxton shrugged. "Got to make sure I get the condemned man's last smoke."

Elzevir grunted, then pulled up a chair and sat down so that he could lean forward in a conspirator's huddle. That's what they were, what they'd always been even here in the heart of their own safety, conspirators.

"So why did you want to see me? My guess is you haven't shown up to see an old man for the sake of it."

"No. You're right. I haven't. Sorry." He fought the urge to smoke. He sighed and forced himself to go on. "Remember how we first met?"

"How could I forget? At the time you were the biggest fright of my life."

"I know. You took a chance on me then. I want you to take a chance on me again. You know the situation out there?"

"Yes. It's not like before, I can feel that in my old bones. This is the End Game."

"The End Game. Almost. It's him or us. Morlock or the *Incunabula*. And when I've finished this," he tapped the manuscript, "I'll be going back to him one last time. To finish the game once and for all."

"He'll *kill* you, Cax!"

"He might. If that happens, then you'll have the information to finish what I started."

"I don't like this. I don't like what you're saying. We have to keep our heads down and survive!"

"Not this time, El. There is no survival – *unless* we get to him first."

"And what has this to do with me taking a chance? Surely, you don't expect me to come with you? I'd only slow you down."

Despite his tension, Caxton had to suppress a laugh. "No, El. It's not *that* dangerous. I hope. It's about the boy. Adam. One of my contacts."

El nodded. "I know of him."

"He's out there on his own. I want… I came to ask that he be brought in."

"These are dangerous times, old friend."

"I know. That's why I need him protected. I can't protect him. He needs bringing in for his own sake."

"Too dangerous to be bringing in waifs and strays. What is so special about this young man? Why would you risk so much for him? We have all, you included, cut loose better prospects."

"I have my reasons."

"Not good enough, Cax. He is a potential liability. No discipline. A misfit, impulsive, a dreamer, a user of the *Gestalt* for God's sake – and you want to bring him in amongst us?"

"I know it's not easy, but I can't leave him unprotected. Not now. *Especially* not now."

"If you want me to even consider this, you'd better tell me. And make it good."

"I have my reasons. Please believe me."

"I am prepared to believe, *when* I hear something."

"Okay. *Okay.*"

He sighed. Took the roll up from his ear and twiddled it through his fingers. Elzevir stared, his face a picture of perfect but undeterred patience. There was no choice.

"I knew the boy's father. Could have stopped something terrible, but I didn't. It's taken me years to track him down. I owe him. More than either you or he can ever imagine."

"I see. You know I have never pried into your past. What I know, I know, and I won't probe any further. But no matter how much you owe this boy, I don't see any reason to do as you ask. If it were just between you and me then I might consider otherwise, but it isn't about you or me or the boy – it's about the future of books, of the *Incunabula* and everyone in it. Too much rides on our survival!"

"You say the boy is a risk?"

"A great risk."

"So was I, once!"

"Yes, I took a chance and you didn't let me down. Though you've always been trouble."

"So trust me now. Look after the boy for me. I can't be there for him. You know what I must do."

The old man looked at him with tired eyes. Tired and afraid. He nodded his head. "Yes. Though I still don't see why it has to be you."

"It *has* to be me. I've been there before. I know what to expect. And I can live with… the consequences."

"You might die with it."

"Perhaps. I'm prepared to take the risk. The alternative is worse."

Elzevir sighed and leaned back. "Okay. Well, old friend, I tried. You can't blame me for that."

"No."

He glanced across at the manuscript and added: "So, this suicide note of yours, how goes it?"

"Nearly finished. I wrote the important bits long ago. I am finishing the rest. My testament. My legacy. Part of my atonement."

"After all these years, you're still tearing yourself up about it. You're not the only one to have defected from *MorTek*."

"I know. That isn't what I'm on about. The *Incunabula* saved my sanity, but I am not certain it ever saved my Soul."

"I am not about to ask what you mean by that. I fear we might be here all day if I did."

"I wouldn't answer you anyway."

"But the boy is involved?"

"Yes." He looked away, unable to meet his old friend's gaze. Bad memories threatened to surface, breaking out of his carefully maintained visage.

Elzevir didn't speak. He only stared until Caxton felt the man was pulling the raw memories of yesteryear from the vault of his skull. He sensed indecision behind the resolve. Maybe the boy had a chance.

"I know some of what you have written," he said at last, "but not all of it. What happens if you meet an unfortunate accident before it's finished?"

"That won't happen. The important stuff is done. Once the whole manuscript is completed I'll be telling what I know to the *Gorsedd*."[20]

Elzevir nodded, and played with his beard thoughtfully. "Even so."

"And if something *does* happen, you'll get the important sections anyway. Laura will bring them to you."

El sighed. "Why you Cax? Why now?"

"It has to be me. I want it to be me."

"*Nobody* can kill Morlock. No one can get near him."

"No, you're wrong. He's vulnerable. More so than ever."

"The head of the world's largest company is *vulnerable*?"

---

[20] The *Incunabula's* Ruling Council. The word is from the Welsh language and means 'throne'. It was used in reference to a meeting of bards and druids prior to the annual *eisteddfod*.

"He's invested too much in his plans now, set too much in place. He doesn't have the room or the time to manoeuvre in a setback."

"And how does the boy figure in this?"

"He doesn't. He's a loose end I want tied up. Please, Elzevir. Don't leave him alone out there."

"I am not happy with this."

"I am not asking you to be happy. I am asking for your help."

The old man looked troubled, his eyes reflecting the struggle of conscience over pragmatism. They *all* had ghosts in this business. He glanced away, picked up a stray paper clip and began to play with it. "I can't make any promises, Cax, but I will see what I can do."

"Thanks El–"

"There's more: you make things plain to him. Tell him the facts of life. And get that *infernal* implant out of his head. I won't bring him in until his mind is free – but I will see what I can do so that he is protected. We won't cut him loose. *Yet.* That is up to you – and this Adam. Make him see that this isn't a story in one of our books!"

He nodded, grateful and reached to retrieve his manuscript. As he did so, Elzevir reached across and gripped his arm.

"You've always been trouble, Cax, bent the rules around your little finger, but I have never known you take unnecessary risks. This isn't like you. I hope you know what you're doing. I hope that young man is *worth* it."

A sigh. An attempted grin. "So do I, El, so do I."

AT times like this, Adam longed to lose himself in the pages of a book, but it was just that kind of activity that had brought him before Lang's sweat-polished features.

Even the *Gestalt* would make for a fair second best, anything to avoid those eyes as glassy as marbles. They stared so hard, they might even be reading his latest book from the impressions left in his brain.

On reflection, he shouldn't have read so much of his latest fix. 'No' was easier said than done. Even now, he could feel the allure, wanted to rush out and bury his head back in the pages. He felt happy there, at peace with himself. Of course, it was always followed by the harsher side of reality. Everything has a downside. Lang was his.

"You're not happy here, are you lad?"

"Sir." He tried to say it with a questioning inflection, but his throat felt clogged. He couldn't say the truth, but he didn't trust himself to give a straightforward lie.

"Do you think I want to be here?"

"Don't know, Sir."

Lang picked up a stylus and began to twirl it through his fingers like a baton. Adam risked wiping his sweaty palms on the thighs of his pants. Then he clasped them in front of him, his head, as ever, downcast.

"Of course I don't want to be here. I'd rather be in the *Gestalt*, like any *normal* person. But I got to be here so I can earn my way in. You see what I'm trying to say?"

"Yes, Sir."

"Do you?"

He dropped the stylus and picked up a sheaf of paper. Casually, he began to sift through the charts and tables. Timesheets and records; cold and functional, on poor quality paper, but still the rustle of the pages sent a tingle running up his spine. Suddenly his nose savoured the half-remembered, half-imagined scent of old books and the tingle threatened to become a revealing shudder.

Lang glanced up sharply.

"You know what these are?" He gestured with the pages, making them rustle all the more.

"No, Sir."

"Time sheets. Work reports. *Yours.*"

"Sir."

"This is the third time you've been late for a shift this week. And for the last three months your time keeping has dropped from just tolerable to abysmal. What's wrong, lad?"

"Nothing, Sir."

"Really?" He dropped the paper back on the desk, where it slithered beguilingly. Adam felt the urge to let his fingers flick through the pages. He had to keep the secret. He had to keep control.

"Just not been well, Sir."

"For three months? Locate a doctor and stop wasting our time!"

"Yes, Sir. Sorry, Sir."

"You don't like this place. You don't like your work mates, do you?"

Poker face time again. "Sir."

"Well, I'll tell you: they don't like you. You're a day-dreamer. They're sick of carrying you. They're a good bunch. Hard workers. Your team's up for *Gestalt* Bonus Time – 48 hours' worth – and they're on target to achieve it despite your slackness. I'd hate to see them lose out because of you. So I suggest you sort yourself out and stop letting *everybody* down."

Adam felt his knees begin to tremble. He wanted to be dismissed, to return to the anonymity of his job, but Lang hadn't finished.

"You just don't know how lucky you are, lad. This might not be *MorTek*, but we're a sub-contractor and that brings benefits. You know what I'm saying? We're in line for increased orders, expanded distribution territory – because we got hard workers. And then we got *you*."

"I work hard, Sir." He felt the sudden confidence drain from his voice, his words turning to a mumble. "At least I try."

"But you can't keep your mind on it! Last week," he shuffled through the pages again, and pulled one out, "we were late with three deliveries because you – dreamy-head – packed the wrong components."

"I did work late to help repack it."

Another sigh as Lang deflated.

"You know, lad, you can be a good worker when you set your mind to it. Settle down, try to fit in better, work at it and in a few years' time you could be a shift supervisor."

"Yes, Sir." He suppressed the shudder of horror. "Is that all, Sir? Only, I should get back to work."

Lang glared at those words, but if fresh anger was triggered, he swallowed it. "Yes, lad, that's it. Get yourself in there and let's see some hard graft."

Grateful, Adam turned to step out of the office. On the threshold, he saw Tracy, one of the clerks, smirking at him, but she quickly turned to a colleague. They both looked up and began to giggle. Adam felt his face flush hot.

Then Lang called out and he was forced to linger in his theatre of shame for a few moments more. "Remember what I said earlier. Cash means more *Gestalt*. No job, no cash. Think on that!"

A deep breath failed to settle his nerves.

Otto wondered why he even bothered any more but it had become part of his ritual of mental preparation. Just like the brisk knock before he flung open the double doors and stepped through. This time, the office was unoccupied. Otto felt his brain slip a gear.

Bill stared from his pedestal on the far side of Morlock's desk. The empty sockets exerted a powerful tug, as if twin singularities were buried deep within the shaded cavities. For a while, the gravitation grabbed Otto's gaze. Then he managed to break free and step towards the desk. *Terapolis* smouldered beyond the window behind Morlock's vacant throne.

He checked his watch and bit down on a curse. Morlock was seldom late for meetings. He stared through the window for a few moments more, and then impatience made him look towards the door of his master's private apartments. It blended with the wall, but to eyes that knew what to look for it was plain. As ever, the mysterious barrier was closed.

Beyond that door, they said there was a *place* that emerged at any of the *MorTek* towers across the globe. Frivolity, of course, but it still caused him to think twice about knocking and entering the unknown on the other side. Better not to fall into the trap of curiosity. None ventured through that door. Except Belial, of course, and – somehow – Creek's less than astute predecessor had found his way to the other side. But *he* had emerged raving and broken, fit only for the *necrolysers*.

Ignorance was safer.

Out of habit, he turned to pace and found himself locked into the skull's field of perception yet again. He shuddered at the grisly reminder, then swore. Out loud this time. It stared as if it resented him, as well it might, but he'd be damned if he'd be cowed by a relic. He met the old bone's gaze with stiff defiance and said: "So, Bill, where do you want to go today?"

Bill, of course, made no response. There was a relief in that, for even though reason acknowledged it as a lump of lifeless gristle, there was still the unsettling recollection of Morlock's many conversations with his 'companion'. Nobody mentioned it aloud, but he was certain he was not the only one to wonder at his master's eccentricity. Did Morlock really perceive Bill's long-silenced voice?

A rich man's foibles. It was only dead bone, and quite harmless. Even so, he couldn't meet the thing's gaze for long. Despite his joking words, he still remembered the face it once wore, the eyes that once filled those empty sockets. In the days when the man had been a powerful figure, a rival of Morlock's, then Otto's prey. After that, just this pampered keepsake. One of his first jobs for Morlock, acquiring Bill.

He remembered.

The old man was full of confidence. Defiant. Tried to buy his way out of extinction. At first. Then he began to whine and plead, just as they all did in those days of relative inexperience, when he took too long at the job. The bullet did its work and put an end to the snivelling. No trace of the entry and exit damage now, of course. He had chosen the bullet carefully for the task. Ammunition sufficient to pulp the cortex without unduly shattering the cranium. The modicum of damage was duly repaired. Where had the bullet struck? Ah yes. Two centimetres or so above and to the left of the right orbit. His aim had been a little off that day. The body twitched for some time before it finally settled into death, pouring out blood over the man's plush furnishing and expensive suit. A grisly task collecting the head – he wasn't a butcher – but Morlock had so wanted it.

And here Bill had been ever since: a dread reminder of human mortality.

Otto broke from the skull's reverie and turned to pace the circumference of the room. Idly, he let his eyes scan the portraits of the subsidiary *MorTek* towers. Grim sculptures of composite architecture, of flesh and bone arranged with no geographic logic. Their names were the last remembrance of places from a world long-vanished: the Oceania tower, *MorTek* Centrasia, Mumbhai, Hong Kong, Beijing, Tokyo, California, Cairo, Manhattan, Europa, Rome, Atlantis, *MorTek* Borealis, *MorTek* everywhere. His master's havens. Each one a transmitter taking a grateful world to the inner mysteries of the *Gestalt*.

Full circuit, he had circumnavigated the globe and re-turned to his master's desk. The damn skull was still watching him, and Morlock had not yet arrived.

He checked his watch and clucked his tongue. There was always so much to do that wasn't being done while he waited. This was unlike his master. He tried to remember the last time he'd been kept kicking his heels like this.

Always a fickle thing at the best of times, memory. He found he was unable to recollect any previous occurrence.

How long had he worked for Morlock now? He frowned. It was… The knowledge failed to materialise. It didn't make sense. He remembered how it began, but the memory carried no date stamp. In a sense, he had *always* worked for Morlock, yet he knew there was a time *before*.

THERE was the time when Morlock was just a commission. In the beginning they had met over the barrel of a gun, their relationship to be nothing but a transaction. A life traded for a bullet.

That's how it was meant to be. In that misplaced envelope of time, he was young. Yes, he had *actually* been young, though he could not really recall the textures and taste of this bygone youth. He was also inexperienced, not just in life, but in his profession of death. There was so much to learn and experience to complete his apprenticeship, and so much respect to earn from his long-lost peers. In the end, that's why he demanded, then begged, for the commission.

The job to make his name, or kill him in the attempt.

A fool's job. He knew it then. He knew it now and winced at the recollection. Experienced men thought twice about it, which is probably why he got it in the end. The odds were not good, the pay below par, and yet he went for it, followed youthful overconfidence, listened to the howling cries of ambition and yelled defiance at fate. Bold youth took a chance, and if it wasn't fate, then at least luck was with him that day.

Almost until the very end.

In those days, *MorTek* was a rising star, though yet to achieve its peak. Much like the young Otto Schencke, he mused. The technology flooding from its research labs was already changing the world with the impetus of a tidal wave, and it terrified the bloated corporations that beheld this bold newcomer with jealous contempt.

In those days it was still legal to print and own books. Journals and newspapers still rolled off the presses, the airwaves screeched with transmitted electronic data, bringing a diverse global culture to a man's fingertips. Otto used many such sources to research his target, and found them frustrating in their lack of hard facts. His prey was the recluse even then. Seldom seen, little heard; he let his innovations do his talking. Yet his company created an endless progeny of analysis, comment and astounded speculation.

All of it useless for a young man in a very different industry. There were other ways to stalk his prey. After months of careful preparation, what he found was astonishing – that his target was so vulnerable.

Getting in was no problem. It seemed so easy. Suspiciously so, in hindsight.

THERE he found him. The man who was single-handedly changing the world. Sat at his desk – this desk – in an office not too dissimilar to this one, yet an ocean's breadth away. Immersed in a pool of light from an old-fashioned banker's lamp, Morlock looked up and smiled with cool confidence.

"Mr Schencke. I am so pleased to meet you at last. I have been waiting for you for such a very *long* time."

Even then, he realised this was not in the script. It wasn't unusual for a commission to haggle for the price of life. Some threatened and blustered. All pleaded before the final inevitability of that hollow point round. None had ever expressed welcome. He'd die all the same. The moment was irrevocable.

All it needed was a squeeze of the trigger. A few kilograms of pressure. The easiest thing in the world. He frowned as he found his finger paralysed.

Morlock simply smiled.

"I'm here to kill you," Otto said. No reason why. That wasn't in the script either. It just came to mind and he said it. If only he could move his finger.

"That is your profession. And you have such potential, but are you sure that you can kill me?"

"Sure. I squeeze the trigger. You die."

Morlock sat back. The epitome of calm control.

"Then shoot, Mr Schencke. Shoot and change the world."

His finger came back to life. The relief dried the sweat beneath his armpits as his finger curled around the trigger. No explosion, just a mild 'phut' as the silenced round left the muzzle and struck its target. Morlock's head jerked back.

After that the moments became blurred. Fragments merged into fragments to create a crazy mosaic of senseless meaning. He – *thought* he – saw Morlock's skull erupt. No blood. No skin. No brain blubber. Just splintered fragments flying free as a searing light blazed from the heart of Morlock's cranium.

Otto cried out against the glare and turned away to shield his eyes with his gun arm. Even then, the red brilliance burned to the core of his Soul. From the radiant depths of the supernova, emerged a voice.

"You are implacable, Mr Schencke. I knew you were a man I can use."

The light vanished so suddenly that for long moments he was blinded by a perception of fathomless darkness. Then he realised there was light. Soft and humble. The light of the banker's lamp. He turned towards the source of the voice and stared through the splashing colours that dribbled through his vision.

Morlock leaned on his desk and stared like a patient predator. There was no hint of any bullet damage to his head, but a hole in the man's chair exuded stuffing like a blossoming flower. A few fibres still floated in the air. The gun smoke smelled acrid; the only evidence that he'd actually squeezed the trigger.

"Now, Mr Schencke, we should discuss the remuneration for your services. You will find me most generous, I assure you."

Without a word, he sat down. For the second time in his life, one Otto Schencke had perished and another was born. And he still didn't understand how or why.

A click brought Otto back to the present. He jumped at the sound, which was too much like the noise of a firearm making ready. The doors swung open. At last –

But it was only Belial.

"Yes, what do you want?" Otto's tone held a gruff distaste. If possible, this creature made his skin crawl even more than Bill.

Belial stared.

Then he spoke. "Master apologises, but he will see you on the veranda."

Otto closed his eyes a moment and uttered a silent curse. The veranda. With a sigh he moved towards the door, trying not to show his disgust at being so near the lumbering bulk of Belial.

The creature – he had difficulty thinking of it as a man – stepped aside. Perfect deference, as always, but filled with cloaked malevolence. Otto stepped past, grateful to be away from such proximity. He paused as Belial closed the doors. Rare curiosity compelled him.

"Tell me, Belial, how long have you worked for Morlock?"

Belial stared at him again. Long and penetrating.

"Same as you," Belial said, "*forever.*"

BACK to the grind. Still only half-dressed, Adam stepped into the warehouse. The cold hit immediately, especially biting after the red-heat of his lecture. It gnawed at his ears and fingers and chilled his face. Every exhalation was a shroud of ice-white mist.

He quickly zipped up the warm-suit over his everyday clothes, pulled the hood over his head and cap and pulled on the mittens. Then he had to remove them again to fumble for his mask and tie it in place. Only then could his fingers find respite from the chill.

He slammed his way through the plastic strips that separated the antechamber from the main warehouse. He stepped out into noise, only slightly muffled by his hood. The hum of the refrigerators, the babble of voices and shouted orders, the buzz of forklift trucks. From afar, the dim roar of powerful engines as trucks pulled up and departed from the loading bays on the far side of the warehouse.

He scurried onwards, past racks and shelves of mysterious components and boxes, all bearing the *MorTek* logo; he dodged whirring trucks, laden with the very same stuff that rested dormant on the shelves. He ignored jibes from co-workers in the other teams as he scurried past their packing stations. He'd heard them all before.

It was just his luck that today his team was close to the delivery bays, it meant more minutes subtracted from his time sheet, more annoyance from his peers, more disapproval from his bosses. But it couldn't be helped, and for once he had a cast iron alibi: Lang's lecture.

Even as he let his mind while away the already dull day, he scanned the rows, aisles, and packing stations for Claire. He hadn't forgotten her enraged message, and he wanted to apologise, wanted to keep her interested. If only she wasn't so pushy about things. She might get them both into trouble before long. When he saw her, he realised, he not only had to apologise, but thrash it into her head that she had to keep the secret. For both their sakes.

He'd be the Caxton to her Adam, her mentor, her guiding hand into a world that was a universe away from this warehouse. And get some good sex too, always a bonus.

"Oy, sleepy head! We're over here!"

Bob strode towards him, his gaunt features recognisable even beneath the hood and mask. His eyes seemed lifeless compared to Lang's. Mere sullen holes scraped out of his skull, but they stung with accusation.

"Sorry, Bob," he said to forestall the accusation of lateness. "Mr Lang wanted to see me."

"Did he now." Bob seemed only slightly mollified by the news. "Well, you'd better get on with it. We've a rush order to sort later, so we need to clear this."

Adam nodded. "Have you seen Claire?" he asked.

"Who?"

"Claire," he repeated, but Bob had already turned to shout at one of the forklift drivers. Adam decided to leave it, and went over to the packing station.

To his surprise, and relief, his team mates didn't bother to rib him about his timekeeping. They just glanced up from their work. They looked dazed, and then Adam recognised the symptoms of prolonged *Gestalt*-use. Of course, there'd been a team outing to a Node last night. They were still coming together, bodies working automatically from long habit while their minds readjusted to this world. A reprieve, then.

He got into his rhythm. He consulted the delivery sheet, selected the components from the relevant pallet, placed it in one of the cryo-crates, then repeated the process. Second by second, minute by minute, hour after hour. The work was repetitive and tiring, but didn't occupy the mind.

So was it any surprise his thoughts wandered? It wasn't like the job gave his mind anything to do but find ways to measure the pace of the day. They could hardly blame him, just because he managed to keep some imagination intact. If they knew, if they had the references he'd found in the books of the *Incunabula,* they'd call him a Billy Liar, a Walter Mitty. He knew that, and he didn't care. He knew he was a dreamer. Knew he was a misfit. It wasn't that he didn't like his colleagues, just that they failed to inspire him. Especially since he discovered books.

It seemed far longer than six months since he abandoned the world of his colleagues. He'd been just like them. Tried to be just like them. Living for the thrills of the *Gestalt*, scrimping and saving and working for the bonus hours to boost his rationed time, making do with Retro-Tek arcades, booze and – too infrequently for his liking – meaningless sex when he couldn't access a G-Spot. Then came Caxton, and books.

He still felt the pull of the *Gestalt*, its dreadful cry wailing through his head, particularly when he was running low on a fix, or couldn't get one for a while, but when he had a book it made him forget all about *MorTek* and the *Gestalt*. At least for a while. In a way, he pitied those who shuffled and worked around him, he pitied them that they lacked what he knew. But he could never tell them; never reveal to them the tantalising wonders that a few hundred sheets of paper could hold.

But Claire was different. Like him, she was some kind of misfit. She didn't belong either. Plus, she had a great body. So he'd drawn her in slowly but surely. And many times since regretted it, when her loud mouth opened to hint – only hint so far – at the secrets he revealed. He'd made her feel special, and she wanted everyone to know that she was too. Women, he considered, were scary at times.

Bob came over with the new delivery order. A big one. A rush job at that. The team was recovering enough to groan a mutual but resigned acknowledgement of the arduous task to come.

So on they went. *Geistmasques* in shrink wrapping, cables and connectors coiled round them. Consoles and attachments that looked like standard polysach boxes, but in a configuration he hadn't seen before. Packs of sealed bags that squidged as though liquid. Worst of all, the largest components sealed again in opaque wraps, but as he carried each one, many of them seemed to squirm sluggishly of their own volition. As the hours passed, he learned to curse his imagination.

Then the time for a break mercifully came. Adam shuffled to the heated rest area and removed his hood, mask and mittens with a deep sense of gratitude. Around him, people from his team and others did likewise before dropping heavily into the worn seats placed around the heaters.

He just slumped into his chair and looked around blearily for Claire. There was still no sign of her, but he felt too tired to ask her whereabouts.

Several of his co-workers started to doze. A few nibbled on packed lunches, or sipped hot coffee. Most, recovered from their ascension through the *Gestalt* last night, talked quietly amongst themselves. Adam felt glad they didn't try to involve him in the banal conversations.

Someone sat in the vacant chair across from him. A newcomer, judging by his fresh face and body language. He didn't speak either. He just reached into a pocket and pulled out a small device that Adam recognised as a portable entertainment console. An *old* one. It must be awkward to maintain. The newcomer placed the mini-headset over one ear, and placed the connector just behind his right ear. Then he set the device's timer and settled back with his eyes closed. Soon his breathing was slow and steady, away with whatever fantasy he'd loaded into the machine.

Adam felt himself doze off the natural way and allowed himself the luxury of a nap. In it, he dreamed of Claire's soft voice reading to him. She'd just got her mouth round to the good bit when the dream was rudely interrupted. Someone smacked his knee and shouted: "Wakey-wakey!"

It was Bob. Adam stared up at him groggily. "Save the wet dreams for later, lad, there's work to be done."

A few colleagues smirked, but said nothing as they shuffled back into mittens and masks. He did likewise, and hurried back to his station. Everyone from his team was there already. Late again. Despite the cold against his exposed face, he felt the heat of redness creep over his features.

The only way to hide from his humiliations was to bury himself in the work, and that's what he did. The same repetitive routine. At least they'd finished the rush order. Back to the standard fare. The day was catching up with him now. Fatigue. He kept going by sheer willpower, forcing not only his body to keep going but his mind. Time dragged like a ball and chain, until *finally*, the shift was over. Before he went, he had to find Claire.

The team shuffled wearily across the warehouse and into the antechamber, milling in amongst the other teams whose shifts had either ended or started. Weary bodies, tired looking faces, but with a hint of satisfaction and anticipation for what the following hours would bring.

Outside the chill air, Adam removed his heat-suit and threw it untidily into his locker. He lingered in a corner, fighting not just the fatigue, but the growing need for books.

People shuffled in and out, waves of bodies, but as the numbers dwindled, there was still no sign of Claire. By now he was beginning to feel afraid.

Reluctantly, he was about to leave when he saw an old woman shuffle out. She hadn't been around long, and he figured her for some retired clerical out to earn a little extra access to a G-Spot. He recognised her from one of the other teams, but he had also seen her in the past talking to Claire. He pushed himself from the wall and walked over. The woman hadn't seen him. She flinched when she turned from putting on her coat, then relaxed a moment later when she recognised him.

Unlike many of the others, she seemed fresher and brighter, despite the long arduous day. There even seemed to be a glimmer in her eye, but Adam rejected that as merely a reflection from the overhead lamps.

"What's wrong, dear?"

"Have you seen Claire? Did she 'comm in sick or something?"

"Who, dear?"

"Claire. You know Claire. I've seen you talking to her!"

"I don't know anyone here called Claire. Do you think you've been overdoing the G-Spot?"

"No! No I haven't."

Anger made him move closer to the woman. He was almost physically forcing her against the wall. He was tired, and desperate.

"What's wrong with everyone? Tell me where she is!"

A flicker in the woman's eyes. There was a sudden sharp pain in his ear. She gripped tight and pulled hard. He buckled his knees and found himself level with her face. The woman's soft, amiable features had hardened to ice.

"Understand, *they* took her and that's *your* fault," she said, tight-lipped. "Now pray that it's only the Cons that got to her and then you forget she ever existed. She didn't belong. She wasn't one of us. So what about you, are you *ready* to join us? You'd better think carefully, my lad, if you don't want to join her. It's time to decide who you are."

OTTO'S business was death, some said – though never to his face. They feared him too much for that. Or, perhaps they feared Marla. Whatever; their opinion displayed only a superficial understanding of his purpose.

The business, these days, was not so much death, as much as *survival*. His employer's naturally, but also his own. Survival. A trait honed to a preternatural edge early in his life in the ruins of lost Hamburg.

Now those survival instincts told him this was to be no ordinary meeting; the future was in flux, melting like a *simulacomm* ready to adopt some new shape. And the man who would mould it waited patiently far above. This day, survival demanded a sense of foreboding.

Belial's last words echoed in his mind. Forever. *Forever.* Yes, it felt like that sometimes. What kind of forever was waiting for him now? No time to ponder. Survival was all. Service was all about surviving, ensuring that you remained useful to the man who played with the world's future.

At the top, the wind moaned beyond the door, like laments for all his victims of years past. Many enemies waiting for him, many scores to settle, many ghosts haunting the dark avenues of his mind. He took a deep breath, and then swallowed the imagined ghosts. A bitter pill, but his grandfather always said the best medicine tasted foul.

He stepped out onto his precarious future. The view from the veranda would take his breath away, if the wind hadn't already snatched it from his mouth. Up here, not far beneath the tower's bulbous minaret, the wind was proud of its strength. It bombarded his body with cold blasts, explored with icy tendrils and ruffled his clothes. It wobbled him on his already quavering feet. He reached out for the wall, seeking balance and security. Instinctively, his fingers flinched to pull way from the strangely yielding material, but he fought back the wired response. Such was his need for support both physical and primal against the horror of vertigo.

The veranda was a flimsy platform of grated steel that girdled the tower. For all the name conveyed, it was little more than some leftover maintenance scaffold for the living structure's man-made accoutrements. These days, it was Morlock's 'retreat'. When he tired of the confines of the office or his mysterious private apartments, he came here. To be alone; to gaze out proprietarily across the city that he, more than any other, had done so much to shape.

Never before had Otto been asked to join his master on this precarious place. An ill omen, for he had far to fall if he failed to meet expectations.

Morlock stood at the parapet. Otto cursed and forced himself to walk across the quivering web of metal. He felt less sure of himself with every step and fought the child-like urge to reach down on all fours and crawl towards his master. It would not look good. It was an urge to be resisted at all costs.

At the parapet he grasped tight to the rail as though his life depended upon it; his anchor to peace of mind, or as much as he could gain up here. Whatever happened, he would not look down. Never look down. His master did not look away from the city, but he spoke first, interrupting the wailing wind.

"We are so close now, Otto. Look, they are ripening."

Otto reluctantly followed Morlock's gaze. Now he mentioned it, those minarets and spires did indeed look as though they were ripening; giant seedpods preparing to spawn, gathering strength to blast their progeny across the city.

Despite himself, he shivered. Mentally he cursed his body's betrayal.

"You are troubled, Otto?"

"We all have our weaknesses, Sir. Mine is a fear of heights."

Yes, a terrible fear of heights. At times like this, he was glad of it. One fear can be used to mask many others. Morlock turned his piercing gaze away.

"Irrational fears. We wouldn't be quite human without them. I have none however."

"Not even of books, Sir?"

"Books? Books, Otto, are a legacy of the past heading for extinction. A former commercial rival. A health hazard. A truly outmoded product, rightly abandoned by humanity for the purity of the *Gestalt*."

"Except by the *Incunabula*, Sir."

"Yes, except for those damned bibliophiles."

Morlock turned away to walk back to the tower's entrance. Hesitant, but with a certain degree of gratitude, Otto began to follow.

"That is why I called you here. There is much to discuss. I have already talked this over with Bill and he agrees. The time has arrived for us to act. We have watched for long enough. So, tell me your assessment of the situation."

"They're good at evasion, Sir. They've had years of practice, but naturally some are better at it than others."

"Quite so. But have we allowed their weaknesses to breed?"

Otto began to speak, but then stuttered. He felt uncertain of the question.

"Forgive me, Otto. We have neglected these bibliophiles for some time. Have they become slipshod, complacent, have they let their defences slip?"

"It's a difficult question to answer, Sir. Many of their newer people aren't difficult to track. But their old hands, well, some we've cracked, others not. Often I am afraid they have discovered our operatives tailing them so they haven't revealed anything useful. In such cases, we have followed a policy of visible observation. If nothing else, it upsets their ability to go about their business."

"Can they not? Do they not lose you as soon as it becomes convenient?"

"Yes, Sir, some are able to do that. But we have made it harder for them."

"But without locating prime centres of their operations."

"No, Sir. They are good at evasion, even if their standards have slipped of late."

"Indeed. The long waiting game has dulled both our edges. Now, tell me of Caxton."

"He's a strange one. He's good. We've never been able to crack his movements until recently. I don't understand it. He has taken what I would deem excessive risks to nurture his latest contact. The lad leads us to him."

"Good. I knew it. We have identified a weakness. It is good that he was not sent on his way, after all. He finds the purpose that he has long craved."

"Sir? What possible use can he be? In any case, Caxton has gone to ground. It appears he has lost interest in this contact, after all."

"Otto, dear Otto, can it be you are getting old? But of course all this relates to a time before your service. You have said it yourself. He leads us right to him. He is Caxton's weakness. Caxton will not leave this tender young morsel long neglected. We shall have him – and the secrets he stole from me. The boy will deliver us both. We have watched and we have waited long enough. Now, it is time to act, Otto, time to put in place the final moves of our little game. We are so close to our goals now. So close. We cannot be upset."

"No, Sir, but surely the *Incunabula* are no threat now?"

"Books are dangerous by their very nature. They have an allure. That is why our task has been so difficult. That is why these bibliophiles have refused to accept extinction."

"Yes, Sir."

"However, we must be cautious. I fear there is a spy in our midst."

Morlock stopped so suddenly that Otto nearly bumped into him. Then Morlock turned, his face only inches away.

Otto tried not to flinch as he felt his master's cold gaze crash like a glacier into his mind.

"Given the size of *MorTek*, Sir, I would imagine we have many infiltrators. However, they are blocked from senior positions, surely. We have too many safeguards."

Morlock held his gaze for what seemed a long time. At last Morlock sighed and turned away. Otto managed to hide his shudder in the motion of his fluttering clothes. The wind had its uses.

"You are probably right, Otto. But all the same, we cannot take chances. Not when we are so close to achieving what we have worked towards. We must finish the *Incunabula* once and for all."

Morlock stopped by the wall. His master stared at the dark surface of the tower, his skin reddened by the dying sun, his dark hair unmoved by the wind. More of his master's eccentric traits that seemed designed to prey on the mind, even as he tried to keep them barred from consideration. These days, with ever decreasing success.

"Will Marla be joining us?"

"In truth I think not, Sir. When I left for this meeting she had just emerged from a G-Spot. You know she is never quite together after a session."

Morlock gently nodded his head. "Ah yes. I thought I sensed her presence earlier. You know it really is a shame that I cannot read minds, only taste them. Perhaps it is for the best, given the nature of our conversation."

"Sir, surely you don't suspect –"

"Marla. Dear Marla?" Morlock smiled. "Of course not. Marla and I have always been so close. Her devotion is beyond question."

"Sir." He couldn't think of anything else to say, beyond his feelings regarding Marla's favoured haven from daily life, and they were best left unsaid.

"You seldom use the *Gestalt*, do you Otto?"

"You know how it fogs the mind after use, Sir. To serve you at my best I feel it is a sacrifice I must make."

"Of course. There is *The Vytez*. That is its purpose. In part."

"Yes Sir. I know, Sir. But I fear to use it in case it makes me less useful to you. It is my loss, but one I am prepared to make for the company."

"It is indeed your loss, Otto. I am sad for you. But when our task is done, you will have rest. All the time to catch up on what you have missed. But there is work for you do to before that time comes."

Morlock turned towards the wall. Otto watched through the fog of a troubled mind. Never before in all his years of service had he been asked to account for his avoidance of the *Gestalt*.

"Watch," Morlock said.

Obediently, Otto turned to gaze at the innocuous patch of wall. Morlock stroked the surface until it began to ripple like some viscous fluid. Otto stepped back in alarm as the surface bulged outwards. A protuberance, like a diseased pustule, emerged from the wall. It ran like melted wax and began to assume a shape. He stepped back further, frightened that the blob might somehow reach out for him.

Don't be a fool — it's nothing but some kind of simulacomm. *Oh, for the days of cell phones...* Fear was overcoming his sensibilities. Dangerously so. If not for a fear of heights...

"Forgive me, Otto, given the nature of your employment there is no reason why you should be familiar with intelligent materials technology. I forget these things at times."

Otto only nodded. The blob continued to take shape. Discernible now. A grotesque human head. It didn't remain that way for long. As though it was clay moulded by invisible fingers, it assumed the defined features of a face. Greater clarity, more definition. Finally colour spread across the features. The typical washed out face of a *Terapolitan*, but this one was familiar.

"I know that face."

"Indeed, you have been following him for me. You have accessed his file?"

"Yes, Sir."

"But not all. There are certain restricted appendices that might interest you. There are details that you are unaware of. That is why it is for the best that Marla is not here. She is not yet ready to know that he still lives. Perhaps there will never be a reason for her to know."

Otto allowed himself a puzzled frown.

"Here is the weakness we shall exploit, Otto, so allow me to introduce you to Adam Caine. Marla's son."

The Fourth Folio

When There's Books, There's Brass To Boot

THEY looked like drunks, but Laura knew better: these were *Gestalt* fodder of the most annoying kind. Loud and aggressive, they were dressed in the typical street attire of some *derm-rat* gang; she eyed them warily from her side of the avenue. Already feeling like the White Rabbit, she didn't need any further delays.

They bellowed incoherently as they tried to swagger with dislocated motor functions. One of them stumbled and fell on his arse, blinking stupidly, mouth hanging open. Laura suppressed the impulse to laugh. She was too close, but she hoped to take the chance to slip by unnoticed, while the other four staggered round their fallen friend.

Laura wished they were c'ol-heads. Drunks were easy compared to *Gestalt*-zombies: the kind that were out of cash and rations too, chucked out onto the street, and hell bent on just getting back into a G-Spot. By any means necessary. She cursed her luck, and knew it was no *Lady*. Luck was too unreliable to be anything but male.

Naturally, male luck proved true to form.

One of the groupies noticed her as she drew level. He looked at her as he helped his friend find his feet. A lecherous grin warped his slack features. They were coming together, brains readjusting back to bodies and gravity and conventional existence. Not good. Too far to turn back and find an alternate route, the way ahead looked longer with every step. She was level with them now, then a couple of paces ahead. Maybe…

"Oy, *cunty!*"

She felt herself stiffen at the insult, but she bit down hard on the snarl it provoked. Mission first. Anger later. She didn't look over, mustn't look over, she just continued as if the groupies didn't exist. One hand gripped the strap of her rucksack, the other slipped into her pocket. She felt the satisfying metal of the knuckle-duster. Fingers slipped through and she gripped it tight. Just in case. In *Terapolis*, a girl needed all the edge she could get. Especially given her precious burden.

"So then, cocksleeve, you deaf? Don't rush off. We're not gonna hurt ya!"

The adrenaline washed over her like a cold shower prickling her skin. If only she wasn't carrying her precious cargo, but the books came first and foremost. That was the Creed of the Courier. Always, no matter the provocation, she had to put their security first, even if that meant gritting her teeth to the abuse of a chauvinist junkie. There were times she hated courier work, especially times like these, but she had to play it cool. They were after all, only *derm-rats*.

"Where do you think yer goin'?"

The game was escalating. She squeezed tighter on the satisfying brass waiting patiently in her pocket. The groupies surrounded her, orbiting aggression polluting her personal space. Stinking bodies and stale breath. Troll faces, rabid eyes, drooling stubbled mouths. Up close and personal, they swayed and swaggered. She kept going, obedient to the courier rules, and forced them to keep pace. They didn't like the game, but she knew better than to play it their way.

The leader walked backwards, merciless face grinning. She stared back unflinching. "Leave me alone. I mean it."

The words provoked laughter. The leader just grinned and winked to his friend behind her. "These are our streets, yer know. Youse gotta be nice to us."

"What's up? Don'tcher like us?"

More laughter. The one behind picked at the bag. It slipped from her shoulder. She caught it and swung it back into place. She felt the books move inside, settling against the disturbing motion, but to her mind it felt as though they moved in alarm. Another book prodded her painfully in the back, urging her to action.

"Leave it!" She turned. Hard stare.

"We're good 'uns, us. We'll do yer right and proper. Make youse scream for more. An' we'll not charge yer. Much!"

"Just enough for a roundie in the G-Spot, eh lads?" His mates laughed raucous.

The vicious humour was draining from his eyes to leave plain vicious. She felt a fleck of spittle hit her face; skin rippled revulsion. "Come on! Give us some. What else a'yer for? Don't be so fuckin' tight."

"We'll loosen yer up."

"Yeah, don't be shy, bitch. Show us what yer got."

Laura felt the tinder smoulder as she considered her response.

"Think yer fuckin' better 'n us?"

In answer, the knuckle-duster smashed into the leader's face. Blood, spit and stained teeth exploded. He staggered backwards with a bewildered expression. Laura followed through by slipping the bag from her shoulder. She caught the strap in her hand and whirled round a dervish. The satisfying weight of books slammed into the head of the junkie behind her. The impact crashed him sideways into a companion. Their heads cracked loud. Another blow with the knuckle-duster sorted out the fourth. The last stood staring, unmoving but for a slight swaying motion on his feet and a trembling of his lower lip.

"Well, you wanted what I got. Not hard enough to take it?"

He stammered, whined and backed away. A few steps and he tripped onto his backside again. Laura watched him crawl away, her face blazing hot.

"Fuckin' *bitch*!"

The one that got the rucksack obviously liked it rough. She side-stepped his awkward lunge and turned to face him, rucksack in one hand, knuckle-duster clenched in the other. He faced her, snarling and salivating, his rage-swilled eyes glared; a blade flashed in his white-knuckled grip.

"At least one of you is up for it!"

His eyes darted between the choices, so she slammed her boot hard into the crux of his legs. His eyes almost popped, his mouth stretched wide around a high-pitched squeal, the blade clattered, impotent, as his hands clasped to the epicentre of grief and he doubled over.

"Oh come on," she sneered, "something so *small* couldn't possibly hurt so much."

She left him to tend his squashed machismo and slipped the rucksack back into place. The wreckage of male pride tried to crawl away from the impact zone. Bloodied, bruised, and still stuck outside the *Gestalt*. Behind her, the damaged *derm-rats* cursed and wailed, but didn't follow. Sometimes, the books permitted a little arse-kicking. When she got round the corner, she started to smile and hum a little tune.

GESTALT Nodes – or G-Spots as they're known in the street parlance of *Terapolis* – were common throughout the city; one never had to travel too far to find the nearest outlet. There were never enough to meet the demands of a populace numbering billions, but it was *MorTek*'s solemn promise to fulfil humanity's need for deliverance.

The Node located on the corner of 48th & Otranto was nothing special, as far as such things went. Indeed, for the most part one G-Spot was much the same as any other. This, however, was one of the older Nodes. Not one of the First Wave, but certainly Second or Third Generation. The evidence of its origins lurked in the shadows, hinted at when lights gleamed their intrusive rays into the deep shaded corners of the interior.

In places, original stonework could be seen, revealing the place as a structure fabricated in the days of the Old World. Like so many not abandoned to ruin, it was assimilated into the organic embrace of the modern. Above this subsumed structure, another of the city's vast fingers of power soared skywards; an obelisk, in this case, that housed not people and offices, but the machinery of the *Gestalt*. The whole living structure was a dedicated appendage for the translocation of its inhabitants to *other* realms.

On the stonework, there were clues to the structure's original purpose. Broken or membrane-thin patches in the skin of *Terapolis* revealed paintings and icons. Pigment faces peered with mournful eyes out of gaps in the *archidermis*.[21] One large patch showed a pale colour to the old stone, hinting at something that once protected the surface from entropy's curse: a ghostly crossbeam that cut across an elongated vertical bar.

The cruciform patch overlooked the booths and alcoves and the walkways where *Gestalt*-wanderers had left their bodies for safe keeping. They might have been residents in an outlandish morgue, but the monitoring equipment and life support systems showed the flesh still lived. Patient almost-cadavers, these hosts waited to be reanimated by the return of their living sentience.

Only the G-Spot's organic systems were state of the art. They grew and evolved in tune to the eugenics of Master *MorTek*; kept always at the cutting edge of the *Gestalt's* transcendental purpose.

Packed inside this space were some 1,500 wanderers. A Geistmasque rendered each one faceless; fleshy rubber fists gripped faces, held them down while sentience took flight. Tubes delivered sustenance to the living corpse; others removed bodily waste. Cables and tangles of delicate datafeeds fed information to a host of bio-monitor arrays that observed metabolic and physiological functions.

---

[21] A general term used to indicate the tough integument that covers the architectural surfaces of the city. Consists of a hard hide heavy in collagen and chitin that protects an underlying matrix of germative and support tissues.

Occasionally the machinery intervened to maintain a careful balance that preserved the host flesh.

Beneath the catwalks and the mezzanines where the somnambulists rested, several hundred more pilgrims sat with forced patience. They crowded in huddled knots, squeezed onto old pews and benches, or slumped on the floor in their wait for a free booth and a trip beyond the earthly plane. There were too many sojourners, too few places, but all ultimately trusted in *MorTek* to provide the way. Patience was not a virtue here, but a humbling necessity.

Outside this sepulchral organism, city life continued. Those not currently blessed with an allocation of time in the Node went about their daily lives, sought release in more mundane ways. Despite the magic of the *Gestalt*, the city's denizens could not fully escape the demands of urban living.

Around the Node on the corner of 48th & Otranto were shops that sold food, clothing, sundries, basic furnishings. Its environment aside, this might have been a high street from any city of the Old World. After all, even in *Terapolis*, city of the *Gestalt*, toilet paper was an unfortunate necessity.

A kilometre up the northern end of Otranto was Otranto Towers, the habitentiary where Adam lived. This is what made this run-of-the-mill Node of such importance: for it was here where Adam knew the *Gestalt*, when his ration permitted, or on those rare occasions when spare currency allowed the purchase of extra time.

Since discovering literature, he came to this place less often, but still, like all the denizens across this global city, he felt its pull. The *Gestalt* was like an ethereal Pied Piper: it ever called the rats home.

Inside the Node, it was always quiet, almost reminiscent of an ancient library.

Just the soft hiss of breath, like gentle waves caressing a distant beach. The soft hum of air conditioners, like a hive in the next field. Occasional bleeps of electronic monitors, like the echoes of I.T's forgotten dominance. A hungry gurgle of liquid tubes, then there was the soft shuffle of feet on stone, or a light clank of a metal walkway, as a Minder made her rounds.

This Minder was middle-aged and tired in appearance. Approaching the end of a long shift, she longed only for the pay packet that would enable her own release into the *Gestalt*.

She walked among the apparent dead, checked bodies, adjusted tubes and cables. She assessed bio-monitor displays and checked data feeds. All so routine. As she walked from one knot of bodies to another, she tried to ignore the rippling her sight perceived. It was a slight flicker, as of a neon tube malfunctioning, or of a heat haze that cast ghosts upon her retinas.

The phenomenon was known to occur at every Node. As always, the Minder told herself it was the light playing tricks, or fatigue. Or else it was the energy field in the structure affecting the neurons of her brain. Something *reasonable*. Something *rational*.

Much energy was required, all Node-Minders knew, to tear open reality's dimensional cluster, to break a mind free of its neuron fabric and yet leave its return passage open.

Tremendous energy and tremendous quantum computational sophistry.

So she ignored the phase shift in reality. She didn't hear the gurgling and sucking noises that were more like the feeding sounds of some exotic parasite. She didn't really see how the man-made objects appeared intertwined with some living organic material above and beyond the vat-growth of *MorTek* that seemed to extrude from the shadows.

Instinct said to stay close to the illuminated places. She heeded the ancient advice without even being aware. She simply rationalised that the light helped her to see.

Almost finished, she stopped by a recumbent figure. It rested alone in a solitary booth. A frequent customer. The Minder didn't bother to speculate how the man could afford so much time in a G-Spot. It wasn't her job to wonder. He wasn't dressed like a wealthy man, so perhaps crime bought him this transcendence. No matter. She neither knew nor cared that he was the fortunate recipient of a winning lottery ticket: a lifetime's supply of *Gestalt* ascension.

Visible skin showed a terrible marbled pallor beneath a sheen of sweat. Bio-monitors fluctuated with the signs of an unhealthy individual, but nothing was apparent outside borderline tolerances.

She didn't appear to notice the cable that disengaged from the flesh and turned to hiss at her with a needle-like proboscis. A drop of golden fluid dropped from the tip. Then the head buried into flesh once more and its long body pulsated with a peristaltic rhythm.

There appeared to be nothing untoward about this recumbent client, after all. Satisfied, she walked away to resume her round. But as she left, a tiny shiver ran through her body and fine hairs stood to attention.

Behind her, the anonymous journeyman flinched and stiffened with a rigour that transcended even death. Dark blotches erupted on the visible skin; liquid bruises flowered from rupturing subcutaneous capillaries. Red turned to black as though the blood had been heated too high for protein tolerances.

A monitor flared a warning: a medical emergency. Light erupted from the flesh of the face. It seared, turning both skull and *Geistmasque* translucent. Face and mask fused from some tremendous burst of energy. All in the time it took for monitors to sound the alarm.

Almost as soon as it erupted the supernovic illumination faded. The body sagged limp and steaming. From the gloom, more irritated than distressed, the Minder returned to investigate the alarm. She clucked her tongue in exasperation when she saw the steaming corpse and felt the heat of the alcove.

"That's the third disincorporation[22] this week," she muttered. That was always a risk for fools who spent too much time here; still, she wondered that the figures were increasing. Not only here, but across the *Locus* and beyond. Her lot wasn't to reason why, she considered, as she flicked through the client information.

---

[22] Heavy and prolonged use of the *Gestalt* can exert harmful effects on human physiology, disincorporation being the most severe mode of mortality. Used with care, the *Gestalt* can provide hours of safe existential transcendence. Users are considered responsible enough to police their own tolerance limits; however, there are always those who for whatever reason see fit to push the bounds. *MorTek* cannot be held accountable for the irresponsible behaviour of a minority of its consumers.

The man was a nobody as far as she was concerned; no one to care or wonder about his loss. She liked it that way, made her job so much easier. She quickly tapped in a code that would register the disincorporation and began the process of closing all files and functions the man had in life. Then she began to unplug and pack the cables and feeder tubes. The coils disengaged and slithered to their reception ports.

The fried *Geistmasque* was easily disconnected from the console; its cables and tubes she coiled up to rest beneath the man's chin, but the mask itself was now bonded to the corpse's flesh. Fluid gurgled hot to stain the cadaver's shirt. The heat from the cooked head stung her fingers, but she was quick enough in her actions to avoid injury.

With a flick of a program stud, a sphincter opened just behind the resting platform. Motors whined as it tilted backwards. The body slithered into the dark hole, its passage lubricated by slick body fat. Down below, the Node's *necrolyser* belly was ready to digest the man's spirit-emptied bio-mass. The sphincter closed.

The chair resumed its normal position. The Minder hurriedly cleaned the cooling body fat from the chair, grateful that with this last duty, her shift was finally over. For some lucky *Terapolitan* in the hall below, a vacancy had arisen…

SOMEHOW, Laura managed the rest of the trip without incident. Maybe Little Boy Luck had gone for the op, but she still didn't trust it. She took any potential shadow on a wild paper chase before she was sure she was truly alone.

Such precautions inevitably made her late, but better to arrive at her destination without unbidden guests than to keep good time. Few in the *Incunabula* could be relied upon to keep firm appointments. Maybe one day it'd form the basis of a joke, but not today. Such was the reality of their existence.

This cloak and dagger lifestyle was exciting. Once. Before she learned the full nature of their deadly burden, before it became the routine of living. Now it was a drag, constantly checking over her shoulder, wandering the streets seeming aimless until she was sure of no pursuit, watching the shadows, always suspicious of every face. Especially every *new* face. It wasn't a life. Not really. But as she pondered the alternatives, she knew it was the best life *Terapolis* had to offer.

She slipped the rucksack higher onto her shoulder for a more comfortable fit and then winced as one of the books within prodded her in the back.

"Okay, okay," she muttered.

There was no living thing around. At least of the two-legged kind. She relaxed a little. All the way her eyes and ears and even her nose scanned for anything that might cause her to abort. She didn't believe in a sixth sense, but she used it all the same.

A few more minutes and there it was; some kind of old abandoned factory lurking in the gloom of the street lamps and the pale light of day that filtered from above. Here, in this relic of Old City, some fluke of *Terapolis* meant that more natural light filtered to ground level. Doubtless that was why Caxton chose the place, that and the fact it was so isolated and abandoned. Maybe some part of him missed the

Old World. She'd never asked him about it. One day, she must get round to the question. For now she just asked the empty air: "Cax, why do you have to live in such an out-the-way shit hole?"

At the murky entrance, she paused. The air smelled damp and heavily tinged with chemicals and rust. How did Caxton stand it? She scanned her environment once more then took a deep breath and slipped inside.

Caxton was typing again. The sound was music with a rich and mesmerising beat. The metallic clatter echoed through the dark factory and bounced off the rusting hulks of obsolete machines.

Laura enjoyed the sound of Caxton's archaic composition machine; the evocation of the man's raw thought had a beat and rhythm. It struck a chord with the pounding bass of her heart, with the timbre of her pulse, it tickled her ribs and made her breathe all the faster.

A tinge of jealousy, but only brief. She didn't begrudge Caxton's ability to capture the living essence of thought in visible words. She just wished he'd share it with her sometime. Every time she asked, he rebuffed her curiosity. *Wait and see.* Always *wait and see.* So infuriating. That was Caxton.

She ascended the metal stairs that led to the old mezzanine office. Once it overlooked this cavern, in the days when it was a hive of industry. Now its windows were opaque with a cataract of untold years of grime. Still, the light glowed through Caxton's hearth and home. Welcoming, after the dreary streets of *Terapolis.*

For a moment the clatter of composition ceased. A brief babble of speech filled the rusting silence. Caxton talking to himself, to the muses in his mind, to the ghosts of authors past. The clatter resumed with all its vigour and power. Laura approached the door and, as always, she knuckled the glass strip down its centre and shouted – "Cax! It's me!" – before she slipped inside.

Caxton maintained his door was always open, but she frequently felt a little reticent about going straight in, especially when he was writing. As for the place itself, it was like entering Caxton's mind, always a shock to those who did not know him well.

There was no break in the flow, but Caxton spoke up from his cluttered desk. "Laura! Take a seat. Nearly done."

She looked around for a place to sit. Easier said than done. The clutter seemed to increase with every visit. The walls were lined with shelves, filled – naturally – with books. On sideboards and cupboards were even more. Stacked on top of them were papers and documents and bulging files. Notebooks and spare ribbons spilled from their nests and slumbered on the floor. Old clothes stuffed in piles. Caxton might be fastidious about his appearance and his dealings but it broke down when it came to his garret.

She looked around for a perch; the clearest was an armchair. She stooped to clear away a couple of jackets and yet more documents. Finding a new place for them was almost as difficult as finding a seat. She settled for a sideboard that seemed a little less overburdened than most. Then she gratefully slumped into the chair and watched Caxton work.

Even his workspace was cluttered and cramped. Several cups huddled together in a corner. Notebooks were spread open on the far side, a pile of clean paper rested just behind them. Laura watched, amazed at his blurred fingers. They danced across the keys, never seeming to miss a beat. Caxton hunched in his swivel chair, the stuffing protruding from rips in its covering. His brow furrowed by concentration, his eyes darting from the keys, to the paper, to the notes at his side. Just watching made her dizzy.

"Sorry, Laura, nearly done. I promise."

She nodded mutely.

She'd tried typing once and almost immediately vowed never to try again. That mechanical contraption might not be alive, but it had a taste for fingers. Hers at least. Those keys mashed and bashed, and all she ever got on the paper was a similar mash and bash of meaningless letters.

A clatter came from the corridor that led to the kitchen, bathroom and the place where – she found it hard to believe – Caxton actually slept. Hard to think of him sleeping, he always seemed so full of energy. The clatter materialised into the living form of Maggie.

"Is he still making that infernal racket?"

"I like it. It's like music," Laura said. Caxton laughed, but didn't break his stride.

Maggie turned to Caxton. "I bet you haven't even offered her a drink!"

"Sorry, slipped my mind."

Maggie's glance said *'men!'* Laura smiled and nodded her head.

"You're lucky I've managed to salvage some clean cups before you arrived. Cax, you really ought to tidy up sometime. How can you live like this?"

Caxton let out a laugh. "Maggie seems to think I need mothering."

"Mothering is not the word *I'd* use. Shooting maybe. I don't know, Laura. Behind every great man there's a woman picking up the pieces and cleaning the snot from his nose."

Laura giggled at that, but the sound died when she saw Caxton's profile. Ever so slightly, the frown had deepened. For a moment she sensed a profound sadness. Secrets. So many secrets. Her curiosity was piqued, but she knew she'd never get anything out of him. Maggie left her comment hanging in the air, and vanished into the kitchen.

Caxton continued to the end of his page, then he pulled the paper from the machine with a flourish. He added it to a stack of pages behind the typewriter. He sat up and sighed, massaging his back as he did so.

"So, how's it going?" she asked.

A brief smile, then he swivelled the chair to face her. "Almost done. Technically it's finished. I'm just putting the final draft together."

"Can I read some?"

"Not yet. Patience. Soon, I promise."

She sat back in the chair, disappointed but not surprised. Maybe she'd sneak a look later, if she got the chance, only for curiosity's sake. The rebuffs only succeeded in raising her interest. She hoped the wait would be worth it.

"Okay, I'll wait," she said, trying not to sound too resigned. "So, why did you want to see me?"

"Ah! That's my Laura. Always to the point." He wheeled the chair a little closer and then swivelled it round so that he could use the backrest to lean forward on his elbows. He looked at Laura for a while as though reading the thoughts skittering across the back of her skull. For some reason, she began to feel uncomfortable.

"I wanted to talk to you about Adam," he said, and the discomfort turned to disdain.

"What about him?"

"I want your help."

"With Adam."

"Yes."

"Haven't I done that already?"

Caxton paused, as though uncertain what to say next. That in itself was unusual; it made Laura feel uneasy. What was he after? What could possibly make this man so concerned that he needed her help – beyond *Incunabula* duties that it is.

"I thought you liked the lad."

She sighed and folded her arms.

"I did. I do… in a way, but he's so… unreliable. He's such a dreamer."

"Blessed be the dreamers, for they are navigators on the voyage towards tomorrow."

Laura frowned, and flicked a strand of hair from her face. She couldn't tell if Caxton was serious or taking the piss. "Sometimes, Cax, you talk like a book."

"Well, I *am* a writer these days, so that's not such a bad thing, surely?"

"I'm just a reader," she said in a quiet voice.

"There's no such thing as 'just a reader'," Cax said, taking her aback with the strength of feeling in his voice. "A book is nothing but a potentiality until it grounds itself in someone's mind. Without a reader, a book is a coffin."

"What's this got to do with Adam?"

"Nothing, really. I just want your help again. You don't have to. You didn't have to before, you know, though I was glad you did."

"I owed you."

"You make me sound like a pimp!" Caxton bellowed, but there was no offence. She was glad of that; she didn't want to upset the man. "Get to know him, make friends, bring him to me. That's all I wanted. I never said for you to sleep with him!"

"I know… I just…" she squirmed in the seat. This was everything she had feared. Why did Caxton have to bring up past mistakes? "What was I supposed to do? You're the one who wanted to fast track him."

"Not like that!"

"You wanted him. You got him. You know how long people are normally groomed. *I* didn't even see a book for a year. Adam gets regular drops and meetings and you're talking about bringing him in – and it's barely been six months. What's so special about him?"

Caxton sighed, and looked at her with sad eyes. "Everybody's special, Laura. Books make people special."

"Not like this."

"I'm sorry, Laura, perhaps you're right. I don't know." Caxton sighed. "I know things didn't work out, and I didn't want to embarrass you by bringing up the past. I just worry about you. You're always so alone."

She shrugged. It was true. There was safety in isolation, less ways to be hurt, but she didn't dare express the full depths of her thoughts. "I like it that way," she said. "Besides, I'm not alone. There's you, there's Maggie, there's the whole *Incunabula*."

Caxton sighed, and this time it carried a weariness that surprised her.

"Laura, you don't want to end up like me. That's what I'm afraid of."

"Why not? What's so wrong with being like you?"

"More than you could ever possibly imagine. One day you'll find out – and then you'll know enough to change your mind. Be yourself Laura; let Laura be herself."

Laura stared at him, confused and puzzled. Caxton looked down at his feet and didn't see her shrugged response. Maybe that was for the best. She wasn't used to such a contemplative Caxton. Somehow, it scared her.

"So why do you want my help?"

The question brought Caxton out of himself.

"He knows you, Laura. He trusts you. I want you to keep an eye on him, keep him supplied with books, make sure he stays out of trouble. Can you do that for me?"

"I guess. But why?"

"He's alone out there. I've asked Elzevir to bring him in, but in the meantime I need someone to keep an eye on him. In case something happens to me."

"Nothing's going to happen to you! Cax – don't talk like that."

He smiled, but there was no strength in it. "No. No. But just in case."

"You haven't answered me, Cax. Why? You've cut loose so many contacts who are more reliable than Adam. What's so special about him? Why are you taking such a risk?"

"It's important, Laura. He can't be left out there alone."

"That's no answer. If you want my help, then I deserve to know."

Caxton lowered his head and sighed again. When he spoke, his voice was so soft and muted that she barely heard what he said. "Let's just say I owe the lad more than you can possibly imagine."

She was about to press him further when Maggie returned with the drinks. Caxton looked up, and the pain in his manner vanished as though the shutters of his street personality had crashed down. Laura let it pass and thanked Maggie as she was handed her drink. It was hot and she blew on it a while to cool the steaming coffee.

"That Adam is bad news," she said as she handed Caxton his drink. "You want to cut him loose."

"So I am told," Caxton said. "You haven't made one for yourself?"

"No, I have to rush off. Are those books in your bag, dear?"

She swallowed hastily, almost scalding her tongue, and nodded her reply. "Mostly returns for the library. There's a few to hand out to contacts."

Maggie nodded. "I'll save you a journey. Sort them out and I'll drop the returns off."

The offer was too good to refuse. She placed the cup carefully on the carpet and then moved towards the entrance. She fumbled with the rucksack and tipped the books out to begin sorting them.

"The stupid boy has been trying to *recruit*," Maggie said. Her voice was always brisk and sharp, but there was a petulance Laura had never heard before. "Did you know that? Morlock's people got the poor girl before we could sort the situation out."

"He's keen and enthusiastic."

"He's a bloody liability. That girl was quite inappropriate – and she's paid a terrible price for that boy's impetuosity. What next?"

"The boy will learn. He will grow. With our help." Now Caxton's voice was rising, an underlying anger that again was so uncharacteristic. Laura wondered vaguely what was going on, but she pushed the thought from her mind and focused on the books.

"Well, I had a word with him. Warned him off. I don't think he'll pay any heed, even though I put the fear of God into him. He's dangerous."

"No. Our times are dangerous and the boy is adrift. We need him. He needs me."

"Caxton, in all the years I've known you, I have never known you to be a fool – until now. You'll get yourself killed over this. Worse, you'll probably get us all killed. What is so special about him?"

"Nothing. And everything. I have my reasons. I'll say no more. Have you finished, Laura?"

So many secrets, Laura thought as she stuffed the last return into Maggie's bag. She wanted no part of this argument, but she looked up and said: "Yes."

"Good. Maggie was just leaving. We'll finish our talk when she's gone."

Maggie glared, then reached for her bag and turned for the door. Laura sat down. The anger and the tension in the air felt like choking smoke. She dreaded the talk with Caxton now. The pleasantry of the visit was gone; destroyed by secrets and politics that had seldom entered her life.

"What I said was for your sake, Cax," Maggie said as she opened the door. "Please think about it. I'd hate to lose you. We all would."

Caxton just nodded his head and waved her away. Laura sat and waited. Everything was changing, she sensed that with a terrible dread, and it looked as though there was no choice but to play a part in whatever was to come.

As she sat there, waiting for Caxton to compose himself, she rued the day she had ever met Adam. This was his fault. Of course. He'd always been trouble. Oh, he didn't mean to be, she knew, but he was all the same. A risk. And she felt a surging fear for Caxton, that he might endanger himself to no purpose. She couldn't let that happen.

"I'll help," she said quietly.

Caxton still brooded, apparently deaf to her words.

"I said I'll help."

He finally looked up and gazed blankly at her. Then he blinked as though switched on.

"Thank you, Laura. I can't tell you what it means to me."

Laura nodded gently, then a thought occurred to her. "On one condition."

Both eyebrows flew up on Caxton's face.

"Read some to me."

"When it's finished, Laura, you can read it. I promise."

"No. Read some to me now. You want my help, right?"

Caxton stared at her, then sighed. "Okay," he said, relenting. He reached for the manuscript, tapped it on the desk for effect and began to flick through. His eyes scanned the flurry of pages. Then he paused.

"*Yes*. I'll give you this," he said, and then he began to read aloud…

LET us consider Silas Morlock. Little is known about him. Since the days of his beginnings to the height of his power he has been a mystery to the world.

Even in the days before the Gestalt, when Man still pampered his curiosity, Morlock aroused much interest but seldom any real knowledge. He was the multibillionaire head of MorTek. Known to be reclusive, known to protect his privacy with a jealous hand. Eccentric also. That much filtered from the whispering passages of his Empire.

Everyone knew MorTek—or rather <u>thought</u> they did—for its innovations in interactive technology that evolved quickly into semi-immersion and full-immersion artificial reality. Before our awe-struck mouths could even close, these gave way and crumbled into obsolescence with the advent of the all-embracing technology that became the Gestalt.

It marked the true beginnings of Morlock's mysterious goal, the culmination of his ramifying empire. The beast that was MorTek went forth and multiplied, and today it is the hive in which we live. From cradle to grave, we live in MorTek's bosom. We are its workforce, its customer, its clientele, its debtors and its creditors, its very nourishment.

And MorTek boasts that from rich man to poor man, none are excluded.

There is something for everyone within the mysterious realms of the Gestalt. Thanks to the complex system of rationed access to a G-spot, none are denied. None are banished from tasting the pleasures of MorTek's ultimate glory. The Gestalt is a sanctuary and an escape from a dreary and heartless world. It has become the opiate for the masses.

In the days when books still lived in the world above, when periodicals and newspapers were still printed and sold, when the world was still bound by an electronic web of information, many thousands of words expressed society's speculation, its hungry curiosity and its lack of hard facts.

They knew with astonishment the wonders that came from MorTek. They pulled apart the intricacies of his business, but never could they get to the heart of the man. They chattered from the sidelines as once proud corporate giants stumbled and fell before him.

And all around us, as we pondered this enigma, this mystery that was Morlock, as humanity marvelled at the machines and wonders that came into the world to make MorTek a name on every mouth, the world changed around us. The sun set on our history, on our words and our curiosity, and the twilight descended as the towers of Terapolis grew and flourished.

As the light went out, as the printing presses rolled to a halt, as the Hazamat raised their matches ready to strike, the world's last lament of curiosity was a singular question: "Who is Silas Morlock?"

Indeed. Who is he? What is he? What is it that he wants?

This last question died on the lips of the Old World.

Unanswered.

For the books perished in flame, the newspapers blackened and collapsed into fragile ash, the World Wide Web dissipated, and the Gestalt absorbed all that was Humanity.

Nowadays, some among us call him evil, a canker of malice filling—eating—our world. Morlock is not evil. Not in the traditional sense at least. He is not driven by hate, or cruelty for its own sake, or the lust for power and wealth. He simply wishes to serve us through the fulfilment of our deepest most spiritual desire. Or so Morlock himself believes.

He seeks to grant us absolution.

Yet here, among us, he is the consummate businessman. He is shaped by this world, by its structures and its relationships. However much he may bend them to his will, he cannot undo them, for they are the mechanism of his ability to shape our destiny.

In an earlier age, he might have been a priest offering desires through the absolution of prayer, or he might have been a nobleman granting favour to his courtiers. Better still, perhaps, he might have been the sorcerer, granting loaded gifts from the dark vaults of his forbidden knowledge.

Instead, he gives us the Faustian gifts hidden in the heart of his Gestalt. And as he gives, so too does he take...

SILAS Morlock stared at the burning ember in the sky. Eyes wide open, he almost dared it aloud to leech the vigour from his flesh. He could feel it; the rays cascaded through the molecules of his being, weakening the bonds of electrochemistry, vibrating and wearing down the fabric of his protective shell.

"One day," he whispered to those golden rays, "you will be nothing but a stream of photons. As you were in the beginning so shall you be at the end."

The words silenced Bill's latest melody.

"It was nothing, Bill. Just thinking out loud. Please, sing for me again."

Bill complied. Morlock closed his eyes and let his mind float on the soothing resonance. Something about it struck a chord; a symphony of the heavens, beautiful in its lack of consciousness. Merely the delightful hum of the universe cruising the ocean of eternity.

Still, his restless mind turned to the world beneath his feet, to the cursed bibliophiles that crawled through the sewers and tunnels of *Terapolis*. Diseased rats, spreading their plague through the populace. He opened his eyes again, to scan the city as though looking for those febrile rodents.

"They are out there, Bill, spreading their poison. But not for much longer. Marla and Otto will not fail. Things are coming into place, and we have found the mechanism to silence their words before they might threaten us."

Again Bill stopped humming.

"We should have finished them in the beginning. It was a mistake to leave them, but they seemed doomed at the time."

Morlock straightened a ruffle in his frock coat and listened.

"Yes Bill. Even I make mistakes. I am not infallible. But the mistake will soon be rectified. Forgive me, I did not mean to cause you concern. You have earned your rest, and I would not deliberately upset your repose. If you can, sing for me once more. I will try to keep my thoughts inside."

That pleased his partner; seldom did he get asked so frequently to sing. But instead of commencing his soothing hum, he talked. Morlock felt no choice but to express what was on his mind. Bill alone deserved his frank attention.

"I was wondering, Bill, which of our weaknesses will our enemies exploit?"

Morlock nodded.

"Yes. We have weaknesses, Bill. Nothing in creation exists without them. As we use our enemy's weaknesses against them, so they will seek to use ours. Our size for instance, that is a great weakness. We are as big as a world. How well does a world notice the tiny creatures crawling upon its surface?"

The skull said nothing, but seemed to contemplate the words.

"Consider Caxton; he is a fool, yet Marla and Otto have so often failed to untangle his movements. And now this boy turns up and Caxton reveals himself. He may have gone to ground, but not for long. He will not leave this foundling to its fate. Not this one. *Guilt* compels him."

A thought occurred. He mulled it over for a few moments, while his companion digested his explanation. There was more to Bill than good companionship and soothing melodies; there was still a hint of his earlier days when his sharp thinking had played so great a role in *MorTek's* strategies.

"Have you ever heard of the theory that there are only so many *real* people in the world, while the rest are there only to make up the numbers? It is nonsense of course. Who should know that better than I? The strange thing is that for millennia, Humanity has struggled to make the theory truth. They have fought to render the many but shadows of humanity. *Humanity.* So often its own worst enemy, but then isn't that only a manifestation of its deepest and most cherished desire?"

He paused at a twinge in a tendon and clenched his fist against the head of his cane to apply a little feeling into his ancient frame. The sinews creaked noticeably, a leathery sound. He frowned, but let it pass.

"Life is full of such ironies. The entwined avenues of fate bring *them* together again. Out of all the multitudes."

Caxton, Marla Caine. The boy. Yes, he thought. So strange that he should resurface, after all these years. Of course, he knew the boy had lived. And the boy had gone on, ignored and unknown, a seed of potential waiting for the *Incunabula.*

"I see you now," he muttered. He saw and understood. This boy, he was the deliverer, he was the tool to prise open the cracks within the *Incunabula.* Such a delicious irony, that this ghost of the past returned to play a new role. And he shall be rewarded, he vowed. The rewards of all humanity shall be his.

"He will join us, Bill. Marla's child shall be one with us."

Bill said nothing, but it mattered not. That he was there to listen was more than sufficient.

"He is a misfit. He has never found belonging. Perhaps that was made by the manner of his birth. Perhaps it is something within his essence. It matters not. I shall end his restless search. I shall give him a place to belong, a place of meaning. I will absolve this boy and shape him for what must yet be done."

Morlock listened, and gently nodded his head. Most of his companion's concerns he disregarded, but the final point needed an answer.

"Books?" He thought a moment. It was an important concern. "You are right. He is torn. Torn between the lies of paper and the truth of transcendence. But when the books are finally no more, his mind shall lose its confusion and he shall find the peace of the *Gestalt*. Then I shall make him anew."

A thought made his lips curl in a half smile.

"In time, I shall be the *father* that Caxton failed to be."

Bill laughed at that. A melodic tinkle, almost child-like in its sound. Morlock felt the rare urge to join his partner's mirth, but another twinge aborted the humour. He raised his hand to stare at the parchment skin, then he flexed the trembling fingers. He stared hard at the wasting flesh. The lines and blotches were deeper. Wriggling veins almost looked like words scrawled on the back of mildewed paper.

Morlock frowned. So much decay in so short a time? He had left it too long again. Too long. But there was always so much to do. Time and entropy were taking their toll. He sighed, wearily.

"I am fading again, Bill. It takes more every time and the effects are less."

He flexed the hand once more. There was no choice.

"I am going for a lie down, Bill. Keep an eye on things."

Bill watched quietly as Morlock slipped into the darkness beyond and closed the door. For long minutes nothing happened. Then, if Bill still possessed his eyes, he would have closed them against the bright glare that burst from the faint cracks. Finally, the intense light dimmed to normal levels, before becoming extinct.

Bill kept his silent vigil.

THERE was something disturbing out *there*.

Not out there in the lab, beyond the peaceful confines of his study, but out *there* in the mental landscape of his mind. A perception, like a rising of the hackles; an intrusion that defied definition.

Boris Creek tried to shrug it off and focus on the beautiful simulacrum taking form in the processing array of consciousness. He watched his synaptic cortex at work: his brain mixing imagination and knowledge ready to bake them in the crucible of inspiration. All without much in the way of any conscious mental button pushing.

Breath-taking, he considered, the way the brain expressed itself; the way his genius worked.

Processing in process. Creation unfolding.

Problems deconstructed. Solutions manufactured.

All while he dozed lightly in his office.

It was often the case, he found. After the days and the weeks of hard work and mental toil to solve the innumerable technical and scientific problems that were his daily bread, the solutions often emerged in quiet moments like this. Inspiration detonating with the explosive force of realisation.

So it was now. The *Gestalt* enhancements he had worried over for weeks were finally taking shape. And his understanding mentally slapped its forehead and yelled *'of course'*. It was so obvious. Once his subconscious mind showed him the way towards the 'eureka' moment.

In a way it reminded him of a Nano-Mator, the AR/Sub-*Gestalt* machines that allowed him to manipulate matter down to the sub-atomic level. Even down to the level of the quantum exo-dimensional.

There was no Nano-Mator plugged into his implant. He merely sat at rest, with his cap pulled down over his eyes, his feet at rest on the desk.

Boris Creek, the self-contained entity within that brain, took mental notes, ready to turn this vision into reality in the genuine Nano-Mator out there in the lab.

Components self-assembled in the heart of darkness. Molecules ticked. Quarks spun their dancing pirouettes. Alpha helices unzipped, unwound, kissed and replicated and then reassembled. Languages encrypted, ready to direct the molecular dance of primordial assembly. Complex molecules processed, turning raw chemicals into the nanotech he needed to complete Morlock's vision.

Concepts and additional ideas whispered on the cerebral breeze. Notes and thoughts, theories and technical explanations. A grunt as he shifted position in his chair. A yawn. Loud. Then he turned his attention to the voice that explained what he saw. He understood, mentally laughed at the simple oversights, the mistakes of the past, the omissions made up to now. Unconsciously, he nodded his head as the voice lectured.

Mostly the voice was his. Boris Creek. Occasionally, the voice belonged to Morlock.

It often happened that way. Amidst the technical monologue in his cranial auditorium, Morlock's voice added suggestions, corrections, clarifications. The footnotes to his grand creative essays in thought and virtual design.

And he took note of them too.

Strange, that his thoughts should adopt another's voice. A measure, obviously, of respect for his boss: the ultimate genius behind the genesis of the *Gestalt*. It marked his fear of failure and his desire to prove his worth. To convince himself, if no other, that he was no fraud, no technician promoted beyond his status because of a predecessor's professional demise.

He owed it to Natalie, too, of course, that her selfless sacrifice was not in vain.

A stab of guilt lashed out at the beauty in his mind's eye. It began to collapse. Boris reordered his thoughts, pushed aside his doubts to stabilise the birth taking place in the uterine shade of thought. Something else stabilised too. That niggling itch that tried to suggest something wasn't quite right.

Something out *there* in the ocean of void that formed the backdrop to his creation. No longer amorphous black. Now it had texture. And depth.

Instinctively, he felt uncomfortable with that fuzzy backdrop. It wobbled slightly, as though it was not quite in phase with the universe of his mind. The magical construction, *his* fabrication, floated above this uncertain background, and even seemed to emerge from the depths of this strange mental substance.

He swallowed, and felt a ligament in his throat strum unease.

What else could it be but his own creative processes laid bare? Yes, that was it. He was perceiving the hidden quantum mechanics of the mind, laid out before him as mental metaphor. Not that it reined in the deep sense of unease the vision caused.

He tried to ignore it and focus instead on the germination of genius.

The more he watched, however, the more his brain deciphered the patterns latent in the fuzzy background. Against his will, his neural machinery was making sense of the senseless. It reminded him of something, but there his vision thus-far failed.

From beyond his vision, from the depths of that unfathomable *machina ex deus* he sensed the presence of Silas Morlock. The unease grew in strength; it pushed him back into the waking world, as if to get away from the sense of his all-pervading master.

The nagging doubt emerged with him, crawling bestial into the light of his waking mind. He did not understand why, but suddenly he had the feeling that there was something profoundly *wrong* with the universe.

And it had something to do with his precious *G-Tek*.

WHILE one mind pondered the possibilities inherent in existence, another mind was incapable of pondering at all as it dissolved and slowly ceased to be.

Silas Morlock savoured both.

He was curled at rest, deep in the soothing shade of his private universe hidden far inside *MorTek Prime*. Eyes closed, he perceived them as two amorphous patches of light glowing against the opaque backdrop of the human aura.

Perception was not achieved by the actions of organic cameras called eyes. Nor was it achieved by the electrochemical processes of a cerebral cortex.

Morlock simply relaxed and unfocused the exotic wavelengths of his essence so that he drifted beyond the confines of his corporeal shell. He drifted through the fabric of matter and space, until he stirred the quasi-particles of himself that lurked always in the dark lacunae of creation. And there were so many in *Terapolis*.

From the dark shadows between the synapses of two brains, and the shadows cloaking the framework of their existence, he watched. The one Mind soared on the thermals of genius, the other faded like an ancient photograph.

For the first, he felt satisfaction and approval, at the second curiosity and a vague sense of disappointment.

Creek was proving more than adequate for his new post; silently, Morlock wondered if his predecessor should not have been exorcised at an earlier date. But that damaged sentience had proved useful for the duration of its service, and now Creek was succeeding where worn out faculties had slipped into obsolescence. He was increasing the pace at which *MorTek's* purpose was made flesh.

Morlock smiled in the darkness, or rather his physical anchorage did. Then he turned his attention away from his servant and on to the second mind.

There was little left of her now. In truth there had been little to begin with. Just another *Terapolitan* in so many ways.

But she had been useful.

One of many scattered throughout *Terapolis*. Bait. Spies. Informants. The label was irrelevant. Most became nothing. Seeds scattered on the wind only to land on infertile soil.

Not this one.

This one informant turned up the boy. And *he* led them to Caxton. She might have gained further use, if the *bibliophiles* had not begun a counter-move and forced *MorTek* to bring her in. What information they might have reaped from her dismantled brain had she been able to insinuate deeper into the *Incunabula*...

Even the boy told her little, beyond hints and feeble fantasies. No matter. She had served her purpose. She provided some morsels of information beyond the major prize.

Now the dregs of her essence gurgled away as her body dissolved: digested to nourish the organic superstructure of *MorTek Prime*. He listened to the dying echoes of the girl's cortex and watched the dimming glow of her spirit as it evaporated from its physical root structure.

There was no self-awareness now, only the embers of what had once formed a mind; a feeble thought repeating, "*Claire... I'm... Claire...*" Not quite a disincorporation, but what lingered would find peace in time.

The darkness was fading. Morlock squeezed his eyes together and gritted his teeth against the pain and the flaring illumination to come. It was brief. It was necessary.

And then perception exploded into supernovic light. Morlock allowed himself to scream out the agony. Then it was over. The soothing darkness slowly returned.

Bathed again in that purest liquor his highest servants craved, the fluid did more than rejuvenate; it steeped the fabric of his being to ensure he was emulsified with this brane of existence. Agonising, to so conjoin, it helped to think of it as rebirth.

He wondered if the girl's rendered soul was part of the dose that had just immersed his entropy-damaged substance. But no. The disused female was but a tiny drop milked from the billions. A small price for the species to pay for the rewards he was to grant them.

Silas Morlock allowed his being to focus again.

Before he withdrew entire, he heard a tearful voice faint with distance.

"*Uncle Boris!*"

In the darkness, Morlock smiled once more.

"*Please! Help us! We can't get out. It won't let us out!*"

So, they were gathering. The lost ones. As if they had any choice. Another sign that the completion of his long-developed mission was near.

"Soon, my little one, *soon*," he whispered. "All good things come to those who wait."

THEY sat in the gloom and stared at each other across the table like a pair of duelling cats, but it was a fight Elzevir knew he couldn't win. His guest played tougher games than this; too tough to ever allow a tired old librarian to best him.

He sighed and raised his glass to his lips to sip a taste of wine. It was an excellent bouquet, well-matured but a bad year; it was of the last vintage before the Old World fell on its sword. For a moment he savoured its aroma, then he set the glass down but toyed with it nervously. Sitting back in his armchair, he studied his guest. The man hadn't moved a muscle.

"So, you have some information for me?"

"Of course. Do you have the books?"

Still no movement from his guest; the man might have been carved in stone for the lack of reaction. He was a man used to shadows, to stealth, to the minimum of gestures that might give him away. Obviously, the traits were too deeply ingrained. Only the muscles required for speech moved across his gloom-masked features.

Elzevir nodded his head gently, slid the volumes across the table. "Sun Tzu, *The Art Of War*; Nicolo Machiavelli, *The Prince*; and a couple of Jeffrey Archers. You can tell a lot by a man's reading tastes."

"In my case it's professional curiosity – and a little escapism."

At last his guest moved. Otto Schencke leaned forward and reached out with a hand to stop the books sliding off the edge. His features ignited suddenly in the glow of the candles, his dark eyes flashing, his beard hairs gleaming in the soft luminescence.

"It usually is." Now Elzevir also leaned forward, eager to receive the information that would hire these volumes. If the rest of the *Gorsedd*[23] knew of his contact with this man… but it was worth the risk, however distasteful, and he was careful, always so careful in the places where they met. The man's information was not always useful, but it was sufficient to keep him at arm's length.

"So, Mr Schencke, what do you have for me?"

"Something you won't like."

---

[23] The Incunabula's ruling council.

"Probably not, but I assume it's something I need to know, otherwise why are you wasting my time?"

Schencke shifted in his seat. At last motion betrayed his inner turmoil, it made him seem a little more human, especially the farting noise the expensive cloth of his suit tended to make on these old leather chairs.

"I have been ordered to take you in."

Elzevir felt his thoughts scatter like frightened sheep. It took him a moment to recompose himself.

"When?" A simple question, a simple word, but his tongue stumbled over it all the same.

"No precise time. As opportunity allows. Not now, of course. I need you… to make arrangements. But soon. The next few days."

"Why?"

"Why do you think? You know the location of the library. You know primary contacts. Your information is valuable."

Elzevir couldn't help the smile that pulled at his face. "No. I mean – why now, after so long?"

Schencke only shrugged. "Why anything with Morlock? The man's a mystery to me. All I know is he's given the order. You are to be taken. And you will be. No matter how good you are at evasion, I know enough of your patterns to pick you up."

"Patterns can change."

"Yes. But you have too many obligations. I know more about your movements than you guess. You have grown careless in your old age. Or complacent. Either will be the death of you. And it won't come easy."

Elzevir fidgeted, while he let the news sink in. Yes, he had become complacent lately. They all had. Each side grown too accustomed to the other. He realised that now; they had settled into the game of hide and seek, and forgotten the one burning issue – that the game might end sooner than either expected. He'd been a fool. How many more of the *Incunabula* had done likewise?

There was no point in trying to stop the shudder that ran through his body. He was the condemned man. Didn't he have a right to some display of emotion a few days before the inevitable? That was something. Time to correct the drift towards folly. A small mercy that must be taken with all his might. He struggled to remain outwardly calm.

"I can make it easy for you," Schencke added, as if he was helping with an unfamiliar menu. "In this game accidents happen. You will endure no pain."

He swallowed. "What about your… other half?"

The man smiled. "Marla, dear Marla. We have worked together for years. She is talented, shall we say, but she is not the professional she thinks she is. No, Marla is an enthusiastic amateur. She will notice nothing."

As ever, Schencke's eyes were dark and terribly focused; they portrayed a man hardened to the hideous necessities of his occupation. No remorse. Never remorse. Nor regret, but perhaps there was a hint of pity in those eyes, a little pity struggling against the man's strong sense of self-preservation.

There was no way to avoid this fate. Not really. He could run. He could hide. Move to another part of the city, perhaps flee the city entirely, change his name and have… but that meant living as an unperson. And without books, was there really any point in living further? This was too much to think about, in too little time. How to betray his family, his companions of so many years? For that is what it would be. Face the fear. Face the end. Was there any other choice? Is this what sacrifice feels like?

"No." There, he'd said it.

Schencke stiffened.

"You are Morlock's attack dogs. You will – you *must* – bite. Even the hand that feeds you."

"There is no telling what you will reveal."

"I will never reveal the whereabouts of the library."

"I did not think you would."

Sudden realisation. "You are concerned for yourself."

"You have no idea what Morlock will do if he finds out."

"Yet, as you say, I am doomed to find out."

Schencke said nothing. Only let his head fall forward so that he might stare into his lap. He sat there for several minutes. Elzevir took the opportunity to refill his glass. It seemed he must finish his stock of precious wine. Schencke sighed.

"This was not supposed to happen," he said. "I thought I was stronger than this. I thought I was immune. Infiltrate you, that was the plan. Only infiltrate. Instead, here I am hooked. Hooked by dusty old books."

"No. By what they give."

Otto nodded his head. "Now I know why Morlock forbade us to try infiltrating you. I knew better. Or so I thought."

"Books have power. Morlock knows that."

"Not enough to save you."

"No."

"*Damn it!*"

The sudden animation, the explosion of fury, took Elzevir by surprise. His glass half way to his lips, he flinched and spilled wine on the table and his lap. Such a *waste*. Otto's fist slammed the table and even the books jumped.

"Morlock will make you talk! I can prevent that. Fast. Painless."

"Kill me and Morlock will suspect."

"No. Like I said – accidents happen."

"No, Mr Schencke."

"You stubborn old fool! You don't know what you are saying!"

"I have lived my life for books, Mr Schencke, never more so than now. In my youth, I took them for granted. I suppose we all did. Then it was too late. If my death will somehow help their survival then so be it."

"But it won't help! You'll damn yourself. You'll damn your precious books. And you'll *condemn* me!"

"Don't you deserve it?"

Schencke didn't respond. Not at first. He looked stunned by the question. Then he reached out and stroked the books with a sigh.

"Perhaps," he conceded in a quiet voice. Then louder. "At least run and hide!"

"No, Mr Schencke. Your information has been useful to us. If I run, you will be suspected."

"Morlock suspects –"

"You?"

A brief smile curled the man's beard. "No. No. But there are people we can make suspect."

"Sacrifice another?"

"Of course."

"We don't think like that, Mr Schencke. To save myself by condemning another, I find that… *distasteful.*"

"You sanctimonious prick! How many people have you given to prison – how many dribbled away in *MorTek's necrolysers* – because they didn't fit your *precious* values?"

"And how many people have you killed because they had a price tag attached to their big toe? Don't lecture me, Schencke. Never have we turned someone away lightly. What we have done is for the survival of more than any one individual."

"Semantics!"

"*Survival!*"

Otto scowled and reached for his books.

"You will be taken care of, Mr Schencke," Elzevir said before the man could depart. "Don't worry on that score. I'll see to that before… Someone will keep you supplied. For information, of course."

"My information will die with me if you go through with this. Please! Listen to what I say!"

A weary shake of the head. "No…" he paused. A thought. A lovely, precious thought. He stared at Otto, his face grim. "There is something you can do."

"What do you mean?"

"When the time comes and I am before Morlock, slip me a book and loosen my bonds."

"Why?"

Elzevir smiled, so grim and mirthless, that even a man like Schencke backed away. "I must make one *final* delivery."

The Fifth Folio
For What We Sow, Let The Children Be Eternal...

MIDNIGHT beckoned like a sore loser out to settle a score. Adam wasn't up to it; not the fight, not the taunting passage of painful time. Now his number was coming up all over again, and he sat there watching the old clock flick it into place.

Another twenty-four hours without a book, another day of waiting for Caxton's unfulfilled promise. Another fight to keep it together, to stay clear of the junk that sullied his head; he didn't know how much longer he could hold it together.

It ain't my shit that's tearing you up. Books and the Gestalt *don't mix.* Sure. How many times had he heard that? How about some answers. Like, why? The longer he waited, the more he began to wonder if the old dealer wasn't full of shit.

Adam stared through eyes watery with fatigue and despondency, listless while the old wall clock melted slow into another wordless witching hour. The digits of its circumference ran bottom heavy under the weight of seconds. Time liquefying along with his sanity.

A twitch of the minute hand, and one day was poised to drip into the next.

Another day of abstinence.

No books. He'd finally exhausted his last fix, read and re-read until nothing remained but the urge for *more*. No *Gestalt*. That was taboo, however much it called. Nothing in between, but the void of longing.

Adam groaned.

Midnight descended.

The new day was born.

The siren-cry of the *Gestalt* was rising in strength; calling to him with its promise of release from all his woes. The urge to resist was fading, as the muscles of will-power throbbed cramp in his mind.

Days. Weeks. When was the time going to be right? So much for the promise of untold secrets. Caxton was gone. The books were used up and he had been abandoned. A sob smacked his epiglottis and the watery fatigue became tears in free-fall frustration.

No words.

No books.

He needed them. He needed *something*.

All day and night, he'd searched through the broiling crowds of *L-Prime*, the desperation stalking him just as he'd stalked Caxton. Everywhere they'd ever met. Anywhere he might potentially find the man. All the bars and clubs where they'd conversed and transacted. Nobody had seen nor heard even a ghost or a whisper.

"I'll find you – when the time's right." He had to hold to that, because he didn't think he could face the future without ever surfing a book again.

For now, there was only one way to get him through the lonely hours of the night. Already, he felt Caxton's disapproval as he reached for his old console. A battered thing, bought second-hand years ago. A handful of upgrades and retro-fits furnished sub-*Gestalt* capabilities, but it was still little more than an obsolete artificial reality engine. A poor substitute for what he *needed*, but it was all he had to silence the *Gestalt's* pleading cry, or his hungry need for words on paper.

The rest of the room seemed to ripple against the machine's promised solidity of escape, insubstantial as a heat haze. The machine was real now; all else was the illusion.

"Join me," it might have whispered, but that was only his sanity running loose at the edges. He lay back on the couch and rested the machine on his chest. Then he slipped the mask over his face and shuffled it into a comfortable fit. A quiet 'snik' in his ear as it made contact with his implant. The machine began to hum soft as his fingers caressed its *chakras*, ready to reward him with its seductive pleasures.

An explosion of crimson photons as he breached the portals to a realm beyond his mundane existence. It wasn't a book, but it wasn't the *Gestalt* either.

For a moment, he was poised on the event horizon of compromise. Then the waveforms of possibility collapsed into darkness with a few barely conscious motions of his fingers. The coagulating portal collapsed into nothing. He broke the lifeless connection with his implant, and peeled away the mask.

In frustration, he swiped the console from his chest. The mask slithered with it into temporary obsolescence. Then he rolled on to his side and buried his face against the couch's stale-scented back in search of sleep and solace.

One more day. One more chance. That was all he could take, then he was done with all the *bullshit*.

THIS *wasn't right. He'd not been back to this place since that former life; the time following that terrible deed when three lives altered forever. The place still haunted his dreams though, not that this felt like a dream. This visitation, not even like memory crystallising out of old sorrows; it felt like what it was… a place that had no belonging.*

Nobody was ever supposed to come here, not that it had stopped him then, or now, or once more; nor had it stopped those fool few who came before. A lethal curiosity compelled them; disbelief of the senses combined with a denial of mortality held their hand along the way. Fury and guilt had been his *driver, until dread staunched resolve. After that, a dark gravity had tugged him onwards into the depths of unease.*

So, here he was, the latest explorer, looking for some way to make sense of his misdirected life; he followed lamenting voices to some apparent source only to arrive here. A lone figure in the shadows, walking where Angels feared to tread and even Demons stepped foolhardy.

Lights glowed distant. Bright and strong they gleamed like over-sized stars, but against the gloom here, the light had little more strength than those cosmic baubles possess against the night, not that anyone in Terapolis *saw stars any more. No, in a city that drank much of the sunlight before it might ever reach human eyes, what hope of a glimpse of the heavens?*

The shadows in this place were darker still; they yielded an overwhelming physicality, as though they had actual substance. Beneath the ringing catwalk lurked a depth of shade that suggested abyssal proportions. Down might have been fathomless; it might also be mere feet. Impossible to tell, at least by sight. The catwalk joined more of its kind, where some form of growth covered the fragile construction of metal. Hideous and organic, whatever it was glowed ever so slightly and glistened putrescent.

Man-made structures here were nothing but a trestle for this tangled organism. The strands and fibres intertwined and bundled into thick-knotted clumps that in turn became weaved into giant root-like vines.

Faint smears of light gleamed in the distance. It wasn't long before they resolved into shape. The interloper swallowed down the bile-marinated vomit that gurgled in search of a way out. The smell here was as nauseous as the sights. The mildew stench of this xenomorphic matter cloyed at the throat.

Huge sacs dangled from some unseen point of attachment far above. Some sagged, nearly empty, like an eviscerated scrotum. Others were bulbous and swollen to obscene proportions. Thick, rubbery veins bifurcated through the membrane-surface. Whatever fluid was within these giant sacs – sap or pus or something else – it radiated a sickly glow.

The breeze whispered with a million half-heard voices. Or so the imagination suggested. A shudder ran through nervous flesh; this was not a place for a vivid imagination. Further on, the catwalk met others. Peering into the gloom, illuminated somewhat by the glowing pustules, it became clear that this was a meeting of ways. He knew he was close now. Close to the secrets hidden in the shade.

Fear was sensible and begged retreat. Morbid curiosity displayed its blind death wish and urged him on past yet more rows of those fluid-filled sacs.

Beyond and around the sacs, beneath the catwalk and overhead, the tangled growth was thicker and closed in to create a grotto filled with a looming malevolence.

Curiosity was such a fool. It stepped forth.

And found something. He felt it brush against his spirit. A presence.

Here, in the centre of all things; the Heart of all that is Dark.

At first, it appeared to be yet another putrescent sac dangling from the unseen rafters. Until, that is, it pulsed brighter and forced the darkness to retreat.

The interloper took a step back in shock. Medical students would know this thing, and wish they did not. Suspended amidst the thick vines and fibres, hung a gigantic and bloated womb. Where fallopian tubes and ovaries should have been, there were twin bundles of fibres, veins and arteries of rubbery flesh. They pulsated with a sickly rhythm and glowed from within. The glow was spreading, pumping into the womb itself so that its membranous surface joined the light.

Eyes play tricks, especially in places of poor light and sullen fear, but the shape that resolved was no artifice of shadow and contour. It was real. Seen through the opaque wall of the womb, a body was huddled within. Curled in a foetal position, it appeared to wear clothes, though these might have been ruffles and folds of some inner membrane.

Motion caused the interloper to stand back. The womb writhed. Muscles bunched and trembled with excited tension. The thing inside moved; there followed a sense of malignant awareness. What could only be a head had shifted and a face appeared to be pressed against the inner membrane.

The veins on the womb pulsated and thickened. The glow became brighter as the flow penetrated the body of the womb until the entire organic apparition blazed like a beacon. For a moment, the thing within was revealed as a translucent wisp against the scintillating brilliance.

Light flared. A silent scream exploded from the interloper's mouth, but the coruscating fire of energy drowned even sound. Before his body erupted and scattered in this explosion of photons, the light faded.

He turned away to gaze at the returning shadows. Darkness cooled his eyes, and as his vision returned he realised in silent awe that several of the giant pustules had shrivelled with the loss of their load.

The gurgling faded. A dull pumping thud pounded at the thicket around him like a distant heart beat. Voices muttered in the distance, another screamed a tormented lament.

"Join us. Be one with us."

A choral resonance, many voices spoke almost as one. The interloper shuddered; fear seared his heart just as the light seared his eyes. He wanted to turn and run, but he was caught in the moment, perfectly balanced by the fear of what confronted him and the fear of the unknown waiting for his flight.

And of course, there was the Watcher in the Womb.

Ancient fears rose from the primordial pits of human existence, buried deep by the cultured sophistication and reason layered like silt during the millennia of civilisation's flow, and he understood. This was a place worse than damnation; a fitting place to expunge the savage guilt congealed in his frozen heart, but the rising fear smothered even this latent ghost of reason. It was a fear of the dark things lurking in the shadows beyond the firelight, and it was a fear for which the modern man was ill-equipped to utilise.

And there, within, lurked the ancient progenitor of all humanity's nightmares.

The interloper collapsed to his knees. The light was dimming. The shadows closed in. He sensed the purpose of this terrible place, felt the knowledge soaking into his spirit; the secrets hidden in the Heart of Darkness, but comprehension was yet to come.

The thing in the womb spoke sibilant.

"Such a pity; I saw such pleasing things for you amidst the patterns of causality. Now your patterns are in flux. You should not have come here, but now you know. And what can you do with the knowledge but go mad from anticipation? At the end of days, when It is made Complete, then we shall meet again. You and I and all things Aware. Then we shall join. Our deepest most secret desire shall be unleashed – and creation transformed."

A shrill scream erupted from the distance. Something slithered; he heard the snapping and cracking as of wood in a forest. More screams. The thicket came alive with dreadful sounds. The ghost voices lamented and mocked. The interloper was the centre of a closing noose of dread.

The spell of terror was broken. Now the ancient primate survival instincts unlocked his limbs. He turned and ran the way he came, heedless of the dark. Shoes clanked on the metal, breath harsh and loud in the dark, his heart thumped like miniature explosions in his chest. Behind him, the screaming things from the heart of darkness were closing in from all sides. There was no time. He couldn't get out…

Behind him, the voice: Soon, soon now, your guilt shall find absolution… "Caxton!"

THERE was no escape. The screeching *thing* leapt from the shadows. A demonic manifestation half-morphed into a parody of the humanoid, the rest just crumpled membranes oozing mucous, bound by too many vermiform tentacles. Eyes like globs of congealed pus irradiated hate. Foul breath washed over him as another soul-piercing shriek almost ripped the sanity from his mind.

On instinct alone, his arm rushed forth to ward off the finality of the moment. It struck something solid in the darkness. There was a thud followed by sodden dripping. Only then did he realise. He was safe. He was *home*.

Caxton rubbed his sweating face and then laid his head back down on the desk. His solid, familiar desk where his work lay cluttered after a session of hard toil. The smell of old wood and oil and stale tobacco soothed his senses. He sighed in the darkness and waited for the trembling fit to pass.

Ancient men knew there was a power in dreams, when the mind's complex framework touched ethereal dimensions, but his modern descendants had forgotten so much. This was no dream though. No, this was memory, a haunting legacy of the epiphany that finally changed the course of life.

"Why now? Why *now* after so long?"

The answer was all around him. The darkness was closing in. Not just here in this room, but out there in that metropolis of darkness. Morlock was close. Not to this point in space, but to the destination of his desire.

Caxton. The realisation was a throttling band squeezing his chest and threatening a bronchial barrage. Never before had the nightmare vision included an invocation of his chosen identity.

He shuddered at the thought and switched on the desk lamp for comfort and security. The shadows rushed away from the explosion of light to huddle in the corners of the room, there to lurk and watch resentfully as he tidied up his papers and wiped clear the drool of slumber from his sheaf of notes.

Coffee pooled on the edge of the desk, fortunately nowhere near his work, but the cold dregs of the overturned cup dripped monotonously onto the old carpet. He cursed under his breath and moved to find something to mop up the mess. That was the solidity he hit when he jerked awake from the climax of his haunted past.

Solid. The *other* had not been so. Not then, when he barely got out with his sanity, let alone his life.

There was nothing to clean up the mess close at hand, so he strained upright and then stretched to ease the tension in his back. He hadn't meant to fall asleep at his desk, but the demands of work often kept him there until he was mugged by slumber.

The chair squeaked in protest as he pushed it back and raised his bulk. More light tormented the shadows as he flicked the hall switch and stomped towards the kitchen. He returned in moments with a damp rag and meticulously cleaned the spilled coffee. Then he mopped the brown-sodden patch of carpet. Maggie, he mused, would be speechless to see such domesticity.

Still, the shadows watched from their haven beyond the light. They might have whispered, were they shadows of *Terapolis* rather than those of his hearth and home. He threw the rag aside and sat down again on his old swivel chair. It creaked in friendly protest as his bulk settled into place. Then he leaned against the desk and stared at the familiar place that had been his home for so many years.

And for all that time he had been haunted.

You can run, you can hide, but *things* have a habit of catching up. The Damned can never escape, but a few – only a few – gain one precious moment to redeem their salvation. Yes. *It* was still out there. Watching. Waiting, as he had been waiting, for the moment to arrive. That time he lacked the armour of the *Word*, but the next time… Well, he would see.

He turned in the seat and picked up his manuscript. He flicked through it, then placed it to his face so that he could savour the scents of paper and ink and oil from his ancient Hermes. There wasn't much left to do now. It was almost finished.

There'd be nothing to hold him back.

From what he – and he *alone* – must do.

Redemption was hard. But it was no longer about him. No, it had ceased to be about him the moment he had ventured into that *place* and found what lurked in the shadows.

On impulse, he cracked open the top drawer of his desk and peered inside. He felt his face soften as he looked at the old faded photograph. There he saw a younger version of himself grinning at the camera, her arms around his shoulders. Her face – ghost pale even then – beamed happy, her dark hair a lustrous cascade over her shoulders.

"I'm so sorry," he whispered, fighting back unfamiliar tears. "I took away the one thing that might have saved you. It's too late for us, but I'll see *him* right."

He closed the drawer on memory. For what was to come, he had to be the tough, confident, streetwise figure declared by his street persona. The visage that had kept him together in all the years of business in smoky bars nurturing contacts and delivering books, or wheedling, bribing and forcing information from contacts so he might fill in the gaps of his research for his soon-to-be-completed work.

He needed to be strong.

For a little longer.

Until Humanity reclaimed its *Soul*.

He grinned at the thought. As he had learned, it wasn't what the Old World theologians had thought it, but the metaphor still had a certain appeal.

The grin died grim. He tapped the manuscript on the desk and then placed it carefully beside the typewriter. Then he looked up at the grime-stained windows, as though staring at the city beyond.

Out there was the *Gestalt*. Out there was Morlock. The place of his nightmares was now out *there* in *MorTek Prime*. The certainty filled him with dread, but there was no other choice. He had sired his fate long ago.

"Books are a poison to the *Gestalt*," he mumbled. "But do we still have *enough*?"

To that, the shadows had no answer.

THE doorbell didn't work when she pressed the button; that came as no surprise since the lift was out of action too, and the old palm-reader was long since supplanted by more reliable mechanical locks. It said something about *Terapolis*, but Laura had too much on her mind to consider it.

She knocked instead, and silently urged Adam to hurry. The slog up the stairs had tired her out more than she wanted to admit.

A door across the landing creaked open to reveal a slice of pallid, wrinkled face and a suspicious eye. Laura glared back until the eye retreated and the door closed.

Adam still hadn't answered.

She didn't bother to knock again, but leaned forward to peer at the lock in the weak, flickering light. She smiled. *Easy pickings.*

It proved as straightforward to pick as it looked. Maybe even easier, and in moments the door swung inwards.

The smell of stale cooking, nutrient glands, and male laundry – unwashed, naturally – escaped onto the landing. Laura wrinkled her nose in disgust. The odour was not entirely dissimilar to Caxton's place, but there the worst of it was masked by the rich scent of his tobacco and the incense sticks he burned. Both scents combined to overawe the rest.

Though Maggie played her part too, she had gathered. Well, she was not about to become Adam's Maggie; she'd keep an eye on him, but she'd be damned if she'd cook and clean and wipe *his* snotty nose.

She stepped into the gloom and closed the door.

"Adam?"

There was no answer, but she thought she heard a sound coming from somewhere inside the flat. She paused on the threshold and strained to hear. Two lines of illumination, the colour of stale piss, framed the door to the living room. She pushed it open and the light spilled into the hallway. Still the same pigsty she remembered.

She didn't see Adam until she moved into the living room and looked around. Then she saw what lay discarded on the floor by the couch. Her heart skipped a beat. *"Adam…"*

She was surprised to feel a tear spill, then her anger brushed it away.

He was stretched out on the couch, sleeping now, but on the floor beneath him the old console and mask lay in a jumble of cables. The useless junkie just couldn't leave it alone. She kicked it out of the way. Adam grunted and twitched in his sleep, but he didn't wake. He just rolled and slumped into another position.

"Adam, why can't you leave that *shit* alone?"

She kneeled down beside him and contemplated waking him, but he looked so calm and peaceful. All those troubles and confusions in his head gone. For now. She felt the anger slide away and become replaced by memories of the better moments they'd shared. She reached out tenderly to cradle him in her arms.

"Why can't you be more like Cax?"

She stroked his chest, and felt his heart beat. She pressed her cheek against his head and felt his tightly curled hair tickle her skin. How she had missed that. *Don't* cry, she thought harshly.

For not long enough, she held him close and soothed him in his sleep. When he showed signs of returning consciousness she quickly disentangled herself and moved across to the armchair.

There she sat, and kept watch.

ALL the arrangements were made. Now it was just a matter of waiting. Always the waiting. Impatience wasn't healthy in this kind of work, but for once Otto couldn't help the frustrating sense of urgency. Doubtless it derived from his sin of personal involvement. The sooner this job was done the better.

He shifted in the seat to look around at the café. This was one of the livelier establishments in *Locus Prime*. No doubt that's why his target favoured the place. The smell of real – not *ersatz* – coffee massaged his palate. The babble of voices stroked his ears with a human animation that was like a resurrection of a memory from the Old World. Well, the old man had managed to keep this haven a secret. Pity. He sipped, and made a mental note to return. Only for the coffee, of course, *only* that.

Elzevir walked in at that moment. The game was afoot. The old man moved towards the counter and placed his order. Otto watched as his prey took his drink and then made his way towards a table in the far corner, away from the window and the fishbowl onlookers outside. The way the old man sat spoke volumes of old habit and familiarity, as much for Elzevir as the other patrons. *Complacent*, old man, his mind growled. The table was secluded and empty. He sat with the air of a man ready to open and absorb his newspaper. Not here, not now. Not any more.

Again, Otto felt uneasy about the job, but he had to concede that Elzevir played the game well; he gave no sign that he was aware of his observer. Years of clandestine practice, no doubt. Not that it mattered if he knew or not. Otto watched the old man from the corner of his eye, just there at the periphery. He raised his cup and drained some of the coffee, savouring its rich sensuality, and then he let the cup guide his arm back down to the table.

Elzevir's last words came to him. He reached gently into his jacket and felt the pocket. As he did so his fingers brushed against the hard metal of his deadly purpose. Metal, and then cloth. And through the cloth he felt the solid lump that was the old man's last request.

The Bible.

A bible, at any rate. Religion had never meant much to him, even as a child when such notions still held their grip on the human race. Evidently, it still mattered to Elzevir. Funny. To think there was any latent faith in the old man's heart. Except for his precious books. What he aimed to achieve with this one, beyond some misplaced personal solace, was best left to the dead deity it spoke for. Once again, he had his doubts, but a morbid curiosity had gained the upper hand.

There was more with *this* book, though. Inside it, when he flicked through in idle curiosity, he found the scrap of paper scribbled hastily in the old man's script. He mulled it over now.

"Though he has lived in the shadow of the valley of death, at the end of days he must fear no evil but walk proud and tall into the light."

The words were as baffling as the man who scribbled them, but reminded him of some old religious incantation. No priests today. *Certainly none for you old man.*

Elzevir was making ready to move. Otto caught the body language from the corner of his vision. He felt himself go tense in anticipation. This was it. The moment of dread.

Elzevir stood then and began to shuffle towards the door. When he reached it, his eyes finally met Otto's. A chance encounter of two strangers in a crowded place. There was just the barest nod of the head, then the old man stepped out onto the street.

ADAM jerked awake with a sleep-strangled cry of terror when he realised there was someone else in the room.

"Don't be afraid. It's only me."

"Laura!"

The soft voice kissed a memory and soothed his nerves. He slumped back on the couch and hugged a tatty cushion in lieu of the warm body he remembered. She hadn't changed. Hard exterior, yielding candy within. A new jacket, he noted, but still the loose fitting garments she favoured. Nondescript and baggy but hard wearing: a kind of urban camouflage, nothing to make her stand out against the crowd.

The hungry heat dribbled down to his lap as he remembered; there was nothing nondescript about the body beneath the veil. He realised he was grinning at the memory of that cute little mole just above...

"And you can stop those eyes undressing me, if you don't mind," she snapped. "I'm sure it sends you blind."

"I wasn't!" Hot flush of guilt. "I just... I *missed* you."

She snorted. "You miss the sex, that's all."

The comment stung, but he couldn't help pushing it. "Well, it was good wasn't it?"

Laura just grunted a response. Agreement, denial or contempt, he couldn't tell. Better not to push it any further. Take it as the flattering option.

Laura looked around the habitat.[24] Adam remembered the mess with a rush of embarrassment. "Have you ever

---

[24] Personal living space for a *Terapolitan*. In Old World terms an apartment. Entire towers, or those sections of towers given over to residential purposes, are called habitentiaries.

cleaned this pigsty since I was last here? You're worse than Cax!"

He sat up. More important concerns barged aside his embarrassment. "You've seen Caxton? Where is he? I've been going out of my head here!"

Laura stared. "I noticed."

"Well? Cax said—"

"He's busy. His life doesn't revolve around you, you know."

"I know, but I've used up the books. I need more!"

"If it was up to me, I'd leave you to fester with that shit you Gack."

"I haven't!"

She nodded towards the discarded console. "Oh, so what's that then?"

"I didn't Gack. I... Look, I needed something, okay? I was going out of my skull here on my own. But I didn't. I *resisted* it. You have to believe me."

She nodded unconvinced. "I don't get you junkies. How can you plug that shit into your heads?"

"You wouldn't understand."

"No. So what's it like?"

"I could show you."

"Not a chance!" Then she tapped behind her ear. "And no implant, remember?"

He shrugged. "Okay. It's like... I don't know how to describe it."

"Try."

He sighed, frowned, almost gave in, then he thought of something. "It's like sex. You have to experience it to really know it."

"So, it's not actually that great, then? Or did you mean sex with someone who knows what they're doing?"

The word 'bitch' flashed in his head, but his tongue knew better than to say it. He just looked away and swallowed the hurt. "I knew you'd never get it," he said.

"No. I don't want to. Books are better."

"I *know*. But if I don't get some books, then I *need* something. Where is Caxton? I need some books!"

He hadn't meant to shout, but he was too strung out for this grief. Laura stared at him, unperturbed. She was cast iron, sometimes. He'd forgotten that. So there she sat. Stern. As always. If only she'd loosen up, let herself out of those shackles of self-control. On the few occasions she did...

He buried the pleasant memories. No point going there. Maybe he'd tried too hard to bring her out of herself, maybe they'd still be together if... if only. That was just wishful thinking. When she was like this, though, did he really want the wish fulfilled? A clunking spring brought him out of his thoughts. Laura stood up and strode towards the hall.

"Laura?" He frowned, on the verge of upset.

"I got you some books."

She disappeared. He heard the commotion with her bag. She never left home without one. Then she came back and held out a bundle of volumes. He reached up for them gingerly and then felt their supple forms beneath his fingers. He quickly clutched them close to his body, along with the cushion, and then he looked up hopefully at Laura.

She didn't sit beside him. Instead she returned to the chair and slumped into its battered seat. Adam had to make do with the disappointment.

The scent of old paper was soothing incense. That was better than her cold shoulder. The aromatherapy began to settle his fraught nerves. He flicked through the first volume and enjoyed both the sensation and the sound. He let his mind drift with the sensual moment.

"We had some good times, didn't we?"

"Occasionally."

Was that a smile on her face? A smirk of pleasant recollection? Yes. The way her head tilted to the left, and a lock of sandy hair draped her eye. She flicked it back. Just as he remembered. An unconscious mannerism he knew well and adored. A chink in her armour. She pointed at the books in his hand.

"You got no more excuses now. You can stay off that junk."

Adam suppressed the groan. Why couldn't they leave it alone? "Maybe," he replied.

"No maybe about it! Books and the *Gestalt* don't mix!"

"Why not?"

Laura opened her mouth, her eyes blazing, but she said nothing. She only stared for a moment. Then she found her voice, and it was harsh. "I don't know, okay? I just *know*."

"That's no answer! There's nothing wrong with my machine. It's only AR – not *Gestalt*."

"I don't care what it is – it came from *MorTek*."

"There's nothing wrong with the *Gestalt*!"

"Oh really? I remember what you were like after trips. A *fucking* zombie. Why do you think I walked away? How do you feel after hitting a G-Spot?"

He looked away. "Like death."

"So why do it?"

"Because I *need* it."

"No, you don't. It only makes you think you need it!"

"You don't understand what it's like to hear it calling you. The pain of this city, the emptiness of living in this place. If I can't get a book, then what else am I supposed to do? In the *Gestalt*, or my console – then at least I am away from the... hollow *ache*."

"We live it too, Adam, but we don't succumb. We don't have that shit buried in our heads. You should have been weaned off it by now. If you want to be one of us – truly one of us – then you'd better deal with that junk and get it lifted."

"Why? Why can't I have both? You never explain anything!"

Laura stared hard. He'd seen her before like this. Usually before she hit someone, but he wasn't backing down. Not on this. He was tired of being told what to do without any reason.

"Adam, the *Gestalt* sucks your soul."

"I don't believe in the soul."

"Okay, then it sucks your mind – what's left of it. Believe in that?"

She fell silent. Her eyes glared. Adam couldn't look back, nor could he think of anything to say. *Just go*, he thought bitterly.

"Adam this is serious. Don't Gack. Get that shit out of your head."

He waved her away. "Leave me alone."

"Okay. I tried. It's your choice. Enjoy the books."

She stood and walked towards the door. Adam looked up sharply.

"Laura... Wait! Don't go..."

She paused to meet his gaze and hesitated. He felt a moment's hope and reached up with his hand. Then she looked away.

"I can't stay," she mumbled. Adam let his hand fall. The hall swallowed her form. He heard the rucksack shuffle on to her shoulder. The front door open and then slam closed. She was gone. Just like that. All over again.

TERAPOLIS brooded on the horizon like a gathering storm. Boris squinted at the view until his forehead ached with the effort, but he endured and stared at the shadow of home with a deep sense of foreboding.

The place was calling him back to continue Morlock's purpose. The *Gestalt* beckoned. Dully, he realised he didn't want to return. Not yet. Perhaps never, but he still felt the place pulling every cell of his existence like some gravitational tidal wave.

From this distance, the city was a dark and sombre cliff stretching as far as the eye could see, a dark prophecy reaching out to fulfil its temper. The sky above it was smothered by a sullen cauldron of grey cloud, but even with dark glasses the light glowing from within the translucent depths was still too bright for *Terapolitan* eyes.

The clouds appeared to pour from the city like the noxious breath of a burning volcano. Fronds of utter black extended into the grey clouds, bleeding out to cover the world in darkness.

Urban spread. Irrevocable. Unstoppable. The advance of the modern, coming to claim this quaint relic of *outcity*. He might run, until he ran out of Earth, and still the city's patient encroachment would reach out to engulf all that he was. Another chilling thought.

Boris sighed, and turned his back on *Terapolis*.

The gravel of the path crunched beneath his feet. A strange sensation after the yielding *pedederm* of home. The grass felt more familiar, the way it accepted his tread with a soft embrace, but there was something more *human* about its texture. Perhaps it was only his mood. It was a strange place, this, far removed from the familiarity of *G-Tek*.

A few more paces and he reached the nearest standing stone. Vaguely, he was aware that a human form was interred on this spot. No *necrolyser* bellies for those born of bygone days. There were letters carved into the simple tablet of weathered rock. Hardly discernible now after who knew how many years of the elements. Patches of lichen stained the edifice and filled in the words. Blobs of moss, thick and pungent, clung to its edges and crannies, like some proto-*Terapolis* ingesting the ruins of its predecessor.

With a sigh, he turned away to look at the stone structure built amidst the field of standing stones. A church, his sister Shona said it was called; he understood neither the word nor its purpose. Yet, he understood with the stiletto pang of guilt why family and old friends gathered inside. They were strangers now; he felt an intruder in the midst of their grief, not merely because he was its cause. He had left them behind, been absorbed into the new family in the vaults of *MorTek Prime*. Until his ambition – and his *cowardice* – instigated this sombre reunion.

The priest had known what he was. Somehow. Boris thought of the man who led his former family in their ritualised grief; a sharp faced man with wild hair the colour of the clouds. Dressed in white flowing robes over a sombre black suit, he wore a strip of white cloth at his throat and around his neck was a cross with an elongated vertical bar: a strange uniform for an outlandish anachronism.

The talisman he wore was a smaller version of the one that dominated the far wall of the building. On it, the gaunt figure of a man was apparently nailed to the cross. A gruesome image on which to focus, he reflected, still bewildered by the peculiar belief system he had never realised still existed. Who would have thought Shona followed the macabre cult of this tortured god they invoked inside the old building? His work had kept him away from them for too long, perhaps beyond the possibility of return. Now he was alone out here, a stranger in a strange land, fearful of discovery.

All through the sermon, the priest stared at *him*. Eyes hard and piercing, as if he knew. *Knew* it all. That's when he made his graceful retreat from the church's cold pews. Perhaps it was an urge triggered by the mention of 'innocence' that forced him to remember what – who – resided in the small black box placed before the altar.

Safe from the piercing scrutiny, he listened to the chant of the mumbling voices carried away like seeds by the wind. More of the same litany that drove him to wait out here. This was where his ambitions and dreams led: to this place of crumbling monuments.

At least the *necrolysers* wouldn't taste Natalie's remains. He felt strangely grateful for that. Instead, she was to nourish the soil and the creatures that dwelt therein. To rest, and digest, in the belly of the Earth. The thought should be distasteful, but somehow it appealed more than the bellies of

Terapolis. Poor Natalie, she should have grieved for him in time. So much for his promise.

"I'll make you some wonderful toys."

The memory resurfaced on a gust of wind. He'd whispered the promise in Natalie's ears what seemed a lifetime ago. Four years and eight months later, he was here in this wild and empty place, startled from the memory as the door to the ancient church opened with an ominous creak.

THE cell door screeched open. Otto gritted his teeth, but it wasn't the noise that provoked his discomfort. The old man lay on his side within, trussed up with his head covered in a cloth bag.

In truth, it wasn't a cell at all, just an old lift shaft; the derelict remains of a London skyscraper long forgotten since being absorbed into the flesh of *MorTek Prime*. Long ago, they'd welded the old doors permanently open, bolted a simple but effective steel door in place, and with the addition of a grated metal floor and ceiling, created a functional holding pen for Morlock's *special* guests.

The old man had proved a difficult quarry. Deceptively difficult, for all that their little arrangement had made him a collaborator in his own capture. The need to make it convincing had seen him put up a spirited resistance. A few of his men bore bruises and black eyes from the encounter; who'd have thought the dried-out old librarian had it in him? Not Otto. The *Incunabula* were full of surprises. In the end, he'd had to intervene and taser the old man into submission. That was not part of the plan.

For a moment, he didn't know whether to curse or congratulate the rent-a-cops who staffed his department. No way of knowing the payback they'd inflicted on their guest while his attention was elsewhere. He barely dared hope, but then he saw the bag flutter. So, they were doomed to play their little charade to the very end.

Otto sighed and stepped over the threshold. The grated deck shifted slightly beneath his weight, causing a wobble of vertigo deep in his guts. He closed his eyes briefly and steeled himself to the task. Marla, of course, had no such apprehensions. She breezed past and prodded the old man with her foot.

"Don't be dead, Darling, it's impolite to leave without saying goodbye!"

The old man groaned and slowly raised his head. Otto squatted and helped the man to sit up, leaning him against the concrete wall. Marla's view was obscured by the bulk of his body, a convenient moment. Otto took the opportunity to slip the bible into the man's pocket and then he checked the bindings securing his wrists: rope, not the plastic tie he'd feared. That was good; he could carefully work it loose as they guided Elzevir to his destiny.

Satisfied, he pulled the bag from Elzevir's head. The old man blinked in the weak light. His face looked haggard and bruised, one eye blackened, his teeth worked on the crude gag the men had forced into his mouth. The old man could swear like a trooper, and loud too.

"Your hospitality needs a little work," Elzevir said, once the gag was clear. He glanced up at Marla, then back to Otto. "No last meal? I could *murder* for a decent curry."

"Don't worry, Darling, where you're going you'll soon loose your appetite."

Elzevir rolled his eyes and sighed theatrically. Despite himself, Otto grunted amusement; grudging respect bursting through his usual controlled façade, but beneath the old man's bravado he saw the exhaustion and wondered if the man really had the strength to go through with this. They'd find out soon enough.

"Marla, get the door! Come on, old man, it's time."

He pulled Elzevir to his feet. Once his burden stopped swaying, he dragged him out into the corridor. When they were clear, Marla let the door swing closed. The metal groaned in a tone to match Otto's mental burden. The physical burden lessened, but only a little, as Marla took up position to bear some of Elzevir's weight.

Otto tried to bury his fears as they enacted a parody of the traditional dead man's walk. From the holding cell to the execution chamber, he and Marla carried the burden that was the *Incunabula*, but Otto felt as if *he* was the man walking the final steps to perdition.

He wondered, perhaps now was the time for Elzevir's untimely but merciful demise? No. Not now. The time for such an 'accident' was gone. There was no plausible explanation this late in the game, not one to convince even Marla, let alone Silas Morlock.

For better or worse, after their shared bravado in the cell, he faced judgement too. The strongest test, and he must place his life in the hands of a doomed man. Otto didn't want to admit it, even to himself, but there was no time that he remembered ever being so afraid.

Don't let me down. Be strong, for your bibliophiles if not for me; but, make sure I'm covered too. Is this how his commissions felt, as they tried their impotent negotiations for life? He gritted his teeth and tried to stop thinking. At this rate, the old man wouldn't need to turn him in.

"Stop dragging, Darling!"

Marla's outburst surprised him, so much that for a moment he actually wondered if she was addressing him. Aside from her comments in the cell, she'd been uncharacteristically quiet; a further worry to gnaw at his mental defences. Perhaps it was impatience. She enjoyed her work far more than was healthy. A death junkie and a practitioner of pain. Two of the elements that worried him as much as they made her clinically fascinating.

Elzevir picked himself up somewhat. More of his weight descended on his shuffling feet. Marla's outburst might have done some good.

Work with me old man, he thought as he and Marla struggled to manipulate his mortal frame. In position at last, breathing heavy with the exertion, Otto kicked the doors open. They swung inwards to reveal a darkness as deep as any abyss. One of the many vast and unadorned vessels within the flesh of *MorTek Prime*; most given over to storage, this one was left to a far darker purpose. As Elzevir was doomed to discover.

Come on, he breathed, dragging the old man across the threshold. Marla shifted and the old man stumbled. She lost her footing and Elzevir pitched forward into the darkness. He landed heavily; his head thudded against the grime-laden *pedederm*. A cry of pain brought Otto relief; it meant the man was still conscious.

Before Marla could react, he stooped and put one arm under the man's armpit and began to drag him to his feet. Marla moved to the other side to do likewise.

On his way back up, Elzevir turned his head slightly and glared from his one good eye. A shock of recognition. Otto understood the old man's signal. *So it begins.*

NATALIE'S coffin looked pathetic, suspended over the yawning hole in the ground. They gathered round as the priest beheld his congregation with his piercing and naked eyes. Some quiet sobs from the mourners. The man's hair fluttered wild in the wind.

The funeral was approaching its climax. Through this latest ceremony, the priest stared and Boris found he couldn't return the gaze. Instead, he watched the ground, focused on the scuff marks and the slight traces of mud on his shoes.

The breeze flapped his trouser legs and tried to push him into the grave. It whispered mocking in his ear; the air knew his hidden secret too. He shivered, and tried to tell himself it was only at the chill weather.

"Uncle Boris!"

His head snapped up. His body went stiff. The air froze in his lungs. All the mourners listened intent to the priest's litany. Shona stared at the coffin, slug-trails of fluid dribbling from behind her dark glasses to leave gleaming streaks on her cheek. Her lower lip trembled. She had heard nothing. Nobody had. It was just the wind.

"Help us! We can't get out!"

A pounding heart didn't quite drown the voice. Blood pumped in his ears, crashing like the waves against the beaches of his brain, trying to batter down his mental defences.

"Pleeeeassssee… Uncle Boris!"

Behind his glasses, his eyes darted, looking for the speaker, someone huddled within the mourners. Nothing. Nothing at all. Was he going mad? Were the guilt and the fear finally tripping his switches and shutting off his sanity? Now, he finally started to understand his predecessor. What dark secrets were hidden in that man's conscience, festering until his mind exploded? He didn't want to go the same way. Somehow, he had to escape. Shona's hand slipped into his and gripped tight, as if she'd read his thoughts. Bound to the woman he betrayed.

"We commit this body to the ground."

Ropes creaked as the small coffin was swallowed by the soil.

"Earth to earth."

Natalie made her final descent.

"Ashes to ashes."

A gentle thud as she made landfall in the New World of the dead.

"Dust to dust."

The gathering shuffled forward for some arcane part of the ritual. He watched them stoop before the hole and throw in a handful of soil, then move away. To his horror, he felt Shona drag him forward.

"Come on, Boris," she whispered. "Time to say good-bye."

She was the strong one. Why was she the strong one? How can she believe Lorelei's crafted cover story? Did she understand nothing? He wanted to shout the questions aloud, but like a robot, he followed her towards the gaping wound in the earth. He stooped to follow her motion and pick up a handful of soil. It fell wet from his fingers and he heard the dull patter it made on the coffin below.

Across the grave another hand released a shower of dirt. Boris looked up as he rose and gagged at the face that stared intently from the other side. Silas Morlock rubbed his hands free of clinging soil and spoke.

"Grieve not for your niece, Creek, for she shall find the peace of the *Gestalt* in time," he said as he stood. "Hurry back to us. The *Gestalt* needs you. There is still so much to be done."

The phantasm turned and stalked through the assembled mourners. None appeared to see him. Only Boris watched him walk into the wind-blown landscape and vanish into the expanse of rippling green.

He almost choked on the breath going stale in his lungs. Hands gripped his body and pulled him round. Shona stared at his face. Eyes somehow meeting through twin sheets of darkened glass. She mistook his fear for grief, and put her arms around him to guide him from the grave. He almost stumbled again as they staggered into the midst of the standing stones.

Boris couldn't think, couldn't speak beyond the storm of terror in his head. He knew only one thing: he didn't want to return to the haunted city and his lab deep in its heart, but he saw no escape. No future beyond Morlock's pale face.

Shona pulled him close in a tearful embrace. Boris allowed her to do that, and let his own tears spill over her shoulder.

"You shouldn't have gone there," she whispered. "Come back to us, Boris. Come back to us if you can. Before it's too late."

WHERE there was nothing, suddenly there was infinity. In the flinch of an over-burdened eye, a singular photon exploded into the creation of a universe so bright it drowned any semblance of self. For Elzevir, it was not the birth of a cosmos, but the final flourish before the shade of forever.

Otto turned away from the overloading light, his muscles aching with the grimace. As the light faded into something comfortable for mere organic senses, Otto perceived the silhouette on the far side of the light well: Silas Morlock; stood as ever on the boundary between the light and the dark.

Then he stepped forth and gazed with predatory delight at the old man. "Welcome Elzevir, to *MorTek*," he said. "I am so pleased to finally make your acquaintance."

The light was now only a pool of radiance cast from the shaded rafters. Otto recovered enough to push the old man forward. Any part he had in this affair was over. He was a Morlock-man again – even if one with a guilty conscience. The old man was on his own. Time for him to hold true or fade forever into shadow.

Fortunately, Morlock was too intent on his guest to perceive any treacherous preamble in his manner. As for Marla, her own bloodlust was surging now; he was cloaked by their respective desires.

A moment's pity for the old man, quickly quashed by Morlock's deceptively conversational tones: "Was he a difficult catch?"

"No, Sir. Not difficult." Brusque, business-like, no trace of his inner turmoil. He might get through this yet. "He's just a cantankerous old man, long-since set in his ways."

"Indeed. Then let us see what we might do to *unbind* the restraints of routine."

Otto hesitated at the statement, his mind made frigid by the memory of their captor's loosened bonds and the book slipped discreetly into a pocket. When Morlock turned away, Marla offered her own relief to his tension.

She pulled the man forward. "This will be such fun, Darling."

Beyond the barrier of light, Otto saw a presence betrayed by motion. Belial shuffled forward and met his gaze with a lingering and disinterested stare. It was the unwitting moment where they all played into the old man's plans.

"Damn you, Morlock! DAMN YOU!"

The cry was frenzied. Suddenly he was charging forward. Otto felt himself fall as the man's lunge caught him. Marla's harsh cry was shrill as she collapsed onto all fours. Belial never flinched. Morlock only turned towards his guest.

Elzevir swung his arm. A blur of motion, even as Otto's hands slammed into the *derm* to arrest his fall. He looked up and saw the book soar towards the face of his master. Marla leapt to her feet and was running in slow motion towards the raging librarian.

So calm, Morlock's arm rose with the cane, a sweeping arc that swept the book from its trajectory. Marla's body cannoned into the old man and brought him down. They landed in a heap of limbs and bruised flesh. On the edge of the light pool the book crashed into impotence with a dull thud. Time returned to normal, faster than Otto's wits or breath. Damn, he was getting old.

Marla dragged the weeping man to his feet and then, still gripping his lapels, her fist smashed into his face. A tooth broke free and clattered to the safety of the shadows. Belial still stared. At Otto. Sweat emerged beneath his armpits, but mercifully his face remained composed.

"You didn't even search him?"

"He's just an old man, Sir. We thought—"

"Insufficiently!"

"He *was* bound, Darling!" Marla's voice was an octave shriller. Eyes wider than usual. Her lower lip shivered.

"Again, *insufficiently!*"

Otto dragged himself to his feet and winced against a few points of pain as he moved to help Marla with their guest. The old man was no longer passive. He screamed and struggled as they moved him to the chair and forced him to sit. Marla provided a vicious slap. The whimpers coming from his swollen lips were pathetic, but he was stilled enough for them to bind his hands and feet to the chair. The game was over now. The inevitable had begun; Otto just hoped there was time for him beyond this final meeting.

Morlock turned around abruptly and stalked towards the fallen book. The hapless volume lay open on its broken spine. A few pages hung listless from the layers of its composition. There was no breeze in this place but as Morlock approached, the pages ruffled as though caught by a curious current. Morlock stopped and took a half step back.

To the shadows, where Belial still lurked he hissed: "*Burn it!*"

He flicked the book with his cane. The Bible slithered across the *pedederm* until Belial reached down and stopped it. Taking the book in his hand, he stalked into the shadows. Moments later he returned with a metal waste bin in hand.

Elzevir's battered face tried to freeze in indifference as the lumbering creature stooped to place the bin at the man's feet. Then he fumbled in a pocket and withdrew a small lighter. The object appeared so out of place in Belial's meaty fist, more so when he placed it between his teeth and turned his attention to the book. That was the moment when Otto realised Belial wore a pair of surgeon's rubber gloves, as if there had ever been any truth to the contaminated nature of book paper. Even here, they preserved the old lie.

A sharp crack bespoke the book's sundered spine. A soft groan from the old man. His eyes bulged as he watched Belial tear the book into its constituent pages and let them flutter into the bin's waiting mouth. Belial himself was expressionless, as if he conducted any one of his many mundane tasks. He did not even glance at the old man as he took the lighter from between his teeth, spun the wheel to ignite the flame and applied it to the last bundle of helpless pages.

They illuminated Elzevir's face with a golden tang as the flames took hungry hold. Belial let them fall into the bin, where the dying pages shared their end with the book. The creature stepped back towards the shadows. Elzevir made a pitiable whine from the back of his throat. Otto felt a sympathetic response emerge in his own gut, but he gripped his jaw against its birth.

Flames ascended from the bin. Bright and lively, flakes of incinerated pages took flight on the thermals and danced for the audience until the book was nothing but smoking ash in the bottom. The chamber, dark as it was, felt darker still as the flames guttered and died. All Elzevir's dreams and hopes interred forever.

"Ashes to ashes, dust to dust." Morlock's soft sibilance replaced the crackle of fire. "Where are your precious words now?"

Elzevir's glare burned with pure hate. "Every burned book enlightens the world!"

"Indeed. Then let us see how enlightened it may become."

The old man's defiance stirred an unexpected admiration in Otto's heart. Perhaps Morlock was right; there was strength to the *Incunabula*. A dangerous strength, but could it persevere in the days to come? And what did it all mean for him? *MorTek* and the *Incunabula* – a servant to the one, drawn to the other. How long before he was squashed between them? No, he mustn't think like that. There was a way through this.

"Curious," Morlock added idly, "that he made no attempt to evade capture."

The comment streaked through his mind with the slick motion of a disembowelling knife. Before the fear caused him to spill his blurted guilt, Marla came to the rescue.

"Why don't you just kill him, Darling?"

"Knowledge is power, my dear, and he holds a tiny morsel that I require."

Morlock turned towards Belial and offered a gentle nod of the head. Belial moved into action. He wheeled a trolley into position and then checked the mysterious and archaic-looking machines. After that, Elzevir could only watch helpless as sensor pads were attached to his head and body. Displays flashed into life, charting the last moments of Elzevir's physiological existence. Otto hoped that soon they might be dismissed; he'd never been expected to linger this long. To kill or capture a man was one thing, but to participate in what followed, even as an observer, was another. This was beyond his remit, and his capacity to stomach. A bad time to develop a squeamish sensibility, let alone a conscience.

"I am told they call you the librarian," Morlock said. "Why is that?"

"I *was* a librarian, you bastard! Before you had them all destroyed."

"A vicious slander. Oft repeated. What was done was for the good of all. Even you. Now you must help me set things right."

Elzevir looked taken aback by the statement.

"Tell me where it is, this library of yours, so that we may add to this light of which you are so fond."

"Over my bleeding corpse!"

Morlock clicked his tongue. "Bookish melodrama. I expected better."

Belial stepped away from the machines and stared. "All is ready, Master."

"Good. Make it easy on yourself, *librarian*. Tell me."

"Go *fuck* yourself!"

"Now that is hardly literary language."

Morlock took a step closer to his prey and pulled back the fingers on the man's left hand. Elzevir winced. Morlock raised one eyebrow as he studied the gnarled appendages and stroked the callused index finger.

"You write as well as read. And you use a pen. How quaint. Quite the scribe."

Elzevir began to struggle against his bonds. As if there was any way he might alter the future. "I'll never betray the library. You hear? *Never!*"

Morlock smiled. "I did not expect you to. Belial."

"Master."

"It is time."

The creature bowed his head and then returned to the shadows. When he returned he held...

"A *Succub-I*. What use is that?"

"An opening, Otto, merely an opening. Young Mr Creek made for us far more than an interesting toy."

The *Succub-I* was strangely quiescent in Belial's grasp. It slipped over the old man's frightened face like the hood of a condemned man. He shook his head to try and shake it free but the creation came alive and its claspers gripped tight. The tentacles coiled and wrapped and found their way inside the prey. Elzevir screamed like a violated virgin as the machine forced its way inside his pristine brain.

"Step back everyone. And watch. I sincerely doubt you possess Belial's fortitude."

Belial stood immediately behind the old librarian, his face a portrait of perfect indifference as he stared ahead. Otto shuffled backwards to the edge of the light. Marla followed, confusion lining her artificial youth. Out of sight and far overhead, something gurgled and slithered. A glance upwards revealed nothing. The old man, blinded by the *Succub-I,* voiced his confusion and fear. Something leapt from the shadows. Otto cried out and nearly stumbled.

What resembled a gigantic glob of mucus and damp leathery sheets descended into view. Tentacles extruded from its amorphous mass and snaked towards the old man.

He screamed as they wrapped around his helpless body. Others moved for the *Succubi-I* and began to merge with both man and *G-Tek* machine. The old man wailed like a terrified child as the obscene emergence invaded his flesh. The air stank of mildew, soon augmented by the stench of the man's bowels as his remaining dignity fled.

Still Belial stood and stared, unmoved by the scene. Morlock stood nearby, eyes closed, frowning in deep concentration. To the side, out of sight, Marla wept in terror.

Elzevir screamed shrill from beneath his envelope of alien flesh. The wail died to a bubbled gurgle as the mass of organic matter shivered and throbbed. The still-visible portions of the man twitched and shuddered. Otto wished he could turn away and flee into the depths of the shadows, but now he feared what lurked beyond his sight.

"We have it!" Morlock cried, his eyes snapping open. "The location of the library is ours! That and more!"

Then as one, both Morlock and Belial turned to stare. Otto felt their combined gaze reach into the depths of his soul as his master spoke: "Be thankful, Otto, that there are no secrets between *us*."

The Sixth Folio

Old Legends Never Die, Only Bide Their Time

MINISTER Vaghela emerged from the *simulacomm's* plinth with a rippling liquid motion. The final addition to the fluid bust was the amalgam of colour. The chromospores[25] emerged as spots and patches of pigment that slowly blended across the man's features.

The colour was hardly worth the effort. Despite the man's standing in *Terapolitan* society, his face was bleached the same bloodless grey as any average citizen. Perhaps the eyes were a little sharper and more alert, but then again that might only be the glimmer of the *simulacomm's* exotic substance as it formed into Vaghela's molecular cocktail.

Morlock discarded the thought, sat back and steepled his fingers. The man's head turned to meet his gaze.

"Minister Vaghela, It's good of you to see me. I appreciate you are a busy man."

---

[25] Tiny packets of pigment assembled from the raw matter of a *Simulacomm* that spread through the animate and provide appropriate colour and hues.

The head tilted to flick a lock of putrid hair from its brow. Vaghela's lips rippled liquid and strands of flesh bonded them together until the *simulacomm* stabilised the sudden motion. *"For you, Mr Morlock, I can always make time. You are after all our city's most gracious benefactor."*

"Quite." So much for the ritual of social etiquette.

Vaghela's right ear dribbled down the side of his head, but quickly reformed and began to crawl back to its correct place. The man spoke, unconcerned as his ersatz flesh composed itself. *"What can I do for you?"*

"A matter of a serious nature has arisen. It has come to my attention that we have a number of libraries in our midst. The largest right here in *Locus Prime*."

"What? Here? I know some old library buildings remain, but I thought Locus Prime *was long since purged of the contents."*

"Sadly no. But I do not refer to a dead shell; I mean that I have obtained the location of a living specimen. I expect to learn the whereabouts of more in due course."

"It can't be. There are surely none left."

"Books remain, alas. The *Incunabula* sees to that."

"I've heard of this organisation, though I must add, I fail to see the concern."

Morlock suppressed a frown. *Politicians.* Always concerned with the wrong priorities.

"They keep books alive, *Minister* Vaghela. They keep alight a flame that is best extinguished for all concerned."

"A few dusty old books. What harm are they to anybody after all these years? Curiosities. Nothing more."

"Curiosity is a powerful urge. Books have power. And it is always wise to be wary of a power other than your own. Don't you agree?"

"Perhaps. But they are no threat to me. Or – I would suggest – to you."

"Again, you are sadly mistaken."

"They're as good as dead, Morlock. Relics and curios from a bygone age, and so are these Incunabulites *who stockpile them. Surely a man of your standing has more pressing concerns. I know I do."*

The tone grated. It was an effort of will to suppress the anger; Vaghela was, alas, not an underling as such. A more delicate game was therefore required.

"Books are a *pestilence*. Must I remind you of the Folio Plagues?"

"Of course not, but even so –"

"And now we have unearthed a substantial stock of books in our midst. Survivors of the Plagues and the burning. Ask yourself what might be festering in this library. If not disease, then surely the toxin of sedition."

"I must say I really don't follow you."

"You are a Minister in the *Interregnum*.[26] A regime that has gained a certain permanency that belies its name. Have you ever wondered why?"

The head didn't have shoulders; all the same it gave a good impression of a shrug.

"The *Gestalt*," Morlock provided.

Again, the head did an impressive display of body language.

"The wishes of Government are to rule free from the interfering quibbles of the citizenry. The people wish to be

---

[26] The city's governing body. It began existence as a temporary executive committee superseding former national governments as *Terapolis* absorbed the geographic and political entities that had gone before, but in the world of the *Gestalt* has come to linger.

governed free of worry and doubt over such quibbles. They wish to be free to pursue their happiness and fulfilment."

The head nodded. Understanding perhaps dawning at last.

"The *Gestalt* gives you this. It provides the freedom to play your political games *sans* real world concerns. It gives people an outlet for their fears and their hates and their passions. In turn that grants you the passivity you crave. Without the *Gestalt*, Minister Vaghela, you would be out of a job."

"I still don't see what the concern is over a few dusty old books!"

"They have power. Power to subvert the *Gestalt*. Power to subvert *you*. If that does not move you then consider this; books are *filthy*. It was bad enough in the days of the Plagues; imagine the nightmare of such disease festering beneath the streets of our overcrowded city. Public health is paramount. We cannot allow this filth to linger longer than necessary."

Morlock realised he was leaning forward in his anger. He forced himself to return to a calm state and settled back in his chair. It had been so long since he had dealt with anything other than a deferent servant.

"I... suppose I can issue orders to the Constabulary."

"No."

"Then who?"

"The regulars are nothing but plodders. They dawdle through their day dreaming of the *Gestalt*. Indeed as they should, for their role requires little more. This task is beyond them, and it would be unfair to put them at risk of... *contamination*. We need specialists. We need the men of the *Hazamat*."

"They were put in storage years ago."

"They can be resurrected. I supplied you the means for this."

"I... I suppose so. Yes. There are still records locating the containment facilities. But—"

"If not, then *MorTek* can provide the information."

"I'll issue the order."

"Good. How long before they are resurrected?"

"A few days. A week at most."

"I knew I could rely on you."

"Of course. I'll see to it right away."

The head collapsed into liquid. The plinth bubbled and rippled for a few moments until it settled down. Morlock leaned back further into the chair and turned to face his old companion.

"The final chapter, Bill," he said, "the final chapter: the *Hazamat* awaken."

WHEN the last ripple on the flat panel *simulacomm* died, Vaghela wiped his forehead with a handkerchief and then turned to face his guest sat out of sight by the door.

"It's always the same," he said. "Whenever I speak to Morlock I feel as though he's stepping over my grave."

"Nevertheless, you did well. Thank you."

"You have a few days. That's all I could give you."

"We're already using it to the full."

Caxton reached down beside him and retrieved a slim bundle. Vaghela licked his lips and stared at the paper package as Caxton moved towards him.

"Read and anticipate," the dealer said. "Better days are coming."

"Do you really believe that?"

"I don't believe. I have faith."

"There's a difference?"

The big man tilted his head, smiling slightly. "Yes. Subtle, but there is a difference."

Vaghela stared at Caxton and swallowed. He wished he could believe, but he didn't. He took the books anyway; they might well be his last.

"The *Hazamat* —"

"Have been a threat since the beginning. This day was destined to come."

"No! You don't understand. The *Hazamat*, they're not what they were."

"What is, these days?"

Vaghela suppressed a curse. Caxton had to understand. "I mean he's done something to them. *Changed them*. They're not —"

"We'll survive," Caxton said, grim-faced. "Whatever the cost, we'll *survive*. We've no choice."

Something in Caxton's tones turned his bones to ice; his gravesite was fast becoming a popular thoroughfare.

THEY'D never save them all. The thought was a heresy, but Laura found she couldn't stop it. Like the aches and pains in her fatigued body, the doubts throbbed in her mind. There were far too many books and not enough people to clear the library before the *Hazamat* arrived. That wasn't heresy: it was an awful truth.

The next load of books was dumped into her arms. She sagged under the weight of words, paused to find her balance, then swung round to deposit the load into the next pair of waiting arms. An endless repetition on this human conveyor belt that took its toll on both mind and body.

For Elzevir, this evacuation was a poor memorial. This was *his* library, his charge, and his *failure*. It should never have become so huge. The *Incunabula* had failed him by failing to suppress the largesse of an old man's cherished haven.

Laura tried not to think as she passed another batch of books back to the next link in the chain. She struggled to become an automaton. Her limbs and torso said otherwise, but they were willed into submission. Then a shrill whistle blew three times. A voice barked the order to disperse. The command brought in its wake a chorus of relieved murmurs.

"At *last*," Laura muttered.

"Back in *four* hours," the supervisor added, waving four fingers to emphasise the point.

The relieved tones turned to heartfelt groans of dismay.

Four hours. It didn't seem anywhere near long enough for her strength to recover. She was exhausted beyond her capacity to express. Everyone was; it was written in their faces, voiced by the sheer lack of even muttered conversation. Laura shuffled off in search of a place to rest as much as to find a familiar face. Behind her, she heard new volunteers and rested workers moving to replenish the lines.

As she shuffled to the sidelines, she felt like a soldier on an ancient battlefield. Bloodied and wearied, but at least still on two feet. Elated to be amongst the living, saddened for the lost, suddenly dismayed at the news the war was far from done. *They* were coming, and anybody, *anything*, left lingering within this place was doomed to a fiery end. A shudder rattled her ribs. The Pyre Brigades. You didn't remain long in the *Incunabula* before the tales were told, like ghost stories around bygone camp fires. Nobody in the *Incunabula* could fight the *Hazamat*. Not literally. Evade and hide. Blend into the shadow; that's the war they fought. And it all seemed hopeless now. A bitter end to their dream.

She pushed her way through the gaggle of weary volunteers, trying hard to hold back the tears of fear and grief that had gained in strength as she grew ever more weary. Everything was falling apart, everything was doom and foreboding, but still everyone around her held their weary heads up and stared defiant at what was to come. She was beginning to wonder if she was capable of living up to their example.

Laura reached the wall, close to a tunnel mouth. A soft breeze flapped the plastic strips that closed the library from the labyrinth beyond. She savoured its cooling touch as she leaned against the wall and gratefully gave in to gravity. She slid down the wall until seated on the ground, then slipped her legs out in front of her.

From where she sprawled, she watched her fellow *Incunabulites* work. An army of strangers drawn from other Chapters, from far-flung *Loci*; long-standing rules broken by the overriding rule to survive. She thought she recognised a few of them, faces in the human tentacles, supervisors parading around overseeing the work, barking orders in fretful voices. Huddled groups clearing higher shelves, others stacking them ready for collection and passage down the lines. Most of them unknown to her. She longed for a little company. Someone to share the grief of the day; even Adam's presence would be acceptable for the moment.

She closed her eyes and breathed deeply, savouring the musty odours of the library and willing it to enlighten her soul. This great disturbance had kicked up the dust of years, and with it came the scents of old paper and ink and bookbinding resins. Aromatherapy, but for the fresh scents of human sweat and fear. Still, her mind was lifted on the wafting odours and it wasn't long before the voices and clatter of the library rescinded as she drifted off to inner places.

MARLA Caine stared down the sights and squeezed the trigger once, twice, thrice in quick succession. The sharp reports merged into one deafening roar, but her ear protectors muffled the blasts. They could do nothing for the weapon's kick; she savoured the shock waves that trembled through her flesh like the rough hands of a lover.

Technically, and Otto always scolded her for this, the weapon was too powerful for her build, yet she had learned to master the implement and she enjoyed its sheer overloaded vitality.

Far away in the gloom, at the practice range's extreme distance, she knew her bullets had hit the target. Today, for practice, it was but a general purpose dummy: a brainless lump of metabolising meat grown in one of *MorTek's* subsidiaries.

Mindless flesh. Arteries, muscles and sinews torn apart by high velocity metal. Hardly a kill at all. Never mind. There weren't so many these days, but another time, perhaps tomorrow, it would be a real target, a being of flesh and blood and a mind to contemplate the great void of oblivion into which it was about to be hurled.

Yes. Some *dermrat* caught at the end of a thrilling chase, when her adrenaline was flowing. The sharp buzz of excitement tightening in her loins and then the prey, cornered at the climax.

Soon, it would be Caxton.

The most satisfying kill of all.

Anticipating the big man in her sights almost made her shiver and miss her aim; that wouldn't do, no, not when the moment finally came. A quiet sharp chuckle as a thought thrummed in her mind: not as big as he makes out. Not very big at all, really.

She would shoot his death, as he once shot life, and let the young one watch. In the gloom, Marla smiled, her artificial youth moving almost genuinely.

It would be wrong to say Marla Caine remembered all she had been. For she did not. It would be equally wrong to say that her memory was a totally blank slate. There were loose fragments of recollection; a stained glass mosaic of a broken whole. Ghosts of a younger version swirled in her consciousness like flurries of snow. She hated Caxton, she remembered hating him. She remembered life, she remembered feelings, she remembered moments *before*... but they were a haze. Places, faces, actions and words were elusive, lost in the muddy pool of yesterday.

There was enough left to give shape and form and function to the entity that called itself Marla Caine: the woman who lived for the moment to gratify the senses, salve the urges both primal and more urban esoteric. Thought and reminiscence were unfamiliar companions, but ponder now she did.

For Morlock. Always for Morlock who healed the pain *after*... For *MorTek*, which gave her purpose as well as escape. For fulfilment, for those screaming feral urges that haunted the shadows of fitful sleep. For the Voice; that long ago, once-hated torment, then the friend who remained when all others had gone. The Voice that told her how to salvage the best of life and which guided her on the path of existence, until she joined with *MorTek's* corpus.

Ghosts now. Half perceived. Residues of another existence, another being. Echoes of a time long gone, and now obliterated in the gunshot roars of target practice.

She might ask the question: what came before Morlock? She might as well ask an Old World cosmologist what came before the birth of the universe. There was Morlock today. Only Morlock. There had always been Morlock. The only reality she needed, but that truth never quite muffled those echoes of that other existence, nor blunt the shards of the broken future that cut to the core; the hard shell of purpose slashed to reveal a glimmer of the weakness that still wept within.

There, through the wet blur, a ghost rising: Marla bit down hard against the unbidden haunting, focused on the target, squeezed off rounds, but still the weak woman beseeched...

Somewhere, some when, the vision lost to time and space, the woman wept as she had done when she was a little girl after her mum had scolded her. As the tears streamed down her face, so she stroked her swollen belly.

Slick, like her face, but not with tears. Blood soaked through her fingers and dripped sullen onto the floor where she lay. Her own life blood mingled with her baby's, to dribble into the amniotic deluge that had gushed from between her legs.

Around her, the paramedics hurried their work, but she thought nothing for them, saw nothing of what they did, heard none of their soothing voices. Through the tears she only saw that face: the once-loved face twisted insane with monstrous rage, the hand that once caressed sensual now lunging with the blade.

What had she done? Why had he done it?

And her baby, draining from her belly, its life ebbing through the hole he'd punctured.

And then the Voice, shushing her as if she were a child, it promised her things would be better. Later, it helped to ease some of the pain, until the coming of another gave her new meaning. At that moment, beyond consolation, she had paid it little heed. The pain, not of the wound, but of the fading life inside was her entirety, and in desperation she reached out for the medics.

The woman who had been Marla sobbed: "Save my baby…"

A shudder sent the last bullet awry; memory died its latest of endless deaths. The manifestation of loss crashed back into the shadows as the surety of Morlock enveloped the entity she was with the soothing certainty of purpose.

With a dainty finger, she wiped a solitary tear from her eye and stared puzzled at the gleaming moisture on her fingertip. She frowned as it evaporated, and once gone, she paid it no more heed. There was only the *now*.

With a flick of that moistened finger, she activated distant motors. They whined far away, the pitch increasing as the engine moved closer. The target dummy swayed in the gloom like a ghost emerging from its tomb.

Marla saw it clearly now: the blood trickling from the bullet holes; the neat group to the chest, a single shot in the forehead. She frowned at the shot that went astray to pulverise the muscle, bone and sinew of the dummy's right shoulder.

A flash of light as an old-fashioned digital camera recorded the day's shoot. A monitor flashed as the image was displayed, overlaid with performance analytics and annotations. Then the bio-mannequin dropped through a sphincter at the head of the range. The digestion bellies far below its final destination. Purpose fulfilled.

ADAM looked at the stash of books then flicked his gaze to his battered console. Torn in two, that's how he felt.

The *Gestalt* was humming in his bones; the deep-thrumming discomfort was something only the books truly soothed, but they were finite – and who could say when his next supply might come along. Laura was nagging in his head; Caxton stared disapproval through a haze of cigarette smoke.

Fuck this shit!

He slumped into the armchair, picked up a book and flicked through the pages, savouring the scent that wafted into his nose. Three volumes. He could easily digest this one in a night. The other two, fatter; they'd take more time, but his voracious mind would soon lap them up nonetheless. And then...

The console wasn't the *Gestalt*. It didn't come close, well, maybe it wasn't that far removed. Like Laura said, it came from *MorTek*. The upgrades he'd scrounged for it certainly did. But no, it *wasn't* the *Gestalt*, whatever she said, and what did she know about it, anyway? Take a little time out, that was all; a night surfing the unreal made the books last longer. No harm in that, right?

Got to make them last! And stay off the Gestalt!

Sure. He could do that.

The book gripped firm, yielding to his fingers; he brought it to his face, closed his eyes tight, as if trying to squeeze the *Gestalt* out with his tears of restless frustration. Then he placed the book on top of its two siblings stacked on the floor at his feet, and snatched up the console.

The battered device rested snug in his lap as he caressed it, still undecided; the books' allure pulled at his mind, but he reached for the mask all the same. Ribbed, rubbery, an ancestor of the *Gestalt*'s *Geistmasque*, it slipped on easily: a second face. In the darkness, breath hissing slow and sure through the gill vents, everything seemed that much simpler.

The nagging complexities of life vanished, replaced by the sense of Self expanding to fill the void. Far away his fingers worked unbidden. The flesh knew what was required, as if guided by the device rather than the other way around; they connected the mask, then moved to stroke and probe the console, finding the *chakra* nodes to open the way out of himself.

A faint 'snik' – more felt than heard – as the mask connected with his implant. The darkness began to swirl into a whirlpool. Adam sighed as he felt his body settle back, a dead weight left behind as his sense of being peeled away and ascended to a plane far beyond the confines of *Terapolis*. There was more than one way to escape...

OUT in the hall, the *simulacomm* began to glow with an incoming animate, but there was no shrill alarm to announce its emergence; not that it mattered. Adam was oblivious to the intrusion, his mind translocated somewhere between the outermost fringes of the *Gestalt* and the legacy worlds of archaic simulation.

Adam was reposed on his reading chair, faceless beneath the mask, his fingers slowly working the console.

Back in the hall, the *simulacomm* glistened organic. The surface rippled. A liquid gurgle measured the frantic pace of activity. The upper surface bulged outwards like a boil about to burst. For a few seconds it pulsed and wobbled in its own iridescent light. Then it popped.

Matter spurted into the air and arced towards the floor. A long thread rested in a tangled huddle, still linked to its progenitor by a long umbilicus that emerged and dangled from the *simulacomm* like a string of viscous slime. The strand thickened. The long cord came alive; it undulated and twitched like an angry snake.

Rapid sine-wave motions propelled the emergence towards the living room door. There it paused. The bulbous head explored the crack and then slid cautiously into the room. The long body whiplashed its 's'-shaped curves as if gathering strength. Then with another leap the head landed at Adam's feet. Too close to the books.

The entity made no noise, but its sudden partial retreat suggested a snake hissing at some unexpected threat. It regrouped and slithered forwards, keeping a distance from the paper packages. The manifestation slowly coiled around Adam's ankle and slithered up towards the console.

Here it extruded a bundle of slender threads. Each one grew in mimicry of the mother-cord's emergence. While the main body made its way towards Adam's head, so these threads insinuated their penetration through vents in the console's casing. Inside, they sub-divided further, until a parallel network of unnatural matter had completed its link to upgrade the host.

The machine began to register the invasion. Alarm LEDs flashed insanely on the console fascia. Adam's body shifted in its pseudo-sleep, but the invading synaptic web overrode the safety systems.

Above this parasitic conquest, the primary head reached its target. The body slithered round to find the connection between man and machine. The proboscis merged into skin where it pulsed in sympathy with the host's blood-stream. The claspers grasped flesh to hold it secure. Then the bulbous sheath split open and a nest of fibres spilled out in a wriggling mass. They merged with man and machine, crawling into ears, beneath the mask to infest mouth and nose, completing the overall symbiosis.

In the hall, the *simulacomm* continued to gurgle and ripple. Adam's breathing became laboured and erratic. Sweat gushed from his pores. Slowly, his pallor turned deathly. A long moan of anguish rumbled from beneath the mask.

WHEN she woke, there was a warm weight resting on her shoulder. Still muggy from sleep, Laura shifted against the wall and turned her head towards the source of the comforting radiance. Immediately she moved, the presence retreated with a troubled murmur.

"I'm sorry, Dear," Maggie said, her voice slurred by the residue of sleep. "I didn't mean to use you as a pillow. Never thought I'd sleep at a time like this."

"That's all right," she yawned. "Never thought I'd drop off either."

"It's the work. It's so exhausting. And it seems so hope-less *now*…"

Maggie stopped abruptly with a low gagging sound that might have been a badly suppressed sob. She looked worn out, the way she slumped against the wall. A far cry from her usual fastidious appearance, her blouse and sober trouser suit was creased and grimed from her labours. Most of her face was hidden in profile behind a greying cloak of ruffled hair, but she looked as though she was studying something in her lap.

Curiosity took hold. Laura shifted position. Light gleamed off something in Maggie's palm. A locket. A finger of her free hand stroked the object, then pulled away as it was snapped closed. For one moment, Laura saw the faded photograph before it was shut away. A middle-aged man, a happy grin spread across his face. Despite the lack of years, she recognised Elzevir.

Ashamed and embarrassed by the realisation, she looked away. It was hard to imagine the old man being romantic, let alone *sexual*.

"He won't betray us you know. Not Elzevir!"

Guilt sidled up to carouse with shame. The woman must have noticed her prying eyes. Laura looked down at her feet. "In *MorTek* everyone talks. You know that. We can't take the chance."

"Not Elzevir."

"Even El. I'm sorry, but it's true."

She hated herself for saying it. For parroting the *Gorsedd's* line and adding to Maggie's grief. Elzevir would *never* wilfully betray them, but tortured and reduced to a broken wreck by the servants of *MorTek*, how could he *not* talk?

Poor Maggie. Her mistake was to get too close to someone. Laura reached across and put her arm around the older woman's shoulders. As she did so, she made quiet 'shushing' noises and tried not to weep too.

They didn't live in that kind of world. It was gone. Maybe forever. Laura promised herself she'd never make that kind of mistake, never suffer her friend's pain, never experience such a heart-wrenching loss.

At least, not again.

"Has Caxton been in?" she asked after a while, once Maggie's sobs began to subside. She asked to change the subject, as much as to soothe her anxiety. If Elzevir was a target for abduction, then surely Caxton was marked too. Then again, weren't they all?

Maggie sniffed and pulled away. She used the sleeve of her blouse to dab her eyes with a deceptively dainty manner.

"Earlier today. After he'd been to see Vaghela."

"Who –"

"A friend, Dear. He's bought us some time." At last Maggie smiled. "We have friends here and there. Including high places. You can thank *Cax* for that one. The other Chapter Heads didn't like the *risk*, but Caxton made it happen. And we've had many a reason to thank him for it over the years, I can tell you."

"I never knew," Laura said quiet.

"No reason why you should. He's a right one, is Caxton. Makes his own rules. Could have been a Chapter Head, on the *Gorsedd* even, if he hadn't been such a maverick."

Maggie turned away. Laura watched her profile for a moment, then gazed down at her lap. They sat in silence. Tired to the bone, but no longer quite so exhausted.

Then the thought. *He* ought to be here. Helping. But he was off, doing his own thing. The dreamer, the waster, probably in some bar or arcade. Maybe jacked into that Morlock contraption. She shuddered at the recollection of that vile machine. A hideous intrusion, an intimate violation of everything that made them human.

She pulled her knees up beneath her chin and hugged herself, as much to contain some body heat as to crush the tremors. Maggie didn't notice. That was one small mercy.

"I don't know if I should say this, but do you know anything about why Caxton is so keen about *that* boy?"

Laura shook her head, a sinking feeling in her belly. "No."

"Caxton looked bad when I saw him earlier. Never seen him so agitated. He's been like that for days. Last time we spoke he kept going on about Adam, about atonement, about that book he's writing. I'm worried about him."

"I don't know Maggie. Last time I saw Cax you were there. He's never let me near that manuscript, he's so secretive."

"Always has been. 'Specially about himself."

Laura nodded. That was true. The mystery was all part of the essential Caxton persona. Part of the appeal of the man.

"Can you go see him tomorrow dear, before you come here? Let me know how he is?"

"Of course, but why me?"

"I'm needed here, to look after El's life."

She looked away and gazed at the dismantling library. Laura stared at Maggie's face, trying to read beneath the lines of her weary face.

"Sure, Maggie."

As an after-thought she added: "On the way, I'll go see Adam."

Maggie frowned, but she said nothing.

"It's about time he started earning his keep."

SOMETHING had gone wrong with his reality, he realised; it felt a little like the Gestalt, impossible though that was. But he was here all the same.

With a sense of deep foreboding, Adam understood that he knew this place. He'd passed through before on journeys to other places when he was trans-linked to a G-Spot. Somehow, it had managed to mask itself from recall, then, until these sights and sounds revealed suppressed memory.

Slow and uncertain, he progressed into the pits of amnesia, pulling out the raw vision from the darkness. Yes, he had been here before. Others too. Curiosity had him now. So he plodded on, burying the guilt as he thought of Laura and Caxton and their endless lectures, but if they refused to tell him why books and the Gestalt failed to mix, then he must find out for himself, in the very heart of the forbidden. After all, isn't that where knowledge resides?

An armchair emerged from the shadows. Bemused, Adam stepped forward to find more relics of his life lurking in the shade. Here was a perfect representation of his living room, even down to the piles of abandoned and unwashed clothes. The walls were missing, but the darkness made a fair substitute.

Now the manifestation was nagging; if that was the point, to tell him he was a slob. Well, he knew that already. He ignored the mess, just as he did in the other life. There was a book resting on the cushion. He picked it up and tried to read the cover, but it was stained and cracked with age. Even so, the vibrant print of the title said it should be readable. The letters appeared out of focus.

At least the words on the inside were clear. He sat down, only vaguely aware of the absurdity of the act here in this place. Then he reopened the book at random.

The Gestalt is the flower that traps the bee; its mysterious enigmatic allure is the pollen that lures us in. And when it has us, while it has us, it imbibes our essence, draws out that precious nectar that protects the human light from the shadow that seeks to engulf it. [Get OUT!]

Adam frowned as the letters dribbled down the page. He scanned further, flicking at random through the pages. It was difficult in the light from those obscene pustules, but the more he read the more he was convinced. Even here, Caxton lectured.

Ours is a haunted city, for those who left us behind have nowhere to go. The nets of the Gestalt catch more than the souls of living Terapolis. Indeed, there are many more souls in this great conurbation than a body count permits. For Morlock's great machine embraces the dimensions of our world, and leaves none with the avenue of escaping into the vast beyond of this cosmos.

The seeds of our being are stockpiled in readiness for the days of Completion; little choice then for the lost ones to do anything but linger amongst us, or wander the labyrinths of time and mundane space that bind us to this reality. [He's coming you fool! Get out now!]

For those seeds, wandering from afar, spreading into the trans-dimensional deeps of creation's complexity, there is the dense gravitational well of dread—ever pulling them hither to the point of primordial origin. And so the light of sentience is pooled, and emulsified with its eventual undoing. Until the Master Maker of the infinite end is ready to conjoin with us all.

The words made little sense; what had they to do with books and the Gestalt, with living and hungering in Terapolis? The consideration vanished. Something was crawling around the back of the chair. Spindly things brushed and probed his shoulders. Instead of leaping out of the chair, which was the sensible thing to do, his body froze.

Tentacles wrapped themselves around his arms and legs to bind him in the chair. Another slipped round his throat and held him tight against the back until he gagged for air.

The book fell into his lap. Its pages rustled, and for some reason, it made him think of a frightened cat arching its back and bristling its fur. A face leered at him from the side. Pale, gaunt, as skeletal as it was capable of being without actually losing all flesh. The apparition dribbled something onto his lap. The book dissolved and its liquefying remains soaked into his crotch.

The thing had a body like the mating of a Geistmasque *and a spider. It leapt for his face, spindly legs clasping tight until his skull felt as if it might crack. Tendrils uncoiled from its abdomen. He felt them as they slithered and probed. Then they found his nose and mouth and slipped inside. Cold to the touch. They smelled like spillage from an infected nutrient gland, left to rot. His eyes bulged with revulsion and horror as they slithered down his throat.*

As if a connection was made, hissing words slithered into his mind: "Greetings, young one. I have been waiting…"

SOFT hum, soothing melody. There was barely any discernible tune, more the rhythm of a sanguine purr. Silas Morlock allowed the honey tongue to caress his ears while he in turn caressed his companion's pate.

Circular motions. Gentle with the silk kerchief. Bill did so enjoy his grooming. Beneath the delicate motion, the lint and dust of time surrendered its hold on Bill's bone, to reveal the polish of ancient care. When the carapace of his friend's mind was done, Morlock moved down to the ridges and furrows that once were the foundations for a living face.

Empty sockets stared as the finger motion swiped the cloth inside and around the rims of the orbits. Across and over the chasm of the nose, along its defining edges, down to the teeth and around to fondle the delicate mandible.

"Does that feel good, Bill? We'll soon have you good as new."

Morlock continued the gentle action of cleansing. As he stroked, he let his gaze glance out through the window, towards the towers of *Terapolis* gleaming ashen in the moonlight.

"Soon, Bill, soon."

The hum took on a questioning tone.

"The pieces are moving towards final play."

The hum paused for Bill to ask a lazy question.

"The library will burn. Caxton's protégé will join us. And he shall bring us what was stolen long ago. But it will cost us."

Morlock increased the soothing motion on his friend's surface, reaching to the point where once the gristle of an ear had bonded to bone. Bill murmured his appreciation.

"Sacrifices are necessary. We must have the manuscript, lest it be read and some other foolish mind is spurred to act against us. We might search in vain till the end of time. Better that one of our opponents brings it to us."

Bill's curiosity was not to be so easily settled. Now was as good a time as any to indulge his faithful companion. In any case, it often helped to talk things over.

"Everything has a weakness. It is a paradox, but as we approach our final goal, so do we become weaker. We must remove any potential threat, no matter how trivial they might seem, while we have the strength and the opportunity to do so."

Bill hummed an agreement, but said nothing, as though thinking on Morlock's words.

"The boy will become one of us. Let that haunt Caxton until the end of days. Let it torment his mind, as he awaits Completion of the *Gestalt*'s purpose: that he delivered me the boy and stirred his own undoing."

A chuckle from Bill felt like a tickle. Morlock savoured the sensation, felt a tingle in kind begin in his throat, but he suppressed it with the motion of a speaking tongue.

"But you are right, Bill, we must not trust to fate alone to do our work. We must set the wheels of destiny in motion. Yes. We must bait the trap."

Morlock finished polishing Bill's skull with that thought resonating in his mind. He replaced the kerchief in his pocket and gazed at his companion's gleaming dome.

"*I* must bait the trap he set for me." He gently shushed his companion. "No, Bill, now is the time for silence. Just guide me. Guide me to where I must go."

He stood erect before Bill's plinth, but as he closed his eyes his head sagged as though nodding to sleep. Soon his forehead rested against Bill's and there he stood in the moon glow. As his mind seeped from his shell and began its search, the shadows thickened around him.

Bill watched his master and remained faithfully silent.

THERE is a realm that has no name; there is neither word nor definition that captures its essence, for those who create words and ponder creation know nothing of its existence.

String theory never untangled its mysteries. Quantum mechanics never found the right algebraic spanner to unlock its properties. Cosmology, the notion of parallel universes, even the concept of the multiverse: none have ever considered the depths of existence that might create or incorporate such a realm. Even philosophy and theology have never dared to begin to explore its paradigms.

Art might have grown close, through coincidence, chance, sheer insanity, or just chemical concoction, but in truth only the wanderers in the mysteries of the Gestalt *have ever peered within its formless infinity.*

This void is a suspending meta-fluid, and acknowledged or not, it is there, between the light and the dark, packing the spaces between the components of sub-atomic particles, the trellis of not-quite-nothing on which the vines of meandering space-time grows.

It has neither planets nor stars. No dust, nor atoms. Only energy, of a kind. Certainly, it possesses no living things.

Call it a dimension, call it a parallel universe if you must. Such terms are of no meaning, here, but this realm must be called something. Better still, call it the antiverse.

Find its opening at the heart of every soul, in the darkness growing to consume the afterglow of every synaptic firing. Consider it the filmy membrane that encapsulates every self-awareness and sub-divides each individual, cell-like, from all others.

But as it was in the beginning, in the deeps of this meta-space resided…

Nothing whatsoever.

Until there came the light not born of photons.

In the darkness that is meta-space, something emerged in response; an expression of awareness brought into reluctant existence. The barrier of brilliance that resists the darkness imprisoned this manifestation in its primordial environment. Vast but impotent, it waited and probed the membrane of its enclosure, until the light that is not photons dimmed enough for it to find the breech, and flood into the dazzling realm beyond, in search of unity…

THE Gestalt *was screaming. That made two of them. The siren cry of its need tickled his implant and set the sub-neural strands vibrating in his head with a dissonance that went beyond sound.*

For a moment, he saw them, burned into his mind's eye like a retina highlighted by bright luminescence; there in the fragile tissue of his brain, the complex web of the Gestalt's *gateway throbbed and pulsed. Strings of tangled dark matter enclosed the ghost light of his own mind's root, both merging into the folds of space-time itself.*

Raw knowledge flooded into his head to overlay the fabric of his old need. Images and sounds, voices and memories, until it seemed the entire universe was becoming compressed and pumped into the space of his skull.

The pressure squeezed until he was ready to burst. His mind was becoming a black hole, sucking this flood of knowledge into a dreadful singularity that only strengthened the gravity and imprisoned the light of understanding. None of it made sense to the tiny flickering flame that knew itself as Adam. He pleaded for Caxton's salvation with the modulated tones of pure distress, even as he failed to latch onto this flood of awareness.

Tears soaked his face. His heart thudded in his chest. Blood pumped into his skull, crushing his reason. He gagged, nauseous, against the tendrils that filled his mouth and nose. The thing that clung to his face hissed a knowing laugh.

Yessss. Scream. Struggle. Bring him forth. Light the way to his anthropus…

Let me go. Let me get though this and I'll never Gack *again. Just let me get through this…*

A hissed chuckle. "In time..."

Light and dark were merging until he no longer knew how to tell them apart. The tiny bubble of reason that screamed against the nightmare spilling through the door of perception began to come apart. One last residue of coherent awareness puzzled at the hint of tobacco smoke, and then a particle of light exploded to vaporise the gushing darkness.

The thing binding his face let out a shrill shriek that almost completed the eradication of his sanity.

"A room without books is like a body without a soul; naked and defenceless against the waves of dread seeking to engulf all that we might ever be..."

The words boomed from afar, centred from deep inside the glowing orb of burning brilliance. Or maybe they were a memory, leaking out from the dying core of consciousness. The besieged entity that remembered being Adam felt an awakening.

It emerged from the light, a frequency signifying sound. It became a scream, a primal scream from some ancient pit of memory that found root in the flesh until it became a bellow of resistance. The death mask manifestation joined the chorus, the gripping fingers loosened their hold, but its cry was more triumph than rage.

I see you now...

An explosion of red light. Waves of agony. Thrashing limbs. Something snapped and cracked. Suddenly, his arms were free. He reached up to wrestle with the thing on his face. Tearing, stretching. The tangled knots of thoughts reformed in time to suffer. A sharp knife punched behind his right ear. With a feral cry of pain, he tore the ghastly masque away and slumped back, exhausted.

WHEN Adam dared to open his eyes again, he found he was back in his habitat. The four honest walls once again defined the boundaries of his existence. A lingering impression of Caxton left a suggestion of 'I told you so…' spoken from deep inside his brain. The thing was gone. The ordeal over.

On his lap, where he'd left it, the machine sat dead and lifeless. A small frond of smoke writhed from its cooling vents. At his feet, the mask lay discarded. He thought of the thing in the trip and hurriedly kicked the masque out of sight across the room. When he sat up again to lean back against the chair, he felt another sharp stabbing pain behind his ear. He winced, and reached for the throbbing source. The flesh felt slick and raw. The fingers came away pinked by blood.

Now he understood: his implant had blown. Possible, but as far as he knew unheard of. He swallowed a vortex of nausea and took a deep breath to combat the accompanying giddiness. It didn't work. He groaned in distress, wanting only to rest.

Without warning, not even the slightest tingle, he sneezed. Something emerged to dangle obscene. He reached up to extract the congealed thread of snot. It resisted at first. Then began to ease its way out. He pulled more, as though he was unravelling a loose thread. After too long, it came clear in a small eruption of blood and slime.

One of those hideous tendrils; the severed end still oozed vile fluid. His stomach heaved. He reached the bathroom almost in time. With a roar of torment, his stomach disgorged its contents across the floor, the edge of the bowl and finally into the toilet itself. There amongst the mundane matter of digestion floated more of those lifeless tendrils. They floated like putrid spaghetti. The sight made him retch again, but there was nothing left to eject.

When it was finally – mercifully – over he splashed his face with water and looked at his haggard face in the mirror. He looked washed out, as if the colour was leeching away to make him as pale as the thing from the visitation. He shuddered at the thought.

"No more implant, Cax," he moaned. "No more *Gestalt*. You got what you wanted. But what was that *thing* – and what did it want with me?"

The reflection never answered. There was no time. The world span from beneath his feet. He stumbled and slumped onto the cold floor, claimed by a mercifully more human darkness.

CAXTON spluttered and gasped for breath. This was not the time for weakness. Not when the shadows were gathering to stifle the last haven of light. Not when Morlock's plans were so close to fruition. And not when he most needed every granular morsel of strength.

He told himself this through gritted teeth while he gripped the sides of the washbasin until his knuckles popped. His ribs ached from the internal pounding. His throat felt like it was chafed by sandpaper, but he tried to will his body into submission.

Yet there it was. His *weakness*. The putrescence erupted from corrupted lungs. And the decay was accelerating.

Now, more than ever, he needed to be *strong*. Strong as people perceived him. Strong as they believed him to be; as he needed them to believe, because perversely he did gain strength from their faith.

Proof, wasn't it, that he was all front. *Elzevir* was the strong one. Always had been. He'd possessed the inner steel required to pull him from the self-destructive road that had claimed his youth. Elzevir had seen the lost soul inside, and opened the door for it to find its way back to the world. But the old man was *gone*. And for all his streetwise pretensions, Caxton never expected to lose him. Just like that.

At last, the iron bands were loosening their hold on his chest. The rhythm of breathing was returning to something more akin to normal. He knew he wasn't destined to linger too long behind his old friend. The vile proof dripped in glutinous strings like something from one of his nightmares. And the blood. Rusted clots spattered on the mirror. Crimson splashes spreading across the basin.

Caxton leaned forward to stare at his face in the mirror. Bloodshot eyes cosseted by bags met his gaze. On the sagging flesh of his face, more lines etched the scribbles and drafts of fear and experience. Too many. Far too many. His face told a story; this night it was a sombre one.

"You're getting old, Caxton. You can hide it from others, but you can't hide from yourself."

It wasn't just the illness that scrawled lines on his face. A troubled mind added its own flourish. A brief shudder, as he remembered the nightmare. For a few moments he closed his eyes to rest; he must have been more tired than he realised, because all of a sudden he was back *there*. Mental delusion though it was, it always left him horribly drained. For a moment, as he gazed past his own reflected face, he wondered if that's how *Gestalt* users felt in the aftermath.

The ordeal was different this time. He frowned at the recollection. Adam was in there. In that baleful place. The focus of some dreadful hunger. Caxton sensed it, had fought it for dominion over the lad. Did that mean anything? He did not even dare to contemplate an answer.

With a weary sigh, he flipped on a tap to sluice away the wastage of his anxiety. Then he washed his hands and splashed water on his face. The chill liquid helped to revive his wearied mind and postponed the urge for sleep a little longer. But coffee was the true restorative he needed.

Without bothering to dry his hands he swivelled round and padded to the kitchen. His arms trembled a little under the weight of the percolator, but the caffeine urge kept his limbs steady enough.

He flicked the light off on his way out and padded back into the gloom of his garret. As he walked he blew on the steaming liquid and then took a sip. The sip became a grateful gulp and he felt the hot fluid soothe his wasted throat, warming his lungs and waking the fibres of his being.

By the time he creaked into his seat, the mug was half drained. He placed it beside the old Hermes, careful not to spill on his precious testament. In the homely oasis of the desk lamp, the stack of pages glowed with a reflected luminescence that was the purest satin. He lovingly brushed a few stray fragments of tobacco from the topmost page and then tamped the edges into a neater bundle.

There it was. The product of his solitude. Hours of blood, sweat and tears, amalgamated with the accumulation of too many dark secrets. Caxton flicked through until he found the section that recorded the burning discovery that had haunted him for too long. He let his eyes scan the type, but he didn't read the words. After so long, he no longer needed to. The information was etched indelibly in his brain.

"They'll say I've gone mad when they read it, you know," he told the shadows, "but by then it shouldn't matter."

The shadows made no reply, which was just as well for these weren't the dark pits of *Terapolis*. Just places where the light failed to reach. There were too many *other* sources of illumination in here for *Terapolis* to reach his safe haven. Not that the darkness needed to. It had plenty of flesh and blood servants for that. Another reason to live here, hidden away in the bombed-out ruin of Old City. Where, out of necessity, few knew how to find him.

There was one other reason to live in this place.

Far above the *Terapolitan* canopy it was a clear night. And there was a full moon. He'd checked his old almanac, then made the necessary calculations to bring it up to date. It *was* full. And a single moonbeam glowed like a translucent messenger from the Heavens. Cold, white light cascaded through the skylight. It found its way through some fault line in the overbearing lattice that was the city overhead.

And there, where it splashed like quicksilver, it lit up the books stacked on and around the armchair. There'd been no time for finesse. Only time to gather what he could and ship them here. There were more, so many more, and the horrible question remained: how many could they save before the kerosene was spilled and the matches ignited?

A sombre thought. With Elzevir dead, or worse, there was no choice but to assume the library was compromised. He felt grief for his old friend and saviour, but knew there was nothing to be done. Grief couldn't save them. Nor could his guilt. He should have saved more; but the

Incunabula had plenty of hands. His task resided elsewhere now.

It was more urgent than even he had suspected, but Vaghela had bought them some time. Soon there'd be no more hiding in shadows. No more solitude. And Elzevir's death would not be in vain.

It was a compelling hope; one that raised his spirits against the shadows outside and the growing shadow eating away his life. His own light was fading, but he had enough. *He had to have enough.*

The chair squeaked again as he pushed it back to stride into the light. He stood there, like a man enjoying a soothing shower. His face upturned, he gazed into the brilliant moonlight and imagined the photons enervating his nervous system; pure light chasing away all those ghosts and shadows draining the motive force of his mental machinery. He closed his eyes.

Nice fantasy.

It was only moonlight. Good for the soul, uplifting for the heart but no miracle cure. With a sigh, he stepped out of the lunar shower and seated himself back at his desk. Time to indulge another hunger. He reached for his tobacco and rolled himself another cigarette.

He knew it was killing him. At least hastening the decay in his lungs. The inevitable was set in stone, however, and it was not to be his death, after all. Perhaps its handmaiden, but given these dark times and the uncertainty that any of them might survive, did it really matter?

"Of course not," he barked and flicked his zippo open. In a well-practised movement, it burst into flickering flame.

For a moment, he watched the light and the shadows dance and wrestle all around his desk. As always, the light seemed so horribly outnumbered, yet still it held its ground. There was a hope there. Then he ignited the cigarette and killed the flickering light. Under the glow of the moon and the bubble of his desk lamp, the opponents retreated to their lines of armistice.

Caxton risked a shallow inhalation. Felt the smoke stroke his innards, was rewarded with the flooding rush of nicotine. Life was but chemicals, he mused, suddenly realising he sounded like a *Terapolitan*, but *living* is books. That was pure *Incunabulite*.

He finished the roll up and stubbed the butt out in the already too-full ashtray. Then he picked up the smaller pile of pages and began to sort through. He worked quickly now, flicking through the main pile, checking the page numbers and then inserting sections where they needed to go. For a moment, he felt like Frankenstein assembling his creation from bits of cadavers gathered here and there. Yes, he had done exactly that in a way. Written a bit here, collated a section there. And the information, culled from too many sources to remember. All of it built up from that first terrible revelation.

The one that turned his life around; that led him to Elzevir and the *Incunabula*. If only it had taken place *before* the terrible moment that cloaked the rest of his life.

Sometimes, he wondered if the disease digesting his lungs was a manifestation of that terrible guilt. A romantic, *literary* thought, but the truth was nothing such. Just too many years spent in seedy bars marinated with cheap booze and poisoned with too much tobacco smoke. And don't forget *Terapolis*. It was little consolation that lung diseases were common in this haunted city, where the air was perpetually cold and damp and laden with mould. Or at least *something* exuded by the towers that smelled like mould.

The light dimmed suddenly. A flash of shadow.

Alarmed, Caxton stared at the lamp. Then he let his breath escape in a hiss as he relaxed. A minor interruption of power. That's all. Hardly surprising given the hack into the city's power grid; he'd never got round to rendering it more permanent and effective. That didn't quite explain the cold, but considering his state of health it was a wonder he didn't feel more frequently chilled. He let the puzzle go and returned to his work.

The last few pages added to the pile. It sat there on his desk, a little untidy but complete. Of course, in his heart he knew it would never really be perfected. There was always an extra polish, a little extra phrase to add, but the thing needed to be finished. As much as the feelings of literary art had taken hold in the years of its composition, he knew this was not meant to be a disinterested thing of beauty, standing aloof from the passions and pains of the world. It was a functional thing. A message and a messenger.

After all these years of researching, and searching, and writing and rewriting, the thing was complete. And to get it finished, he had become a virtual prisoner in his own home. Strange. That all the years of effort should be condensed into a few weeks of intense solitude.

But there it was.

What he lacked was any sense of closure, of achievement. Indeed, he felt hollow. As though he had put too much of himself into those pages and left not enough for the living man. Did every author feel that way about completing a project? In all the years of his reading with the *Incunabula*, he had found no answer to that one.

It was just the mood of the times. That was all. So much had happened in such a short time. And his health was failing faster than he'd anticipated. The end of days was approaching, and there was still so much to take care of before his sand finally ran out.

Caxton shook the manuscript and manhandled it until the pages sat together more comfortably. After that, he took hold of the edges and banged the manuscript against the desk to tidy up the bundle. TAP. TAP. TAP. A good solid sound.

There was another noise. Or so he thought. He frowned a moment and strained to hear. Nothing. Not now. He shook his head and raised the manuscript once more. The last time. It was neater now. The pages coming together.

TAP. *Tap*. TAP. *Tap*. TAP. *Tap*. *Tap*. *Tap*.

Pages rustled as they slipped through his numb fingers and fluttered over the desk and floor. Hackles erect, he turned towards the windows and cursed that he couldn't see beyond their ancient curtain of exterior grime.

Tap. Tap. Tap. Tap.

For once the chair didn't creak when he stood. Caxton paced towards the books, quickly passing through the moon's electrifying ray. Quickly, he grabbed a book at random and hurried towards the door. There, he paused to listen intently. Beyond the glass, the tapping was louder, mingled with footsteps steady and confident. There were no other sounds. Whoever it was, apparently they were alone. That was at least something.

For a moment he stood undecided. To be caught like a rat in its hole rankled. There was always the back way, out through the warren of this empty shell, but that clashed with his self-image. In any case, self-preservation wasn't yet a necessity. He glanced at the book in his hand; but instead of the sense of security he'd hoped to gain, he was shocked to wonder if the title wasn't somehow prophetic.

For Whom The Bells Toll. To hell with it, he decided and wrenched open the door.

The darkness swept in with the cold, rust-laden air, but the light counter-attacked and forced its retreat back into the machine hall. All in the blink of an eye while Caxton's senses adjusted to the gloom beyond the mezzanine.

The tapping was louder. The origins of the sound were hidden behind the hulks of machinery. Caxton stepped out onto the landing and leaned on the rust-flaked railing to peer deeper into the gloom.

Tap. *Scrape.* Tap. *Scrape.* Tap. *Scrape.* TAP.

All noise ceased with that final tapping punctuation. Then.

"I know you are near, Caxton. I can smell your Mind, even if I cannot see you."

Caxton turned his head towards the voice. Caught in more stray moonbeams, the figure stood in elegant silhouette. One hand on his hip, another on the slender thread that was his cane. He recognised the stance from images seen in the *Incunabulite* books: it was the stance of the perfect Edwardian gentleman, even if it was taken to the austere. One of Morlock's personal foibles.

"I can even smell the death growing inside you," Morlock added, "Marla will be so disappointed."

The door fell wide open to slam against the wall. More light flooded out and bathed the figure in yellow hues. Caxton realised the figure wasn't looking at him, but staring ahead into the shadows. He clutched the book a little tighter and edged along the platform so that he might better see his old adversary.

"You're so silent, Caxton. Nothing to say? That's so unlike you. Has the Reaper lopped off your tongue by mistake?"

"How did you find me here?" He scanned the shadows with suspicious eyes, but it really did appear that Morlock was alone. His heart began to settle down a little.

"*Here?*" Morlock sounded genuinely puzzled. Then he laughed again. "Yes, there must be a 'here' mustn't there? Some physical locus associated with this meeting. Alas, that I cannot read minds, nor can I pinpoint their location in the fabric of material reality. Life would be so much simpler if I could."

"You haven't answered me."

"Tut. So impatient. Very well. I simply allowed my mind to wander. I am sure that as a… *writer*… you can understand that. As ever, the source of your guilt leads me to your undoing. Sooner or later."

"Elzevir," his voice almost broke, "he is dead?"

"In matters corporeal, quite. In matters spiritual, not quite. But his pain shall end in time."

Caxton squeezed his eyes free of tears, and forced himself to focus on the here and now. "So, what do you want?"

In the shadows, Morlock smiled. It wasn't sight that told him this, but some sixth sense. And then, to his cold horror,

Morlock turned to face him and Caxton knew – *just knew* – that Morlock was *seeing* him.

"I want what you want. What all creatures of Mind and Soul truly crave."

"And that is?"

"But you *know*. Don't you?"

"I still want to hear it from you."

Another unseen smile. "Completion."

"That's what you call it."

"Don't you?"

"No."

"Then what?"

"*Oblivion.*"

"Poor Caxton. You still do not understand. After all these years of contemplating the knowledge you took from me, you still shy away from what you know to be true and necessary. You are incomplete. I am incomplete. Until we meet in the *Gestalt* and we join as one. Then creation shall be as it was in the beginning, before we were split asunder, before the ignition of Mind."

"Before the light of Mind there was nothing but darkness."

"Indeed. Then what do you call that?" The cane snapped up to bathe in the stray moonbeam cascading through a hole in the old roof. Somehow, Caxton just knew the gleaming silver tip was aimed direct at the lunar heart.

"You're playing games, Morlock. For the purposes of our talk that's just photons. Takes a Mind to make it light. And what you want will switch it off forever."

"Not 'switch off'. *Complete*. When we meet in the *Gestalt*, we shall return to the Universe. And then it shall know peace. That is what it wants. That is what you all want. Deep inside. Oblivion, as you put it, is just an expression of archaic flesh. The bio-chemical imperatives of those precocious apes you inhabit."

"You're wrong!"

"Am I? Then how is it that the *Gestalt* is so close to completion? Why has it become the centrality of human existence if it does not promise what you truly crave? And why do *you* scurry in tunnels and caves like rats?"

"So that we might survive beyond you."

"Indeed. And even now, your comrades work like ants to clear their nest before the exterminators arrive to cleanse it. Survival is not an option for you bibliophiles. But salvation, Caxton, the salvation I know you want – that lies within the *Gestalt*."

"Salvation lies in finishing you."

"And who will finish me? A bunch of scattered and frightened bibliophiles?"

"*I'll* stop you."

"That you might. The cauldron of reality contains many possibilities. Even that one. But how far will you go? Everything has a cost. I will share with you that finding my way here has already cost me precious reserves of strength. So what price are you prepared to pay? What sacrifice are you prepared to make in order to unseat my final moment?"

"There's no sacrifice too great to rid the world of you and the *Gestalt*. I'd die to stop you. I'll even damn my own soul to restore the light of living for everybody else."

"How very noble, but I don't think the life of a dying man is acceptable payment in this day and age. Nor the costs you must bear to thwart me. A young man, on the other hand, one who means much to the self-styled martyr. Now, fate *might* accept that little morsel."

"What do you mean a *young man*?"

"The pawn you moved into play, and thereby revealed your whole strategy. Really, Caxton. You should have left him be. He was nothing to me. Forgotten flotsam of past policies. You wanted to save him, didn't you? You couldn't save him before, what ever made you think you could save him today?"

"No!"

The book, its cover slick with sweat, slid from his hand and flopped into the abyss of darkness beneath the mezzanine.

"Leave him be. He has nothing to do with this."

"Oh but he has everything to do with this. I never did commend you on your dramatic approach, and such energies I expended to protect you to no avail! Well, alas, he cost me Caxton, but Caxton did deliver me Marla. So, you see, he has everything to do with this. With *us*. And he too looks for completion. Death is no barrier to that. You were prepared to sacrifice him once for me; can you not do the same now for all humanity? Symmetry, my dear Caxton, symmetry; one life to balance probability and redeem all you fear lost. And there *must* be a sacrifice worthy of the cause."

"It's me you want. Why don't you take me?"

"All in good time. Be patient. What you failed to do in the beginning, Marla will complete at the end. I must confess I rather enjoy the irony of it all. Marla has become quite the… *mortician*… since then."

Morlock turned, and stepped deeper into the shadows. On the verge of vanishing, he paused and turned his head.

"Go see him, Caxton. Say your goodbyes. I give you this for old time's sake. But make it quick. Tomorrow he is... *disembodied.*"

With that, he stepped forth and merged into the blackness. Not a sound to herald his exit. Caxton squeezed the railing, feeling the flakes of rust crack and bite his skin.

"Morlock! Not Adam! Come back! *Not Adam!*"

Silence.

The shadows had become once more nothing but a lack of photons. Caxton felt his muscles tremble and he succumbed. He sagged until he was curled up like a frightened child at the top of the stairs, clinging to the banisters.

Fear brought the past to life as he sat there, staring at the patch of air where Morlock had stood. He saw the visions clear in the light spilling from his home, heard the voices that had tormented his sleep now clear in the air.

Marla's face. Ghost pale. Sodden with tears. Saw the fear. Saw the eyes widen. Her scream pierced his heart, like the blade in the assassin's hand pierced her pregnant belly. And then the blood. The blood that seemed to burn his hands, even after so many years.

"*My baby,*" the ghostly wail vanished into the shadows like the last lament of an exorcised ghost.

Reason, rendered powerless in the prison of madness, looked on helpless. He couldn't stop it. Morlock's taunting voice in his ears, exhorting him onwards. Telling of the future with a voice of certainty. Talking. Promising. Whispering. *Cajoling* him until he couldn't think straight, couldn't pull together the fabric of his own being, until he didn't know what or who he was any more, until he was a tangle of denial and excuses.

With the full force of the recollection the tears came. A torrent. Year upon heaped year of hoarded grief and shame. He bawled like a frightened child and no longer cared if anyone arrived and saw Caxton wailing.

At last, the tears ran dry, but the grief and guilt and fear continued their taunts. He leaned his head against the railings and stared with sodden eyes. The powdered rust on his hands was the accusing colour of old blood. There was only one way to wash away the stains. Morlock was counting on that.

The Seventh Folio

From The Sins Of The Father

THERE was a word from beyond the void.

"ADAM!"

Accompanying the word was a thumping eruption of distant thunder. Together, they reached into the mindless abyss and triggered an emergence to begin its ascent from the primordial sludge.

Another thudding dissonance, another invocation.

"Open up. Dammit!"

As a mind ascended unwilling from its deep dark hiding place, the body that gave it a haven twitched. Sound followed; a low, sepulchral groan.

With that advent of sputtering cognition came pain, an agony with a tempo and rhythm seemingly born of that external pounding.

"ADAM!"

Suddenly he jerked awake. The light seared his aching eyes even through the sealed lids. He was cold, and the floor refused to surrender any of the heat it had leached from his body. The hard tiles tortured his unused muscles and bones, so they ached and throbbed like his head. There was a bitter taste in his mouth.

The voice pounded his skull again. Insistent. Persistent. Annoying.

"*Enough*!" He sent a command to his limbs ordering them to rise. He opened his eyes against the glare as his body struggled to fulfil his orders. As he sat up, he gingerly felt behind his ears. The blood was scabbed but still sticky. It felt almost crystalline beneath the pads of his fingers.

He struggled to the hallway. Another series of hammer blows rocked the door on its hinges; he managed to find the strength to rush forward and throw the lock.

The grim-faced visitor was the last he expected.

"Get your things together, we're outta here!"

"Caxton... what? I thought you'd abandoned me. Where have you been?"

The last words raised to a near-plaintive wail as he staggered behind. The big man didn't stop; he was a sickening flurry of energy.

"We ain't got time for this. We got to go."

Then he turned around and saw Adam properly for the first time. He stopped.

"You look like shit!"

He didn't say: "So do you."

Caxton looked terrible. The flesh of his face was lined and sagged, and his clothes wore the appearance of weight loss beneath. In the weeks since he last saw the man, he'd aged terribly, but the power was still there. In the eyes, focused and concentrated into an energetic stare that might ignite at any moment.

Adam stepped back, afraid as much as sick.

"I... I," he began, looking to claim a hangover. Then, the simple truth: "My implant blew."

The face that threatened thunder didn't bellow rage or lecture. Instead, the man sagged with a long and weary sigh. The light in the eyes dimmed, and there was the unmistakable impression of tragic disappointment. Worse than the pain of bludgeoning fists, or a lashing tongue, the sight of Caxton as a despairing old man hollowed him out and poured liquid grief into the space.

"I'm sorry. Cax. Sorry. I…"

He fell silent as Caxton continued to stare despondent.

"Are you a lost cause, Adam? Have I risked the future for a lost cause?"

"No," he said. "You haven't. I won't–"

Strong arms assaulted his shoulders and spun him round. He cried out weakly. One hand released its grip and pushed his head down and to the side.

"Nasty. Looks worse than it is. At least you haven't got the brains to blow with it. I don't know how you people can stick that *MorTek* shit into your heads."

Adam winced as it brought a sting of pain from the sore spot behind his ear.

Caxton released him. "I won't ask if you're up to travelling, 'cos you got no choice. Get your stuff together."

His body obeyed the command, even while his brain whirled bewildered. He rummaged through a pile of clothes by the side of the couch, looking for something clean.

"Just grab anything," Caxton growled as he stuffed clothes and other items into a rucksack. "No time for finesse here, you're not going out on the pull."

"Where *are* we going?"

"Anywhere. Away from here, that's the important thing."

He paused, a limp shirt dangling from his fist, suspended in limbo over the yawning maw of his bag.

"We'll go to my place. Yeah, that's best. Take the tube north to Stoma 57. Head up 51st and 8th, at Stoma 63 take the eastbound. Then head north again. You'll find your way to Old City easy enough. Not far… my place. An old print works. Inside. You'll be safe there."

"*Safe?* I'm safe here."

A barked laugh. "Not any more. You got a date with a certain *femme fatale*."

"What? Who…? *Oh shit…*"

"Yeah. '*Oh shit*' is right."

"When?"

"Too soon for comfort. Already lost a lot of time getting here, but we've enough to lose ourselves – so long as you stop dawdling."

Adam felt his face flush. He quickly fastened the shirt and pulled on his jacket, then he stooped to slip his trainers onto his feet. In his haste his fingers fumbled with the laces. He had to take a deep breath and force them to slow down before he could complete and tie the loops. From beyond his sight the sharp timbre of the rucksack's zip sounded an urgent finality.

"Let's go."

Caxton headed for the door. Adam stumbled after him, fumbling with the fastening of his jacket. It was a wrench to leave everything like this, but even so he realised how little he had. Nothing, in fact, to regret leaving behind. It was a snippet of self-discovery that stung nearly as much as Caxton's dismay.

"Wait!"

The big man was already hurrying down the steps, the rucksack swaying pregnant in his hand. Adam raced down the steps, breathing heavy as he maintained the pace. The exertion took its toll on his abused body until he felt sick and feverish.

Somehow, his wobbly legs supported him all the way down and into the building's entrance. Just in time to see Caxton barge through the door out into the street beyond.

No time for a rest, not even a curse, he forced himself forwards and crashed headlong into the maelstrom of *Terapolis*.

The noise was a viscous liquid pouring over his head. The maddening clamour of thousands of voices babbling and shouting from all around. The traffic from the highways above. The rumble of a tubeworm in its tunnel, turning to an eviscerating roar as its blasted free of one tubule to descend and vanish into another.

As he stumbled against the flow of bodies, bounding and bumping and cursing through the moving obstacles, he watched through tears of frustration as the flesh waves seemed to part ahead of Caxton, only to reform behind him. Something about the man's attitude communicated itself to the hordes and they cleared him a path without even realising.

He wished he had that kind of *presence* to lubricate his passage, but he was stuck struggling to stay in the man's wake.

"Cax! Wait!"

Ahead, Caxton stopped. Adam felt a wave of relief, and he struggled to catch up. Then he realised something was wrong. Caxton's head turned this way and that. Ever more agitated. The relief died; adrenaline drowned it.

"*Move!*"

Cax rushed back. No time to respond. A hand grasped the scruff of his jacket and pulled him forward. Ahead, he glimpsed a face that turned his bowels to jelly. A furtive, rabbit stare behind and his terror was complete.

Marla Caine cruised the sea of faces, unhindered by the waves that broke on the bow of her predatory aura. He caught the flash of triumph in the eyes, saw the half-smile on her ghostly face, and then he was yanked into the obscurity of the *Terapolitan* swell.

"Down here! We'll lose 'em in the alleys."

"Cax! *No–*"

Before he finished the sentence, he was half dragged into the maw of the alley that led into the netherworld. Utility lights gleamed and blurred in the growing mist belching from vents or exuded by the skin of *Terapolis*. Deeper still until it became a tunnel, claustrophobic even by the subterranean standards of baseline, but there was still no desired maze where they might lose the hunters.

They stopped. Adam peered through the fog belched from the building's vents and skin; he saw, piled high and stinking rotten, weeks of refuse from the block's inhabitants.

"Guess I was overdue a fuck up," Caxton muttered. "Sure picked the right time."

"There's no way out."

Caxton growled. "Tell me about it. I thought the building ate this shit."

"It's been sick for weeks."

"Then lets hope it recovers its appetite *real* soon."

Behind them, the sharp rapid clicks of the hunter. Coming *closer*.

"*Move*. We'll climb."

Too late.

"How appropriate, Darling, that we find the *rat* amongst the refuse."

FOR all the colourful metaphor, however sincerely it was invoked, fire had long been the fear of the *Incunabula*; not just the flames of Morlock's malice, for even mundane fire was capable of destroying much.

An electrical spark, the careless disregard of a cigarette, a misspent match, indeed any accident in the plans of mice and men, and Morlock's work would find an inadvertent ally. In such a dire mishap, even the mechanisms for tackling any blaze would cause irreparable damage to the fabric of the *Incunabula*'s purpose.

As in so much, then, prevention was better than cure.

So, no naked flames were permitted within the confines of the library. Not even shielded lanterns were permitted anywhere where there was paper to ignite. Electric lighting only was used, the power derived from batteries, or culled from ancient and carefully maintained generators, even stolen from the power grids of the city far overhead. Practicality had to veto metaphor.

The same was true as the library was dismantled, and the precious volumes stacked and packed and shipped to new havens, temporary or permanent, elsewhere in the hidden labyrinths beneath *Terapolis*.

In back rooms and tunnels, portable lights showed the way to safety. Hard hats with integral lamps and battery packs provided personal, mobile illumination, along with old caving equipment, mining helmets, whatever permitted people to see. All of it was archaic gear, salvaged and restored for such terrible eventualities. Libraries had been threatened before. The task was nothing new, only the scale; for this remained the greatest, the oldest, of the *Incunabula's* libraries.

Never before had it seen such a gathering, but for all their efforts, it was still a trove of precious books. There was light aplenty, but time was famished. That had always been the case, but never more so than now. Too many tomes remained exposed on the shelves, and the people needed to save them were as finite as time...

MARLA stepped forward and raised her arm. The gun looked hungry in her hand as it eagerly aimed at the old dealer's chest. Adam turned and saw Caxton step backward, matching Marla pace for pace.

Alone, vulnerable, Adam trembled and collapsed to his knees, waiting for the bullet. He didn't want to die. He didn't understand why people must die for the sake of old books. Marla's shadow touched him and was gone as she stepped past his trembling body.

"Cax!"

He leapt to his feet, but Caxton turned to glare and stopped him cold.

"Adam! Go!"

Even now, Cax was stern and commanding, but he couldn't do anything but stand there and watch. Marla was too enraptured in the moment to even sneer in his direction.

"This is between me and Marla," Cax added sadly.

A figure loomed out of the shadows and grabbed the collar of Adam's jacket. He looked up at Otto Schencke's equally stern face. The man's eyes glinted; for a moment he thought he saw sympathy, but figured it must be a glint of the utility lights.

"Listen to him, boy. This is no place for us. This is a matter for... *old friends*."

Adam tried to pull free, more for the sake of it than anything else. He watched Caxton, alone in the refuse and the dark as he faced Marla. So helpless. Adam related to that feeling, but never thought he'd see it in the face of the old dealer.

Otto said softly, "We must talk when Marla is done."

Adam struggled, but Otto kicked him behind the knee. As he went down, his arm was yanked up behind his back. He screamed against the pain as he hung from his twisted limb. Then his tormentor relaxed the pressure by crouching down behind him.

"Watch," he said, almost as if to a child, "this is a lesson for life."

Helpless, Adam managed to raise his head and stare at Caxton, who stood grim-faced. Armed only with words against Marla's deadly resolve. The bullet. The pen. Flimsy paper against *MorTek's* Reaper Girl. Where was the power in books, if it all ended here?

Caxton spoke, and there was a power in his voice, a resonance that sounded desperate but not afraid. It wasn't enough to fuel dying hope, but he still urged the flesh of *Terapolis* to recover and consume. Come on, he breathed, *come on*.

"Marla – the boy. Not the boy. He's–"

"Nothing, Darling. It's just you and me. *It's always been just you and me.*"

She stepped forward. This time Caxton stood his ground and watched Marla with melancholy eyes. "Been a long time coming, then, this reunion."

"Too long, lover, but it's sweeter for that."

"Would it help if I said I was sorry?"

"Too late for sorrow, Darling."

"I know. I never wanted it that way. I wish I'd done things different, played the hand better."

Marla's gun arm trembled. *"You played it well enough!"*

"He was in my head. I couldn't think for him. Couldn't stop it. I let him in and I couldn't get him out. In time. I was… young… and stupid."

"And now you're old – and dead!"

The gun flared. Adam flinched. Marla's expression never changed. Face blank. Eyes empty. The only motions her finger pumping the trigger, the arm trembling from recoil, spent shells flying through the air.

Caxton danced like a marionette on tangled strings. Every bullet a new move. Blood burst from his body, magma rising hot and wild. Arms twitched and flicked, body bent back like a man in a gale. Teeth clenched and eyes shut. Until the final impact released him and he toppled backwards on to the pile of garbage. For a moment his legs and arms twitched and his back arched, then he sagged limp.

So did Marla. Almost. Her arm fell to her side, the gun held loose in her hand. She stared at Caxton's remains with vacant eyes. Then a single tear gleamed a trail on her cheek.

She turned and sleepwalked back towards the main-streams of *Terapolis.*

Adam only stared, a living, mindless camera incapable of anything but surveillance, until Otto switched him back on.

"Well, my friend–"

The words triggered his scream of impotent rage. Eventually words, a stream of grief translated into profanity. Otto took it calmly, until Adam tried to follow through with fists. One hand deflected his blow. The other released his arm and grappled the back of his neck. A tight squeeze. The other hand clamped over Adam's mouth and nose. He pulled and clawed at the hand but he couldn't break the grip. He felt his face flush, the pressure in his lungs rising until his eyes bulged. Otto pitched him forward and held him face down, hand still clamped tight.

"Another lesson in life is needed, I see," Otto said calmly. "Time is relative, they say. So for your friend measuring his last, you might say he has all the time left in the world. No hurry. No worry. You and I are different. We remain creatures of time. Finite precious time. As precious indeed as air."

The words buzzed in his ears. His face was burning, bursting. His lungs ached like a pair of lead bellows.

"Now that I have your full attention…"

Suddenly he was released and he sucked in air, wheezing and coughing.

"Good. There's a certain manuscript that Morlock wants. Something your friend over there was writing. Bring it to him. And he'll let your *Incunabula* live. You can have your books and your libraries, in return for that one manuscript. Find it. Bring it to *MorTek*."

Otto stood up and brushed himself down. Then he stared down at Adam. His dark eyes glinted in the lamplight. Adam rolled over and tried to crawl away.

"One more thing," Otto growled, "and this is from *me*. That manuscript puts *you* in a powerful position. It makes for a unique opportunity. Think about it."

NO one had visited this place for many a long year. It had been sealed from the surface during the cataclysm that brought the Old World to its knees. At one time, many human feet scurried along the avenues of busy and crowded lives. Nowadays it was quiet, forgotten and locked in darkness.

The rats scampered over and under the rubble. They stalked and devoured the insects that lived alongside them. They ran on their way to their foraging grounds in the tunnels and city far above. They built nests, they fought, shit, fucked, they gave birth. Everything, in fact, their kind has done since time immemorial – both as individuals and as a species.

This timeless pattern of activity was interrupted by a pattering of dust and stone fragments hitting the ground. A vibration resonated through stone and old steel, followed by a distant rumble. The rats were alarmed at the unprecedented intrusion. They hid where they could, in holes and cracks and crevices. Even the insects scattered as the rumbling grew louder and the entire cavern seemed to shake.

An explosion of rubble cascaded from a corner of the cavern. Bright light seared the cathedral of night. Blocks of masonry and concrete tumbled and clattered to a gradual halt. The pattering of gravel gave way to silence. Clouds of dust curled in the air, dancing like wraiths.

Slowly, the glare withered back into its source in a mound of time-compressed rubble. There was something there. An intrusion. Two metres in diameter, it tapered to a small orifice that dribbled a corrosive fluid. The snout was shielded by a bony carapace, split into segments. Between the plates, long blisters of some bio-illuminant slowly sagged as the light faded. Behind the snout, powerful muscles shrugged deeper entry.

The rats watched, fearful.

A snap of bone. The tear of leather. Fluid discharged through cracks in the bony shield. It washed a small channel in the rubble beneath. Suddenly the head split open, the segments sprung back and pressed against the old concrete. New blisters formed on the surface of the segments and filled with renewed light. The creature's gullet extruded and bulged to the point of bursting.

The slick, membranous material ripped open. More of that corrosive liquid spewed to flood the cavern floor. Rubble and insects were flushed from sanctuary. A rat, engulfed in its hiding hole, twitched in the flow. Its legs were dissolving; fur rendered a sticky mass on its body. The head was already made a naked skull, the creature's dying breaths bubbled from its bony nostrils.

On the edge of light, the fluid erased a faded sign on the floor as it spilled over the edge. 'Mind The Gap'.

Behind the drainage, the beast's gullet pulsated to disgorge the first pod. It tumbled over the floor, sliding and rolling. More pods followed until twenty such birthings had settled onto the corroded floor.

Still, the rats watched helpless.

The first pod began to shrivel. Then it started to split, punctured by sharp spines from within. The membrane writhed with some inner motion. The material was shredded and something arose. It shook clear the remnants of its chrysalis and turned to watch its brethren likewise arise.

Bipedal, the birthed creature stood erect. In the now-dying light from the segmented snout, it resembled an insect. Its carapace gleamed in the wash of photons, but its head was marked only by a curving 'V' that was utter black. No reflectance at all, as if it absorbed all available light. They might be eyes; they might be something far more perceptive.

Gill-like slits fluttered at the sides of each 'V'. The carapace bristled with blade-like spines; most emerged from joints at the knee and the elbow.

For all its alien intonation, there was something humanoid about the newcomer. Each wore a surcoat of some silicon-ceramic fibre, in the manner of Mediaeval knights, each one bearing the old symbol of the bio-hazard. The surcoats were belted at the waist, but no sword adorned these creatures. Instead, each one bore a short tubular device attached by a ribbed hose to a carrypod on its back.

Inside that carrypod was the dragon fire that was their trade. Their appearance, the manner of MorTek: anthrodermic suits that lived in symbiosis with their still human flesh.

The Hazamat.

Revived from the long dormancy of metamorphosis, ready now for the climax of their dominion.

The Hazamat lined up along the platform. Military precision. As a unit, they unshipped their burners. Each one ignited with a soft yellow flame. They approached the edge of the platform, synchronised by silent 'voices' of G-Tek communication. An adjustment, and each jolly Bunsen flame tightened to a threatening blue lance of heat.

As one they leapt from the edge of the platform, then turned and begin their march into the yawning maw of a tunnel.

In the near dead lights, the surviving rats watched the Hazamat fade from their world like old legends. They shuddered as a darker shadow spilled in the pyre men's wake…

FAINT, rasping breaths from the mangled bundle that had been Caxton told Adam that the old dealer wasn't done with yet. He crawled over; shock giving way to the first pangs of grief, and he reached out with a trembling hand. Then he pulled away in fear, as if death might be contagious.

Blood erupted from Caxton's mouth in a tortured gasp. Adam nearly wet himself and stated the obvious: "You're alive…"

"Yeah? That… must… be why… I feel like… *shit*."

The words gurgled fluid. Harsh and breathy. Blood oozed and bubbled with every unbelievable word.

"Cax… Cax… Oh, man…"

"Forget it. Pocket…"

"What?"

"Pocket… *Tobac*… co…"

"I don't know how…"

A strangled gurgle. Caxton's eyes rolled up and the lids descended to hide the obscene whites.

"Cax! Cax!"

A fresh gasp sprayed blood on his face; he recoiled and wiped the splashes.

"Time. Time I quit anyway… those things will be the… death… of me."

The old man gurgled a pained, strained laugh, more babbling of fluid than the sound of bitter mirth. Infectious all the same. Adam felt the laughter bunch the muscles in his chest. Then he remembered the blood and the laugh died at birth.

"Cax…"

"Forget it. Listen."

Caxton closed his eyes against a wave a shuddering agony. On instinct, Adam took the man's hand and held it. Then he winced against the bone crushing strength still latent in the muscles and sinews fighting to hold on to a few last dregs of existence.

"My place…" Caxton strained to raise his head, but the effort was too much. Adam leaned forward to listen better.

"My place… Inside. A manuscript. Get it to Laura. She'll know what to do with it. Just get it to Laura. Make sure it's safe, it's all any of us have left…"

He'd make himself heard at the end of the world, and now his was ending. The voice was nothing but a husky whisper now. He could hardly hear. Just stare at the face, watch the eyes lose their focus as the last dregs of strength whispered from his torn chest.

A limp hand managed to rise in one last resurrection of flesh. Adam flinched as it passed his edge of vision and wet fingers stroked his cheek. Then the hand fell across the ruined torso.

"At least… I found you…"

A low rumbling gurgle.

"That's something. Kept you safe… despite everything…"

A grimace that might have been a grin; a spasm briefly animated the ruined body.

"Don't… blame your mother… she's not herself…"

Adam frowned. "My mother? I never –"

The last of his puzzled words died with Caxton. Adam stared into the empty orbs that had once held so much power and felt the loss eviscerate his soul.

"CAX! It's me!"

Laura frowned. The door was ajar, but there was no sound coming from within. She rushed up the stairs, hand sliding and gripping the rusting rail as she hauled herself upwards. She shouted again as she pulled the door open.

"Cax!"

There was still no reply. She hadn't expected any.

"*Damn.*"

Of all the times for him to be out. She slipped her bag from her shoulder and placed it down by the chair.

Immediately she saw the spillage of papers that cluttered the floor around the desk. That's what you got for leaving the door open. She clucked and muttered and then smiled at the sudden inspiration. No better opportunity to peek at his baby. It was wicked, but she couldn't resist.

She scooped up the pages from the floor and placed them on the desk. Then she unzipped her jacket and threw it onto the chair to keep the bag company. With a grateful sigh, she sat at Caxton's desk and began to sort out the pages. Before her eyes were to scan the words, they needed placing in order.

She wondered vaguely where he'd gone, and wondered how long she had to steal a glance, then her attention was drawn into the task and her thoughts began to merge at random with the flicking pages…

… The darkness that surrounds our havens of light has known many names in the past. The name of now is but the latest of many. Unlike those that came before, however, this is the first time that He has adopted one for himself.

In stepping from the shadows into the twilight, he has made an act of taunting definition.

As an Incunabulite, I can only speculate, but I find the means to inform my hazardous guesses. The mind of our

Nemesis might not be fully known, but in a precious mimeographed copy of an old book, I find my clues.

There, in those pages of <u>The Time Machine</u> by H G Wells, I find my metaphor for our times in the <u>Morlocks</u> and the <u>Eloi</u>.

Siblings they are, born of a defunct humanity. The one underground, hiding in the shadows, coming out only at night; the machine tenders, haunting the shadows to feed on their enfeebled <u>Eloi</u> cousins.

What is in a name?

All, or nothing. Obfuscation, perhaps, or else a clue or a key to some hidden meaning. Morlock flaunts his nature before us, and we blindly flock to the siren call of his machine: the <u>Gestalt</u>...

She heard Caxton's booming resonance reverberate from the pages she scanned. Saw him in her mind's eye, pausing as she skipped the pages to light his roll ups. He took a drag, and resumed speaking...

... Even with the Folio Plagues raging like a fearful dreadnought, the book did not relinquish its hold on life without a struggle. There were enough advocates to hold back the tide of flame for a while, even as the flow of disease flooded through the populace. They doubted the veracity of the contagion's source, fought against the dread harbingers howling for their destruction.

That is when Morlock stepped out from the shadows and made himself the spokesman for those who would condemn the book to death. As he passed sentence, he added what seemed the merciful life eternal for what was once conveyed on paper. All that was precious in the printed page was to live eternal, unsullied and immortal, in the spirit of digital preservative.

It was the promise that broke the back of opposition.

The books duly burned.

Now we should ask, do these fabled digital archives exist? Should we ever gain the opportunity to sift the wreckage of Morlock's Empire, will we find these lost treasures of human past?

We shall not know until the darkness is lifted, until we can crack open the vaults of our Nemesis and map the hidden labyrinths.

It may be that much has been lost forever...

A metallic clamour alerted Laura to impending discovery. With a thrill of guilt she put the manuscript aside, and left the remaining pages in a bundle by its side. She stood and walked towards the door.

"Cax! It's me. Where —"

Her words collapsed as she reached the door. Guilt turned to fear. Beneath her, foot on the first step, a haggard vision of horror.

"Adam." Her voice quavered. He looked terrible. Stained in blood. She half-expected him to collapse at any moment. She was about to move towards him until the look in his eyes froze her heart.

Eyes staring, blood screaming in vivid colour, his mindless stutter managed to form words: "Cax, he's..."

"IT is done."

Morlock didn't respond. If it wasn't for the slight motion of the chair he might have taken the room for empty. Even the ominous presence of his master felt diminished in the shadows clinging to the room.

"As you predicted; the boy was the perfect bait."

"*Yesssss.*"

The voice was a parched, papery rustle. Otto stepped back, shocked at the dreadful whisper. A hand slumped into view to dangle listless from the side of the chair. Flaking, corpse-like, as desiccated as the voice. Otto gave it a shocked glance, enough to sear the frightful image into his mind, before he looked up and away.

To take in Bill's hollow gaze as it turned out. He swallowed his fear and his distaste and silently cursed the skull.

"Death is such a tragedy, for it deprives the Gestalt *of a living soul, and the soul the* Gestalt. *Sometimes it is necessary. Still, we will collect our lost ones when the time comes."*

For a moment, he wondered if his old master was dying. Was that why the sudden resurrection of his ancient hatred for the *Incunabula*: must he rush them to the grave before he found his own?

He felt a sense of hope, of impending release, but then realised that if Morlock suspected anything of his ties to the old library he might join it at the crematorium. He squeezed the shudder into acquiescence and remained sternly at attention, eyes focused on the cityscape beyond the glass.

In the corner of his eye, Bill stared. The sweat tickled the corner of his eye and he blinked furiously to quell the itch. The stare held a dreadful *knowing*, as though Bill read every thought, every treacherous wisp of fear in his brain and then relayed the information to Morlock with his silent tongue.

Terrified paranoia. What else? It was only dead bone. He should know. He killed it. So how long had it sat there, awaiting its chance for revenge? Another foolish thought, his head was full of them, created by this room of shadows and impending doom.

A horrible consideration dawned; that Bill indeed had a voice only his master might hear. And why not? It made a kind of macabre sense. The Hall of Whispers, filled with the voices of the unseen damned, though lately they seemed to have wandered further from their chilling congregation hall. So why not a visible lump of bone with an unheard voice? There was symmetry there.

Suddenly, he had the urge to smash the old bone, but not here, not now, not in the presence of Morlock. He would only seal his own fate. No, it was foolishness. Ride the storm. See it through to the other side; no matter what else is destroyed in the maelstrom, there'll be a place for Otto Schencke in the beyond. Focus on the job: always and forever the job.

"As you said it would be, Sir. It was only a matter of time. He came to us. Marla did the rest."

"And the boy? You told him. He will bring me this manuscript?"

"Hard to say, Sir. I can't see why not. The life of the *Incunabula* for one scrap of old paper. He has little choice."

"No. Indeed. Is he that trusting?"

Otto suppressed a shrug. Morlock might not be able to see him, after all. "I couldn't say, Sir. You might say he's had a rapid and shocking introduction to the harsh realities."

"No. He will come to us. You have done well, Otto. You both have. You have earned your rest. Soon now. Soon. Only a few duties for you, and then your reward."

"Thank you, Sir. It is reward enough to serve."

"Indeed." A long sigh, like a hiss of escaping gas. *"I feel like I have lost something, Otto. So strange. Is it always thus, that long anticipation turns the moment to anti-climax?"*

This time he did shrug. "I couldn't say."

"No. Marla. She understands. Of course you do not. It's what I admire in you, Otto. Survival is your game. To that end you anticipate everything and savour nothing. You have been the perfect defender of the Gestalt. *And I can rely on you, always, to follow survival's path in the actions you must take. Such is why I know the boy will bring me the manuscript. You yourself will ordain its delicious inevitability."*

"Of course, Sir… but…" he almost choked on the question, "what *is* so important about some old manuscript? The man is no more –"

"*Secrets.* Secrets. *I must have it back.*"

The deathly hand gestured. It took a moment to realise it was a dismissal. Then the hand plucked the cane from the shadows.

"*I have waited long for your news, Otto. Too long. I must rest, resurrect, but before you go, I too have some news to share. The* Hazamat *is ready. Tonight the library burns. All shall be ash. Rejoice! For all shall soon be complete.*"

Otto nodded stiff and turned to leave. As he pulled the doors closed, he witnessed his master stagger into view. The apparition captured his gaze and he only just suppressed the gasp of horror. The spectre detonated a word in his brain with all the force of a hollow-point bullet: *Nosferatu.*

SHADOWS clung to the far corners of the room where the lamplight failed to reach. There, a thousand ghosts lurked; spectral mourners gathered in a wake for Caxton. Laura sensed them, lingering in the particles of their words.

She tried to find solace in those books that lay scattered around. Caxton's eclectic collection. And nearby, nestled in the hall leading to the rest of his den, the plastic bags and rucksacks of evacuees from the library. Suitcases even, one burst open, its precious contents spilling onto the floor in an avalanche of old paper.

She sniffled and felt the first tear spill. Then her wandering gaze fell upon Adam, and the tears chilled dry. He sat in the chair Caxton always kept for visitors, squeezed in beside her bag and squashing her coat. Adam slumped, almost nonmoving but for the rise and fall of his chest, gaunt, bloodstained face, mouth open, his eyes unfocused.

She turned away to gaze at the manuscript in front of her and began to pick up the pages and place them into some kind of order. She was the guardian now of this precious burden. Nothing must interfere with what they had to do. Not even her grief. Now more than ever she had to be strong, but she wanted to collapse into a sobbing heap.

"He... wanted you to have it."

She didn't turn, just tapped the assemblage of pages into a neater bundle.

"It is Caxton's, right?"

She paused, not wanting to speak, but equally wanting to *know*.

"You spoke to him? Before..."

"Yes. He said to get the manuscript to you. Guess that's it?"

She nodded, but didn't trust herself to speak. It was an effort to ask: "What else did he say?"

"Not a lot. He said he was glad he'd found me. Said he was sorry. Told me not to blame my mother."

She frowned in surprise. "I thought you never knew her?"

"I didn't. Maybe he means for dumping me."

"He knew her, then?"

Adam shrugged. She only knew by the sound of his clothes shifting. "I guess. Maybe. I don't know. It's just, he was dying... there was so much blood; I didn't know what to say. And then... he was just gone."

Laura tapped the manuscript again, but there was no strength to it. The pages flopped like a broken concertina.

She placed it down gently. The chair creaked, just the way it did when Caxton sat in it. The sound was nearly too much, a burden that threatened to break her imposed and brittle calm.

"There was nothing you could do," she said, contradicting her thoughts.

"So, is that it?"

"What?"

"His manuscript?"

"Yes."

"Only… only, Morlock wants it. The man told me."

"No! He can't have it!"

Her voice was sharper than she intended. Her hand came down of its own volition. A protective gesture that slammed hard against the paper.

"He said they'd let the library live."

"And you believe them?"

"No." He shifted in the chair, his hungry eyes averting their gaze from the stack of paper. "I'm only saying, that's all."

"Don't even think it," she snarled.

She picked up the stack and moved to pull her rucksack from the chair where it was jammed at Adam's side. Then she rolled the slim manuscript as best should could and placed it inside. Clearly, it wasn't safe here. There was a look on Adam's face that suggested more stupidity. Enough to crack her already crumbling trust.

"Come on," she said.

He looked up from his brooding. "What?"

"Get yourself cleaned up. We have to go."

"Why? What's the point?"

"There's work to be done at the library. You can fetch and carry like the rest of us."

Adam snorted. "How can you think of books at a time like this?"

"Especially at a time like this! That's why!"

"Caxton is DEAD!"

She reached him in a heart-broken beat and pulled him from the chair. One hand clutched his jacket, the other bunched into a fist ready to strike. She caught her rage just in time.

"He's dead because of you,'" she shrieked, all the energy of her fist spent in the voice. "It's your fault."

"You think I should have been shot? You think that would have saved him, me taking a bullet?"

"Yes. You for Caxton. Why not?"

"Don't you think I want him back too? I didn't kill him."

"And do you want him dead for *nothing*? We can't... he can't..."

Tears flooded unbidden. She released Adam and turned away as the sobs took hold. It was a storm finally bursting, and in the middle she still struggled to tame the turmoil of grief and loss. Hard, painful, to turn away from the flood, but she knew it had to be done.

The moment seemed longer than it was, but she managed to pull herself together. She turned her sodden, throbbing eyes back to Adam. He stood there, lower lip trembling. She couldn't bear to look at him and pushed him away. *Hard.*

He slammed into a bookshelf with enough force to make them wobble. Books fell down around him. A large thesaurus slammed into his head. He went down to his knees and burst into tears as books hammered his back.

"I couldn't stop them. Marla and Otto. I couldn't... He came for me. They were waiting. They shot him. I couldn't. I thought..."

Hot tears flooded his cheeks, sluicing pink as they washed the dried blood from his face. Laura felt the anger soften as she watched the shuddering sobs quaking Adam's shoulders. He slumped on all fours, heavy drops of grief pattering onto the carpet and the spilled books.

"It's not your fault," she said, as if soothing a child. "I didn't mean what I said. I'm sorry. You couldn't stop them. Cax took it on himself. He was strange at the end. Everyone said so. It's not your fault."

Adam's sobs began to subside. Or maybe the salt-water of his tears was hardening him inside. She hoped so; he needed to be tough now.

"Come on," she said, more gentle this time. "Get yourself cleaned up. I'll be back in half an hour for you."

"Where... where are you going?" he asked, sitting up on his knees and wiping his face with a bloody sleeve.

"Just outside. I need to be alone for a while to clear my head. To think. Be ready when I get back. We can't save Cax, but we can still save his life."

The Eighth Folio
Every Burned Book
Enlightens The World

THE old shopping trolley was a temperamental beast at best, but even so Adam thought he was beginning to get the hang of its wayward momentum. Now all he needed was some way to cope with the backbreaking monotony.

He negotiated another halt close to a smattering of fallen books, then stooped to gather them up in his arms. The movement provoked another whinge from his spine.

He didn't bother stacking them neatly any more. He just let them drop. The books flopped into the wire basket where they settled haphazardly on top of their fellow refugees. After two round trips of the same repetition of lifting and pushing, his body was beginning to protest against the strain. It blunted any zeal, and then some, but the aches and pains and the erratic contraption did have a perverse way of keeping his mind from recent tragedies. As Laura said, in her typical harsh logic, grieve later, once the reason for grief is secure.

Eventually, after some pushing and pulling, he got the trolley moving again. The contraption was half-full now and that made it harder to handle. To add to his woes, one of the wheels was busted. It squeaked loud and constant like a high-pitched metronome regulating the pace of tedium.

Apart from these burdens, the job was easy enough, in its way. Pick up the fallen, fill the trolley, take the load back to a collection point for safe shipping, then back again for more.

The trolley tried to pull him along, but he hung back with his weight and forced it to stop. This time he tried to keep his back straight when he lowered himself to the task. The small stack slithered precariously in his hands. He held the books steady enough until he could use their own momentum to tip them into the trolley. Stooping again, he took a couple more. The pages fell from the dust jacket and spewed across the floor.

"Oh, *shit!*"

The second book's spine was broken. He put the gutted remains into the trolley, then went down on his knees to gather the fallen pages. There didn't seem much point in saving this one, but his was not to reason, he thought resentfully. This was hardly the great adventure he'd once fondly imagined. He stood up with the rough bundle of paper and dumped it into the trolley.

"Here lad! Not like that." A large man waddled towards him, face almost as red as the high-visibility vest he wore. He stopped at the trolley and wiped his face with a handkerchief. "How are the bookbinders to know where they go if we don't keep 'em together?"

He reached inside the trolley. Carefully, he tidied the bundle and slipped them inside the battered cover.

The man grinned. "Thought it's fucked, eh? One day, long time ago maybe. But not today. Not the first book to be fixed, won't be t'last either. You just keep the pages together like that an' t'others can get it fixed up later."

Adam nodded mute, feeling like he was back at the warehouse.

"Now, look at this mess. You want to stack them neater. Get more in that way. Books are like people, they need care and respect."

Adam watched as the man began to sort through the trolley's contents and stack them in neater piles. The man might as well have said it, he can't do anything right. He felt his face redden, and then moved to help.

"That's better," the man said. "Hard work. I know. And it's a thankless task, but it's got to be done. Look around you, lot of folks working hard. Harder than they're used to, many of 'em, but they'll do it. Had to send some of 'em off home. Worked 'emselves too hard. They done their bit and can be proud, come what may. They've given up so much time and effort. Not a hero type among 'em like what we're used to reading about, eh?"

He reached into the trolley and briefly patted a random book. Then he continued, a glint in his eye, "But look at 'em at it. They're not heroes; they're just ordinary folk like us. Lot of strength there. That's why I know we'll come through."

Adam nodded, and stooped to pick up some more fallen books. This time he placed them carefully with their brethren. He felt the man's approval, and hoped it was enough to send him on his way. All of a sudden, he needed his lonely anonymity again.

"That's better. Now, breaks over, so let's see some shuffle, eh? We don't want to be leaving nowt for the *Hazamat* if we can help it."

Adam shook his head, but didn't say what was on his mind. It wasn't the fear of these pyre men he shared; such ghost-story monsters couldn't fire him up. No, it was Marla Caine and Otto Schencke who sparked the fear in his heart, but somehow he didn't see this place as quite their style.

"Good lad. We'll save the day yet. You'll see."

WE learned much later that they were called the Hazamat.

For our part, we knew them by their deeds alone, until we named them the better to focus our curses and our loathing.

The Pyre Men.

The Pyre Brigades.

Hardly original, I know, but that's what we called them. They were the book burners; the agents of Morlock's malice. The ones who hunted and persecuted us in those terrible days of burning that followed the Folio Plagues.

We cursed them as they burned. We fled before them, scattered hither on the firestorms like flakes of carbonised paper. Time after time, they burned, we fled, only to re-form and build anew.

The Hazamat did not only burn; they hunted, they stalked, they infiltrated, until it seemed we were doomed. Only hard work and luck saved us: that and Morlock's purpose as he turned to focus on the Gestalt and the mysterious goal of Completion.

In time the Hazamat faded. Morlock's lesser servants took on the task of hunting us down. The beginnings of the long 'Cold War' between Incunabula and MorTek; the long years of huddled shelter, the fearful glances over our shoulders, the game of hide and seek and incinerate.

Yet always the Hazamat was a threat we feared, and hated, until it became almost a creature of dark legend. Morlock made them. Even now in their dormancy, he doubtless makes of them something new and terrible. They were—they will be — the flaming sword of his purpose, ever thrust into our breast, or held in Damoclean suspension above our bowed and frightened heads.

They had not always been such creatures of terror. Once, we might have gratefully honoured the work of the Hazamat, or at least that which was its forebear.

As with the firemen in Bradbury's 'Fahrenheit 451', the Hazamat did not begin as the nemesis of the book, but as something far more beneficent. They cleansed this world of the worst excesses of humanity's manufactured pestilence.

Of the many plagues unleashed by the collapse of the world that was, among the worst were the dread horsemen of biological, chemical and radioactive contamination.

Thus, the forerunner of the Hazamat cleansed the blighted and ruined remnants of our worst affected cities. It was they who rescued precious patches of this benighted Earth so that life might go on untainted.

Yes, only gratitude in those days. Until the coming of the Folio Plagues born of a sinister depravity turned them loose upon us.

Who better to rid the world of the pestilences absorbed into old paper? Yes, when faced with such hazardous material, call in the specialists.

Hazardous materials.

Bio-Hazard.

To the long list, add books. From the most ancient preserved tome, to the newest published pot-boiler. From our astonishment in the beginning to our disbelief, our scorn, and finally—our horror.

Such crude work it was, after the demands of their specialised role, but the Hazamat-in-making soon learned a thirst for fire.

After the clearing of the libraries and warehouses holding stocks, came the scourging of the bookshops. Then followed the house-to-house purges, searching for the hidden stocks not surrendered by their owners, the crackdowns, the book amnesties gathering them in for the pyres. And the hunt began in earnest for those who would become the Incunabula.

As I write these words, the Hazamat has lain dormant for many years. The fear of the Hazamat still lingers. As it must. Though it is now the terror inspired by legend, of a frightening story told too many times around the fireside. Too much, perhaps, of the real horror has been forgotten.

I fear the return of the Hazamat.

I fear what Morlock has made of them during the years of their dormancy.

THEY called the place 'J.B's' back in better days, when it was a vibrant and convivial place to meet and talk. Now it was quiet and cheerless, revealed for what it was; an old stock room basement, a largely empty space, walled and boarded up from the main library.

Laura forced herself to sit still on her perch on the edge of a table, feet resting on a chair, her chin resting in her hands. She stared at the walls with their bewildering collage of old and faded posters; the now unused trappings of a café. She couldn't find it in herself to meet Maggie's gaze. The older woman kept to one side, lost in her own mournful contemplation.

The two men sat side by side to read through Caxton's manuscript in tandem. No sound but their breathing, the occasional cough, and the flick of paper as one turned a page over to the other. Both were senior members of the *Incunabula*, but other than that, they couldn't be further apart.

Dorian was a thin man with sparse hair regrettably combed across the top of his scalp. He wore a crumpled and nondescript suit of the kind favoured by older *Terapolitans*. A tie dangled loose at the throat. The man's face was narrow and bony, with a perpetually nervous aura. A life spent lurking in shadows, forever fearful of a hand on the shoulder, had left him the epitome of the small mammal, ever living on his nerves, and forever dreading the swooping predator.

Maus was anything but: the awesome manifestation, maybe, of that fearful predator in total contradiction to his name. She had no idea why he chose it. Never judge a book by its movie, she thought. An old *Incunabula* utterance, its origins long lost to memory. Maus certainly embodied it.

To look at, he was the epitome – or the caricature – of the Old World biker straight out of the picture books. Not someone to mistake for an *Incunabulite*. Yet he flaunted what he was before an ignorant population. Whatever rules and guidelines existed about *Incunabulites* blending in, Maus had obviously decided to flout *them* too. His presence proclaimed. To think that he was not only a chapter head but a member of the *Gorsedd*.

A bald head gleamed in the weak electric light, but a long braided pony tail draped over his shoulder. He was a large man, with a muscular body, clad in leather trousers and big boots. A singlet revealed tattooed skin, emblems of the graphic novels that were his speciality. Intense blue eyes, strong and piercing, stared at the pages before him. The face was hard – not mean – ready for anything and unafraid of Morlock's world.

She watched him complete a page and retrieve another from Dorian's finished pile. A swift flick of paper; the words meticulously consumed. Laura suppressed a sigh and ended in triggering a yawn. She went with it, doing her best to mask its intrusion with the palm of her hand.

Maggie came over and gave her a sympathetic squeeze of her arm. "What's wrong?"

Laura shrugged. "I should be out there. There's so much to do, and I don't like leaving Adam alone."

"He'll be fine, dear, and they can do without us for a little while if it's as important as you say."

"I thought you didn't like Adam?"

She smiled and patted her shoulder. "Oh, I've nothing against him personally. I'm sure he's a pleasant enough young man. I've just never believed he's the right material for us. That's all."

"Are any of us? This waiting. This... *helplessness*."

"Try to be patient. You can be with your man soon enough."

She stiffened in protest and was about to speak when Dorian cleared his throat. There was a loud thud on the desk. Laura turned and saw Maus tapping the manuscript back into the shape. He stared at her, blue eyes expectant.

So this was it. The verdict.

DESPITE all the books he had read, Luca never bothered to think about minor characters and their tendency to come to a bad end. Not that he saw himself as a minor player in the trials of the organisation. Not when he wore the red vest of a supervisor.

He was an important man. Obviously, for he had been tasked to help with the management and organisation of the library's evacuation. Not important with a supercharged capital 'I', of course, being a modest man, but certainly he enjoyed importance of a lower case sense. It meant a chance to be noticed, and he intended to make full use of the opportunity.

Again, he never considered that in desperate times, desperate measures are required, or that his role was of less importance than he considered. Someone had to oversee the far crews carting and carrying books through the furthest tunnels to places of hiding. Such was Luca.

None of this entered his head as he plodded down the dark tunnel far from the heart of the library. No reason why it should; he had more important matters to occupy his thoughts. The need to instil a greater sense of urgency into his team of book-hodders, for instance, to get them to increase the frequency of their loads. Some, he knew, as all supervisors discussed, had come to doubt the impending danger. The days since the first alert-inspired panic had faded with the *Hazamat's* failure to materialise. The bogeymen weren't coming after all, some whispered.

The inevitability of human nature; Luca shared the doubt but not enough to tarnish his new found opportunity to be noticed and rise. In fact any truth to the doubt was all the more welcome, for it meant he bore the responsibilities and apparent risks without the inherent danger.

So he turned a corner in the old dried-up sewer that led to where his team should be and heard the motion of bodies coming his way. He stopped and swung his head round to catch his crew in his helmet lamp. He raised his reedy voice with all the authority he believed it could muster.

"Come on you lazy buggers! Don't you know the Pyre Men are coming?"

He caught a glimpse of strange shapes in the far reaches of his light and frowned at what he thought he saw. Then he heard a noise. It sounded like distant laughter. At him? Cheeky buggers. He pulled himself to his full and hardly imposing height. Authority was needed, even though an insubstantial harmonic of fear was leaching from the shadows.

"Yes. We. Have. Come."

A volcanic flush erupted from his anus, the bowels the only part of his body still capable of motion. The magma of terror dribbled down his legs.

"Join. Us. Renounce. All. This."

"Join. With. Us. Join. Us. Or. Die."

The choral voice came from all around. From the figures in front. From somewhere behind. From the shadows above his head. Most alarmingly, from a point behind and to the side, like someone leaning close to hiss menace in his left ear.

At last Luca began to think. *Not death. Don't kill me.* The words were important thoughts scurrying scared through his brain. He managed to channel what he hoped were the right ones to his mouth.

"N–No!"

A long hiss from the shadows. The first of the dark shapes revealed itself in his lamplight. The image unfroze his limbs and Luca turned to run. Terror squished in his underpants, but he was well beyond indignity. The red vest felt tight and clammy. His boots weighed heavy as if they'd caught the load released from his bowels. The world moved slowly. A whine escaped his trembling lips and left him far behind.

The world turned golden yellow. For a moment, he saw the old sewers in breathtaking detail. And then his eyes burst and he saw nothing. The pain vanished in an instant of vaporised nerve endings. He stumbled to the ground and lay there, a charred but living cadaver with carbonised and shrivelled limbs still locked in the posture of flight.

Even to the last dying embers of consciousness, Luca never realised the significance of that red vest. Nor did the once-men of the *Hazamat* care. They stepped over Luca's charred carcass, regardless, and continued their passage into the heart of the *Incunabula*.

LAURA slipped off the table and took a nervous step forward. She caught an imagined whiff of tobacco and mentally pictured Caxton leaning against the wall by the counter; of course, he was delving into his tobacco pouch, as he always did when he had a lot on his mind.

The ghost glanced across and gave a weak smile. Even the memory of the man was apprehensive. As if he needed to worry, he was Caxton, the very essence of persuasion.

"Always liked Caxton's style," Maus interjected, with a grim chuckle. "I'd love to wring Morlock's scrawny neck for what he's done to us."

He pushed the manuscript forward and then leaned in his chair until it was rocking on its back legs. He slipped his hands behind his head and turned to look at Dorian.

"I am afraid *that* is something far beyond our capabilities." Dorian's voice was every bit as nervous as his demeanour, but he managed to modulate the authority that bespoke his position on the *Gorsedd*. The ghost of Caxton stood up, expectant. Laura followed his lead. Maus was staring down at the manuscript now, as if he'd withdrawn from the proceedings.

"Thanks for bringing this to our attention, Laura. It could so easily have been lost forever after..." Dorian waited a moment for everyone to fill in the blanks, then he added: "This is a fine piece of work, of course, our times considered, but I am afraid it has little *practical* value. I'm sorry."

"What? Are you saying it's... *useless?*"

Caxton turned away and thumped the wall. Laura felt like thumping Dorian, but Maus had obviously read the urge in her eyes and stared it into submission.

"No, Laura, that's *not* what I am saying, but... well, have you read it?"

"Yes. No. Actually, not all of it. I haven't had the chance."

Dorian looked at her for painful moments, then he broke contact and reached out to flick the edges of the forlorn stack of pages. "Caxton makes Morlock out to be some kind of bogeyman. A demon of sorts, I suppose. I mean, he appears to be suggesting... *exorcisms*... with books and metaphysical mumbo jumbo. It takes some suspension of disbelief, I must say. Now I knew Caxton rather enjoyed his colourful turns of phrase, but this really is going too far. I never realised his mental well-being had deteriorated so much."

"Caxton isn't... wasn't... mad. He wasn't!"

"We're not saying he'd lost his mind. Only that he was perhaps a little obsessed and that clouded his judgement. I suppose he also paid rather too much attention to Elzevir's more fanciful notions."

"You leave El out of this!" Maggie's eyes flashed an unfamiliar anger. For a moment Dorian was back under the shadow of the hawk's wing. "Without Elzevir none of us would be here. Nor Cax for that matter either. We owe them both! The problem was that young man out there. That Adam and Cax's strange obsession with him. He might have been here to speak for himself otherwise..."

Dorian held up his hand. "Maggie, please..."

Only slightly mollified, she added: "Yes, well, I've nothing against the lad personally. As I told Laura, I just don't think he was ever right for us. And now the Jonah's out there in the library. Does *he* have any idea why Cax is gone? Does any of us? So how can we so casually dismiss what he left us?"

Dorian sighed and looked at Maus. The big biker simply nodded.

"This is a valuable piece of work," Dorian said. "It's not something to dismiss out of hand, as you accuse, but it doesn't – cannot – offer us any practical solutions. What will we do? Wave it at the Pyre Men when they arrive and hope it's fireproof? And it seems Caxton would have us march on *MorTek Prime* like some kind of rebelling peasant army! We can't. Be serious. It isn't why the *Incunabula* was founded. We must bide our time and wait!"

"Caxton always said we are running out of time. You can't sit and wait forever. Doesn't what's happening outside tell you anything?"

Dorian's voice rose in exasperation. "Yes, Laura, it tells me plenty. We grew complacent. We made mistakes. We left ourselves vulnerable. We'll pay for that, but we will also persevere – and survive!"

"So we run. And they find us. And we run again. We can't hide forever!"

Maus suddenly leaned forward. "You're right, lass. We can't. I'm game for the rumble. So you coming then? Me and you. Right now. We'll burn out Morlock's nest between us!"

There was a fierce gleam in his eyes, face stern. Was he serious? Laura felt her thoughts scatter like bewildered sparrows. "I can't. I mean. *MorTek?*"

Maus smiled grim.

"Who can? Who will? It's not what we're about," Dorian said.

"I sympathise," Maus added, "I really do. I'd *like* to do what I just said. Burst in guns blazing. We wouldn't last five minutes. Our time is coming, though. You have to hold on to that. Believe it. Caxton did. In his way. And, he gave his life for us, for our books. I know it's not easy, but don't let that be in vain. Trust what we're doing here."

"But the *Hazamat* are coming! Now!"

Did her voice sound as weak and small as she imagined? This isn't the way it was supposed to go. That they'd dismiss the final legacy of Caxton's life. Caxton's presence was gone, leaving her the sole defender of his life's work. Some advocate she'd turned out to be.

"We've survived them before," Dorian said in a quiet voice. He looked down and fidgeted. A fine sheen of sweat had appeared on his face.

"We live in the city of the *Gestalt*," Maus said. "Now everyone in this town lives for that and that alone, but what they don't realise is that this place contains the seeds of its own downfall. We wait. We survive. Sooner or later this whole conurb of cards is gonna come tumbling down around us."

"I don't understand. How can *Terapolis* come crashing down? It's so... *big*."

"Yeah, well, so was the world that went before – and where is it now? You just take a real good look at *Terapolis* sometime. It looks like a bustling city, but it's *rotting*. For one thing, it's beginning to choke on its sheer size. For another, it's losing the necessary human element to keep it going. The skills to sustain a modern society are fading away. So much is being lost. As for what's left, well people are turning away from learning what's needed. They love the *Gestalt* so much, they don't bother with anything else but getting through the day until they can hit a G-Spot. Even *MorTek* is having problems finding the people it needs. So you see? The *Gestalt* must collapse. When it does, we'll be here. With our books, and everything else we've preserved. Not just the stories and the poetry and philosophies of bygone ages, but with the knowledge and the stored skills the human race needs to sustain itself. The *Gestalt* is yesterday. Books are the future!"

Laura just nodded her head; she didn't trust herself to speak. It made a kind of sense, but there was that nagging doubt lurking in the back of her mind. The shadow of fear that was the *Hazamat*.

Maus leaned forward and picked up the manuscript. "Here, take it. Keep it safe," he said, offering it to her. She stepped forward and took it back, feeling its weight in her hands. Somehow it seemed to have grown heavier.

"It was a foolish thing to bring it here at a time like this," Dorian said.

She snapped her head round to glare, but before she might bark or bite Maus stopped her.

"Easy, Laura! We know you didn't have much choice. These are difficult times, and often there is no right move."

She looked away from Dorian to Maus. His eyes held her steady. Ice blue that cooled the heat of her simmering anger. She nodded, and then she rolled up Caxton's memory and slipped it securely into the pocket inside her jacket. It settled in snugly. As if it was where it wanted to be. As if it was where *Caxton* wanted it to be.

With a sigh she turned away and sat down. Maggie came over and began a gentle massage of her shoulders. Kneading a little sympathy and support into her burdened frame.

"So what happens next?" she muttered.

"We go on. Almost as usual. We clear the library. Save as much as we can. You never know, the nay-sayers might be right – the Pyre Men might not come."

"You believe that?"

Maus barked a harsh laugh. "No, Dorian, I don't, but let a man have some pointless optimism will you?"

"Of course." Dorian stood up and straightened his jacket. Then he smoothed the threadbare covering on his scalp. "I'm sorry Laura, that this didn't go the way you wanted."

She shrugged, but didn't look up. "I should go and help Adam," she said.

"Yes. That's a good idea. Listen… I know you looked up to Caxton. I know all you younger people did, and I understand he meant a lot to you. He meant a lot to us all, but he was only one man. He couldn't save the world. He couldn't slay demons. Things don't work that way, except in the books. You have to understand. Life goes on. So do we."

A tear slipped out of its prison. She sniffed it away. Maggie gripped tighter and made a gentle shushing noise.

"Oh Dorian, you really know how to say the most inappropriate things. Can't you see she's upset?"

"Well, it's true, Maggie, what else – wait! Did you hear that?"

"Hear what?"

Laura stood up suddenly, the tears dried.

"Oh my God," Dorian muttered. Louder: *"They're here!"*

THE man in the window looked troubled; but then he had a right to be, after all he had seen and done. There was also the vague worry that he was developing a conscience. A memory of the old man's end almost caused him to shudder. Otto gritted his teeth against the tremor. Not even here, in the privacy of his habitat, dare he show his feelings.

It was almost second nature now, to keep them locked away, but at times they threatened a mental jail break. A man's thoughts were still protected by the privacy of his skull, provided he took care. That's one of the reasons he never used Morlock's infernal machine. He didn't trust it. These days he knew there was too much thought crime locked away inside his skull. Better to keep it to himself.

Besides, there were other reasons to avoid the *Gestalt*. Over the years, he had seen too much of the drain it placed on a person's vitality. The damn thing seemed to devour the spirit. Marla's habit ensured he saw the ill effects of prolonged use. She was a heavy user. She was in there now. Gacked into the habitat's private G-Spot. Perhaps it was the best place for her. Especially now Caxton wasn't around to make her burn with purpose. She was no longer quite the woman he knew.

He sighed and turned away from his troubled reflection. By his arm, the coffee surrendered its latent heat untouched. The *latte* was made the old fashioned way he liked, but it had congealed. He toyed with the cup and stared at the curdled fluid. A waste. A terrible waste. Bovine milk was so difficult to come by these days, even more so than the coffee itself. Even books, and he did not dare consider where he might find his next literary supply. Or supplier for that matter.

The cup clattered as he placed it back on the table. The only other object was his PDA. It squawked and crackled, its screen glowing with an ever-changing mirage of colour and code. For all its resemblance to the bygone smartphones he understood, the device was the latest in *Geist-Tek*. A little something he'd asked Creek to formulate. The sweaty techhead had looked horrified at the request; expressed the complexity of compressing so much high-grade *G-Tek* into so small a package, then duly produced the goods. Otto wished he hadn't bothered now.

He picked it up and stared at the screen. It was trans-linked to the sub-*Gestalt* feed, picking up and relaying information and situational reports from the *Hazamat* teams scouring *Locus Prime*. The book burners were exultant in their pyromanic triumph.

The clicks and whines sounded like an alien language. He had no idea what information the ghastly symphony relayed, nor did he wish to exercise his badly neglected imagination to the task. Better to listen to the human voices. Almost.

They only sounded human because they were in a speech conveyed in syllables that made sense to his ears. The tones sent cold prickles dancing over his skin. Dry, cracked and sibilant, as if the speakers were long out of practice at vocal communication. It was only the hardware that made these voices sound so inhuman. Of that, he only just managed to remain convinced.

So far, the voices formed a standard patter, just the backchat of any routine military operation from times past.

Otto turned his attention to the display. Much of the two-dimensional flow of information was incomprehensible to his eyes, but it was a comforting method of absorbing what little he understood. Quite unlike the disturbing *simulacomm.* Equations. Diagrams. Pictograms. Accounts of the operation. So far, the reports indicated a successful mission. Two libraries destroyed in *Locus Prime* alone, though they were more stockrooms than actual libraries, but each had contained several hundred irreplaceable volumes, and now the *Hazamat* were closing in on the primary target.

An intangible ache began to throb at the base of his sternum. He breathed deep to quell the unease, forced himself to focus on the few words. Not the same as those that enthralled him in the books of the *Incunabula.* The detached, analytical part of his mind considered the information. The main library was a gargantuan task and it would take days to complete. After this night's assault, the labyrinth of surrounding tunnels would be searched in meticulous detail, to scourge every last book. The *Hazamat* was undoubtedly up to that task.

How many had been taken to new hideaways? A question with no answer. Certainly not by this tablet of technology. He scrolled further, sliding his thumb along the screen, casually scanning the information.

"Put it away, Otto, Darling – it's so much better inside the *Gestalt.*"

Marla's unexpected appearance released all the stored apprehension. The shudder rattled his teeth.

"Cold, Darling?"

He glanced at Marla and shrugged. "Somebody just walked over my grave." Or more likely someone had started digging it, but there was no need for her to hear that.

"It was so wonderful. All burning. Pretty fire!"

"You saw it?"

"Through their eyes, Darling. The *Hazamen* see *sooooo* much."

She giggled like a drunk teenager and sat down. Then she leaned on her elbows and placed her tired face in her hands. Her eyes looked like faded paint on an old canvas and about as equally capable of sight. There were fresh liver spots on the backs of her hands.

Otto frowned, but kept his observation to himself. The *Gestalt* seemed bent on taking what little vitality Marla retained. Or better to say, she seemed intent on flushing the last of herself into that mysterious state. She had always been a heavy user, but now… Much more, and she would surely become a candidate for disincorporation. A tiny thought suggested that might well be for the best. No, he would not let himself shudder again. Once was bad enough. Twice would be damnation. Even in this state, it might arouse her suspicion.

"It's more than seeing," Marla slurred. "There's the taste of the smoke. Its smell. The heat of the flames on your skin. You *are* the *Hazamen*. You are the flames scorching clean those filthy pages. You are the books screaming as they die. The sensation is amazing, Darling. Join me. *Join us*. Know it for yourself."

Suddenly she was alive again. Disconcerting: he'd never seen her recover from the lag so fast. He waved his hand in what he hoped was a casual decline.

"You know it blurs the judgement, Marla. I have work to do."

"You *never* use the *Gestalt*, Otto. It has been noted." Her expression darkened.

"And you use it too much, Marla. It is not good for you."

"Come with me, Otto. Join us."

"No, Marla."

She stared at him, a sullen smoulder in her eyes. "Feeling sorry for the book lovers are we?"

"What?" His heart bounced in its cavity. He stood, and forced himself to meet Marla's predatory gaze. "What nonsense is this?"

"I found your books, *Darling*. I burned them, of course."

"Good."

The word erupted naturally after so many years, but Marla's eyes blazed death, daring him to cut the bullshit and confess his guilt. Not a chance.

"You have saved me a job. Tonight's operation has left me with no further use for them."

"What do you mean? What possible use could you have for the filthy things?"

Every word stung. Even he was surprised at the pain this deception brought. Only in denial, he realised, did he discover just how strong a hold books had taken on his mind. Grief for Machiavelli. The last copy. Entrusted to him. Gone forever, like the man who created it, like the man who loaned him the copy. And he had not gained the chance to read but one precious page. Stay focused, he told himself. This is not the time to grieve.

"Entrapment, Marla. Bribes. A book has bought us much information over the years. I am sure Morlock will appreciate the irony."

Marla looked taken aback. She had been so sure of her kill. Now the mention of their master's name and the appearance of official sanction took away the last heat of certainty.

"By the book did we kill the book," she said with a giggle. "I like that!"

"I thought you might."

"So come with me into the *Gestalt*. Live their end with me."

He sighed. "No, Marla. I must go; I still have duties to attend."

He watched the disappointment spread across her drained features. Let her rot in the *Gestalt*. Marla was yesterday, he realised. Everything that gave them purpose together was fast becoming ash. Now he had a new purpose. He closed the door on Marla Caine, without even a goodbye. But then she wasn't really Marla any more. Without Caxton, she wasn't really much of anything.

GOLDEN light bathed the library in a false dawn. A high-pitched shriek brought a contagion of panic. Adam leapt from mind-numbing boredom to heart-wrenching terror in the time it took for the two books to slip from his nerveless fingers and thump against the floor. The fire was faster still.

Already, it had taken hold in the shelves on the far side. The glow was rising, as the flames raced to eat the old wood and paper. People flooded from the maze, some of them already ablaze. In their pain and panic they ignited others trapped in the fearsome scrum.

Smoke belched thick from the heart of the blaze, slowly veiling the scene in a phantasm haze. Columns of noxious smog ascended to the roof and began to crawl to the peripheral edges of the cavern. Like living things, these wriggling feelers descended to embrace the figures running frantic and choke any avenue of escape.

The heat was rising, until it felt like the sweat was boiling from his body. With the heat and the smoke came a sickening stench. Adam coughed as it was sucked into his lungs. The hideous vapours of burnt skin, scorched hair and incinerating paper.

The workers ran like shoals of frightened fish, swerving one direction, then another as fires erupted in the labyrinths of literature. Some of them clutched books in their arms and ran to save just one last bundle. Many of them vanished in coronas of fire lancing from amidst the shelves.

Ash started to rain down. Flakes of carbonised paper fluttered through the air. Thick swarms of dark butterflies. Orange glow-worms, the parasites ate them raw and whole.

And then he saw them. The *Hazamat*. Dark figures, moving with sinister calm amidst the panic. Worse than Otto Schencke or Marla Caine. At least they were human. The *Hazamat* swarmed everywhere, spraying incandescence. An unstoppable force as hungry as the flames they belched.

Adam looked around, bewildered and frightened. He didn't know his way about this place; didn't know the escape routes. For all he knew there was no longer any avenue clear of the flames.

A nearby shelf collapsed in an explosion of sparks and spitting embers. A cloud of stinging fireflies flooded over him. He huddled up against the burning bites. A cry of pain and frustration as smoke added its stinging torment to his eyes. A shadow emerged from the firestorm. Adam flinched against the expected flood of heat.

"Get yerself gone, lad. There's nowt you can do now!"

The old supervisor appeared like a bad prophecy; burned, the whites of his eyes glared out of a blistered and soot-blackened face. His clothes smouldered. The old man swayed on his feet. The side of his head was nothing but a burst blister impregnated with charcoal grit.

The man staggered and stopped himself from falling by reaching to lean on the trolley. Adam moved to give him some added support. The smell of roasted meat and shit made him feel sick.

"Go lad, forget about me. Get yerself out of here while you still can!"

"What about Laura? I can't leave her here!"

Something exploded. The dim crack and pop of bursting timbers. A shrill scream. The old man grimaced even as Adam ducked. The air was getting thicker.

"Can't..." he coughed until sputum dribbled from his mouth. He wiped it clear. "Can't help you lad. She'll be gone too. If she's still alive. Out in the tunnels. Find her there. If you can."

"Show me! I don't know the way!"

"Don't be daft! My time's up. Leave me!"

Every instinct pleaded for self-preservation, but Adam found he couldn't abandon the old man. Some hitherto unknown part of his soul refused. It was a character revelation he knew he'd probably live just long enough to regret. He reached out and put his arm around the old man. Then he struggled to bear his weight towards the collection point.

"Leave me!"

"Just shut up, okay? I don't need this shit!"

They were nearly at the collection point. The way out looked clear. The plastic strips fluttered down at the far end of the avenue of shelves. Books burned on the floor, on the shelves, but not enough to block the way. The rising breeze blustered against his chest as he began to drag the old man towards their escape route. He bowed his head against the wind.

"The fires," the old man gasped. "Sucking in the air. Maybe…"

Two wild-eyed figures crashed, screaming, through the tunnel mouth. Liquid gold burst from the tunnel, melting the plastic barrier, and reaching out to engulf the hapless *Incunabulites*. Both victims screamed, shrill as the fire consumed their headlong flight.

In the wake of the flames, three *Hazamat* appeared. They marched forwards. Demonic figures. Keeping step. They marched over the smouldering cadavers. Others joined them from the labyrinth of burning shelves. Adam backed away, dragging the old man.

"Where now? How do we get out? Just give me some fucking clue!"

"Get yerself gone. Find your lass!"

The old man elbowed him hard in the belly. Adam grunted and let go as he fell backwards. He tried to steady his balance but a foot slipped on a fallen book and he collapsed to the floor. The old man raced back to the trolley and grabbed it; Adam gaped aghast as the cruelly injured man found a final second wind. The wheel never squeaked once as he turned it round and sped towards the advancing *Hazamat*. Obviously, he had the knack.

"Come on my lads – we'll not go out on our arse!"

The *Hazamat* turned to face his charge.

The guttural roar was visceral and terrifying. A roasting stream washed over the trolley and the old man. The metal glowed, sullen in its nimbus of fire. The books exploded into a freewheeling comet. The old man was a shrivelled core glowing red. He collapsed to a burning heap.

Adam crawled backwards even as he clambered to his feet, hastily trying to get away from the reach of that terrible fire. The trolley's momentum crashed it into the first *Hazamat*. The creature stumbled under the weight of burning books and slipped to the floor. The others dispersed clear. A moment, that was all, one precious moment for Adam to scurry clear of their hungry nozzles.

Sacrifice was futile. It wasn't going to be long before he joined the old man. The fires were all around him now. From somewhere on the edge of his vision a stream of fire blasted yet another pile of paper into a cascading flurry of burning sparks.

Stragglers from the *Incunabula* still huddled in panic, or tried to find their way clear of the inferno. Bodies littered the central space. Some burning, others just shrivelled husks of overdone meat still smoking where they fell.

It was only a matter of time before he found his own cremation.

Somehow he crawled towards the stacked tables and crouched beside for some precious cover. There he looked around at the library. What was left of the library. The smoke was beginning to strangle him from inside, despite the fresh air blasting in from the tunnels. The cavern was roofed now by thick smoke. Some of it bubbled and gushed upwards through cracks in the ceiling. The heat was becoming too much; the air was too hot, he felt giddy.

There was no way out. He was alone. The *Hazamat* ran amok, exultant in this conflagration. They were coming closer. Soon, they'd see him.

All his dreams, all his illusion of great adventure and sacred purpose were ash. The *Incunabula* was gone. Gone like Caxton. Gone like any meaning he might have found. Just ash dancing on the edge of the firestorm. Soon, he'd be ash too. In *Terapolis*, what else was there at the end? The tears stinging his eyes had nothing to do with the smoke now. Just despair. That's all that was left.

Then somebody grabbed him by the scruff of the neck and he was pulled screaming towards the heart of the inferno.

LAURA backed away from the door as if it was going to explode and smother her in hungry fire. Screams bled through the old wood and brought with them the rising stink of singed hair, cooked meat, and burnt paper.

A chair scraped and clattered on the floor. Laura turned at the sound and saw Maus rummaging in a bag on the counter. When he turned, he had a gun in one hand. He cocked it, ready for action.

"We're out of time," he snarled. "Come on, let's go!"

Dorian stared at the door, trembling, his face bleached with fear and sweat. Maggie went over and shook the man as if trying to rouse him from sleep. "Come on, dear, we can't stay here."

The old man emerged from of his catatonic stupor. "The *Hazamen*... they're going to kill us all! I don't want to die!"

"Snap out of it!" Maus pushed him towards the back of the room. "Maggie, take him out the back way. We'll go deep and lose 'em in the tunnels. Just like we practised. Go on, Dorian, or I'll sodding well kill you myself!"

Maggie gave her an imploring stare, but Laura felt the moment slipping away into some kind of dream-state, like she was watching it all from afar. Adam was out there; she needed to find him. That's all she knew. She drifted towards the door.

"Laura? LAURA!"

Someone grabbed her shoulder and pulled her back to the present. Blue eyes stared intense. "Not that way," Maus said. "Into the tunnels. You know the drill."

"Adam's out there! I can't leave him!"

"He's a big boy now. He can take care of himself."

"NO! He can't. I promised Cax..."

She turned and ran for the door. The handle felt hot in her hand. The screams vibrated within the metal. The smell was stronger. So was Maus. He pulled her back roughly.

"Leave it, Laura! I mean it. We have to go!"

"Not without Adam! We can't leave him!"

Maus was too strong. She couldn't break his grip, but she couldn't give up. Aside from the manuscript, her promise to Caxton was all she had left.

"Shit to this!" Maus barked. Then he flung Laura towards Maggie and turned towards the door. Laura felt her anger burn as hot as the *Hazamat*, but before she caught her balance Maus had wrenched open the door. The heat flooded in and the large man was suddenly framed in the inferno beyond.

"Don't worry – I'll save your boyfriend!"

Before the protest formed, Maus stepped out into the furnace and closed the door. Maggie grabbed her arm and gently pulled her away.

"It should be me. I promised –"

"I know, dear. He'll be all right. They both will. Come on. We *have* to go."

"COME on you damn *fuckwit* – this is no place to daydream!"

The stranger's pull was irresistible. Adam struggled to keep his balance and match the man's pace. Books slid across the floor as his trailing feet kicked them. The man was unrelenting.

"Who are you?"

"A fucking lunatic, obviously!" Hard eyes blazed defiance back at the fires and the insect-figures running through the library. "Name's Maus," the man added, "but I don't squeak – I ROAR!"

The last words bellowed, a fearful sound that was bound to draw attention. The man was fucking crazy, but there was no one else to trust in this mad place.

"Where are we going?"

"Out of here. Unless you fancy hanging around?"

"Wait! I've got to find Laura," he pulled against the grip, but he couldn't shake free. "I can't go without Laura."

The man swore and pulled him round. Adam found himself staring into the hard face, his nose filled with the smell of smoke and sweat. "She's on her way out of here. We find her at Caxton's place. *If* we're lucky."

He began to move again, dragging Adam. His face streamed with tears and sweat. The shelves ahead were partially alight. Books were huddled in pathetic heaps, charring or bursting into flames. People ran around them, mouths open in one sonorous collective scream. Amongst them, the pyre men were running, burning, alien figures.

Something caught his foot and he almost went down. The man's grip tightened and pulled him up. Beneath him a charred body. The caramelised mouth grinned goodbye.

Smoke stung his eyes. He managed to pull free of the man and keep pace without being baggage. His hair was streaked with feathery ash. The air was full of black butterflies fluttering insane. Fragments of dead books, dancing on the thermals.

"Where are we?"

"Close to the north end. Near some tunnels. Our way out. I hope."

"You hope!"

"Things are a little out of hand right now, in case you hadn't noticed. Come on."

Maus hurried over to the shelves and vanished into the aisles. Adam followed reluctantly, squeezing passed the tongues of flame as if he was pushing his body through a narrow opening. The man was crouched half-way along the shelves, at a point where the flames had yet to take full hold.

His piercing eyes gazed at the chaos beyond. Adam rushed to join him and squatted at his side.

"What if the tunnels are no good?"

The man turned and stared. Then he grinned. "Then we'll just have to stick around for the barbecue."

Maus picked up a sack and quickly examined it. Then he took a few books and stuffed them inside. "Take this. And don't drop it!"

"What?"

"Come on, whatever we save we save. Are you one of us – or one of them?"

He nodded beyond the shelves. A pyre man in the distance, a stream of fire engulfing some hapless book lover. Adam felt sick at the sight of such a death. Any death for that matter. This was worse than Caxton. The feeling of helplessness. The stench of murder. He knew there was no choice; hesitant, he took the sack and tried to sling it over his shoulder. It thumped into the shelf and toppled some burning books.

"Good. I need my hands free." He raised a gun. Adam stared, and swallowed his terror. "Now, follow me and stay close."

He crawled along between the shelves, shying back from the burning sections. Adam crawled along behind as best he could, dragging the sack of books. It was heavy. A burden, but he didn't dare let it go. This was his ticket to safety.

Heat rose to a stinging crescendo, but Maus was relentless. Adam forced himself to go on, pushing himself away from the flames. The sack started to singe. He patted the smoking part and felt the heat as a scream of pain.

Further through the maze of aisles. Crawling, shuffling, dragging the bag, shutting out as best he could the death cries of the library. A body was slumped over a shelf, caught in flames, shrivelled face locked in a terrible grimace. Adam stared at it, trapped by morbid curiosity. Tears of burning fat dripped heavy onto a pile of books from the bubbling eyes. Adam scurried past.

Maus was waiting for him at the end of the aisle. Breathing heavy, face streaked with ash. The long pony tail was abraded and frazzled down. Self-conscious, he ran his hand over his own head and felt the singed hair crunch.

"No need for a hair cut, now," Maus said, but he didn't grin. "Come on. We're nearly there."

He moved on, rising up and hurrying forward. Adam felt relieved to be on his two feet again, even if they did keep low and the weight of the sack pulled at his aching back. They emerged into an open space. Adam saw with relief the dark orifice of the tunnel; dim electric lights vanished into the distance through the gap in the old canvass drapes. A breeze breathed out from the tunnel mouth, cold and refreshing after the heat of the aisles.

"Let's go."

Maus scurried forward. Adam took hold of the sack and followed. Something moved. "Look out!"

Maus ducked and rolled, but the stream of fire caught his leg. Maus screamed, his eyes squeezed shut in agony. The pyre man rushed forward, eager to finish him off. Caught on the wrong side, Adam felt his knees begin to buckle.

"Move!" Maus bellowed.

He came up. The gun barked. Bullets bounced harmless from the pyre man's carapace, but they knocked the alien figure off its feet. Adam seized the moment and took his chance. He rushed forward and round Maus. At the verge of the tunnel he turned and watched, helpless on the sidelines. *The story of his life.*

Maus crawled towards the downed pyre man and leapt astride the struggling figure. He punched like a madman, screaming and bellowing his rage, as he bestrode his armoured victim. With his good knee he held the flamethrower down, while one hand reached out to pin the creature's other arm. He aimed his weapon at the visor and fired. A dangerous stream of bullets bounced from the carapace, but the grim-faced Maus didn't seem to care; he glared at Adam: "Get out you idiot!"

The alien head jerked under the impact of the shots. Finally, the visor cracked. A bullet found flesh. Blood spurted from the broken visor. The pyre man twitched impotent as death stifled his fire.

Just then, another figure emerged from the aisle and raised its flamethrower. Adam opened his mouth to scream a warning. Too late. The fire engulfed Maus and he fell, a burning carcass across his prey. Out of the dying plume of golden vapour, the pyre man stalked forth.

Adam turned and fled down the tunnel. Running hard, the sack slipped from his grasp and fell. There was no time to retrieve it. Behind him, the world flared gold.

BEHIND the café there was a maze of backrooms and old corridors. Already, she was lost. This was a part of the labyrinth she'd never explored and she was now totally reliant on Maggie and Dorian.

If only the man wasn't such a wreck of terror. Maggie's patience and understanding was incredible. Dorian might lead, but it was Maggie who kept him going.

Laura didn't like her own dependence on the two of them. A rare feeling that did little for her mood of fear and apprehension. Always independent, always in charge, her life was no longer her own and she knew it. But they were the *Incunabula*. They only had each other. They had to stick together; something she was prepared to die by as much as live by. So long as it wasn't this night.

Maggie and Dorian paused up ahead. They'd reached a dusty junction of corridors, piled with the typical detritus of the *Incunabula*. Boxes of old electronic junk scavenged and cannibalised as spare parts. Books stacked on trolleys, trestle tables stored tools and various paraphernalia of some sort associated with the upkeep of books.

"It's this way," Dorian said. "I think."

"You *think?*" She couldn't stop herself. Too much time spent dealing with Adam. The words were out before she even considered them. The man recoiled as if about to be struck. He was terrified enough, and he didn't need this extra pressure. Laura cursed her own exasperated terror. She just wanted to get out. For herself, for the last piece of Caxton she carried, and now Dorian was dithering.

"Yes. Yes, it is this way."

"You're doing fine, Dorian. We'll get out of here. You'll see."

He swallowed, and nodded his head. Then he turned around and led the way with hesitant steps. Laura followed, her impatience and terror silently urging Dorian to hurry.

The screams came from everywhere and nowhere. Laura shuddered at the distorted sounds of the library's death. The smell, faint but unmistakable, made her sick. Burning. Wood. Paper. Flesh. The corridors made both noise and smell deceptive; they might be moving further away from the conflagration. They might be heading back into the heart of it for all she knew.

And Adam was out there somewhere, caught in the midst. She didn't dare contemplate what might be happening. She had to trust in Maus – just as she now put her life in the hands of Maggie and Dorian.

They kept going. Eventually the corridors and passages, and flights of dusty stairs, gave way to tunnels. Dark, rubble-strewn tunnels. They kept going, frightened now of what hid beyond their torchlight. There was no noise, but there was still the lingering odour.

"How much further?"

Dorian turned to face her in the torchlight. His face looked like a startled rabbit. "Nearly there. The next junction and we're at the main tunnel that leads to the surface."

"Then what are we waiting for," Maggie said. "Let's go."

The air felt cooler, fresher. There was even a slight breeze. Laura wrinkled her nose at the sensation. Caught a hint of the city's musty, mouldy odour. Free air. The city. Lose themselves in its vastness, until they might find the scattered remnants and establish a new library. Dare she even hope that it was still possible? Yes, she dared. To do otherwise was to despair and lose.

"There it is ahead!" Dorian grinned, eager and relieved. He rushed ahead, half turned to look back. "We're safe. I told you!"

A molten roar. Golden yellow light. Dorian's scream was washed away in the roar of dragon's breath. Through the coloured spots affecting her sight, she saw Dorian writhe and dance within a cloak of fire. Then he stumbled into a burning heap.

A pyre man stepped from one of the tunnels, dark carapace revealed like a living shadow by the light of Dorian's death. He stood between them and the way out. Advancing. Another emerged from the shadows like a nightmare coalesced from its very essence.

Laura backed away. She felt the manuscript chafe her from the sanctity of her pocket. There was no way out. The pyre men advanced. Maggie backed away ahead, stumbling on some unseen rubble. The pyre man raised his flamethrower.

"Laura! Run! Run!"

"Maggie!"

The sight was surreal. Terrifying. The older woman reared up with a broken length of pipe. She screamed at the pyre men, lunged at them. The metal shattered into fragments; the lead pyre men shook his head as though momentarily dazed. Laura staggered backwards.

"Maggie! Don't—"

The tunnel was bathed in a fresh burst of false sunlight. Maggie was at the centre of her own personal firestorm. Her hair shrivelled to nothing. Clothes vaporised. Skin bubbled and charred. Eyes burst and boiled. She turned. The ruined face peered out from the mantle of flame. The charred lips opened wide. A plume of plasma shot out.

"*Goooooooo!*"

She crumpled like Dorian.

Laura turned to seek sanctuary in the shadows, expecting any moment the hot breath of the *Hazamat*. But all she found was the hot breath bursting in her lungs until she could run no more.

The Ninth Folio

In The Cradle Of Gilgamesh

SHE was the first woman to walk the Earth. Created at the command of Zeus by Hephaestus, the ancient Greek God of craftsmanship. From water and earth he moulded her. Mud, in less poetic terms. Aphrodite gave her beauty, Apollo gifted her music, Hermes added persuasion to the mix. Granting her curiosity was probably a mistake; then again Gods always were a capricious breed.

They called her 'All-Gifted' and she was the bane of humanity, for she cracked open the vault that imprisoned all the ills of the world.

Her name was Pandora.

And, of course, Laura thought, she was a woman. When it came to apportioning blame for the sorry state of the world, the culprit was always female in myth and story. Men side-stepping responsibility, as usual, for the mess they made of reality.

In the memory, they were sitting one night at Caxton's place. Talking in better days. At least Caxton was talking.

She just listened, and sipped coffee and tried not to choke on the thick atmosphere of burned plant residue.

Caxton was telling her about Pandora's Box. How it was opened and all those ills of the world poured out to plague humanity forever.

All except hope.

That was still in the box.

"So there's always hope, Laura," he added. Then he took a drag on his awful roll up, sat back with a smouldering sigh and then released the smog from his lungs.

Laura frowned at the memory, as she had frowned at the story.

"That can't be right. If the ills of the world came into being only after they escaped the box, then hope is still imprisoned. If there's going to be any hope then surely the box has to be opened again?"

Caxton choked on a drag. The only time she ever saw him cough on his infernal smoke.

"Laura," he said mid-wheeze, "it's a *story*. An *allegory*. There's always hope, okay? Trust me."

He had to be right. He was Caxton. But he was dead. The library was burned. She was lost in these tunnels. And Adam was out there somewhere. Alone. Or worse. So much for Pandora's Box and its lost contents.

She stumbled onwards.

No. There had to be hope. Otherwise, what was the point?

The rolled up manuscript chafed her, as though chiding her not to give up.

"Let the box be open," she told the darkness, "let the hope guide me home."

To Caxton's place. Sit there and wait. Wait for Adam to find his way home too.

Hope. It's all they'd ever had. The *Incunabula's* foundation stone. It was Pandora's Box, and Morlock's minions had burned it open. Hope free at last to take on the ills of the world.

Around the corner she realised her first prayer was answered. The air was fresher. Cooler. There was light. Cold and white and bright after the darkness of the tunnels, it was nothing like the bio-luminescence of the city.

"Curiouser and curiouser," she muttered. "Now all I need is the white rabbit."

She stumbled forward, and then staggered on all fours up a flight of crumbling concrete stairs. Near the top she felt the fresh breeze caress her face. She climbed the last steps and staggered over the threshold into the outside world. Laura stepped out into the unaccustomed night, and saw for the first time the nature of the infinite.

The sight was terrifying. It was beautiful. It was *impossible*.

THE ghost of Adam moved through the ruins of the dead city. That's what Laura said this place was: an old city. The tunnels and basements, and even remnants of ruined buildings that had once enjoyed the light of day, were now nothing but a catacomb to house the dead. And this one ghost that went in search of resurrection.

There was no need to rattle any chains. Plenty of metal clanked and clattered as he crawled through the darkness. Stone clattered and his own breath blasted into space as grunts and cries when anything bumped, grazed or poked his tender flesh. Not such a ghost then, but he felt like one in this impenetrable blind alley.

Fingers made a poor substitute for eyes, but they were all that was left to find his way through the maze. A slow crawl, feeling his way forward. Listening too. Sometimes, he even sniffed the air to gain some idea of what might lie ahead. For all he knew, he was taking the long route back to the library.

Hardly a comforting thought, but he'd surely hear and smell his destination before he reached the furnace. He doubted he'd smell or hear a Pyre Man in time to avoid a shroud of fire.

He'd die if he didn't find a way out. The thought was colder than the darkness. Death by starvation. Or maybe a thousand cuts from the unseen wreckage that hindered his passage. Yes, Maus had died easy. Easier than Caxton, at least. Easier than this lingering death. That was the truth. A callous thought, maybe, but not as callous as this place. The dark and the cold were hardening him, but probably not enough to help him resist the growing despair.

If this was a book, and he was the reader, then this was the kind of place where he'd skip the pages, leap-frog to the beginning of the next scene and cut to the action. Yes, if only it was a book, he could let the character suffer alone, while he waited for him at the fun bit. So what if that made him a lazy reader, so what if it meant he might miss some crucial point, like the light glowing up ahead.

He blinked. *Shit*. There *was* some light ahead. The darkness was no longer the perfect blindfold; he was aware of shapes and textures and contours. The utter black was growing depth and some perspective to become shadow. It must mean something. If not a way out, then at least the beginnings of one.

He hardly dared to hope as he shuffled forward at a faster pace. The difference overcame the fatigue in his muscles; postponing the inevitable moment of surrender. These subterranean passages didn't go on forever.

Yes, something was glowing up ahead. He saw a patch of wall. Drab and colourless, maybe, but it was washed in a tantalising sheen of light. It turned out to be a door. Almost too good to be true. Little more than a sheet of flanged steel, but it was the best offer he'd had all day. The light was emanating from somewhere behind, escaping from the crack in the imperfect frame. He reached out and felt along the metal where the light emerged. There was a small gap but wide enough for his fingers.

The metal whined when he pulled against the door. He met the hollow sound with his own wry noise of effort. The door moved a few centimetres, then jammed. This was too much. He rested his head against the flaking metal and tried to beat down the frustration. Keep calm. Think. He peered at the base and saw the rubble blocking its lower edge. It didn't take long to pull it clear and then kick away the last debris with his foot. Then another effort.

The door shifted. He laughed out loud.

Again. He strained with all his strength and felt the door shudder open in fits and starts. The hinges groaned and shrieked in protest. Dust pattered down from the unseen ceiling. Something moved beyond the door. A shuffling and a clank of metal. A rat, he hoped.

Despite the wider gap, the light increased little. He understood why as he squeezed through the gap. There wasn't much on the other side. Rust and damp, the stench of oil from neglected equipment. Some kind of disused machine room. Old hulks squatted in the dim light. Across the room, another door slightly ajar. Light filtered through the gap and a grimed window set in the door.

The second door moved stiffly, but it was easier than the first. Dazzling light overwhelmed his eyes. It took some time for them to acclimatise enough to venture into the unknown on the other side, but when he did, he felt like an explorer making landfall after months at sea.

On the other side he found a well-lit corridor, the sub-levels of *Terapolis*. It could be nothing else. At last, he was getting somewhere. All he needed to do was find a stairwell, better still a lift, and he was free. For the first time in his life, he looked forward to diving into the maelstrom of *Terapolis*. The ghost went looking for resurrection.

AN alien sky watched from behind a few fragile fronds of luminous cloud. A bulging immature moon bathed the world in light so that the stars might see her better.

Laura stared back, breathless and incredulous; she had no idea where she was, or how she could have arrived at a place far beyond the towers of *Terapolis*, but the sky – those stars – were proof of a hope beyond the dark city.

The swathing river of dappled light sparkled in the heavens; she recognised it from old photographs – the Milky Way – and was awestruck at the possibilities. Perhaps there was intelligence out there, sharing in the wonder of the heavens, free of morbid woes. She felt her sense of wonder crumble; for all she knew, they might be subjected to the whims of their own Morlock, their own *Gestalt*, their own

Pyre Men. Strangers on strange lands, suffering as their own lights were snuffed by a sinister desire.

Perhaps humans were all alone out here. Subjected to the dominion of the *Gestalt* and the torches of the *Hazamat*. And when they were gone...

There's only us, the thought whispered in her mind, like a breath carried on the light breeze. *Only us, perhaps only ever us.*

The whisper ceased to be a thought and became words. Laura sat up and looked around, wondering where it came from.

"But the seeds are caught in the nets of the *Gestalt*, denied the chance of fertile soils..."

"Who's there?" Her voice trembled, warbling with doubt. Maybe she was going soft in the head. Like Adam.

His name stirred a bubble of guilt. He was still out there. Alone in the shadows. She'd failed. Failed Adam. Failed Caxton. So much for her promise to keep an eye on him.

"I'll find him," she told the heavens. They twinkled indifferent. "I'll bring him to see the stars."

The manuscript chafed and crumpled against her armpit. She reached inside and repositioned it. More secure. More comfortable. It was starting to feel like a living thing, goading her on. A silly thought, but she was tired, and her mind was wandering.

When she stood, she finally saw the stars on the ground. Lively ghosts of gold that for a moment reminded her of recent terrors.

The *Hazamat*.

She dropped to the ground again and crawled to the verge of the hill. Cautiously, she peered over to watch the flickering ghosts of fire. They were immobile. Small beacons, not rampaging monsters. Even so, she felt her heart thud against the sandy soil and half desiccated vegetation that carpeted the hillock.

After a while she began to perceive the structures lurking in the dancing light. They were amorphous in shape, but stood as symbols of human design. Their structure shifted in the breeze, and she realised they were tents. Figures moved between them, others huddled around them, centred on the small pyres of flame.

Human sounds emerged from the breeze now. Snatches of voices. Laughter. The cries of children. The bleats and snorts of animals she'd never known. A homely scene, far from the pyres of the *Hazamat* or the stygian murk of *Terapolis*.

Laura felt a deep well of loneliness open in the pit of her belly as the scene forced memories of safer, calmer days with the *Incunabula*. Then she was crawling forward, climbing to her feet as she moved closer to the camp fires.

They danced in a welcoming motion, seemingly to beckon the weary traveller to the delights of warmth and rest. Almost spellbound, she walked down the hill. She smelled the wood smoke and tempting flavours of cooking food. Her belly growled in anticipation, to remind her it had been some time since she last ate.

She wandered past flapping tents, some with glowing hearth fires outside. Huddled shapes hunched around them, moving in conversation, or staring in contemplation at the fires.

A voice raised itself against the background murmur. Strong and deep and resonant. She turned to the direction of the voice and saw the huge fire on the edge of the camp.

Blazing bright and strong, it was surrounded by huddled figures. She allowed the voice to guide her in among the growing crowd. Like the rest, she responded to the voice as if it was a call to prayer.

Laura took a seat on a rough block of stone. Around her, were men adorned with shaggy beards, or with shaven heads and strange garments, their eyes painted dark. Women in bright fabrics, draped and robed. Golden jewellery glinting in firelight. They ignored her, this alien in their midst, their attention rapt on the fire and the source of the voice. And then they gasped as the speaker strode into view from the far side of the fire. A tall figure, robed in bright colours, face masked in silhouette. She realised this was some kind of performance.

Beneath the performer's baritone rumble, she heard a metallic music faint and distant. A rat-a-tap-tap. Rising and falling to the voice, undulating, now fast, then measured slow. A melody all of its own, tempo in synchronicity with the speaker; it was strangely reminiscent of Caxton's old typewriter.

The rat-tapping metallic composition was louder now, as the strident man circled the flames. It compelled and gripped her senses with a compulsion born of the man's words. She let herself drift on the waves of sound.

"Remember. You are the torch bearer – not to burn the page but to illuminate it."

The voice came as a surprise. Heard from no place in particular, but *felt* from the rear and to the left, as though someone had leaned over to speak in her ear.

"What?" Startled, she looked round.

The man beside her turned his head and gave a sharp shush. Suddenly she was reminded of the library and the stern gaze of a duty librarian. Then the man turned back to the story teller. Puzzled, she did the same.

After that, she forgot about it as the story teller shouted loud. He raised his arms in a bold flourish, raising a ram's head staff to the star-filled sky as though invoking some terrible old god to come down to Earth. The background babble of voices hushed and Laura felt herself become absorbed into the story.

ADAM felt his heart bounce when a sudden loud boom – hollow and metallic – sounded in the distance. Once it faded into the labyrinth, he thought he heard a low murmur of voices.

"Who's there?"

He stopped and listened, but there was no repeat of either the metal thunder, or the voices. The direction was unclear, but he thought it had come from somewhere beyond the next corner, rather than the passageways behind him.

"Hello! Hello?"

He began to walk faster. The squeak of his trainers on the polished floor measured his pace and conspired with the light's reflected shimmer to make him giddy. The sounds must mean a way out. After so many false leads, and dead ends, *let* there be a way out. He reached the junction and stopped, breath bursting from his exerted lungs, blood rushing in his ears like a whispering chorus.

There was nothing but another lengthy corridor. So long, the far end was lost in gloom. The only difference from the rest of the maze was the long series of steel-grey doors on either side.

He leaned forward and rested his hands on his knees, sucking in air until his breathing was something like normal. He stared ahead and wondered where he was.

He was too tired to care what lay beyond the maze now; the *derm-rat* just wanted to go home. Find his way back to familiar ground, then make his way to Caxton's place. Somewhere safe, if there was such a thing. A safe house where he could wait for Laura and figure out what to do next. Eat maybe, sleep definitely. Now that was something to look forward to.

He began to pace forward, one weary foot in front of another. The first door was a tantalising prospect for escape. Cynicism had its doubts, but he had to try. He pulled on the handle. Locked. Of course.

With a sigh, he studied the door. Thick steel, flanged against the wall. There was a peephole at head level. There was nothing to be seen when he peered through it. With a sigh he turned away and wandered down the corridor, trying each successive door. They were all locked.

Something sniggered.

Again he stopped and listened.

"Hello? Help! I'm lost."

That snigger again. From behind. He turned, but there was nothing. He backtracked to the last door, paused to try and listen through the metal. Nothing. He banged against the door. It rumbled hollow, but nothing was stirred to respond.

The snigger chuckled again. From somewhere above his head. A whisper of a breeze caressed his face and made him shiver. The blood rushed through his ears again, but this time it struggled to overcome the sound of voices whispering in the distance.

"Join… us…"

"Oh! Shit!"

He began to run down the corridor. The voices followed.

"Be one with us! It's not too late!"

The sweat stinging his eyes was nothing to do with his long exertion. The tears blurred the corridor further. A shimmering, dancing deluge of confusing light and drab colour added to the unease of the voices.

"Join us – OR HELP US DAMN YOU!"

No whisper. It was a bellow. He couldn't tell from where, but now he doubted it held any clue to his escape. He ran faster. The snigger kept his pace. He smelled a scent of burning paper and hair.

> *Twinkle. Crinkle. Little book.*
> *Burning bright*
> *In Pyre Man's flame.*
> *Charcoal dust*
> *And fragile ash*
> *All that's left*
> *Of printed page.*
> *No more pain, now*
> *Little tome*
> *Only MorTek's perfect gain…*

The voice sounded like a harsh caricature of Marla Caine. Like the taunting ghosts, he didn't know where the words originated. From all around, it seemed. The chilling snigger sounded as if its mouth was right behind him.

"Leave me alone!"

The unseen torment laughed aloud. *"Join with us! Be complete!"*

"Help us! Uncle Boris! Where are you! Please…"

He squeezed his eyes shut. He had to be losing it. Here, of all places. He hoped he was losing it. Madness was maybe better than this as reality. He shivered to think that his old visions of the laughing damned might be alive and well and lurking behind these doors. Were they all locked? He suddenly didn't want to find out.

He wanted to shout for Laura, voice a beacon to bring her to him and save him from this madness. But she'd abandoned him in the library. Left him to his fate, discarded him like a hapless book to be burned.

"Bitch!"

The unseen presence laughed. He stumbled onwards, no choice but to try and ignore it. They couldn't stop him finding his way out. And then there it was at the end of the corridor. A plain door. Not steel like the others. This was just plain old wood, with a sheet of safety glass that gleamed with the subtle hint of day glow. He felt the elation surge; this was his way to the world. Let the voices laugh this one off.

He reached for the handle, grinned relief as it turned beneath his hand. A quiet 'snik' as it began to swing inwards.

Adam stepped over the threshold.

There was no way out of the maze.

There was only Marla Caine.

She looked up and smiled.

IN the beginning there was Darkness and then, from the depths of this primordial shade, there came a whisper.

A voice.

A word.

"I."

Another word followed. "Am."

"I Am."

It was an Awakening.

With that simple utterance, the Light of Awareness exploded into Being. A fire of magnificence cast aside the shade of eternal night and perceived the Universe in all its wonder.

Light became partitioned from Dark. Twilight was the eternal barrier at which they fought. No longer were the stars just sparks in an empty sky; they were an infinitesimal wonder for a newborn Mind to ponder in awe.

And as the Words multiplied, so the stargazers shed their fur and shunned their ape-like forebears to become Man.

So Man was born and He walked naked under the sun and starlight. His journey began; He named everything under Heaven and Earth. So He multiplied the Words, and what began as a spark, became a mighty conflagration of thought and light.

Yet the first utterances of "I Am" brought forth something else.

In the depths of the shade, brought into reluctant existence was the opposite of Mind. Aware in its sluggish way, it was both attracted and repelled by the light of its brother.

He sensed this, Man, as He began his journey of the Word.

And so He huddled around the firelight, comforted by the warmth and the light, and the safety from that which He sensed lurking in the Shade.

In time He gave It a name.

Many names, this Anti-Mind was granted, as It grew in pace with Mind; devils and demons, its naming was Legion in the sundering tongues of Man. Some few even named It a God, in their folly, and worshipped the invocation of Its dark longing to be as one with us, in a silent eternal night.

And so Man wove this living Shadow into the stories told around their oases of firelight, the better to hold It at bay. These sagas and ballads, like the fire, held back the shadows of ignorance and amnesia, but for long generations the words that made their stories and thoughts were but sparks on the breeze.

Short lives, fickle memories. Whispering laments from vanished generations, haunting legacies to the young who walked in their footsteps, these ephemeral utterances were fragile defences. The light led them, the light warmed them, but the blaze they invoked lacked the power to do more than hold the shadows at arm's length.

And so the Darkness entered into uneasy Truce with Light, for as long as the words were left to fade into the shadows of yesterday, the Dark held Light enclosed.

And then.

There came the Word once more.

No longer was it carried on the breeze of time and memory, like seeds scattered to the winds of chance and fate. For now, Man could bequeath not a haunting lament from one generation to the next, half-forgotten, but a booming voice as fresh as if from a living mouth.

Ephemeral thought was inscribed on clay and stone. As hard as the bones of the Earth. As long lasting. The living at last congregated in the auditorium of the Dead, to continue their debates, to stoke the fires of learning and passion and experience.

Stories no longer danced like wraiths on the breeze. They were rendered flesh to live on among us.

Words and Thoughts, sown and harvested, were stocked against future famine. They became a beacon to vanquish the encircling shade, to break out and engage Darkness in battle.

Until the Dark no longer encircled the Light, but the reverse. Mind grew strong and bold, unto a searchlight to penetrate the veils of shade and force it to retreat ever further into the deeps of mystery.

Man learned, and recorded, and stored His Light, until little of the Shadow's domain remained cloaked.

Until, alas, there came the terrible time, when Man forgot the fears of his forefathers. As His light expanded, both physical and metaphysical, He became ever more fascinated with the secrets of the shade. He wandered off the path of light, groped in the half-light, and found new pleasures, new fascinations for His curious Mind.

And the Darkness gathered.

Anticipating.

Man forgot the dangers of the Night.

The Light of Mind dimmed, and the Darkness seized its moment. The Night descended to cloak the world of Mind.

Save for a few havens of illumination.

This is the story of these light keepers, of those entrapped in the irony that they hide in the shade to preserve the light. This is the tale of Man's folly, and the hope that He might turn back towards the light.

Hear my words, as I guide you through this tale of woe and fear. I have wandered in the valley of the shadow of death and fear and learned its lingering secrets. I tell them now in the hope they might re-ignite the fires of our salvation. My words are the flint, your minds the tinder. Heed me now. Fan the flames. For I am the last storyteller, and our time of Doom is at hand.

For I am Gilgamesh...

I am Dante...

I am Gulliver...

I am Frodo...

I am all of you...

I Am...

FROZEN, despite the heat, Laura watched bewildered, as the storyteller strode through the dispersing audience. The face became clear in the golden light. She looked through the mask of disbelief and wondered whether to laugh or to cry.

"*Cax*... ton!"

Caxton's booming laugh greeted her. "Rumours of my demise have been greatly exaggerated," he said. Then the light of joy faded to sorrow, "but not the hard facts of my death."

"But... you're walking... you're talking..."

"And I can chew gum at the same time."

Laura looked at him aghast and confused. She felt the tears brimming. The hated tears stinging her eyes and threatening her control.

"Sorry," Cax said, "a little Old World humour."

He put his arms out. Laura stumbled forward and let them close around her. The familiar scent of tobacco and smoke filled her nostrils. She held him tight and pressed her face against his robed chest. She sobbed. Cax shushed her as if she was so much younger than she was.

"Welcome to Wonderland, Alice."

"I did that one already."

"I bet you did."

She had to know. "How? Where?"

"It doesn't matter, Laura. Reality is folding in on itself, courtesy of the *Gestalt*. Don't ask me how or why, 'cos I'm not a cosmologist or a quantum physicist, nor am I a priest or a philosopher. I don't really understand it all myself."

"But where are we, how are you –"

"Here?"

He smiled down at her.

"We're stuck. Either we hang around, or get caught up in the fringes of the *Gestalt* and trapped. I decided to wander. I've become quite the bard."

"So, am I… dead?"

Cax's expression turned grave.

"You can tell me. I'm tough enough to take it."

"I'm sure you are."

He reached out suddenly and pressed a finger against the side of her throat. He held it there for a few uncomfortable moments. "Strong pulse, a little rapid, but nope… I'd say the diagnosis is you're very much alive."

"This is no time to joke!"

"Death is far too serious to take it so," he said with a wink.

Despite herself, she couldn't stop the humour from moulding her face into a smile.

"That's better."

"So where are we, anyway?"

"Ah! Not a bad place really, once you've learned to cope without air conditioning and the local take away."

"Cax!"

"Okay, okay." He raised an arm and pointed Eastwards. At least she thought it was East. She followed his direction, but saw nothing but the dark encrusted land and the scintillating star-scape that encased the horizon.

"We're close to one of the places where it kind of all began. About a half a millennium that way, give or take, Sumerian priests are doing something profound."

"What? Something to beat Morlock?"

"I guess you could say that; just a shame we turned away from it for all those techno-phantasms." He raised the flat of his hand and with the other he mimed the scribbling motion of a pen. "They've invented writing. The first and last thing accountants or priests have ever done for the benefit of mankind."

"Writing. Sumeria? Where is that? How did I get here?"

"Ah, your reading is sadly lacking, Laura. You'll have to fix that sometime. Sumeria is both a place and a time and an idea. We're here thanks to a kind of meeting of minds, an exhausted and drifting one in your case; figured I'd keep you occupied while you wander topside. As to the how and why, don't try to figure it out, just think of it as a fond memory: it's enough to be here. Although I don't think the priests share that sentiment."

"Why not?"

He shrugged. "I kind of muscled in on the act."

"You would."

He grinned. "Yeah. I took their precious accounting system and made the first ever recording of the human voice. A wandering storyteller I bumped into. The *Epic of Gilgamesh*. Quite a tale. Literature born from the womb of oral storytelling. I'd like to think Morlock squealed at that one, but I never thought I'd play midwife."

"*Morlock*? He's here?"

"He's everywhere, Laura. Just like the *Gestalt*. He's out there now. Watching. Waiting. 'Course, he's not known by that name here. Not yet. He won't get that name for a long, long while. Not until we act like a bunch of fools and dim the lights enough for him to step out of the shadows. I wish I could do something to stop it; but I can't. I'm dead, and the dead aren't ever supposed to be really here – wherever that might be."

"How can he be out there? The others. Dorian. Maus. They said you were mad. They said you claimed Morlock was some kind of bogeyman."

A chuckle from his silhouette. "Not bad. Wish I'd thought of that one." The lighthearted tone vanished as suddenly as it arrived. "Morlock. The thing out there that will be Morlock. He's the antithesis of Mind. The anti-form of matter. He's the dancing shadow wrestling with the tongues of fire. He's a part of us, and he's not of us."

"Is that a quote?"

"Haven't you read my manuscript? You hassled me long enough."

She almost squirmed in a kind of guilt and wondered why. "I haven't had time."

"No. I suppose not. He hasn't burned everything, Laura. There's still hope. Trust me."

Hot anger dried her tears. It flashed. "They burned the library. They're dead. There's nothing… Adam…"

The name choked her with grief; she let the fresh tears flood away the words.

"You did all you could. He's alive."

Laura wiped her eyes and looked up at Caxton's sombre face.

"Yes, he's alive."

"Where? Where is he? I couldn't…"

"Morlock's after him. He wants him."

"Adam? Why?"

"Why anything with Morlock?"

"That's no answer. What's he want with Adam? Don't be so cryptic. Not with this."

"Okay, Laura. He wants to get at me. I'm dead and he still isn't finished with me."

"Why? Why you, why any of us?"

The light faded from Caxton's eyes. His faced seemed to sag. With a sigh he turned away and stalked towards the star-filled dark.

"Adam's my son."

Laura stared at Caxton's back. She didn't know what to say. Caxton's son? Another maelstrom in her feelings. This was too much; she didn't want to know any more.

"Cax –"

He waved her silent. His brooding shoulders rustling the long robe.

"Marla's his mother."

"What? That…"

"Yes. I... no, you don't need to know that."

"Yes, but you and... *Marla Caine.*"

"She wasn't always like that. She was a wonderful poet. Once. Before... I think... she sensed *him.* Something of what he is, what he wanted. And I was too damn macho and full of it to understand. Or even care... Until it was too late."

He strode a few paces into the darkness and peered out intently. When his voice sounded again it was far away and deathly sad.

"Did you hear my story, Laura, were you listening?"

"Yes."

"He's out there now. In the shadows. He's Morlock. He wants the mind-light extinguished forever. You. Me. Marla. Adam. *Everyone.*"

"He wants to kill us?"

Caxton whirled, a sinister smile on his face, a bitter look in his eyes.

"Nothing so simple. He wants that we never existed: the living *and* the dead. He wants that *he* never existed. He longs for annihilation. That's what the *Gestalt* is all about. It's what our books can prevent – if we can ever dare to channel their light into the heart of *his* domain!"

MARLA sat on a hard wooden chair, her hands clasped on the tabletop. She wore only a thin cotton slip that revealed more feminine allure than he cared for. The hem of the slip had pulled up to reveal long, slender thighs. Adam swallowed, not entirely from fear.

Her eyes were wide and red-rimmed. They gleamed with a life that held no place in his memory. She was too young to be Marla Caine, this woman, far too young, younger even than he was, he guessed, but the resemblance was terrifying.

Her smile wavered. "I'm feeling much better today. Honest. I am."

Marla. Not Marla. He stared dumb.

"You're not one of the orderlies."

She rocked back and forth. The chair creaked. She began to hum tunelessly. Rocking faster. Back and forth. Fingers twining hair, eyes focused far away. Then they snapped away from whatever abyss they contemplated to stare intent at Adam. He flinched, as if she'd reached out and struck him.

"He took my baby. Did you know?"

Adam shook his head. He wanted to turn and leave, but he felt bound to this woman by a curious compulsion, a fascination, a dim sense of horror. He felt a thousand questions rise and fall from the mire of confusion in his brain. Before he might catch even one she spoke again.

"Help me! You can help me, can't you? *He's* coming. I can hear him. Please! I don't want to be *her*..."

"Who's coming? Who are you?"

"*Him!* I hear him. I see him. In my head. He treats me. *Help me!*"

"Who? A doctor? Where is this place?"

"Not a doctor! Him! *HIM!* You're in his place! They call it *Terapolis*. They will call it that some day. Help me! Before he gets here!"

"I don't know how! I don't even know how to help myself any more!"

"Then what good are you?"

The chair grated on the tiles as she launched herself from it. Animal rage twisted her pretty face. In a flash of those staring eyes she was on him: a frenzy of fists and nails and curses. He screamed in pain as nails scraped his skin, struggled to fend off her blows. She was slight in build, but strong. So strong. The power of her rage, of her fear, he didn't know or care. She was a spitting, clawing cat and he was a mouse in the jaws of her fury.

"STOP!" For one crucial instant, the flailing claws of her assault left an opening. His fist slammed into her face; the shock of impact crashed up his arm and detonated in his mind with the full force of shame.

She fell backwards, tottering and stumbling until she backed into the chair. Weeping again, she held her face with one hand. Suddenly passive, she lowered herself into the chair. Blood seeped from her fingers. When she removed her hand he saw the gap in her teeth. He took in a shocked gasp of air.

The woman looked up, eyes frightened. "He's coming. He's coming for *meeeee.*"

He heard nothing, but the woman's fear was contagious. It rose like vomit in his throat. He swallowed and felt a chill sweat break out on his face. He turned to look out of the door. There was nothing to see.

He backed away to the wall furthest from the door and watched the darkness advance.

"Help *meeeee!*" Helpless, he watched her sob into her hands. The darkness drew nearer.

A figure emerged from the depths of the shadow, or else coalesced from the fabric of the darkness. An elderly, pale figure, he was gaunt of face and dressed in an archaic style. He stepped into the room and stopped to rest both hands on top of an ebony cane. He flashed Adam a grandfatherly smile, and then turned to gaze at the woman.

"A family reunion," he said. "How touching."

"What?" He meant to articulate the word; it sounded more like a grunt of terror.

The old man smiled.

"Allow me to make the introductions. Adam, this is Marla as she once was. Marla, this is Adam, your son as he shall be."

"That can't be —"

The old man turned to focus his dark eyes on Adam. He felt his words slip away. "And I am Silas Morlock."

"What? *The —*"

"The Master of *MorTek*. The very same."

Morlock gave a small but elegant bow. Marla, the woman — *his mother if you believed this shit* — stared, vacant, into space, as if she had switched off. He wished he could do the same. This wasn't happening. It couldn't be happening. None of this was real.

"I came to see Marla," Morlock continued. "You are a bonus. It is a pleasure to meet you… in the *flesh*… so to speak."

Somewhere he was lying unconscious in the tunnels. That explained the faint smell of burning paper. This wasn't Morlock. This woman wasn't Marla, or his mother; it was all some strange hallucination.

"This is just a fantasy," he told the phantasm. "None of it's real. Marla Caine's not my mother, and there's no way Morlock would want me. I mean, I'm a nobody."

"The son of Marla Caine is hardly a nobody. A member of the *Incunabula* too. No, Adam. This is real. Why do you doubt it? Do you doubt the *Gestalt?*"

"No. I mean. I'm not Gacked."

"You live in the city of the *Gestalt*. The *Gestalt* is everywhere. Given the right conditions, you can enter it for a time without the paraphernalia I give you. This is quite *real*. I assure you."

"Then why would you want—"

"You?" Another smile. "I think you know."

"*Fuck you!*"

"Hardly literary language, my boy. Consider it. I ask for such a little thing. And in return, I will give you all the rewards you ever dreamed of. I will give you back your mother. You can heal her, Adam. You can undo what your *father* did to her."

"She's not my mother."

"No?"

"No!"

"Ah! The certainties inherent in youth. But how could you know what went on before your birth? The terrible thing your mother had to endure?"

"What... do you mean?"

"You have a scar on your back."

"How did you know about that?"

He smiled and stalked towards Marla. "I know many things."

Morlock stopped beside Marla. She cringed and stared up at him with frightened eyes. Adam felt a strange sense of pity, but stood helpless as Morlock reached out and began to stroke Marla's head. He made shushing noises, as though to soothe a child.

"Don't be afraid, my dear. It's going to all right. Show him."

She grinned, wild eyed and perilous. Adam felt his heart begin to bounce in his chest.

Marla lifted the slip up to her breast. He gulped and stared as he saw the soft expanse of her belly. Smooth flesh rising from the triangle of tantalising hair between her thighs. Any erotic urge died when he saw the ugly red scar on her belly. A healed but still puckered blemish, it spoke of a hideous penetration.

"That is where the blade pierced the very heart of Marla's being," Morlock said softly. He tapped Marla on the shoulder and she covered herself again. "That is where *Caxton* plunged the blade meant to end your existence. It burst Marla's waters. Nicked your shoulder. Brought you forth into the world before your time. Fortunately for you, at a time when you might live beyond the womb."

"But… my parents, they abandoned me, I was brought –"

"Brought up in an institution. Yes. Poor Marla. She thought you dead. It was too much. They kept you from her."

"But… Wait! You said, you mean… Caxton's my *father*? But that doesn't make sense. He couldn't… he wouldn't…"

"I believe he was not himself."

"NO! This is BULLSHIT"

"You owe him nothing. Don't you see? I can give back to you so much that he took. In return for so little."

"No! That's Marla Caine. She *killed* Caxton."

"Do you blame her?"

"Yes. No. I don't know. This isn't right. You made him do it. You must have done it?"

"Must I?" He smiled, a little sadly. "Of course, well, I *am* the villain of the tale."

The wall supported Adam as his legs turned to jelly. He stared at Marla. He couldn't pull his eyes away, but there was no help there. In the tumult of emotion, disbelief was the only certainty he possessed. He clung to it in the face of Marla's vacant, pathetic smile and Morlock's mesmerising voice.

Marla Caine killed Caxton. Marla Caine bore him before his time. Caxton tried to kill him. The old dealer was his *father*. No. Not true. None of it was true. He felt sick with confusion.

"Your mother's not bad, Adam. Can you imagine the pain she suffered? Her unborn son – *you* – was stolen from her belly by the man who put you there. The man she loved and trusted. Is it any wonder she burned for vengeance? I took her into the fold and gave her purpose. I gave her the chance to have a life again, but it would always be empty without you. Not even I was able to find you for her. Ironic, that it was Caxton who found you first, again trying to deny Marla her son. For that one bundle of papers belonging to the man who stole your life too; I can give you your mother and everything he took from you."

"Poor baby," Marla crooned as she stared up at him.

"Poor Marla," Morlock added. "They called her mad. Who wouldn't be after all that? But she wasn't mad. At least not until the psychiatrists got hold of her. If anything, she was but a bearer of the melancholy you call depression. And

Caxton overcame *that*. Until his terrible deed undid all the good he'd given her."

Morlock was stroking her head again. She accepted it now, all trace of fear gone. Adam watched as the fingers began to knead her skull. He gasped as they vanished inside her head, somehow merged with the flesh. Marla's eyes gleamed as she smiled with a mother's misplaced love.

"No, she wasn't mad. She just had a broken Soul."

Marla sighed as if a great pain had vanished when Morlock's hand withdrew from her skull. He raised his hand and held a glowing orb about the size of a tennis ball. Inside, the orb glowed like plasma. Fire danced around a central core of dark matter. Some instinct told him that the orb was dull and sickly. The pulsing wraiths and fronds of darkness were stronger than he felt they should be. Dark mist emerged as the plasma leaked from its surface.

"The formation of the Soul is nothing but a meta-biological function of the sentient brain. It is the secretion of mind that builds up this little pearl around the seed of darkness that is the antithesis of mind. A shield, you might say, against the withering shadow of truth at the heart of every conscious thing. Your mother's pearl is damaged. *Malformed.* It could not fully protect her on its own."

With these words he crushed the pearl. Adam moaned as it shattered like a glass ball. The darkness rushed into Morlock and Marla. The weak glowing substance spattered across the floor and Morlock's hands. A few drops splashed Adam's lips. Automatically, his tongue darted out and recoiled against the acrid taste.

"You see. So sour."

Morlock wiped his hands clean on a handkerchief. Marla stared now with dim eyes. The eyes he recalled from past encounters. All the fear and the turbulence was gone. She appeared calm and at ease.

"You see Marla, I keep my promises. I heal your pain. Forever."

Marla reached up and took hold of Morlock's hand. He took it like a suitor as Marla rose to her feet.

"What have you done to her?"

"Nothing, Adam, but take away her pain and all the torment that troubled her. She will burn for Caxton's end. That will give her purpose. That will make her useful to me. You could give her new purpose. More meaningful than I."

Morlock moved towards the door. Marla followed, but then she paused and gazed at Adam. Her eyes were already filling with a predator's focus. He shivered against the wall, and wished he could burrow inside the brick and concrete.

Marla stepped towards him and raised her hand. He flinched as it brushed against his cheek. A delicate caress. She giggled and leaned forward to kiss his mouth. He was aware of her body close to his. Quick, fleeting warmth, a vampish nip as her teeth closed on his flesh. She giggled.

"Remember my offer, Adam. Think on it. You can always find me at *MorTek Prime*. My door is always open for *you*."

"Be seeing you, Darling," Marla added as the shadows absorbed them both.

The Tenth Folio
The Progression Of Pilgrims

DEATH was prowling. Stalking *him* now. That was hardly anything new. Except he was closer this night than he'd ever been, out there in the haunts of *Terapolis,* setting up his prey.

So, like many a dying man since the invention of the scythe, Otto tried to peer beyond the past life flashing across the mental cinema screen. There was no salvation in this recollection, only the gauze shroud of damnation.

Dying. Before his time. Unless.

Unless he'd hidden his cache of books better.

Unless he'd killed the old man in the beginning as he should have done.

Unless he'd somehow possessed the power a thriving world lacked to turn aside its headlong rush to purgatory. As if a seven-year-old boy could abort cruise missiles any more than he could a civilisation's suicidal urge – even if the adult form was somehow able to turn back the clock.

Unless. So many useless what-ifs and buts…

Not even Morlock, for all his power, was able to change what was. *Was he?*

No. There was no prospect of evasion, so he must find a way to survive the coming cataclysm. How? That was the problem.

Marla's suspicions were allayed for now, but it was only a matter of time before they returned to place him in Caxton's casket. And what of Morlock? What else had his master imbibed from Elzevir's dying brain?

"Damn you, old man, *damn you!*"

And damn this remembering that clouded the mind. Was he losing his faculties?

As if in answer, the scent of roses filled his nostrils and he saw the old man again. Not the one who damned him, but the one forced to abandon him. Suddenly, for a fleeting moment, he was the young orphan watching his grandfather prune his beloved roses.

It took a grandson schooled in death to appreciate the irony: that a German who loved English flowers was killed by an American missile fired from English soil. This night, that soil existed far below his feet, along with the rubble, buried in its grave by this modern city. No more Europeans or Americans. No English or Germans or French. Only *Terapolitans*, united in the *Gestalt*.

Except for Otto Schencke: it was a commonality he shared with the burning *Incunabulites* he had spent so long persecuting.

"Careful, Otto," his grandfather's ghost warned, "the beauty is barbed by thorns."

Marla. He smiled grimly. Too late for such advice, she might already be whispering his death into Morlock's ears. Did she fancy herself as the one? Now that pairing would be interesting…

Now the wailing. Sirens and screams. Shrill with the sounds of terror. Curled up in the dust and darkness of a school basement, with more wailing children, impotently soothed by equally terrified adults. Then the distinct but distant thunder and the shuddering earth. Blow after blow after blow. The city and his grandfather obliterated, the young boy rendered just another orphan in the aftermath, truly alone, forced to survive amidst the rubble on wits and sheer determination, until the footfalls of the years brought him to Morlock. And to this place, this altar of choices and sacrifice.

Otto gripped the parapet until his knuckles cracked. He couldn't help but wonder what the young boy might have become but for his rebirth from the womb of a forgotten war.

Not here for sure.

Enough history, dammit, *there is a future to survive.*

He blinked and shook his head. Let the memories fade, like the old photographs of long-dead parents. He didn't need them. He didn't need Marla. He didn't need *books*. He didn't need any of them. Only his wits. Only his skills. Only his desperate need to *endure*.

And the key to its achievement was out there *somewhere*.

Otto sighed and stared at the city. He swore in the dead language of his boyhood and briefly wondered what the word meant. The manuscript. It all turned on that. Why should Morlock obsess over a few tatty sheets of old paper? Whatever the mystery, it made Caxton's protégé important. Many fates might rest upon those bewildered shoulders. Somehow, he must find the manuscript. That meant finding Caxton's misfit foundling.

That was the way ahead, through the boy. That was the clarity he sought in the miasma of past existence, the lifeline for a drowning man. He stood up, grim. Determined. Decision made.

If the manuscript will not come to Morlock, he mused, then Morlock's servant must go to the manuscript. In search of deliverance, Otto immersed himself in the sea of *Terapolitans*.

Let Death stalk in vain. *He* was the Reaper now.

THERE was something wrong. She felt it, but she found herself unable to pull on any one strand of thought without everything unravelling. Only her primal needs kept her going. Always rely on them when all else failed.

There was something wrong with Otto. Or was it Caxton? But no, *he* was dead. Wasn't he?

She watched him – whoever he was – from her lurking place within the shadows between the floods of neon and the restless rivers of skin. What was wrong with him? A frown creased her artificial youth as she dragged recollection out of her turgid, *Gestalt*-fogged brain. The books. The secret cache of books.

Marla Caine stepped from her hiding place and watched Otto's form swallow into the herd of *Terapolitan* flesh. Old purpose and suspicion kept her functioning, but she knew she wasn't herself. Any kind of self.

"What are you up to, Darling?"

The old purpose found its way through the sludge of mental decay. The whirlwind roar of the *Gestalt* faded for now. Marla coiled together and propelled herself after her former accomplice. There was only ever the now. And now there was something she must do. For Morlock. Always for Morlock…

"REST, Bill."

Morlock placed his old companion on his cushion and carefully adjusted him into a comfortable position. Then, gently, he brushed away a fleck of lint from the skull's left eyebrow ridge.

The skull stared.

"Now, Bill, don't look at me like that. There is no need to worry. Otto is coming to the conclusion of his life's work. He struggled with his fears, his doubts, his raging anger and he has found the way. There is no choice; he does what he must. None can harm us. Not now."

The skull's expression didn't change.

"Soon, Bill. Our long labours will be done. I promise. Now, I must prepare for our guest's arrival."

EITHER the boy was learning or else recent traumas were taking their toll on his mind. Otto wasn't sure which was the truth, but he was certainly a tougher game this night. Once or twice, he'd actually come close to losing him in the seething crowds of the city.

Almost, but not quite, and the boy's tougher game plan did nothing to make amends for his fatal error of returning to familiar ground. Since then, the route was suitably meandering and lacked any apparent purpose or direction. The usual predictable patterns were scattered, but the hard lessons – if that's truly what they were – didn't last. The brief challenge passed to boring necessity.

For some reason, the boy had led him here, to this outpost of the older city. Otto didn't bother wondering where this *follow my lead* was going; the answer would present itself soon enough. Instead, he found the vacant shells of yesterday provoking other considerations.

In a sense, he was back where it all began. Back in the Old World. Or what was left of it. Ahead of him a target. A transaction. A life for a future.

He was still having problems adjusting to the concept that this boy held the key. No, that this boy *was* the key. Everything rested on what was to happen, once he had the target cornered. The fate of a whole world, indeed, but he was more concerned with his own.

They once said that walls had ears and these days it was true. In *Terapolis*, they also possessed eyes, but out here, in the remains of Old City the walls were blind and deaf. All the same, they possessed a sense of awareness that even living *Terapolis* lacked. What stories might they tell if granted a tongue?

They retained one aspect in common with modern *Terapolis* – the walls were silent. They had no voice. Here and there, some ancient and fading graffiti remained to plead the reminder of someone's long-forgotten existence. A few old signs registered closed business, and broken dreams, others indicated the ways to long-lost destinations.

For the most part, then, they were silent. They certainly told no stories of the lives lived within their walls and avenues. It wasn't always that way, he remembered. Long ago and far away, walls once spoke bold and loud for those who knew the architect's tongue.

Otto felt an affinity for the Old City. The walls here kept their secrets; their counsel too. The streets and austere shells cared nothing of what he did or let slip from his troubled mind. Here, he might be himself; not the carefully manicured façade needed to survive the *Terapolitan* hive.

The ruins were fickle and treacherous, however. That's why he needed care to maintain his hideaway in the shadows. There was rubble and rubbish aplenty to catch his feet and so threaten to declare his presence. They might not care what dramas transpired beneath their broken edifices and blind windows, but that wasn't to say they might not miss the chance of mischief.

The boy crossed the street ahead and lingered outside a box-like building. Otto watched the boy vanish inside.

Now stealth was no longer necessary, he stepped out of his shaded hideaway and into the street. The boy was pathetically easy, despite all his recent 'training'. That might be the boy's saving grace, or his condemnation. Otto didn't know. Yet. For all their secrets, he guessed even the ruins lacked an answer to that one.

There was only one way to find out.

BORIS realised his mistake as soon as he closed the door to his apartment. He'd actually escaped all the way to the *outcity*, but now he was back for a few things he didn't really need.

A real smart move. Just the kind of cockeyed logic that dominated his life. It all worked fine when it came to the dialectics of *G-Tek*. Shame it fell apart when he applied it to life choices.

That must be why they called him a genius.

He leaned back against the door and sighed.

Now he needed to escape all over again. No, that was stupid. He wasn't a prisoner. He was entitled to leave any time he wanted. So why did he want to sneak out of the place? Easy, he didn't feel inclined to explain, didn't want to go through the formal rigmarole of an official resignation. He wanted none of it. Just a clean break. A fresh start. No consequences. *Especially* no consequences.

The place was so quiet; he might get away with it. *MorTek Prime* had never been so eerily subdued in the time of his residence, like it was waiting for something long anticipated and inevitable. It made him feel more uneasy than usual.

With a sigh, he moved towards the couch and slumped down into it. He peered around the room as he removed his tie, wondering where to start. Cluttered around the place were unwashed mugs, datapads, frozen *simulacomm* animata, and all the other arcane trappings of the *Necrofycer's* trade.

Somewhere in this mess he had the trappings of a life. A few possessions and mementoes that might be worth taking. He'd never been one for an orderly living space; now he wished he'd made more of an effort. Even the domestics gave up on him over the years. He frowned. Stood up. Where to start?

Come back to us, Boris. Come back to us if you can.

"I'm working on it!" The memory sulked.

Boris sighed, slipped out of his coat and threw it onto the couch. That's when he heard the noise. Somebody was singing. *She* was singing. "Lorelei," he gasped.

The wordless melody was hypnotic, captivating, like a seduction. Sweat moistened his tingling skin; his heart beat to a faster rhythm until he felt his cock chafe against restricting cloth. This was not good, he had to… there was *something*… he had to do, wasn't there?

The bedroom door was ajar. He pushed it open. Lorelei was inside, standing with her back to him by the entrance to the en-suite, singing while she brushed her hair. She wore nothing but a flimsy robe, her clothes placed neatly on a chair, a damp towel cast on the floor at her feet. She seemed oblivious to his presence, but then she turned and smiled.

"Boris! *Lover!* I knew you'd be back. I've been waiting for you."

With the song ended, Boris remembered his resolve; he opened his mouth to make his goodbyes, but Lorelei opened her robe and let it fall to the floor. The words caught in his throat; his eyes gaped, his mind stumbled. In a heartbeat, she was on him, deftly removing his jacket, his shirt; he whimpered as her hands descended towards his throbbing loins, took hold of his waistband, pulled him towards the bed. He was a puppet now.

"You look terrible," she said, her hands caressing his torso. "You need to relax, lover."

Lorelei urged him to sit down on the bed. She kneeled before him, working her hands up his thighs. The smile spread gormless across his face. His prick was a tight bulge in his pants. Boris groaned impatiently, reaching to release his straining lust, but Lorelei batted away his hands and teasingly unbuckled his belt.

She held his gaze, blue eyes gleaming, overriding his need to focus on her swaying breasts. She slipped his pants free; Boris gasped and fell back, gazing up over the mound of his belly as Lorelei rose to claim his cock. Then she was astride him.

She took him in slow, a soft whimper registering the release of her own pleasure. A slight film of sweat glistened on her brow as she increased her rhythm. Boris grunted, gritted his teeth as he fought against the hair trigger reaction that threatened climax; Lorelei increased her vigour, as though daring him to finish before she was ready.

"Stay with us, lover," she panted, "stay and be healed. There's still so much for you to do."

The low lights flickered; the darkness seemed to shift around Lorelei. Voices whispered, as if muffled by the shadows. He might have heard the haunting voyeurs if he wasn't so distracted.

"Poor Uncle Boris…"

"You really are fucked, *pal."*

Boris grunted. Giggled. Lorelei yelped, lost her rhythm, leaned forward to grip the bedclothes either side of his head, her mouth a strained 'O'. Then she screamed. "Boris! Oh! Boris! Stay! With! Us!"

He cried out in grateful response. "Yes! Oh! Yes! Yes!"

And then he was spent; Lorelei gazed exultant.

SO, this was Caxton's place. His mind hadn't been on it before, but now he took it all in during one world-wearied sweep; somehow it didn't fit his image of the man. The clutter brought it a little too close to home, but with the books maybe that wasn't so bad. There must be hundreds, thousands of volumes stacked and packed around the place.

He let his eyes slowly scan the precious layers of paper and words; everything he'd once dreamed of, but that was then, before he discovered what the dream really meant. Before the dream died.

With a sigh that hadn't decided whether it was weary or wistful he moved towards the desk and slumped into the chair. It creaked and clanked as he swivelled his knees round to face the desk, where a strange contraption of lettered knobs and metal struts rested in sullen silence. He stared at it, then placed his head in his hands. There was no 'what next' here, but where else was there to go? This was as good a place as any to wait for Laura, or for something to come along and tell him how to make sense of life.

A quiet squeak as he rotated the seat and stared, glum, around the room. The shadows clinging to the corners matched his mood.

The books sat in their piles, or they huddled fearfully on the overloaded shelves. The air stank of Caxton: of tobacco and coffee and the old aroma of incense that he'd always taken for bad aftershave until now. All that remained of the old man's powerful presence.

He looked at the books again. Smelled the burning flames. The scent came from his own body. Mingled with sweat. He reeked of the library's death and his flight from perdition.

No wonder the ghosts were afraid.

There was a clank from outside. He looked round.

A shadow against the glass. Or was that just a ghost playing tricks with his eyes? He stood up and stepped towards the door. It opened of its own volition; he felt his heart lift a beat. She'd made it. At last something was going right. "Laura –"

He stopped, slumped into the chair again as his knees buckled weak. This time the chair didn't protest. Otto

Schencke stepped into the room and closed the door behind him without turning.

The man gazed round the room a moment with dark eyes. They lingered on the books with a hungry gleam. A flash of fire, the smell of smoke; Adam shuddered.

"What a pig sty. Such an untidy mind. I never realised."

Adam felt his jaw drop open, but no words emerged.

"Well, you don't look *quite* the frightened rabbit that I last saw. Although, I must say it appears you've had a fortunate escape from the bonfire. Truly, I am sorry for you."

"You... going to kill me now?"

"Do you want me to?"

He snapped his mouth shut.

Otto smiled, but the gesture never reached his eyes.

"Take it easy, lad, you've had a rough evening." Otto reached into his jacket. Adam flinched. Otto saw and paused. Then he removed his hand and showed him the contents. A small container of what looked like artificial sweeteners.

"Take it easy, I said. I hope there is some coffee in this pigsty. Perhaps I am better off hoping for some clean cups. No don't move. I'll find it myself."

Otto stomped to the far door and vanished into the darkness beyond. A moment later, a light flicked into life and a few shadows scurried away to join their fellows. A rattle and clank of crockery. The hissing of water boiling, furious.

"And don't think of running until we've had a little chat."

Adam felt his muscles flinch at the suggestion. The door was so near, but then he relaxed. After all, there was nowhere to actually go; besides he was too tired to run anywhere. Whatever was going to happen was going to happen here.

Otto returned. A cup held in his hand half raised to his mouth. He stood by the doorway and stared over the cup. Adam looked back, uncertain of what to do or say.

"So, what shall we talk about?"

He stammered, then found his voice. "I don't know."

"How about a certain manuscript?"

"I... don't have it."

"Indeed."

"I don't. I wouldn't let Morlock have it anyway."

"And why not?"

"He'd burn it."

"Of course."

"What do you want?"

Otto sipped the coffee. His manner so refined. How could a killer be so...

"I want your help."

The request derailed his train of thinking. He stared, bewildered.

"My help? What can I do?"

"I have told you before. For some unfathomable reason, Morlock wants you. Not just this manuscript, but the both of you. That puts you in a powerful position to derail events."

"Why me?"

Otto shrugged. "Morlock has always been strange to me. All I know is he wants you. And that tatty scrap of paper your friend Caxton put together."

"I don't have it."

Otto sighed. Then he stepped into the room.

"Is it really so difficult to use your imagination? Look at the desk in front of you. Look in that bin."

He obeyed.

"Good. Pull out those papers. Unscrew them. Straighten them out. Tell me, what are they?"

"Pages."

"Yes?"

"Pages of words. I don't know."

Another sigh. "At a guess I suggest they are drafts of what he was working on. Gather them. Assemble them together, and you have an approximation of what Morlock wants. Enough to get you inside *MorTek Prime*."

Otto's stare was mesmerising. It forced him to obedience. He picked up the pages. He straightened out the ones he took from the bin. He began to put them together. Otto nodded his head.

"Good. Nobody will take a close enough look to spot that it is fake."

"Why? Why do this?"

"You want to see Morlock."

"No."

"Yes, you do. You want to kill him."

Adam dropped the pages. They fluttered across the desk and onto the floor.

"You're the killer. You do it!"

"I tried that once. Long ago, before I joined the company. I failed."

"So what chance have I got?"

"He wants you and that bundle of papers. It buys you a proximity to the target."

"You work for him. You can get close. He trusts you."

"Does he?"

"He must do."

A grin. Grim on his bearded face. "I think he suspects me. Soon he will know for certain, I think, for Marla most definitely knows. She found the books."

"Books? You're –"

"No. I am not one of your *Incunabulites*. My sense of self-preservation is too highly developed for such foolishness. This is about survival."

"Yours or mine?"

"Gut!" Adam frowned at the strange word. "Good, I should say, you are starting to think. So think about this. Morlock has burned your library. I'm sure plenty of you remain, but too scattered to be of any danger to him. Real or imagined. Now, he is close to whatever it is he is after. How much longer will he need me?"

Adam shrugged.

"Precisely. He was once an assurance of my continued survival. Now he is a potential hindrance to that. I do not like hindrances."

"I can't do it. I'm useless. Ask anybody. They never say it, well mostly, but I know they think it."

"Stop your wheedling excuses, boy! If you want to do it, you can. I cannot. I failed before. For reasons I still do not understand. I am certain I will fail again."

"So what makes you think I can do it? I'm not a killer like you."

"Every one is a killer. It's in the genes. All that is required is the right provocation. You have every reason on Earth to want him dead. He has put the fire in your belly. It's up to you to use it."

"I can't do it."

"Can't or won't? Are you afraid? Good. Be so. It will sharpen your focus. He is weaker than he has ever been before. Far weaker than he appears. We must exploit this vulnerability while we can."

"It's impossible. *MorTek* is so huge! So what if you kill Morlock? You think that will *actually* change anything?"

"I have no idea. I care even less, but I do not think that *MorTek* can survive without him. There is no one in that nest of drones who can take over. If you are not prepared, then I will perform my mission. Then I will look for another way out."

Adam tried not to squirm.

"No, Adam. I won't kill *you*. There is a certain young lady, however…"

"NO!"

He glanced at the door, longing for escape. Then he saw the handle turn slowly. The door opened with a glacial motion. Unaware, Otto took another gulp of his coffee. Just when Adam thought the day couldn't get any worse, Marla Caine stepped into the room and aimed her pistol at Otto.

"Darling! Why is it that men *always* let a girl down?"

OTTO turned towards the interruption and didn't seem to care that a gun's hungry muzzle was pointed at his heart. He raised the cup to his lips and took a slow gulp of coffee; his eyes never moved from Marla. Then he lowered the cup back onto the saucer before answering.

"Overly high expectations, I presume."

Marla smirked. Adam felt a hideous sense of *déjà vu* and tried to make himself smaller in the chair. He was used to being a spectator at his own life, but he didn't relish playing the same game at his own funeral.

"You are to be congratulated, Marla. I truly never suspected you were following me. Either your skills are improving, or I am getting old."

He shifted position, stepping sideways. Marla sidestepped also. Her gun remained locked on Otto's broad chest. "Keep your hands where I can see them, Darling. I wouldn't want to make you spill your coffee."

Adam swivelled in the chair so that he might keep both in some kind of sight. It was no comfort that it meant he'd get to see who fired first. They manoeuvred like an uncertain couple on a dance floor, looking to take the moment to its intimate conclusion. And he was the unfortunate matchmaker.

"*He* will not be pleased, Darling."

"I am sure."

"You betrayed *him*. You betrayed *me*!"

"No, Marla." Otto took another mouthful of coffee.

"You're just like the *other*!"

The gun arm trembled. A flash of hate and pain in the eyes. Then the fit passed and she was an ice maiden again. A priestess of death, come to call on a penitent.

"You are starting to remember things, Marla. That is good. You were never meant for this. Life did not decree this for you. Not like it did for me. It was Morlock. Always Morlock. He plays us like puppets. You and I are his knights. Be thankful we are not pawns, but even we are expendable."

Something slithered through Marla's features. A cocktail of emotions. There was doubt. Adam recognised that old companion. Fear too. The rest, he could not even begin to imagine.

"No. NO! How could you?"

"Times change, Marla. This has always been a mating of convenience. I thought you knew that. You always take things so personally. It has always been a weakness."

"Really, *Darling.*"

Marla's finger curled on the trigger, but it relaxed on the verge of releasing the deadly package.

"Life made me, Marla. That and some bad choices. Perhaps this is another bad choice, but you – you have never had a choice until now. So make one. Take back your life. Walk away. For old time's sake *walk away!*"

"What... do you mean?"

Marla was losing her hard-edged resolve, coming apart around the core of her lethal purpose. Adam felt breathless. A sudden tinge of admiration for Otto; there was something of Caxton in the way he faced the end.

"Caxton was just the mechanism of Morlock's purpose, Marla. He wanted your son out of the way so that he might have *you.* Morlock was the master. Caxton was the puppet. Just as we are today."

"Lies!"

"He's here. Now. Sat between us. Your son."

"Liar!"

The confusion almost spoiled her aim. She swayed on her feet. For a moment her eyes flicked to stare at Adam. The ghost of recognition flashed deep inside her dilated pupils and then vanished. In a heartbeat they were back on Otto. Her knuckles squeezed white on the handgrip, but Adam suddenly saw in her the young woman alone and frightened in a hospital slip.

"Pull the trigger Marla and you might finish what Caxton began."

"No! Lies! All of it. He did it! He took my baby!"

This was it. Adam braced himself. The fear was burning in his chest, the heat reaching down to boil the contents of his bowels. His nose twitched at an acrid smell. Fresh tobacco. A hint of oil. The shadows moved and caused the light to flicker at its edges.

A metallic tap vibrated the desk. Adam turned his head to stare at the machine. Marla stared wild at Otto. The **typewriter** clattered again of its own accord. The keys depressing, the strikers slamming hard into the platen. The rhythm **rose** to a fever pitch of composition. There was no breeze but the **books fluttered** on their piles around the room. A whimper from Marla tore his attention away from the ancient machine.

Her **eyes** darted wild, but never for long, **never** long enough to leave her open. She **was sweating and wild** eyed. Her gun arm **trembled**, but never lost its mark on Otto's chest. Looking round as **bewildered as Marla, Adam saw Otto as resolute as ever, his eyes unflinching but showing a hint of puzzled concern. Like Marla before, Adam felt the whimper escape his throat. This was <u>insane</u>.**

"Control yourself, Marla," Otto barked, voice stern, face concerned. "I told you the *Gestalt* was not good for you."

The words scrolled across the wall. Giant letters, smudged and imperfect, as if bashed out by the invisible narrator clattering away on the typewriter.

This isn't possible, Adam's mind screamed. Then he stared bewildered as his inner disbelief spelled itself out on the wall.

A cling from the typewriter. A pause in the rattle. A whirr and a click, and then the composition resumed. Each letter and word bashed itself into existence with a *thud thud*.

Marla stepped back. Adam realised he was caught in her field of fire and he slumped low in the chair, stopped by the desk from getting fully clear of Marla's misdirected aim. Otto moved also, but he never once let his attention slip away from his adversary.

"Make it stop!" Marla's voice was harsh. "Make it stop!"

"I can't! I'm not doing it!"

"Not you too, boy. What is happening here?" Untouched by the impossible words, Otto stood perplexed in the middle of madness.

"Don't you see it? Can't you hear it?"

"Hear what? See what? That Marla is losing it at last?"

"The writing on the wall! You must be able to see it?"

Otto risked a moment to look at Adam, his face baffled. Then his eyes turned towards the increasingly erratic Marla. Adam watched Otto's inner thoughts rattle across the wall. See what, a room full of lunatics? Then he said:

"The writing has been on the wall a long time, boy."

"Turn it off! Turn it off!"

"It's mechanical. I can't turn it off!"

"Control yourself, Marla. This affair does not have to reach its conclusion."

She was too far gone for reason to pierce her panic. With eyes wild as they flicked around the room, she glanced in turn at the books, the typewriter, at the walls, at Adam and Otto. She was a dizzying gyration of lost anchorage.

"Don't do it, Marla. Don't complete my mistake."

Adam stared at the words. Marla's mouth opened. A slow keen emerged. The gun wavered and for a moment its hungry muzzle looked Adam in the eyes.

"Walk away, Marla. Try to find yourself. Try to find the peace I destroyed. Listen to Schencke. He's our boy, Marla. Adam is our son. You can have a life yet."

"No! He's dead! You killed him! You took my baby! You're dead! I killed you!"

"I can't blame you for that. But not our boy."

"Stop it! *Stop it!*"

"Marla! You stop it. *Now!* Before it is too late."

Marla never heard Otto's barked command. Events had moved beyond the voice of sanity. Marla staggered backwards from the desk. Her gun shifted its aim. Her eyes, wild with fear and confusion, stared at the typewriter.

"Make it stop!"

The voice was that of the frightened women from long ago. The gun flared fire. Adam flinched and felt the liquid heat flood from his body. Another blast ruptured his senses. The machine flew apart. Hot metal stung his cheek. The words died mid-sentence.

A whispered 'phut' from behind where he sat. A chilling instant of vibration above his head. A single red rose blossomed on Marla's breast. A metal casing, still smoking, landed in his piss-soaked lap. A coffee cup thunked as it hit the floor.

Marla's rose melted in a flood of arterial blood. She staggered and swayed. Her eyes blinked in puzzled shock, their focus turned inwards. Her mouth mimed words. Adam took his chance to slip from the chair and cower on the floor as Marla's gun swayed precarious in search of a target.

A second 'phut' opened a blind eye in Marla's forehead. Her head flipped back. A soft moan escaped her lips. Her body slumped to the floor. She twitched for a few moments then came to a rest. Adam shivered as he looked into her lifeless, but strangely pleading eyes.

Otto stepped forward, casually removing the silencer from his gun while he looked down at his old partner. "How many times did I ever tell you, Marla? Never be distracted when facing an armed opponent."

He stooped and gently prised the gun from Marla's limp hand to cast it aside. Then he turned to face Adam. He stared at him for a while, as if sizing him up. Then the muzzle of his pistol came up.

"Ohshit!" The words were a spasm of terror, but Otto only grunted and spun the gun around so that the handgrip was facing away from him.

"Take it easy, boy. The dying is done for now. Take this. You will need it."

"What?"

"You want this for Morlock."

He held it forward expectantly, but Adam made no move to take the weapon.

"Come on, lad, it won't bite."

His eyes flicked sideways to snatch a brief glance at Marla, but he said nothing.

Otto shrugged.

"Fine," he said, and placed the gun on the desk beside the remains of the typewriter.

"Think about things, Adam. You might also want to think about changing your clothes."

Despite the situation he blushed. The piss was cooling and felt quite chilly.

"Was… was she really my mother?"

A raised eyebrow. A sigh. "What do you think?"

"I don't think anything. I just want to go home."

"So do I. But Hamburg hasn't existed for some time now. If either of us want a home to go back to, then you must kill Morlock. For Marla. For Caxton. For your precious books. For whatever damn reason you see fit."

Adam nodded and swallowed. Afraid to say anything.

"I have bet my life on some pretty dangerous odds before now, but you…" his voice trailed off. Then, "What *was* that business with Marla?"

"The typewriter… the walls… you didn't see? It came alive."

Otto stared. "Fine. If that's what you say you saw. It was a handy distraction; just don't go funny when you face Morlock. This is a dangerous game, boy. And I am counting on you."

He turned to leave. Just as Otto wrenched open the door, Adam blurted, "How do I know I can trust you?"

Otto paused on the threshold. "Oh, you can trust me, Adam – I just killed your mother."

SHE found Adam standing in the machine hall, just standing, his back to her, staring into the shadows. Even with his back turned, he looked different. There was a gun in his hand and she wondered where he came by it. Relief turned to worry.

"Adam?"

He stiffened, but didn't turn round. She moved forward into the light spilling out of Caxton's open door.

"Adam, it's me."

"You left me."

"I tried to find you."

"Did you."

"*Yes.*"

He said nothing. Just raised the gun and looked at it.

"Where'd you get that?"

He shrugged.

Laura decided to fall back on the old sarcasm, anything to get a response. She didn't like his mood.

"Been posing with it long?"

"I *wasn't* posing."

He turned. The expression on his face was more like the old Adam. She wondered what he'd seen in the tunnels and suppressed a shudder.

"Really," she said. Habits were difficult to break. She turned to the stairs and put her foot on the first step.

"Don't go up there."

The tone in Adam's voice stopped her. The edge in it was new. She looked at him, but left her foot on the step.

"Why not? I've been coming here a damn sight longer than you."

He shrugged again. "Trust me. You don't want to go up there."

She was torn between two curiosities. The one at the head of the stairs. The other down here in the machine hall. Back to the sarcasm again.

"Why? You got Marla Caine stashed away up there?"

Adam just stared. The smiled died on her lips. Then he turned away again.

"Do you have it?"

"Have what?"

"Caxton's book."

She hesitated before answering. "Yes."

"Can I have it?"

"What do you want with it?"

"I want to show it to someone."

"Who?"

"Someone who needs to see it."

"Is that why you've got the gun? In case I say no?"

She'd touched a nerve. His face looked… haggard. "No. *No,* of course not. I just… Can I have it?"

"No, Adam. It's all we've got left of Caxton. He entrusted it to *me.*"

"Doesn't matter, then. I'll find another way."

"What are you going to do with that gun, anyway?"

"I'm going to kill Morlock."

"What?" She couldn't say any more. The laughter exploded through the machine hall, bounced off the rusting hulks and walls until the whole place sounded like it got the joke.

Adam looked hurt. "You don't think I can do it?"

She managed to control herself. This wasn't like him at all. "No," she said simply.

He nodded. "Don't you want Morlock dead?"

"Of course, but it won't change anything. Anyway, you'll never get in. He's too well protected."

"Not as much as you think. Anyway, he'll let me in."

"Oh, really? Bosom buddies, are you?"

"He thinks I've got something he wants."

"Oh yes, and that would be –"

"Caxton's manuscript."

She sighed. "You'll never do it, Adam. It won't work."

"Why not?"

"Because this is you, not one of your antique video games or artificial reality trips. It isn't the *Gestalt*. This is *real*."

"The *Gestalt* is real. More real than this. That's why we have to end it, before it's too late. Do you want to spend the rest of your days scurrying through tunnels like some kind of bookish rat? Or until the *Gestalt* reaches down and swallows you whole?"

Now Laura felt a stab of anger, but she pushed it aside like some *Terapolitan* junkie in her way. She could feel Caxton's dead eyes on her, feel the burden he'd placed on her shoulders.

"You want revenge, is that it? We all do. But we have to keep things safe."

"*Safe*!" A hysterical cry. "*Safe*! He burned your precious library."

"We have others."

"For how long? We need to bring them back into the light. Books belong to everyone. Not a few. So long as Morlock's alive, they'll stay locked away. Is that what you're afraid of – that you'll stop being a cosy little clique?"

"You haven't been around long enough to judge us like that. We've kept them *alive!* You really are Cax's baby!"

"What?"

He looked up. Burning eyes. *He knew.* How much did he know? *How* did he know?

"I mean he's done a right number on you," she spoke hurriedly and sought to change the subject. Her gaze snatched on the gun.

"You'll never do it. Even if you get close to him. I mean, do you even know how to use that thing?"

"'Course I do. I could shoot a glass off your head no problem."

"If anyone's going to do *that* around here then it's going to be me. You never read the *Naked Lunch*."

"What do you mean?"

She rolled her eyes. "I mean you'd shoot your foot."

"Hey! I'm a good shot."

"In the arcade maybe. This is a little different. Okay. Show me how it's done."

He looked sheepish. Good. A little more of the old Adam showing through. With luck, she was getting through this stupid urge implanted by Caxton's talk. Adam really was too impressionable for his own good.

"That drum over there," she added, pointing into the gloom.

She watched him swallow his injured male pride and take aim. His finger tightened on the trigger. The weapon clicked.

"What's *wrong* with it?"

"Is it loaded?"

"Yes!"

He fumbled with the mechanism and managed to release the magazine. He displayed it to her and she peered forward, more for effect than anything. Bullets gleamed in the clip. Adam clumsily slid it back into the pistol grip.

"Is the safety on?"

A bewildered flash of the eyes. He studied the weapon again, then he just shrugged.

"Aren't guns supposed to be boys' toys?" The sarcasm was heavy, and maybe misplaced, but she couldn't stop it. She sighed and stepped towards him. "Give it here."

"You had the safety on," she said. "Look. Here. On. Off. Okay?"

He nodded dumb.

Laura turned to face the drum. Aimed and fired. The blast echoed from the rusting metal. Maybe a few ghosts hidden in the shadows scurried clear. What was it she'd read about old China? Firecrackers drove away evil spirits? Let it drive away Adam's spirit of madness. She turned and handed him the gun. A wisp of smoke coiled from the muzzle and danced mockingly on the air currents.

"Now you try."

He took it nervously. Raised it with a trembling arm. He pulled the trigger and was rewarded with another mocking click. Laura suppressed the smile.

"I put the safety back on."

He fumbled.

"Okay, so what now?" He waved the gun in the air. Laura flinched and ducked.

"Don't do that you idiot!"

He looked hurt. She didn't care. She just pointed down 'range' towards the drum she'd selected as a target. He turned, looked for the target and fired. His wrist bucked against the recoil and the bullet went wild.

"Squeeze the trigger. And it helps if you look where you're aiming."

"I'll remember." He let the gun dangle despondently.

It roared again. A bullet blasted chippings out of the floor and screamed into the shadows. That time a ghost definitely wailed its alarm. Maybe it was a feral cat.

"You idiot!"

He held the gun out at arm's length down range. Apologetic face grinned weak and pathetic. Maybe it was better to leave some of the old Adam buried.

"You take a shot and the thing reloads and cocks itself."

He nodded his head.

"Put the safety back on."

He flicked the switch. "How do you know all this stuff, anyway?"

"I know people, okay."

He looked at her blank. She rolled her eyes.

"A girl's got to look after herself."

"Doesn't everybody?"

"It's different."

"How?"

"Because... Oh, use your imagination. Why didn't you get a gun more appropriate to your weight and build, anyway?"

"This one is..." he paused, and stared at the gleaming metal in his hand. "*Appropriate.*"

"So you're still going ahead with it?"

"Yes."

"Hasn't this shown you anything?"

"Such as?"

"I mean even if you get in to see Morlock, you'll point that thing and probably fuck it up. Marla or Otto will finish you. Or do you plan on making Morlock laugh until he chokes to death?"

He turned away.

"Marla is not an issue. Neither is Morlock. I *will* do this."

"Right. And how will you get in without Caxton's book?"

He reached into his pocket and pulled out a sheaf of papers. He waved the rolled bundle like a wand. "How will Morlock know these are just scribbled drafts and crumpled pages?"

"You can't do this! Caxton doesn't want *you* to do this."

"Caxton is dead," Adam said. "And Caxton is *nothing* anyway."

"No! Adam! Don't do it. You'll die."

"What do you care?"

"I care."

He turned away again. Pushed the gun into his waistband at the small of his back. Then he pulled his jacket over. At least he had the sense to keep it hidden. She reached out to him, but he pulled away and started to walk into the shadows.

She could follow. She wouldn't follow. Not to *MorTek*. Not to this pointless task. Despite what she knew, it was beyond her, beyond Adam.

"Don't go!"

He ignored her and kept walking towards the exit.

"Please, Adam! Don't you leave me too…"

Voice too weak to carry now, she watched his silhouette disappear into the street.

"Don't my feelings count for anything?" she asked in a hoarse voice, laden with potential tears. Anger brimmed.

"So die then! *See if I care!*"

The Eleventh Folio
All Things Come To Those Who Wait

BETRAYAL was so easy, when all was said and done. After all these years, Silas Morlock was still so vulnerable; a matter that had previously caused so many sleepless nights and frustrations, but tonight Otto blessed his master's perpetual indifference to 'mere' matters of the flesh.

There was little to prevent some modern day Otto Schencke from gaining an unscheduled audience, providing he had the verve for such an encounter. Even the boy was theoretically up to the job. He still had doubts about this mad scheme as he stalked towards the security control room. Otherwise, he'd be long gone, but the boy – he *was* the one. He didn't know it but his gut was definitely telling him: the reason Morlock wanted the boy was because – unlikely as it seemed – he carried the potential to be a genuine threat.

So, follow the gut and ease the boy's passage. Then let Morlock's ploy run its deflected course. Some plan. He paused at the door and took a deep breath. Composing himself, though he didn't know why, he slipped inside. In its way, it was all so very *routine*. The air stank of boredom. The men at the consoles and observation stations were typical rent-a-cop material. For the duration of their shift, they were desiccated by boredom and longed for the *Gestalt*.

The supervisor, a slack-faced man with bovine eyes glanced up from a scribbled pad. His face showed fear. The wrong kind. It was the guilt of the schoolboy caught doodling in class. Otto almost felt sorry for the man, but not so much that he bothered to scan his name badge to learn who he was.

"Mr Schencke… Sir!"

Nameless stood up hastily. His three understudies attempted to look alert and keen at their duties. With a sigh, Otto slipped the pistol from behind his back. Nameless widened his eyes in fright then the bullet absolved his guilt. Otto turned with clinical calm and went about his business.

The first underling was slammed into his workstation by the impact of the second bullet before Nameless hit the *derm*. Number two just had time to react, glancing sideways in wide-eyed shock before the next bullet smashed his head to the side and splashed his brain all over a screen.

The third managed to scramble out of his seat, just as his companion slumped from his chair. It squeaked on its wheel as the guard's ascent propelled it across the room.

"No! *Please*… Not outside the *Gestalt* –"

The bullet slammed through his forehead with the force of a lead 'eureka'. His head flipped back and one arm rose to slap the hand against the bullet-wound revelation in his brain. The body twitched backwards, clumsy steps until it hit the wall. It stayed there rigid a moment, eyes staring, mouth slack and trembling as though cold. Then it slithered down to the ground.

The body settled into its final position, knees bent and apart, head slumped over between the knees. The hands rested on either side, the fingers still twitching spastic, as though the guard was impatient to become a corpse.

Dismissing the staff took only moments, but to his mind the scene had been slow and casual. Equally so was his movement to retrieve the spent shells. No point making his calling card too obvious.

Finally, he glanced at the monitors. For the most part, the screens showed empty corridors. A few showed minions at work in largely empty offices and labs. *MorTek* was said to be a 24-hour company, and it was *globally*, but at late hours such as this, even mighty *MorTek Prime* tended to heed the *Gestalt's* call and do little more than tick over. The foyer screen showed one guard on duty, sat staring mindlessly into the middle distance: a stare indicative of boredom, and a mind little capable of dealing with it. Another guard wandered briefly into one of the other percepticon's field of acuity then he vanished beyond consideration.

Otto quickly surveyed the scene. Messy, but there was no time for finesse. This was hack work, not artwork. He stalked towards a junction box on the wall. Locked. He grunted irritation. Stepped back. Raised the pistol. Fired. Shards of cartilage cascaded. The hatch sprung open to reveal the flesh beneath.

Tubes and damp coils like entrails and nerve bundles gleamed in the light. He stared hard at the tangles of flesh and fibres and located the required ganglia. He fired again into the heart of the mass. Flesh shuddered. Fluid splashed and splattered. Then oozed and dripped. The monitors blacked out.

MorTek was blind and deaf.

Morlock had eyes and ears of his own, but he let them linger here and there – never on the entirety. Those eyes could not be punctured and blinded. Indeed, for the plan to work they must not. *He* must see the boy coming. Only the minions needed to be extracted from the equation.

The question now: leave and lose himself in the vast sprawl of the city, or linger for the finale to come? It was a harder choice than he originally expected. The urge to flee was in deadlock with the knowledge that the boy might need assistance to finish the man he had served for so long.

Leave. Yes. He'd done all he could. Time for the boy to measure up.

There was nothing he cared to take. He had all he needed. In a long life, he had amassed little in the way that meant anything. There was nothing to keep him here. The job was done. He headed for the lift at the end of the corridor. A brisk pace but not overly hurried. Be the man of action, brusque and efficient, just in case, not a man potentially running for his life. There was no reason to attract attention. Not at the last hurdle.

WITH Adam gone, the place felt somehow different. Empty. Even the lingering residue of Caxton had gone away with him. Laura stood alone and uncertain in the pool of light that spilled from Caxton's den like a luminous fog. Her anger was chilled now by disbelief at Adam's resolve. It was so unlike him.

He had to come back. He *had* to. But what if he doesn't? A tear spilled. Angrily, she wiped it away. Another insisted on replacing it so she was forced to go with the flow.

She should have stopped him. Tried harder. Gone with him. No. Not that. She couldn't go to *that* place. She'd promised to keep an eye on him, not follow him into a *necrolyser* belly.

"I'm sorry, Cax," she whispered, "I *know*, but I *can't* do that. I'll find someone, but I can't follow him. He's gone beyond my help."

She cursed Adam's stupid pride. That's all it was. Leaving her to fret and worry, while he paraded his male ego to the extent of losing it. This was no time for him to show hidden depths and character revelations. He was as bull headed as Caxton, but with none of the substance. Or the style.

"He'll be back," she told the shadows. She bit her lip and stared into the gloom. "This is just machismo bullshit. He won't even get half way there before he chickens out. You'll see."

She had to cling to that notion. So wait, and play *I told you so* when he returned. Knock the bravado out of him; keep him from doing anything else stupid. But this was beyond stupid; it was suicidal. To go to that place where Elzevir was lost.

Adam's face failed to reappear from the gloom. She sighed. This was useless, floating around like a Miss Havisham. There were things to do. Eventually, she might even remember what they were.

It would take a little while for him to see sense, she realised, so she walked over to the stairs and reached out for the handrail. She placed her foot on the first step and gazed up into the light spilling from the door. She wondered what was up there, then the manuscript chafed her. A reminder. Now was as good a time as any.

Laura swung round and sat down on the stairs. She reached inside her coat and pulled the manuscript clear. Carefully, she unfurled the curling paper, yellowed and worn at the edges. Some pages were grubbier than others where it was well-thumbed by its maker. Laura flicked through. She neared the end of the sheaf. The thinnest, but the most soiled section of the manuscript. The oldest, obviously. Caxton's ultimate purpose behind this construction of words. She paused to stare at the page, the earlier sheet held poised between her fingertips. Here were those secrets waiting to be liberated from their paper haven.

She slipped the pages from the main body and let her eyes pass over the type. How long did Caxton hold those words in the privacy of his skull? How long had this thing been bursting inside him, before he began to commit the words and deeds to paper? Then she wondered how he was able to keep it to himself for so long without going insane.

It was obvious: he discovered the *Incunabula*. He became the *Incunabula*. There, he found the haven to shield his sanity from the darkness that forever threatened to sweep them away. The *Incunabula* was his sanity. Such terrible knowledge. Such a burden. And here the beating heart of his slender book. The one and only section that gave meaning and purpose to its sister pages.

She let her perception merge into the manuscript, reading her old friend's mind. Soon, she found the resonance of his voice. Those rich tones that captivated an audience sat around a fire beneath an impossible star-filled night. This time, the auditorium was her skull. She listened all over again.

THERE must be Completion. And we of the Incunabula must forge it. Not as Morlock desires, but through the imposition of our Will, the fulfilment of our Purpose.

For too long have we hoarded our hidden treasure. For too long have we hidden in the shadows. For too long have we waited for a Dawn that will never reach our subterranean havens.

Our books are too weak now to keep Him at bay. Too dim to stifle his shroud of darkness. He is near to the peak of his ascension, and so, paradoxically, he nears his moment of greatest weakness.

We must take our books to Him. We must venture into the very heart of darkness, so that our precious light might assault the shadows of his fulfilment.

All roads lead to MorTek now.

They lead to Him.

There is no escaping this.

For the Book is the Light and the Life.

Our life.

And the key resides within the book...

Laura snorted a frustrated heckle. "The key? The book? Which book? There's so many..." She flicked through the pages, feeling she was on the verge of some great discovery, but frustrated by the lines and paragraphs of text. Impatient, she implored the silence for answers. "Cax, you never thought of an index?"

She forced herself to take a deep breath, and dived back into the flow of Caxton's words.

... Consider metaphor. Consider Mind. The Light. One entity, one phenomena but sundered into sparks as numerous and myriad as the stars in heaven.

The opposite, the balance, the ancient equal and opposing force: singular and homogenous, a vast and deep abyss of utter antithesis.

Like the stars sailing in the endless oceans of night, so we drift in the currents of the permeating ether that is aware, yet not Mind. Not Light. It is of us, it is not of us and we have brought it here among us...

... I am the Alpha and Omega, the Beginning and the End; what is, what was, and what is to come. Or as He might say: As it was in the beginning so shall it be at the end...

... such is the Gestalt. It is the honey pot beguiled to both attract and bind us. It is the meaning granted to the otherwise empty lives we made in days gone by, it is the crucible made for our union with Him; for in the Gestalt will the light and the dark meet and, like a mating of matter and anti-matter, so the one shall extinguish the other.

All that shall remain are but photons travelling the endless dark domain of the cosmos, hurtling unknown in a universe bereft of perception. For there shall be nothing and no one that is rendered Aware...

... For Silas Morlock is that which lurks in the shadows beyond the firelight; he is the hidden malevolence sensed by our ancient forebears as they sought haven by the hearths; he is the dark oceans between the stars; the binding shadows that seek to engulf the lightening sparks of human thought; he is beyond Death; he is Despair; he is the manifestation of our folly; he is the carbon black remains of the incinerated page; he is quite simply

THERE was more. She knew she should read it line for line, page for page, but the sense of doom he brought to mind broke her concentration and patience. She looked up from the manuscript and stared at the machines. Adam didn't have the time for her patience.

He wasn't coming back. Not unless someone brought him back.

Books are the key...

She frowned. She didn't understand. Not yet.

Morlock is no man. And Adam is no hero. She understood that.

Now she knew what she had to do. There was no choice. There was never any choice. Not for the *Incunabula*. So, it was up to her, after all. She carefully reassembled the manuscript, and slipped it back safe in her pocket. Then she stood up and turned to stare into the light pouring from the open door overhead.

"What's up there? What didn't you want me to see?"

She put her hand on the rusted rail and began to pull herself into Caxton's lair. She paused on the threshold. This was no longer the same, comforting place. Then she passed through the opening and into life beyond Caxton.

THIS was a suspicious time for the lift to develop a fault, but Otto tried to allay his fears with the unconvincing fact that so many systems overlapped his bullets might have damaged more than mere sensory perceptors.

He stared out into the depths of darkness, one hand holding the doors from closing. Somewhere, the ghost of Elzevir was out there. Did the old man bear a grudge? His voice might be among the whispers already softy lapping his ears. They sent a shiver of fear through Otto's spine.

"Don't be a fool," he said. Fear refused to be placated.

Unconsciously, his hand reached into his jacket. Only when his fingers caressed the soothing hardness of metal did he become aware of the movement.

Reassured, he strode into the darkness.

After only a few paces he turned left, another stroll then right again. Memory started to offer clues to his whereabouts and he felt his confidence return. There was a lift on the other side of this labyrinth. Not far now. He hastened his pace, rounded a corner. Stopped dead.

"Mr Morlock!"

"Otto." A gentle, professional nod of the head. There was a faint hint of disconcerting amusement in his master's expression. "The boy is coming."

"Yes, Sir. All is ready."

"So I gather. As always you have performed… to *requirements*."

Otto was about to speak, but his master stopped him.

"I was so very sorry to learn about Marla. Alas, for every deed there are consequences, but I knew this strategy would require sacrifice."

Otto stepped back in fear. Before he could speak he realised there was someone or some*thing* behind him. With a vision of Elzevir's end, he turned rapidly, reaching for the hidden pistol at his armpit.

He *almost* reached it too.

MARLA Caine stared at the desk; one stiff arm followed the gaze, delicate fingers of the hand clawed but for one. To Laura, she appeared to be pointing towards Caxton's desk, her dead face almost pleading.

The shadows watched Laura shiver as she stepped over the legs of the corpse. Blood still dripped turgid into the carpet from wounds in chest and head; she tried not to stare, but her eyes knew a morbid fascination. What happened here? She felt her blood chill as cold as Marla's.

There was a gun on the desk, perched besides the broken remains of Caxton's typewriter. More mystery. The gun was old, clearly, but well cared for, gleaming the colour of a bluebottle's carapace.

Laura felt a thrill as her fingers brushed against the metal and composite instrument. She picked it up and tested its weight. Then checked the magazine and chamber to find it filled with deadly potential. She made it safe, slipped it into a pocket and then turned to scan the room.

Books everywhere. So many books. You can never have too many. She knew what she had to do and it made her afraid. No choice after all; but that was the life of the *Incunabula*. She began to fill her bag with the articles of Caxton's faith, hoping she shared its strength.

Marla stared. Did dead faces change expression? Laura shivered as she stuffed the last book into place and fastened the rucksack. She didn't know, but Marla's face held impatience now, not pleading. The finger had curled away from the desk.

Laura turned away and hurried out. She didn't bother to close the door. Somehow, she doubted Marla would mind.

THE sheer magnitude of *MorTek Prime* cast a pall over Adam's sense of perspective. Out here, alone in the Plaza, he began to realise the foolhardy reality behind his mission. The gun was a dead weight in his waistband. The manuscript rolled up in his pocket was nothing but a limp and tatty fake. And he was just a *derm-rat* dreaming of playing the hero.

All the real heroes were dead.

Like Caxton. Like that guy Maus.

This was their job; Adam just knew he wasn't up to filling dead men's shoes.

Silas Morlock wanted to see him, though. Alone amongst the multitudes, he had the open invitation. Proximity to the target, as Otto put it. That scared him as much as the prospect of taking aim and pulling the trigger. It all seemed so different, back at Caxton's place, after the insanity of Marla's extinction, with the fire of the library's destruction still burning in his belly. After Laura's scorn...

He'd show her.

Some other time. Some other way.

He turned away from *MorTek's* shadow and squinted at the blazing neon fire of *Terapolis*. Indecision and fear pulled at him. There were no books over there. None that weren't burning. He turned back to the shadows. This was pathetic. He was pathetic. Laura was right about him; he was just a junkie.

He pictured the contempt in her eyes when she said: "See, I told you so!"

The thought angered him even more, because it was right. He didn't want to prove her right. How could he go back and show her what he really was? The fear burned inside his chest, as if the *Hazamat* were making a bonfire of all his tinder-dry vanities in the library of his soul. Laura's scorn poured fuel on the fire and it exploded through the shield of indecision.

A couple of tottering steps towards *MorTek* and he realised what he was doing. The breath was heavy in his lungs. He expelled its weight, sucked it back in, the bellows of terror.

So the book ends here.

Like this.

No.

It can't. A life without books is... *unbearable.*

Adam craned his head until his neck bones creaked. The tower vanished into the thickening murk of night at some dizzying point far overhead. At this hour, the sun was long since masked by nightfall and so the inverted well of sky merged into the regular *Terapolitan* canopy of shadow. Only a singular star winked at him from the other side of the veil. A weak and trembling signal that might have been a blessing to those trapped in the gutter.

Morlock was only a man.

So *MorTek* was vast, world-embracing, but its heart was only human. All he had to do was aim and pull the trigger.

He could do this.

The way was open. He didn't have to do a thing, except walk through the doors and wave the manuscript. They'd take him all the way to Morlock.

Yes. He stepped forwards. Felt some of the burden of terror and doubt cascade away. *MorTek's* foyer loomed larger. Morlock was finished. The end was coming. He'd show Laura. He'd show them all.

Already, the memory of Laura looked at him with fresh interest. The contempt was gone, a promising gleam in her eyes. Like the old days, before she got to know who… *he had been.* All because he was going to *do* this.

With a deep breath he stepped forward into the belly of the beast. For Marla. For Caxton. For whatever damn reason he saw fit. The book was not coming to an end, but to a glorious beginning. And the name on the spine was his. Adam. Adam… *Caine.*

HE had waited for so long.

Waited. Patient. Impotent.

There, in that esoteric continuum that dwelt on the other side of shadow.

There had been no other choice, until *they* opened the way into themselves.

Now, the waiting was nearly over; he felt a hint not of regret but of nostalgia. For the heady early days, fresh and strong and vibrant in this world, learning to function in the unfamiliar medium of mundane matter. The thrill of setting up the fabric of the New World, of heading off and dismantling opposition, of all those internecine strategies and Machiavellian manoeuvres.

Of Empire Building, he supposed.

Strange days, but essential, the way that older order was so structured. Not too dissimilar to the modern, but of course now everything was focused towards the *Gestalt*. As it should be.

All except… the *Incunabula*.

The *late*, unlamented *Incunabula*.

In the darkness, a leathery creak interrupted his thinking. A soft putrescent dribble was followed by a muffled groan. Morlock opened his eyes and a ghost of a smile slithered through his lips.

"Patience, Otto. Caxton's protégé is coming. Your work is almost done."

The Twelfth Folio
At The End Of All Days

"MY name's Adam Caine. I'm here to see Silas Morlock."

Despite all the confidence he tried to feed into the words, the guard looked less than impressed. He slouched in his seat and stared over the security station, as if this kind of entry was a common occurrence, even at this late hour.

The man looked older than he probably was. The bland face was as lined and sagged as the uniform. Most of his hair had long-since abandoned its anchorage. Only a few strands, grey as ghosts, remained to be teased across his scalp. The eyes stared blank and bored, but with a hint of musty authority. Adam felt his conviction curdle to a lump in his throat, but he refused the urge to swallow.

At last the guard moved. With a sigh, he reached for a screen and began to tap its surface. "Got an appointment, have you?" The tone added 'of course you don't'.

"No. I have a package to deliver. *Personally*. It's of the highest importance."

To add weight to his demand, he retrieved the bundle of counterfeit pages and waved it like a staff of authority.

The chair creaked as the guard stood up to his full height. Not much if truth be told, but the elevated security platform allowed him to glare down from an imposing height. His stance registered calculated indifference and a boredom that was doubtless genuine.

"I'll see he gets it."

Adam snatched the manuscript away.

"*No!* I have to deliver it personally. I am expected."

"Sure. He loves visitors does the Master. 'Specially from little *c'roaches* just passing."

"I mean it. He said his door is open any time."

Adam felt his voice crack. His confidence was half way back to the entrance, running hard and fast. Already, he saw Laura's smirk. It looked better on her than it did on the guard. That only made things worse.

The guard grinned, beginning to enjoy asserting himself. This was not in the plan. He should be in by now, not a source of amusement for a bored junkie. The man leaned forward, his clenched fists leaning on the counter.

"I'm sure you and the Master are good friends," he said, "but –"

I will see him now.

The voice came from everywhere and nowhere. The little colour on the guard's face drained as pallid as his sparse hair. A glob of matter spat from the *simulacomm* plinth resting between his fists. The man backed away just in time to avoid the glimmering substance from colliding with his face. The deluge subsided. The dark matter bubbled and rippled as it moulded into the effigy of a head.

"Mr Morlock. Sir!" The guard tried to stand to attention, but his body had long since left such firmness of flesh and will behind.

Adam felt his spine stiffen. He just managed to crush the autonomous urge to turn and run for the doors. The manuscript – the forgery – creaked as he squeezed his sweating fingers around it.

"*I am expecting our guest*," the Morlock-head said in a metallic hiss. Then it turned around 180 degrees, the ersatz flesh of the neck creasing and folding against the impossible rotation. The face gazed at Adam in triumph.

"*You are late my boy, but that is not important. What matters is that you are here. Come. Come to me. The west wing. The far end. A lift is waiting. It will bring you to me.*"

For an eternity the head stared like a vulture waiting for its victim to lie still. Then Morlock ended the connection and the head gurgled back into the plinth. Adam felt himself released and he stepped back with a breathless gasp.

The guard did the same, slumping into his seat and leaning against the desk. After a few gasps, he recovered enough to point the way. "Back... back there," he said. Then he hid his head in his arms and trembled. Adam left the guard to recover and made his way cautiously into the gloom.

A row of lifts waited. One of them was wide open, a weak light glowing from within its patient maw. Adam reluctantly stepped inside and the jaws closed behind him. He waited for the swallow. The manuscript was sweaty in his hands. Something lurched inside his belly. The lift gave a steady ride, but Adam felt as though the world was ready to drop from beneath his feet. He stepped back and pressed himself against the wall. The gun clanked on the metal panelling, no comfort. A dribble of sweat stung one eye.

He closed his eyes and took a deep breath. His heart thumped in his ears. Loud pounding. His skin was trembling. For the first time he had a purpose in life. A terrifying purpose. He had to go through with it. He had to pull it off. *Pull the trigger.* Or... he stopped there. Before he fell apart.

He was all alone here. In the dark, with his eyes closed.

So he opened them. Accepted the comforting light. Where was Laura? Wasn't she his friend? So why wasn't she here to help? He cursed and almost closed his eyes again. The light was his friend. As it was for his dim and distant ancestors. The ones Caxton told him about, gathered around their fires for warmth and protection as they listened to stories. They might listen to his story someday. About the guy from the street who took down Silas Morlock.

Yes. He was the Hero.

The centre of the story.

Well, at least this chapter.

Adam the Hero – facing impossible odds and coming through to tell the tale and win the girl. Laura was never going to forget this. He grinned. There were other stories where some other bastard got the girl. Not the hero. That'd be just his luck. He frowned. His teeth chattered. The lift stopped.

This was the moment Caxton had plotted for so long.

And unwittingly bequeathed to his son.

Thanks. *Dad.*

He slipped the gun from his waistband. Now it no longer felt like a dead weight. It began to come alive in his hand. A frightening buzz of power emanated from the metal. It felt slippery in his grip. He slipped it under his armpit and wiped his hands on his jeans. That didn't seem to help at all.

The doors began to open with a thunk. Adam stepped forward, psyched up and ready for action.

The light died.

Adam didn't curse. He whimpered. He blinked. There was a sense of moving air. A coolness on his face, but nothing to comfort his eyes. Helpless, he backed up against the wall and then slid down to a frightened crouch, the gun cradled, impotent, in his lap.

"As it was in the beginning, so shall it be at the end. Welcome, Adam… to the consummation of our *Completion*."

"BORIS! Boris! BOOooOORRRIiiIIiSss!"

Lorelei's eyes closed and her mouth opened wide for a banshee's shuddering shriek. Her whole body went tense and jerked. Her latest climax lasted only seconds, but it seemed longer. What was it, again, about the law of diminishing returns? He gazed up at the frenzied woman with a sense of boredom and a vague concern that she might go on screwing him all night. She'd kept him too long already. So much for his one for the road.

At last the passion fled her body and she relaxed astride him. Her hands gently caressed his chest and ample belly until her panting breaths subsided to a normal rhythm. Then her throat purred like a mythical cat's.

"Hmmm! Boris. It gets better every time."

He stared up at her pink, shining face and grunted. "You know, for a marketing executive you really need some acting lessons. That performance was not convincing."

The expression of contentment slid from her face, her lifeless eyes glared. The chemical brighteners had worn off, which always made him feel uncomfortable. With the artificial gleam he could pretend that there was someone in there.

"I know I am not that good," he added when she made no reply.

"Why do you say that? You're getting better. You know how I feel about you."

She slid off him, her sweaty body moving with silken grace. Lorelei stretched out and moved her thigh across his loins. One hand stroked his chest; the other propped up her head.

"That's what worries me."

"You know it's you and me. Only you and me, Boris."

He suppressed a bitter laugh. "And all the others. I know you've screwed pretty much all the senior staff. Except Morlock and Bayle."

Lorelei giggled. "Don't forget Otto and Belial."

"Marla would kill you. And even you're not freaky enough to seduce Belial."

Another giggle. "I wouldn't be so sure of that."

He didn't reply, only tried to roll away from his shapely captor. Her limbs tensed to stop him.

"Boris, you're not jealous are you? You know it's only you now."

"Right." He sighed.

"Oh, poor Boris. Don't be like this. I'm having a good time. Aren't you?"

"You're like *The Vytez*, aren't you? Part of the perks to settle me in. When a new boy comes along you'll screw him into place next."

A flicker of anger became apparent on Lorelei's features, even a glimmer of life returned – briefly – to her eyes. He'd been flattered at first. She was a beautiful woman – far beyond his league – but she just went through the motions. He never felt close to her, never felt like he mattered. A man can only lie to himself for so long. And how could he be fooled by anybody with such hollow eyes? They looked at him with the same emptiness he felt growing inside his own soul.

"You don't care about anything but your career and the corpus."

The bed shifted suddenly, sending ripples through his belly flab. Lorelei strode naked around the room. Her voice was shrill with anger: "Stop it, Boris! Stop being so *boring*! I hate it when you're like this."

"So go, then."

She glared. Yes, there was some life igniting in those eyes, but he knew it wouldn't last. He watched her retrieve her robe and slip it over her slender arms. Then she wrapped it tight around her body, the tantalising morsels of flesh veiled.

Boris looked away. He stared up at the ceiling. He felt bored and depressed. No, he felt ashamed and guilty. He should be long gone by now. Lorelei's plaything, that's all he was, and like a dumb puppy he'd come drooling every time she called.

She loomed over him suddenly. The anger was gone. Her face tried to adopt the features of concern and conciliation.

"Let's not fight, Boris."

He just looked up without replying.

"I know you're under a lot of pressure. I know the Project is weighing you down. You have to be strong, Boris. For all of us to be Completed."

Boris sighed. "And what is it? Really. I mean do any of you – us – know?"

"*Transcendence*," she breathed.

He barely heard the word but Lorelei's face was enraptured. He wanted to say 'bullshit' but the flash of liquid glitter in her eyes almost stopped his breath. It was beyond the rhapsody of sex.

"Transcendence, Boris. To leave this place behind. To live forever beyond the *Gestalt*. To be ourselves and break free of limitations. To complete our evolution. We won't be trapped inside these greasy post-apes any more – but Gods."

"Lorelei, I'm a *Necrofycer* not a damn prophet."

"Yes, Boris, you're both. And we're your chosen ones. We shall be Gods among Gods."

He slumped his head back against the pillow. "Okay, okay, you've sold me. So why do I feel so uneasy about the whole thing?"

"It's only natural. So much rests on you. Poor Boris. I know what you need."

He groaned at the suggestion. Hadn't she had enough? "Not again, Lorelei. You've worn it out!"

She giggled. "I didn't mean that. *The Vytez.*"

"We've run out of that too."

"So? I know where Belial cooks it up. I can slip in and get us some more. That'll make you feel better."

That would mean more of Lorelei's company, rather than the solitude he craved, but he couldn't bring himself to say it. *The Vytez*. Yes, Lorelei's company would be a price worth paying for some of that, it might even help him to cope. He can always pack later.

"Go on, then."

"I won't be long, keep the bed warm for me."

He grunted an affirmation. Moments later, the door banged.

Boris enjoyed the silence and the solitude. He stretched and then settled back on the bed. He closed his eyes and listened to his steady breathing. Sleep was enveloping him, a soothing somnolence. He floated on it and felt satisfied. Deeper now into the realms of sleep, still semi-aware but well on his way to the private realm of dreams. This was bliss, far beyond Lorelei's cloying reach…

"Uncle Boris!"

His mouth flopped open with a nasal snore.

"Oh, Uncle Boris! Wake up! You have *to wake up…"*

Boris slept, oblivious.

"Okay, pal! We tried. You've really *had your oats now!"*

THIS is a lesson in darkness. A lesson about defeat. Light fails in the end, Morlock was saying. Darkness will always defeat light. The match burns out. The torch batteries fail. Stars die. Minds perish. Even time dies, here, in this primordial pit of despair. All it has to do is wait.

For now, the dark whispered: *"Our time is at hand. Come. Come to me."*

Not a request, not even an order, merely a prediction. Even so, Adam found it an effort to move. He slowly managed to crawl to his knees and shuffle forth, refusing to let go of the gun, so that he was hobbling on three limbs. He felt the lift's threshold beneath his fingertips, then his knees. A little further and he was out in the Abyss. The doors thunked shut. There was no going back. There was nothing to go back *to*.

The fear tasted bitter in his throat. It ached in his bowels. Adam was scared to move, but he was also afraid to remain in one place. He wanted to curl up into a huddled ball, a foetal stance of a young child beneath the bed sheets, and cry for a mother he had never known.

Finally, he braved his own two feet. He moved forward, one hand outstretched against whatever was out there. He felt unbalanced. He closed his eyes, and that seemed to help him navigate the shade.

If only Laura could see him now. She wouldn't be contemptuous. Not now, as he stalked the shadows. No she'd be proud, he wasn't the loser she thought him to be. That thought provided a little strength, only a little, but it might be enough. He let it lead him to the hate he felt for Morlock, and that strengthened him some more.

Yes, he hated Morlock, hated him enough to want him dead, but he realised with a sick feeling he had never killed before. Laura was right; this wasn't the *Gestalt*. It was real. Real and he was going to kill someone.

A light exploded and seared his vision. One hand clamped over his eyes, he turned from the glare and snarled in rage and pain: "Where are you, you bastard?"

The answer sounded horribly close. "Where I have always been; stood at the event horizon between the light and the dark."

Adam tried to look towards the source of the sound, but his eyes were two balls of hot pain boiling in a bath of tears. Morlock laughed somewhere beyond the pain.

"Eyes are such fickle things. Take your time, my boy. We have all the time left in the world."

Slowly his eyes evolved to tolerate the glare, until he could turn towards the light and see what it contained. Not much, it turned out. An oasis, or a spotlight revealing his weakness. As his eyes adjusted further, he finally came to discern its outer edges, and there on the far side he found his quarry.

"I knew you would come," Morlock said. "It was inevitable once Caxton moved you into play. Now, give me that which I asked you to bring and your rewards will be great. All the meaning and purpose you have ever sought will be yours."

Kill him! Kill him now! The thought was a shout in his mind. An overriding passion, a beacon in the darkness as bright and clear as his fear, but his limbs had turned to lead. He fought for control. Morlock watched him calmly. He managed a twitch. He stepped closer. Closer still. The arm moved, slowly levelled the gun. He gazed into his opponent's eyes through the sights. The eyes remained unchanged, still calm, serene even.

"Your mother's pistol. How touching." Morlock smiled. "Very well, before we discuss our business, we shall let you get this urge out of your system. Call it a rite of passage if you wish. But first, indulge me a moment."

Another light flared a few meters away, but this eruption lacked the power to overwhelm the eyes. He didn't want to look away from Morlock, but all the same he felt his head jerk to the side. He wished he hadn't. It took every ounce of self control not to drop the gun.

Otto stared. Eyes pleading. Tentacles and damp folds of masticating membranes held him in a mucous shroud. The coiling tendrils met and entwined into a gigantic vine-like protuberance that soared into the darkness, a tether to something unseen far above. Otto swung gently in this hideous cradle, all but his pallid face hidden beneath the binding membranes. Monstrous machine, or alien creation. It was both, it was neither; to Adam's terrified mind it was a nightmare straight out of a bad *Gestalt* trip. He stared into Otto's bulging eyes; horrified to realise they contained awareness, unable to look away until finally a chuckle from Morlock broke the spell.

"Poor Otto. He never realised just how close Marla and I always were."

Something wet sloshed inside his stomach with a stab of cramp. A wave of nausea gurgled all the way down his bowels. A hot streak, he barely managed to prevent from flowing down his legs. Swallowing hard, he gripped the pistol. Now or never.

There was an impotent click. He closed his eyes in horror. A liquid groan from the remnants of Otto.

"It helps if you release the safety catch. Or so I am told."

His arms trembled. It made it all the harder to fiddle with the gun and release the catch. Hurriedly, he struggled with the implement in his hands, fought back the whine of pure terror. Somehow he released the catch and aimed the gun again. A panic stricken twitch of his finger and the muzzle flared fire.

The gun boomed. Kicked. The energy rippled up his arm to detonate in his shoulder with a muscle-wrenching ache. The bullet went wide. Morlock moved in a blur, his arm sweeping up as the bullet crashed into the shadows. The cane impacted. Pain exploded in his face. The gun fell into the shadows.

Another pain as Morlock's arm swiped again. He yelled and fell back, his arms up to protect his body from further blows. The impact jarred the breath from his lungs. The cold floor chilled his heart. He felt the first sob of defeat well up inside like magma from the fiery depths of the Earth.

He had failed. Everybody.

"Join us. Be at peace. It's not too late…"

Adam panted with fear and squeezed his eyes shut. As if that was capable of blocking the voices or making Morlock vanish into the night. The cane tapped in the fathomless void. Closer. He realised Morlock was clicking his tongue. Soft, repetitive, as one chides a child.

"You know, Caxton was meant to go insane when he turned against me. That's why I let him learn what he did. As he hid from me, it was meant to gnaw away his mind until there was nothing left but a longing for Completion. Alas, the seething sea of possibilities saw another way."

The whimper was less a sound, more a crushing pit of terror breaking open his soul. Adam hated himself for this display of utter breakdown. No Caxton-style defiance in the face of the inevitable. He was not his father's son. A bitter thought.

"Instead," Morlock continued, "he found the *Incunabula* and nurtured the information until he might actually threaten me. Can you believe that? Still, no matter. Such considerations are of no relevance now."

Something hard but thin struck his arm. A tap, none too hard. His eyes opened against his will. Morlock's face stared from on high. His cane gently wrapped against his arm. The skin tried to crawl away from the impact zone.

"And you helped, my boy."

"N-NO!" The sob rippled through his body. He felt so alone. So horribly alone. He tried to crawl away on his elbows and shoulder blades but the cold *pedederm* clung to his clothes and defeated his attempt to slide clear.

Morlock smiled again. "The best agent is the unknowing one. I am proud of you."

The smile faded. One hand unclasped from the other as it rested on the cane. Pale and glowing, it left trails of unearthly light in its wake. Adam watched it extend towards him and the fingers uncurl.

"Now, surrender the manuscript."

"Why? Why do you want it so badly?"

"Secrets are for keeping. In the dark places. Complete your purpose."

"No! You want it – you take it!"

The hand closed and returned to the cane. One eyebrow raised briefly. Adam felt giddy at the hidden depths of defiance, but it was futile. It achieved nothing.

He never even saw the movement, but the cane's silver tip was suddenly pressing into his face. Hard against the flesh beneath his nose to grind gum and bone beneath. Sharp pain bellowed in his head. Through the tears of agony, Morlock's face remained the epitome of disinterested calm.

"The *Gestalt* is here, Adam. It has always been here. All around us. Every mote of darkness leads to its blissful realm. You can have that. I promised you all your heart's desire. Everything you ever wanted. I stand by that. So much. In return for so little."

Through the agony, he found his speech. "Can you give me books? Can you give me my mum and my dad? Can you?"

"All that and more."

The cane pressed harder. The silver tip became the centre of his existence. It was too much. His teeth flared a white-hot agony worse than a back street dentist. His nose was cold numb. A distant thunk-clunk of a lift door taunted the impossibility of escape. The voices were a hissing roar flooding through his ears.

"Surrender the manuscript and the pain shall cease."

Trembling fingers found the sheaf of papers and slowly withdrew them from the holster of his pocket. He held it up to Morlock, but the man flinched as the paper neared his fingers.

"No! Don't give it to me. Cast it aside."

The paper struck the floor and slithered. The singular tone collapsed into a flurry as the paper dissembled and fluttered broken. The cane withdrew. The pain collapsed like Caxton's forgery.

"You see? I take away your pain forever."

"Let me go... let me go..."

A weak voice, but Morlock heard. His face held an expression that suggested he fully understood the pain. "Of course," he said. "Peace, Adam. You go to the *Gestalt*. I shall release you – and all the just rewards hidden in your soul."

A luminous claw coming closer. Helpless, Adam watched as Morlock bent towards him. Calm face glowing. Hideous, but holding him frozen like a rabbit.

"GET AWAY FROM HIM!"

Morlock looked up, startled. The clawed hand retreated. A hiss from his thin lips. A boom thundered through the shadows. Matter exploded from Morlock's chest. Another boom. A crow-like outcry as more flesh blasted from bone and sinew.

Morlock staggered, face twisted in fury. Another boom and his temple exploded. Light seared the night. It stung Adam's eyes. The building began to shudder and vibrate with a distant resonance like a visceral roar of pain.

It made no sense, how Morlock kept his feet – *kept breathing* – but with one last baleful glare, his tormentor turned and fled into the deep shade beyond. The radiance escaping his body flickered like a stellar event then even that faded, leaving Adam bewildered and not at all relieved that his ordeal had finished.

Laura emerged from the languid spots of colour and looked down. "I knew you'd get into trouble without me."

BEHIND his back – even though they feared him, *especially* because they feared him – the minions of *MorTek Prime* called him the 'odd job man'.

It was an appropriate name on so many levels. Belial was odd, even for a city like *Terapolis*. Odd because he had none of the same needs as its other denizens. He never entered the *Gestalt*. There were no lusts apparent in that great lumbering assemblage of matter. Odd again because he was like no other and he did all the odd jobs; not in the manner of Marla Caine or Otto Schencke who did the odd jobs of a 'political' nature. Just odd as in menial, trivial, unimportant. Yet, there was nothing of this in his demeanour. He projected a powerful, intimidating presence that demanded, if not deference, then certainly a civility to someone who was not registered in the conventional hierarchy of daily life.

There was no official title to justify his existence within the company; the origins of his semi-unofficial reference as Morlock's personal assistant were long lost to corpus memory. In the end, it was probably for no greater reason than they had to call him something.

In the midst of the busy functionaries forever in the service of the hive, Belial was the bee buzzing to no apparent purpose. Another reason, perhaps, he caused so much disquiet. It would have surprised them, then, to learn that he was an integral component of the *MorTek* organism.

Nobody knew what he thought of all this, of his place in the fabric of existence, or indeed on anything.

But he did not think. No thoughts currently occupied his cranial contents, for he was the very epitome of focus. Not out of loyalty, or personal idiosyncrasy, not out of mental debility. He was simply what he was.

A servant.

Of *MorTek*.

Of the *Gestalt*.

In ways none but his master might understand.

Alone of all *MorTek's* minions, he was the only creature allowed to venture into Morlock's mysterious apartments. The only one indeed who might enter free from fear and emerge unscathed of mind. Not even Bill had ventured into that unknown place.

Nor did they know that it was Belial who concocted the alchemical brew the higher echelons craved second only to the *Gestalt. The Vytez.* The self-same amber fluid that seemed to discharge the very essence of life into every cell of the body, and fill every trough and peak of their spiritual waveform; a replacement for something *missing*.

He did this now.

Dark eyes unblinking in the paltry light.

He was silent; the room was not.

Equipment hummed softly. A Bunsen flame hissed. Fluid bubbled and gurgled. Footwear shuffled with Belial's motion. Glass clinked and chinked as he performed his surprisingly dexterous activities.

There was no sound of breathing. He was not breathing. Needed no breath, except on the few occasions that he was required to speak.

Belial was odd.

The room was an office on the periphery of Morlock's private apartments. Much of the level was unused and dusty, but for this partition that had been turned into a lab. He moved towards the end of the bench.

On the edge, where he left it, a sac of flesh pulsated gently. It looked like an egg sac and glowed dim with an inner luminescence. It sagged as his big hand closed around it. He raised it to his mouth and used his teeth to tear the membranous enclosure. A few drops of amber ichor splattered his work clothes. They glowed bright and strong for a few moments, before they faded to a soft honey pallor.

Belial carefully moved with the shriven sac towards the alchemical production line. He poured the glutinous contents into a beaker. The light bathed his face with golden sunlight. Then he lifted the beaker ready for the next stage of his mysterious work.

Belial's chest exploded.

The beaker fell from his hand and detonated in liquid fire across the floor.

Another explosion punched a hole in Belial's torso. Threshed cloth filled the air with fine particles of pulverised thread. No blood. No quivering blobs of sundered flesh. Just worms. Or tentacles. They thrashed, writhed, hissed from the new orifice. Amber fluid spurted and dripped from the pulverised flesh. Curls of shadow spilled from the wounds and writhed as if grateful at this unexpected freedom.

On the bench were fragments of his physical shell blasted from his frame. No resemblance to skin, fat and muscle. The lumps of ichor-soaked matter were hard, and flaked at their edges. A closer look in better light might have revealed a dark series of stains. Almost, the stains resembled blurred and sodden letters on rain soaked paper left to harden.

Belial groaned.

Another explosion erupted from his body.

Belial staggered backwards, clutching his body in every evidence of terrible pain. He roared his suffering and found a word: "Master!"

Then the fabric of *MorTek Prime* shuddered. The sympathetic shock cascaded through the odd job 'man' and into the neuro-muscular organism that was *MorTek Prime* to provoke a deadly counteraction.

"Master... hurt!"

He turned for the door.

Before he reached it, his temple exploded. Bright beams of light emerged to cast writhing shadows against the walls. Yellow, filthy ichor glooped down Belial's face. Thrashing tendrils writhed and beat against his flesh. He stumbled, but managed to catch himself on the edge of the bench.

He shut his undamaged eye, breathed deeply, and somehow gathered his strength. Then he lurched towards the door and the labyrinth of *MorTek Prime*; bound by preternatural symbiosis to a distressed host organism, he was called to his true nature and purpose.

Woe betide those associates who crossed his path; Belial was beyond odd.

FAR above the crowded lives of lost Humanity, the Moon shimmered indifferent, as she had done since before the birth of Life.

Across the hemisphere facing her craggy and ancient visage, nocturnal creatures navigated existence by her cold illumination. On the surface of lakes, and the still vaster pools of oceans, the light gleamed silver, transmitted into the darkness of night.

Beyond the urban sprawl a few humans tilted their eyes skywards, to absorb her splendour and admire the shimmering, scintillating Heavens. Only a few, for where it came to Terapolis *the moonlight failed, and the billions of primates called Man dwelt in ignorance of the cosmic angel shimmering overhead.*

Terapolis *shimmered not silver, but the dead colour of ash. The putrid hues and shades of the city's flesh were bleached, like the pallor of a faded* Terapolite *who has spent too much time in the embrace of the* Gestalt.

Still, the light illuminated the endless vista of minaret and mono-lith, vanishing beyond the clustered horizon of the Earth's curved and ever-pregnant belly. No Human awareness had ever witnessed this sight. So there was no one but the Moon Man to attest the tepid palsy that rippled outwards from the axis of MorTek Prime *to the outermost fringes of the stygian labyrinth.*

This was no earth tremor, for Locus Prime *resided in a region of geological stability and the mighty monoliths knew how to absorb the energies of Mother Earth's raging truculence. The shivering flutter was the lingering residue of another trauma; one sourced of flesh and bone and the mental radiance of rage and agony.*

The shivering towers the Moon perceived was but a subtle display of the truism that Terapolis *was a cybernetic organism of global proportions, forever bound in spirit to its Master Maker deep in the core of the Mother Tower. And this night it had suffered a violation unprecedented in the history of its magnificence.*

Even as the convulsion passed, changes were inherent in the sprawling canopy of the city. Easily missed by the casual observer, but the Moon's gaze was broad and deep, and the unearthly radiance revealed the ripening transformation taking place.

Far from uniform, random and without apparent purpose, mina-rets retained the shivering energy. Out of the millions, thousands spasmed with the muscular contractions deep beneath their integument. Some cracked open, like pine cones, to reveal the darkness within. Still more split in spiralling gashes. Leathery hides parted and tore as the great interlocking plates unfurled.

Deep in the cracks and chambers revealed within, were pools of utter darkness, in stark contrast to the shimmering quicksilver swimming on the surface of each broken minaret. Moonlight began to spill into the gaping wounds, and discovered the shuffling movement therein.

An effervescent fluid rushed out to breathe the air, alive and gushing, energetic and restless, it flowed out over the surface of the tower. Under the light of Moon, the progeny slowly revealed itself as it thinned and spread.

No liquid was this. Many-limbed things *scurried. Young spiders, they appeared so small, yet no arachnid birthed these creatures. On closer inspection, they might yield clues to their origins and nature. The coiling tentacles, the bodies shaped and contoured like a* Geist-masque…

This was not yet their time. Many appeared incomplete. Some were but amorphous blobs of gleaming flesh; still-born and pushed aside by motile kin.

Many flooded down the length of their towers of gestation; seeds scattered to take root in human minds. Here in Locus Prime *they were assured a welcome among the* Gestalt *exiles, but for the others gathered at the apex of their birth the welcome was destined to be one of horror.*

They left the nest, carried on the air currents far outcity – *in search of virgin minds and the untimely Completion of their purpose…*

ONE look at Laura's face told him all he needed to know: she was *never* going to let him forget this. At least she hadn't said 'I told you so'. That was a small mercy.

"Are you going to lay there all day?"

Despite his aching teeth, he managed to make a face. "Gimme a break!"

"Tough day?"

"What do you think?"

She smirked while she slipped the gun into a pocket. The rucksack on her bag shifted heavily. Even now she had the damn thing, as if it was any good here, but he was too tired and relieved to ask about it. She might have answered and forced him to think.

"You brought this on yourself, you know. I have no sympathy. Just lucky for you I arrived when I did."

"I was biding my time. *Actually*."

"Sure. You had him right where you wanted."

Adam gave up. He knew when he was beaten.

"My poor eyes," he said, trying to blink the coloured blobs clear, "what was that light?"

"Not here, Adam. This isn't the time – or the place. Just get up and let's get going."

"Okay! Okay – hey do you feel that?"

He frowned. The *derm* shivered. Something was rumbling far off, like a tubeworm approaching its salmon junction ready to leap.

"Machinery or something. I don't know. *Come on!*"

She held out her hand. Adam groaned against the aches the movement provoked, but reached out to take it. She pulled hard and got him to his knees, then he pushed himself up to his feet. The movement made him feel dizzy.

"Up you come."

His vision swam. A nauseous wave. He groaned and swayed.

"You okay?"

He nodded.

"Deep breaths. I'm going to let go now."

He nodded again. Breathed deep. He was starting to feel better.

A high-pitched shriek almost blasted his brain out of his ears. He clamped his hands to his head, watched Laura do the same until he squeezed his eyes shut in agony. The floor lurched. Shuddered from side to side. An instant's free fall. A siren of pain from his backside when he landed heavily. Laura on her knees, toppling onto all fours, her mouth was wide in a cry of terror, but he couldn't hear for the fading shriek and *MorTek's Prime's* rumbling groans.

Then it was over. The quake seethed back into mild tremors. The banshee wail was fading into the distance. A few pops and groans added an ominous afterthought. A creaking rip gave way to the gush and gurgle of angry fluid somewhere far away. Something slithered overhead, somewhere much closer.

"What was that?"

"I don't want to know. I just want to get out of here."

"Okay. Okay, let's go." Laura began to climb unsteadily to her feet. Adam picked himself up to follow.

That's when the light went out. A dreadful reminder just how deep the shadows were in this place.

"Adam! Stand still! Don't wander off!"

And just where was he going to go? He felt the angry retort burn his throat, but annoyance was cooled when the air stirred overhead. Something slithered. Something else shuffled. He hoped that was Laura. A stench filled the air. Noisome, organic and foul. Definitely not Laura. A spattering of some thick fluid hitting the *derm*.

"Adam... I think there's something in here."

"There's... there's only Otto."

And that *thing*, but he didn't mention it.

"What do you mean?"

"Otto. Hanging… around. Kind of."

"I don't think I want to know."

"Trust me. You don't."

"I was afraid you'd say that."

Adam squatted down and reached out for the *derm*. He stroked his hand over the yielding surface. Sensing by feel, for all the good it was. The shiver was still running through its fabric, but he gritted his teeth against the awful living sensation. There was no sign of it. He dropped to all fours. Reached out further with exploratory fingers. It had to be here somewhere; but he didn't want to stray too far.

A snort of frustration. "I can't find it!"

"Find what?"

"Marla's gun!"

"So Morlock's got it! Forget it, Adam, we need to find a way out of here."

"How?"

"I'm working on it. Use your eyes. Can't you see any-thing?"

He waved his hands in front of his face. Nothing. Only the motion of air on his sweaty face told him he still had fingers. There was no way to decide which was worse – the darkness or Morlock armed with something more than a cane.

Laura muttered: "Where's the bad guy when you need a light?"

"Is that supposed to make me feel better?" Some rescue. Something landed on the *derm* with a series of heavy thuds. It sounded like heavy-duty cable, except for the slither of moving coils.

"Cax got me into this," Laura added, as if there was nothing out there. "I'll *kill* him next time I see him."

"Don't talk like that. You're creeping me out!"

The smell was stronger. Mouldy and foetid. Air moved in a long slithering hiss. He couldn't tell the direction of the noise. He had no sense of direction at all.

"Adam!"

His heart almost stopped with the fright.

"There's a light. A way out. Over... *Sorry.*"

He looked around wildly. "I can't see anything!"

"Stop moving. Calm down. Now just turn round slowly until you see it."

Trembling, he forced himself to comply. Turning, ever so slow. Something touched his face; he recoiled with a cry of horror.

"It's only me. Don't panic!"

He reached out again, his heart racing. Fingers. He took hold of them. They squeezed tight. Pulled him to his feet. Helpless again, he put his trust in Laura.

"Don't let go," she said. "Don't squeeze so tight either."

"Sorry. How far?"

"Hard to say. Do you see it yet?"

A sigh. He squinted out into the unyielding darkness. Turned his head this way and that. Scanning with a beacon of pure hope. Wait. There. Two perpendicular smears of light. Faint. A door. Left ajar.

"I see it!"

"Good. Then let's make a run for it."

Her hand released him. He felt naked and alone. Footsteps stamped over the *derm*. No choice but to follow. He broke into a shuffling run. The distant smear of light was his navigation. Behind him, something was moving fast. Homing in on his slapping footfalls.

"Laura! Wait!"

"Stay close! Hurry up."

She was way ahead of him. Almost at the safety of the light.

It was a door. Best of all, it was open. Laura was already there, widening the orifice, letting more light flood in. She turned to stare wild-eyed at something; he didn't want to know at what. He ducked at a sensation of moving air above his head.

There was a fire burning in his lungs. His heart was thudding too much. Time was slowing down to match the pace of his leadened limbs. So close.

Something tangled around his foot and gripped tight. He fell heavily onto the *derm*. The last of the wind grunted from his body. A slithering gurgle close to his ear. Something damp touched his cheek. He felt himself pulled backwards and he dug his nails into the *derm*, but all his fingers managed to do was tear wet tracks in the thick integument.

Then something moved in front of him. He looked up to see a pungent mass of membrane and mucus hover a foot from his face. The smell was disgusting. It cracked open to reveal something inside that moved with all the semblance of a *Geistmasque*. Bony, leather-clad claspers snapped eager for his face.

The cry rose like vomit: "I've had enough of this shit!"

The monstrosity flew apart. Fragments of bone and scraps of leather spattered in all directions. He ducked just in time to avoid a globule of pungent gore from hitting his face. A harsh boom rolled back the shadows.

Laura had her gun out; in her other hand she held the rucksack. She swung it in sweeping arcs. More of these monstrous tentacles swayed clear, retreated back into the shadows. She was at his side in a heartbeat, swinging the bag, batting aside these monstrous extrusions. The binding on his legs lurched free.

He got to his knees and dashed for it, half running half crawling. Somehow Laura grabbed the collar of his jacket and added to his momentum by pulling him forwards. Light was all around him next. Light to soothe his eyes and dusty concrete supporting his hands and knees.

A sharp screech. A hollow boom. He sank back to sit against the wall and watched as Laura secured the rusting door. Something banged against the metal. Slithered against it. Then lost interest. Slowly, some sanity began to unfold.

"We… were," he began, panting heavily, "we were made for each other don't you think? Like an old married couple."

"Oh shut up, Adam, this isn't the time."

"I only meant I'm always getting you into trouble, and you get me out of it. We're a great team. A match made in heaven."

"Somewhere a little lower, maybe," she muttered un-convinced.

"So what… what's in the bag?"

Laura just shrugged. "Only some books."

"Yeah? Guess those *things* didn't like your selection."

"I guess not."

She stared up into the soaring heights of *MorTek* with a preoccupied air. Adam sat back to focus on his breathing. He never got the chance. Laura stepped over his legs and began to climb the stairs.

"Oh come on! Not that way! Can't I have a rest at least?"

She didn't reply. Her footsteps shuffled further away.

"Women," he muttered, once he was sure she was beyond hearing.

BEREFT of Boris, Lorelei let her façade slip. The features of a vibrant but adventurous virgin melted into the pores of her painted face. Revealed were the hard and calculated lines of the ambitious *MorTek* executive she really was.

A thwarted executive in these latter years.

Some might say bitch, but never to her face.

There were no further peaks to climb, for she would never fill Morlock's shoes. At least, no method of succession had yet formulated in her mind. So, there was nowhere else to go, except into the *Gestalt's* glory when it came to Completion.

Why else did she mollycoddle flawed genius like Boris? Why else was she wandering these neglected and dusty levels that maintained a distance between Morlock and his minions?

Somewhere around here, Belial worked his magic brew they called *The Vytez*. She wasn't supposed to know, nobody was, but once she had encountered the strange man and followed him. She – barely – caught a glimpse. A useful if risky venture. It might bring Boris out of this mood; make him tolerable if not pleasurable company.

She chuckled at the thought of seducing Belial. The notion tickled her. No, not *that* way. The thought of getting intimate with such a creature made her skin crawl, but the maudlin jealousy inherent in the comment was so amusing, it almost – *almost* – eased the discomfort of the assignment.

She was tired of coddling him through his mood swings. Stoking his ego, whispering platitudes in his ears, trying to generate some stimulation from that pathetic protuberance he called a prick.

If it wasn't for the symbiote grafted inside, then she'd have to fall back on fingers and falsehoods while satisfying his pitiful male ego. It guaranteed climax to her fullest satisfaction regardless of how minuscule the worm they put inside her.

She began to consider the conclusion of her report – whether to damn or acknowledge Boris fully into the *MorTek* corpus – when the high, pierced shriek tore through the walls and seemed to slice through her brain. The tremors that followed in its wake knocked her off her feet. She stumbled into a wall and then collapsed in an undignified heap on the bare floor.

"Fuck!"

Lorelei brushed hair from her face; the motion provoked a sharp stinging on her elbow. A quick examination revealed a red weal of grazed skin. It matched the raw patch on her right knee. Together with her bruised shoulder, the pain was threatening to tip her temper over the edge, but she just about held it in check. Then she noticed a broken nail.

"Fuck! Fuck! Fuck *you*, Boris Creek!"

Let him go the way of his predecessor. Let him end up like that raving old *scrote* after what they did to him. She shuddered at the memory of what he became and was glad she didn't know the details. Not even Otto and that psycho bitch Marla knew anything about that. It was Belial's doing. Old Belial. Well, he can have Boris too. Plenty more where Boris came from. Someone else can forge the *Gestalt's* Completion. Decision made, she clambered painfully to her feet, and began to trace her steps though the maze of corridors.

She limped and cursed at the pain. Then she cursed at the failing lights. First the main illuminants faded to the dimmest embers. The emergency lamps flashed into operation and cast an unearthly glow over the dusty corridors. The darkness only seemed to thicken and consume the light.

"Give me a *fucking* break."

The light dimmed a little more, but retained enough energy to let her make her way back down to the habitat. Once she got her bearings, that was.

Another ear-chilling shriek ripped through the maze. She stopped halfway down the corridor. Uncertain. Something shuffled into view down the far end. She backed away from the obscene shadow. Whatever it was, it shrieked again as though in agony. It stumbled forwards.

Light revealed its features.

"*Belial* –"

The apparition wore the odd job man's shapeless, heavy clothes. Half its cumbersome features were his, but the rest... As the light revealed more, she stifled a scream of terror.

Worms or slender snakes writhed in a frenzy. Tears in his clothes revealed membranous sheets oozing mucous. The tentacles and pseudopods of some hideous organic monstrosity clung to Belial's head and body. They thrashed in his flesh. Belial roared again and stumbled forward.

Consumed alive. By *something*. Lorelei felt sick and staggered backwards. At that moment, her knee betrayed her and she collapsed to the floor. The thump brought Belial out of his private realm of pain. He looked up. One mad eye, the colour of congealed pus, flared with rage.

"*M-o-r-t-e-k...*"

He reached out with his good hand. Lorelei saw the tentacles writhing and burrowing in the flesh. She struggled to stand, her knee refused. She began to shuffle away, sliding backwards on her backside as Belial lurched forwards at a frightening speed.

"Belial! NO – Belial! It's me. It's Lorelei!"

He growled. He roared. He moved closer. Finally her scream escaped, the only part that could. She realised those wriggling monstrosities were not consuming the lumbering man-shaped thing. *They were part of him.*

"Belial! *Noooooooo!*"

He was on her. One clumsy hand raised her high into the air. She hung in pain, thrashing with her legs, kicking at Belial's obscene body. Her gown fell open, but she no longer cared about her exposure, only the slithering damp sensation of those things touching and entwining her body.

And more.

They burrowed.

Lorelei cried and watched helplessly as things that looked like jack cables, rendered organic, burrowed into her belly. Others coiled round her thighs and buried their heads into her groin. Still more slithered and found the opening between her legs. They undulated through the veil of hair, entered in a horrible parody of a man's sticky palp, an obscene penetration deep into her inner cavities. They pulled her closer to Belial, where more of his extrusions found her naked flesh.

She screamed again. Screamed for Boris.

"Help me! Help *meeee*!"

She couldn't thrash and kick any more. She was bound too tight. Belial growled, face up close, vile stench filling her mouth and nose. Nothing human glared out of his one functional eye.

The spillage from his head reached out for her face. Tendrils probed her nose and mouth. Crawled deep into her ears. Burrowed in and around her eyes. Tears spilled, the only response she had left.

Her body was filled with the wriggling appendages. She felt them *moving* inside. They pulled her ever closer to Belial, close with a lover's intimacy. She managed a tortured gargle from the back of her entangled mouth. Closer still until she was no longer touching Belial's deformed body. She was merging *into* his flesh.

Then she was on the floor. Somehow he had passed right through her body and then disengaged to leave her kneeling. All pain gone, she swayed in shock and latent fear. Even the tendrils had withdrawn. She gagged and coughed. An attempt to speak, to scream, she didn't know, but she couldn't vocalise. She felt weak.

She managed to stand and turned to watch Belial depart down the corridor, her gown caught on his foot to trail in his wake. As she moved, she placed her weight on her left foot and felt something crumble. She looked down. It *was* her foot. Unbalanced, she collapsed onto her knees. The impact cracked them. They powdered and crumbled, widening fissures that ran up her thighs. Not just disintegrating, the dust itself was evaporating to a smoking nothingness. Dark plumes of shadow blended and merged into the shade congealing thicker in the corridor.

"*What… did… youuuu… doooo… tooooo… meeeeeee?*"

Harsh words. Dusty. Barely speech at all to her ears. She felt teeth and gums become exposed to cold air as her lips crumbled away like dry sand in a breeze. Belial ignored her. She watched in dull dismay as the tendrils oozed back into Belial's form and became overgrown with a mantle of flesh. The creature stretched, invigorated.

From the shadows breathed a sigh of air. Sibilant and lingering. The tones became words, and as she recognised the voice, she wept tears that eroded grooves in her face. *Find them, our guests. Disarm them. Harm them if you wish, but let them come to me, let them see, let them know…*

She watched Belial shuffle away. Felt the dust that was her grief tickle the still biotic nerves of her face. The voice lingered.

Farewell, Lorelei. You have served well, even at the end. Farewell. Until the Gestalt *consumes all you might have become…*

Lorelei felt herself diminish ever faster as her naked body continued its unnatural disassociation. An arm detached and dissolved on the floor, her breasts dribbled down her belly to vanish in the shadows between her broken thighs. Her spirit was abandoned by the flesh, to haunt the shadows until the *Gestalt* opened itself.

That was the only ambition, the only hope left to her now. In that moment of final revelation, she knew just what she had dedicated her adult life to achieve.

Too late.

The scream of rage and pain and loss cracked her dwindling remains asunder before it added to the ephemeral voices already awaiting the mystery of Completion.

THE dreadful nightmare was already forgotten the moment he awoke with a start. The sheets were sodden with fear, tangled with his primal turmoil. Awake, the nightmare was far from over. The bed still quivered from whatever seismic turbulence had dragged him from the depths of sleep.

"Lorelei!"

His call explored the empty suite and found nothing but emptiness. He thought he'd felt her close. Tasted her terror, even as her sense of existence passed through his body and dwindled into some quantum distance. A legacy of his nightmare, nothing more, he remembered – she'd gone to find *The Vytez*.

He was surprised at how badly he wanted to see Lorelei walk through the door, with or without that magical elixir.

"She ain't coming back, pal. She ain't never coming back."

Boris cried at the sound of the voice. He sat up and looked around.

"Leave me alone. Whoever you are. Whatever you are. Please!"

"Uncle Boris!"

"Noooo! *Goawaygoawaywayaawaay...*"

"Hurry, Uncle Boris. Get out while you can."

"Leave me alone." He began to cry.

"He's coming. Hurry. Hurry, Uncle Boris! You have to get out now."

A beaten man, he crawled from the bed and began to look for his clothes. The voices ceased their harassment, but he sensed them all around. He pushed the thought away as he struggled into his clothes.

Come back to us, Boris.

That wasn't a voice. Only a memory. It came to him suddenly; he remembered his determination to leave. So strong an impulse, until Lorelei snuffed the resolve between her thighs. So he was weak. Yes, weak, to allow Lorelei to sculpt his whims and urges like clay. No more.

Come back to us if you can…

"I'm leaving. I'm going *home.*"

Whatever had spoken before – imagination, guilt or ghosts – said nothing to this as he left the bedroom, but he felt a yearning triumph lingering in the air around him. Grabbing his coat on autopilot, he reached for the door and then yelped as though the handle was electrified. There was an energy there of a kind. A vibration that set his teeth on edge. An urgent tension that somehow felt alive.

MorTek Prime was alive, of course.

And this habitation pod, this door, was but a manmade capsule implanted inside the living heart of the tower. The jolt reminded him of how he was deep inside a vast chimera that should not *be* alive. For the first time in his life, he doubted his trade, doubted *G-Tek*, doubted every dream and aspiration that ever made him.

"Oh God! Please let me get out of here."

He didn't know who God was, but he fervently hoped that didn't matter. Shona knew, surely that was enough to embrace him too?

He braved the door again. Winced at the fresh jolt. Gritted his teeth and flung the door wide. There was a thick and unpleasant darkness outside, but he'd been living with that for too long now. Too long to really pay it any attention.

He plunged into the shade and on into the uncertainties of *MorTek Prime*. Behind him, a faint whisper: "*Hurry, Uncle Boris. There isn't much time.*"

The Thirteenth Folio
On The Cusp Of Completion

THE stairs were long and winding. They twisted up into the heights of *MorTek Prime* like some kind of endless column of concrete vertebrae. The dull walls were stained and mildewed. In places the concrete was cracked and skewed and only the shell of *MorTek* kept the giant blocks stable. The air in the stairwell was stale with the odour of mould and damp. Even the scrunch of crumbled concrete beneath their feet sounded subdued and old.

Things were not right. Nothing had been right since he'd let that head talk him into the lift. No, if he were truthful with himself, then he'd have to admit that things had *never* been right. This was *Terapolis* after all. Still, he seemed to have lost his desire for the *Gestalt*. That was something. Wasn't it?

Laura's footsteps skipped lightly above his head. The shuffle of her heavy rucksack didn't slow her down. He was worried that she'd leave him behind and he did his best to match the pace, but the only part of him that seemed capable of catching up were his wheezing breaths.

"Hey! Slow down," he called.

Laura's voice drifted from afar. "You junkies! No stamina!"

With a curse that came out as a grunt, he gripped the handrail and yanked himself up the next couple of steps. The handrail shuddered uncomfortably, but he really didn't want to let go any more than he wanted to look *down*. The higher they moved, the more he felt the vertigo. He handled it by staring right ahead at each endless step.

"There's got to be an easier way," he muttered.

His legs ached in protest. Even his arm was starting to throb from sharing the burden of the climb. He forced himself to go on until he reached the next level. Then he scraped round on the dust and put his weary foot on the first step of the next stage. Laura was still out of sight above him.

"Wait will you? I'm fucking dying here!"

"Then die a little faster!"

No sympathy. He bit down on the insult that tried to bludgeon its way out of his mouth. She probably *would* leave him if he let that one out.

Laura moved as if she had a map. She ignored the tantalising doors they encountered every few flights. Nice, *level* corridors where they might locate a lift. No more of this exhausting climb. He was beginning to wonder if this vertical forced march wasn't some kind of punishment. All he'd tried to do was save the day. Was that so bad, even if he had fucked it up?

"Why are we going up, anyway?"

"'Cos it's a long way down."

"But that's the way out!"

"Is it? You know where we are? You know the way the lifts moved? You know which floor to take? You got a map stashed somewhere?"

He felt his face flush hot. Not with exertion this time. "No! Have you?"

"Nope. Don't need one. Morlock knows the way."

He stopped and stared up at the dizzying array of flights, as if he might see Laura through the concrete. "You're crazy! You're following Morlock? I thought you were looking for a way out. We can't do this!"

"You started it. So now *we'll* finish it."

"No way! You shot Morlock I don't know how many times. And that light. I mean what–"

"Hey! You got us into this – going off half-cocked as usual."

"But…" He gave up and reluctantly resumed the climb. He remembered he never won when she was in this mood, but those fights had been over usual things. Kind of. "So how do you know Morlock went this way?"

"Use your eyes instead of your mouth."

"What…"

"He's bleed… well, leaking something."

He looked more closely at the steps beneath his feet. "What is *that*?"

"Damned if I know."

Damp patches in the dust. Thick globs of amber jelly, congealed in the damp air. It reminded him of something. Then he remembered the tongue-clenching taste of *sour*. Adam tried to avoid stepping in the splattered patches and wondered how much he'd already trodden in. He decided he didn't want to know and tried to find solace in the mundane.

"So how did you know where to find me?"

"Wasn't difficult."

"I mean, inside *MorTek*."

"*I know.* The guard in the foyer. A real mine of information."

"He let you in?"

"He didn't have a lot of choice."

"You didn't…"

She clucked her tongue and Adam's face fell. "What do you think I am? I just persuaded him to hit a G-Spot early, that's all."

Adam felt a strange sense of relief. "Sometimes Laura, you scare me!"

There was no response this time. He looked up and realised he couldn't hear her moving. He frowned at the silence. He didn't like this. Suddenly, he felt extremely alone.

"Laura?"

A loud boom thundered from above. Hollow and ponderous. Adam found the energy to begin a sprint up the stairs. Another boom reverberated down the stairwell. Then he heard a sharp crack and something clattered.

"Laura!" It was a wheeze, not a shout, but he cleared the flight, then half-way up the next one he saw Laura's feet at eye-level amidst a scattering of broken glass. He stopped to look up.

"Here!"

She threw something. He flinched but managed to catch the missile broadside in both hands without falling backwards.

"You could have had me down the steps doing that!"

She grinned mischievously. "What – a hero like you?"

He closed his mouth and sighed. The object in his hands was an axe. Sharp pointed edge along with the classic cutting blade. The handle painted red. It was in surprisingly good condition. No trace of rust.

"Feel better with a shaft in your hands?"

She smiled and turned to climb before he thought of anything to say.

"I want to go home," Adam muttered, but he forced himself to follow. The axe was heavy and unfamiliar, but at least it was something to put between him and Morlock. Yes, a shaft in his hands did make him feel better.

A little.

MORLOCK staggered through the labyrinth of *MorTek Prime*. He felt his strength waning, his flesh desiccating, as the stuff of his primary essence flooded from the breaches in his shell.

It gathered like a veil of smoke. Thick and dark, coiling into tormented fronds in his wake. Where it touched the natural shadows, it blended perfectly.

The amber fluid continued its ominous drip, but it was no longer an arterial flow. The loss was manageable. It oozed glutinous like a pale tar, but the crystalline scabs were insufficient to prevent the eruption of dark matter. He retained within his corpus enough of the essence imbibed from living humanity to emulsify him with this universe, but there was little enough to shield him from the ethereal torments of the sapient maelstrom.

It stung his eyes. Burned his shell. Sapped his strength further. There was no choice but to plunge through the spectral nebulae of burning light. Photonic – *ordinary* – light.

The rest, the worst, the lingering glimmer of human minds, the searing flares that were minds ejected from their dying material root structures. The backwash glow of the soulscape, the languid lost souls drifting around the baleful eye of the *Gestalt*. So much exo-dimensional radiance to torment his weakened senses.

With the pain and the disorientation came the first mocking doubts. Alien thoughts. The nagging fear that he might indeed fail, might actually return to *that* place. In turn, the doubt fuelled anger; an all too human emotion. He had spent far too long in their midst. Becoming like them. It was so... *intolerable.*

Morlock tightened his grip on Marla's gun. There was energy, a kind of *life*, within it. The molecules of metal infused with Marla's essence. Not her soul, not her mind, but the feral residue that had made her so useful over the years. Marla's imprinted aura would not fail him. Not even after the end. In a sense, he drew strength from the thought. Enough to tear through the web of alien doubt. He began to chuckle. Yes, he was becoming all too human.

"You're leaking, Morlock. A few bullets. Is that all it really takes? If I'd known it was that easy I would have done for you years ago."

Morlock felt his humour evaporate. "You! I should have known you would not be content to linger."

"Can't keep a good man down."

"Indeed. And what do you think you can achieve? Dis-embodied that you are?"

"Me? Nothing. I just wouldn't miss this for the world. So I came along to say bon voyage.*"*

"You believe your spawn will do your dirty work."

"I have faith in the lad."

Morlock snorted. "Faith. An illusion. A legacy of *extinguished* belief systems."

"Maybe. I have faith in humanity. In my son. He's finding himself. Overcoming the life we made for him."

"It was you who wielded the blade, I might point out." There was a cold silence. Morlock smiled. He had touched an ephemeral nerve. "And now you send the boy to finish the job. You should have finished him then. This way is so *cruel*. You send him into the crucible of souls. You know what he must do. You know what he must face. Is he strong enough to endure damnation for *your* sins?"

"He'll find the strength. Laura is strong too. She'll help him. They will finish you."

"I pity him, Caxton. For he knows not what he must do. Nor the consequences. Pray for him. Pray that he fails. It is best for him. It is best for you all. Completion is inevitable."

"Even you cannot predict the future."

"As my current predicament testifies, you might think. No, I do not predict. I lack the arrogance of you mutant primates. I sift patterns of probability. Balance possible outcomes. I retain the favourable balance of causation. It is fate. It is the natural order of creation. There can be no other outcome. Only details remain to be filled in."

"Oh? Such as, hmm – a bullet in the head?"

"*Quite.* Enjoy your amusement, Caxton, it will not distract me."

"We'll see," Caxton added. *"The Gods of Mount Olympus were just as bound to the whims of Fate as we mere mortals. But even Fate was subject to the whims of Kaos. We'll just have to see what the old butterfly can conjure, won't we?"*

Morlock ignored the jibe. He sensed a better retort ahead, a dribbling presence of leaking terror and adrenal energy. The nervous odour of Boris Creek. *So, he finds* other *uses. An opportunity to buy some precious time at least.*

Around the corner, he found the root of that trembling aura. Boris Creek, frozen in shock, as he found the release of his maker.

"The *Gestalt* needs you Creek, for a most unexpected duty. I have every faith in your capabilities."

"S… Sir?"

A deft motion and the gun was in Creek's unresisting hands. Morlock swept past him like the shadow of a winged predator. The *Necrofycer* was but the vehicle. Marla's residue would do the rest. *In death, as in life, still they served the greater purpose.*

"And what good do you think he'll be. *He's about ready to piss his pants."*

Morlock allowed himself a tiny laugh. Grim with potential. "The patterns of probability, Caxton. The patterns. As you say, we shall see. Whatever the outcome here tonight. I shall receive your son – and I shall absolve him. In time, I shall absolve us *all.*"

MORLOCK was running.

From them.

From *him*.

Nobody had *ever* run from him before.

In a way, for all his terror, Adam found it kind of invigorating. The most powerful man in the world was fleeing for his life from two *Terapolitan derm-rats*. Words had power all right: and right here, right now, the word for Morlock was *fuckyou*.

The quarry was no ordinary man, though. How could he be? No one should be capable of running from such devastating damage. Adam didn't know how many bullets Laura pumped into Morlock, but he was terribly aware that a shot in the head should have at least slowed the man down.

And that light.

Suddenly, the word was *ohfuck*.

What were they dealing with? What were they doing? What *was* Morlock? And, now he thought of it, why hadn't Laura expressed any kind of wonder? Not even a mild comment in passing? She knew something. Had to. But looking at the determined expression on her face, now didn't seem like a good time to ask.

Adam tried not to think about it. Such thoughts weren't good. He clung to the feeling that Morlock was running and they were hunting. But nothing was *ever* this easy.

"YOU should have stopped him, pal!"

The morphless words held no sympathy.

"He… he had a gun! What was I supposed to do?"

"He gave you the gun, didn't he? You could have stopped him."

Another voice, suggesting an old man: *"Bullets won't stop Morlock. But they might have weakened him. Weak enough…"*

"Why didn't you help us?" Natalie. It was too much.

"Shut up! All of you! Leave me alone!"

Boris leaned against the wall, fighting the spastic tremor that made a mockery of his flabby flesh. The gun felt heavy in his hands. The burden of indecision was an even greater weight.

He had to get out. He had to escape. But, Morlock. Morlock, how was it possible? That darkness clinging to his body. The shattered temple. It was impossible. He didn't dare disobey such a creature. For that matter, he didn't dare obey. He was caught between flight and fight. Fearful of the consequences of whatever decision he might make. No, that was foolish, how long ago had he made an actual decision of his own? When he grew the courage to leave *MorTek* behind forever, of course, and look how long that lasted.

Reluctantly, he stood up and shuffled down the corridor. He thought he heard a deep rumbling laugh on the very edge of hearing. Possibly. It might be another distant tremor in the autonomic fabric of *MorTek Prime*.

He definitely heard the voice.

"Bad choice, pal!"

MORLOCK crashed through the doors and stumbled into the side of his desk. He struggled for breath, although his damaged shell had no genuine need for its oxygen content. The impositions of this form, growing stronger as his strength waned. It renewed his rage.

All it took was but one fluctuation in the streaming chaos of possibility, but he was still tied yet to this framework of existence. He struggled to straighten his stance. Then he wiped the oozing essence from his face. A phosphorescent glow streaked the air as he flicked it away with disdain. More of his own essence, torn from its sheath, smoked and coiled back into the shade as though it were one and the same.

Bill stared.

"Not *now*, Bill."

No change in the skull's expression.

Morlock sighed. Despite the setback, it was no cause to vent his outrage on his old companion.

"Forgive me, Bill. And fear not. They cannot send me back. They have not the strength. Nor the means. Not any more."

He did not wait for his old companion's response.

He turned towards his private apartments and pushed the door open. A soft, putrescent glow sidled out of the darkness to join the harsher glow of the cityscape, then Morlock vanished into mystery.

BORIS Creek, award-winning *Necrofycer*, *MorTek* rising-star and utter fool squatted in the cloying darkness of some corridor in the residential levels. Exactly which one, he was no longer certain, but he was sure that – yet again – he'd made a bad choice.

There was still time to back out. Find another way of escape. He listened to the voices that mingled with his own bewildered thoughts. Frankly, he wished they'd just shut up so he could figure out what to do.

Everybody who worked in *MorTek's* haunted halls learned to shut them out eventually. Ambition helped; he let its loud booming demands drown the whispering laments. Now the ambition was silent. It skulked afraid somewhere at the back of his mind, wondering just what the hell it had got itself into. Boris thought the same, as he sat there in the dim glow of emergency lamps. And even they seemed to be failing, or else something was smothering their energy.

The gun felt heavy and strange in his hands. There was also something, he swore, resonating in the metal. An essence, a force, a presence, he didn't know what to call it. The damn thing seemed to hum in his hands with an energy that had nothing to do with chemical propellants and kinetic mechanics.

Maybe it was just absorbing and re-transmitting his terror. He didn't know. He was beyond *G-Tek* now, beyond anything that made any kind of sense.

So he waited, and he listened, and tried to shut out the voices so that he could detect the sounds of the living. That made sense. That he could understand. Just what he might do when the time arrived was another matter. Aside from wet himself.

He wiped his face on a sleeve, then rested the gun in his lap so that he could wipe his hands. It didn't help. The gun was still slippery in his grip.

Right now, he really needed *The Vytez*. More than he'd ever needed it before. For a moment he thought he heard the sounds of weeping; a woman's voice, familiar somehow, lamenting.

Boris…
Boris…
the Gestalt…
help me…
… Boris…

He shook his head to try and clear the enigma from his mind.

Another noise did that for him. A real sound, from the real world. He looked up. Gasped 'ohshit' and then winced at how loud his voice sounded.

There it was again. The living were coming his way. Slowly, he slid upwards against the wall. His heart pounded fit to shake loose of its mounting. He couldn't breathe properly. Sweat dripped from his nose.

A girlish laughter heard against the background of whispering laments.

"*Oh, Uncle Boris.*"

He gasped again. "Nat… Natalie!" Not here. Not now.

"*Baaaad Uncle Boris.*"

More laughter. Taunting him. Punishing him? The whispering grew louder; he imagined a crowd of fragile wraiths gathering in a crowd of anticipation. He cursed and prayed. Cursed and prayed to a God he did not understand, nor believe in.

"You're not real. None of you are real. This gun is real. I am real. And I *am* getting out of here. Whatever it takes."

Footsteps. Mocking whispers. Cautious sounds of movement. Swishing cloth against cloth. Closer. Near to the turning in the corridor.

He can handle them. He has a gun. The gun is his friend. It won't let him down. How difficult can it be anyway?

He swallowed his heart. Mastered his trembling limbs. Then with a bellow of fear and determination he leapt into the corridor, the gun raised and pointed forward. A brief sight of two figures in the gloom, startled ahead of him then he began to pull the trigger.

NOT MY BABY!

The shrill voice, resonant and metallic, flared in his head. The gun seemed to yank itself to the side. A loud boom as the bullet discharged and left the muzzle. In the split moment that the cartridge ejected and spiralled through the air, a flicker of movement caught his eye.

He looked up, mouth agape. A brief crunch and flash of impossible red light and he found his way out after all. Somehow, the voices became clearer too.

"Told you that guy was a *fucking* undertaker!"

TOGETHER they stalked the corridors of *MorTek Prime*. No longer the hunted denizens of *Terapolis*, or the despised outcasts of the *Incunabula*. They were the hunters; the arrow-point of human self-determination aimed at the heart of the persecutor.

Or they would be, once they got Morlock in their sights, Adam added ruefully. He shuddered at a brief sensation; a mingled sense of approval and worry, tinged with stale tobacco. Funny time to think of Caxton.

They saw no one, which was strange, because this level had all the appearances of a residential block. More up-market than many of the habitats he was familiar with, but still just a habitat. And that meant people. Sounds emerged from some of the doors. Unpleasant. Slithering. Not the kind of sounds associated with people at all. The kind of signals that forbade investigation, even if they had the time. Once he thought he heard a human whimper from behind one of the doors. A sad, pitiful sound. He hurried past that door, and wondered why whatever was on the inside didn't try to come out.

They advanced, with Laura slightly ahead, frowning in concentration. Fear pinched the flesh around her eyes, as though she was ever-expectant of a sudden blow from the thickening shadows. Her mouth was set in a determined line. She was suddenly more beautiful than ever to his eyes, pale and rigid with fear, shape hidden by her bulky jacket, hair bedraggled and impatiently tied back.

He was enjoying himself, despite the fear. A strange observation. It felt like a game. No, even a game felt more real than this. As they penetrated deeper into Morlock's domain, reality seemed to grow progressively blurred at the edges. Threadbare and faded. Like they were somehow leaving mundane reality behind.

Maybe that explained the noise, like waves heard from afar as they crashed against rocks. These were voices, the old familiar voices, and if he listened carefully he was just able to snatch the odd word from the meaningless babble. He'd be seeing *them* next, the old hallucinations; maybe the dead had always been real… He turned to Laura.

"Do you hear them?"

"What?" She tried not to look irritated.

"The voices."

She shook her head. "This is no time for you to go weird on me."

He shrugged. He envied her immunity. There was something unsettling about them. He hefted the axe. Old it might be, its weight still felt reassuring.

"It's just the place that's getting to you, that's all," Laura suddenly said. Her voice was a whisper, as if afraid something might overhear. "Those 'voices' – they're probably people elsewhere in the building. Carried on the air ducts. Nothing more."

So why did she sound as if she was trying to reassure herself? Adam held the axe out like some kind of shield. Suddenly, it wasn't quite as reassuring as Marla's gun.

Morlock was up there somewhere. Adam anticipated the meeting. This was their moment. The moment the *Incunabula* had waited to receive for too long.

The voices whispered louder. They had gained an anticipatory note, a sense of rising excitement. Amidst the babble, he heard the faint tinkle of girlish laughter. A name, a garbled rasp of air. He frowned as they came upon a turn in the corridor.

Adam looked at Laura and tightened his grip on the axe. They both sensed it: a presence hidden from them. Laura raised her weapon cautiously. The faintest 'snik', 'click' as she removed the safety and cocked its lethal load. The weapon looked a natural part of her body. Once again he couldn't help but wonder about her past.

Laura hugged the wall, stalking towards the edge. Adam took the far wall, peering into the shadows ahead as the abyss of the turn slowly came into view. His forehead and neck ached with tension. Sounds from the depths. Unclear. His skin creaked like leather on the axe's haft. Sweat dripped from his nose. He squeezed his buttocks against the loosening sensation in his bowels.

A deep bellow almost purged his resolve. A cry of desperate fear was followed by an apparition of insanity. Caught in the dim light, Adam saw a flash of gleaming flesh with glittering holes for eyes, a wider orifice gaping in bellicose thunder.

Instinct propelled the axe above his head. A shot rang out, deafening in the closed space. Impact jarred his body, then he felt the axe slip from his slick hands. He stepped back, panting with the heavy burden of adrenaline. Laura stared wide-eyed, mouth agape.

"You... *you* killed him."

She didn't have to sound quite so astounded, he thought, then he took a good look at the figure on the floor. Only then did he truly comprehend what he'd done. A man now, not the terrible bellowing demon he'd initially perceived. It – *he* – was a rotund figure flat on his back, as if he'd merely slipped. He was dead. His coat opened out like an unfinished shroud. Legs apart, arms splayed out. The man's fleshy face still glimmered with sweat. The eyes, small in his pouched flesh, stared up in a bewildered attempt to beseech pity. The mouth was open as if he'd just thought to ask a question.

The axe was embedded deep in his skull, the haft extending upwards from his scalp. There was a thick mulch of bloody gore squeezed out of the wound. Adam felt his stomach flip. He turned and felt the vomit gush hot and sticky.

"It's no game, is it?"

He said nothing. Just coughed and spat sputum from his polluted mouth. Then he wiped his sleeve over lips. Laura squatted beside the corpse and prised the pistol from the man's unresisting hand.

"Yours, I believe."

He spat once more. Took a deep breath. Accepted the package. He mumbled: "My mother's. *Apparently.*"

Laura raised an eyebrow with what might have been sympathy, but she said nothing.

"What good is this thing going to be anyway?"

"For *Morlock*? No use at all. But we don't know what's between him and us, do we?"

423

Not the answer he was looking for. He still felt weak and shaky, the gun now an extra burden. He felt its dead weight numbing his muscles. He struggled to find further words, something to express his need just then for a hug, but Laura turned back towards the shadows.

"Let's find Morlock," she said. "Let's finish this. Once and for all."

BILL sat silently. Biding his time. Dreaming, perhaps, of bygone days before the bullet, when he was Master of a Mighty Corporation in a world long dead, or perhaps only dormant.

Alone now on his pedestal. A disembodied Ozymandias.

Helpless and vulnerable and forgotten.

As only old, polished bone can be.

His empty eye sockets stared at the doorway.

Waiting. Watching.

Nothing else for him to do.

Footsteps stomped from the corridor outside. Heavy, they managed to imperceptibly rattle Bill's slender pedestal. The doors slammed open; a repeat of their master's ascent to his domain.

Bill stared at the creature that panted heavily as it held the door open, like a weary man using it for support.

"Master!"

Belial closed the door, shuffled into the room and glanced around, uncertain.

Then the creature cocked its head and listened intently. A snarl that might have been a rattle of phlegm, he – *it* –

shuffled to the side of the door, and squatted in the shadows.

Waiting.
Like Bill.
For the End.

The Last Folio
The Exultation Of
Fireflies

LAURA had been getting Adam out of trouble for all the time she'd known him, but this had to be the pinnacle of his career. Now, she was beginning to feel the strain. She'd play it tough before Adam, of course, but the truth was she'd never felt more fragile.

All her life, she'd lived in the shaded underbelly of *Terapolis*, but it was never any preparation for *MorTek Prime*. Every step took them deeper into the unknown, into the shadows that birthed all their fears and loathing. This is where Elzevir was ripped from their hearts and minds, where the library's destruction was plotted, where Caxton's end was decreed before he might ever tread the dark paths of salvation.

So she'd gone in guns blazing – just like Maus said – and lasted a damn sight longer than five minutes, but that didn't count for anything if it all went wrong around the next corner. Following now in the footsteps that Cax never trailblazed, she felt nothing but a poor substitute. Even so, she wondered if Maus was grinning, wherever he was, maybe sat with Caxton around some metaphysical hearth fire, slapping the old dealer on the back and grinning as he urged her on: "Go on, lass, give him Hell!"

That was the plan. No, hardly a plan really, more an idea triggered by circumstance. They'd been lucky so far, but luck was fickle, and she lacked faith in Morlock's supposed vulnerability. She'd caught him off guard, that's all, played the wild card but the gun hand was played to death. Morlock was beyond bullets and he knew they were coming.

With every step the sense of dread clotted harder in her chest. The meandering journey through this labyrinth provided plenty of time for doubt to infiltrate her defences. Tonight, she bore the entire weight of the *Incunabula's* purpose, along with all the heavy expectations of too many dead dumped on her shoulders. It was a tremendous burden. Naturally, she bore it alone.

Adam was up ahead. A typical man in so many ways, he was oblivious to the conflict rumbling in her head. Well, let it stay that way; she'd be damned if she'd display any weakness around him. Some habits were difficult to break, no matter the situation, but if that was the scaffold she needed to hold herself together, then she'd use it.

A few emergency lamps glowed wan beneath the tumid shade, fighting bravely to show the way, but the feeble rays were more like Canute against the tide. In this place, the shadows were perverse even by the standards of *Terapolis*. The floor felt solid beneath her feet, but it was lost to sight by a thick mist of restless shadow. Still more of this utter darkness clung like a primordial sludge to the walls and ceiling, where it rippled as if alive. It had the slimy appearance of a spilled *simulacomm*, but it was all too easy to imagine it as some membrane barely preventing a nightmare amalgam from reaching out to make her a part of its substance.

She shuddered, hackles rising and falling, her skin prickled by a sense of watchful malice. The darkness was seeping into her mind and freezing her spirit. She mustn't let it. She had to be strong. Caxton managed to carry this foreboding alone for years, so she must carry it too – for the little while needed to return it to its maker.

The shadows loomed as if to mock her determination. They crowded in like a pack of *derm-rat* junkies eager to roll her for a ride, but their insubstantial malice was beyond the reach of her fists. That made it a threat beyond her experience.

She closed her eyes and felt a tear squeeze out as the whispers explained how easily she might lay aside the burden. Adam was oblivious. Just slip the rucksack from her shoulders – *that's it* – turn and run out on the nightmare. No one would blame her. No one would even know.

Without any conscious will, her hand reached for the strap of her rucksack and began to lift it clear, but the books shifted their weight and moved to prod her back. The other strap dug into her collarbone with a painful bite. The pain dried the tears with the heat of anger she needed to sustain her spirit. At the same time, it made her aware of the action and served a sharp reminder of what – *who* – she was.

She was a courier – one of the best – and this was courier work. So it was a strange job, but she had a bag load of books, hazards to negotiate, a destination to reach, a delivery to make – and come what may she was going to do it.

Couriers had to rise above all the shit or keep it locked away until the mission was over. They were never permitted to put their own interests first. No matter the provocation, no matter the fears and doubts, the books were to be preserved and delivered. Even here, in the heart of *MorTek Prime*, there was no fundamental difference from any previous job.

Adam had never understood that; never appreciated the internal victories she made before she even stepped out onto the *derm*. He just expected the books to turn up, with never a thought to the arduous path they took to reach his grubby fingers. His head had been too full of his own demanding needs. He never thought about any of it, not even after she'd walked away. So, what's changed there, really?

The thought made her wonder what tricks the shadows played with his mind. She stared ahead at Adam's partially shrouded form as if it held a clue. Maybe he was oblivious to this place too, she realised. He was a junkie. This was a junkie's place, the palace of the *Gestalt*, so why should it hold any fears for him? Besides, wasn't he supposed to be here by invitation? She on the other hand was a bearer of books, bringing the poison chalice into the heart of Morlock's realm. Yes, it made sense that it would focus its rancour on her uninvited presence.

Perverse, perhaps, but it suggested she was a threat. That meant there was a possibility of success, however remote. They might pull off this mad scheme yet. Suddenly the darkness didn't seem quite so mournful. The books even felt lighter as she hoisted the rucksack into a more comfortable position, the weight evenly balanced for the hard road ahead. There was a strength in books and she took it for all it was worth.

"Hey! Don't wander too far! Stay where I can see you, okay?"

The words sounded forceful; certainly, they hid the troubles that had tried to be her undoing. Adam turned and shrugged as if to say 'hurry up' then he turned to stare at the wall. She had almost caught up when he reached out to touch the smothering shade.

"Adam – *don't!*" She rushed forwards. Too late, his fingers vanished into the darkness. Ripples undulated along the passage.

Laura lunged forwards and grabbed his wrist to pull his hand clear. Where his fingers sliced though the darkness, deep furrows were left behind, as if it was some kind of sludge. As she watched, the scars puckered and sealed.

"Give up! It's only shadow!"

Adam pulled away from her grip then he raised his hand and blew on his fingers. They were clean; she'd expected them to be stained by this muck. Repulsed at the idea, but equally needing to *know*, she reached out and watched her fingers disappear. A sharp chill ached down to the bones but other than that it was mere air unflustered by the passage of her fingers. She shivered and almost convinced herself it was from the cold wave.

"So why does it look so *real?*"

"It is real. It's from the *Gestalt*. It's all around us now. It'll lead us to him. I can hear it. Or something."

Adam's eyes lost focus as he looked inwards to some dream-state. She shook him, worried for a moment. This was definitely a junkie's place, but she needed to keep him grounded in the real.

"Stay with me! I thought you blew your implant, how can you be–"

"It's not like before. It's like a ghost of before. Just a leftover. I can't explain it, I just feel like I know where I am now."

She stared at his face. The old troublesome but well-meant Adam. The infuriating dreamer she'd never been quite able to leave behind.

"Lead on, then," she said, "show me the way."

"You want me to carry the books for a while, if they're getting heavy?"

"Not a chance! This is what I do. If needs be, I'll carry them *and* you. Now, lead on. We have a delivery to make."

IN the darkness, Silas Morlock waited.

He waited for what was inevitable.

First, he closed his eyes and gritted his teeth against the pain to come. It would be brief. It was necessary. Indeed, it had never been so urgent before, but the end remained inevitable. The second consideration would arrive in due course to find true resolution. And there they were, navigating their way towards his primary locus.

Two pale spots of light sparked in his awareness, drifting specks awash in the deep pools of shade. One ember was brighter than the other; a flickering brilliance fuelled by the glittering sparks piggybacked to its light. The curse of the written word, he knew. This ember refused the dark's entreaties to lay down the burden and join the peace of the night.

No surprise. No matter.

In another locus of the present was a seething manifestation of the Gestalt's *profound purpose, an old companion that lurked as a deeper knot of shadow. Like the master, so it waited.*

He sensed the pilgrims' touch, their manifestations of sentience, felt the probing exploration they made in the fabric woven by his purpose. The ripples provided a rare insight into a physical location. Not far away, not far away at all, in the perspective of the material dimensions.

A gurgle from beyond the confines of his organic enclosure heralded the rising sun of his resurrection. A soft glow increased its vigour, washing away his perception of the two fireflies venturing into this realm. Then, suffused in the brilliant nectar siphoned from raw human sentience, he screamed his agony through the deep vaults of creation.

The screaming lasted an eternity, before the light faded and collapsed into beautiful darkness. Healed, renewed, he waited. As he had always done.

"It is time."

Somewhere, nearby in the physical realm, even closer in the metaphysical, the old companion heard – and made ready.

SECRETS lurked in the dark places, but the secret of the *Gestalt* was that it *is* darkness – and it never hides. Always it is waiting; inviting those who dare to do more than just sip its potent spirit. Like most in *Terapolis*, Adam had tasted its bitter pleasures, whilst shunning the true depths of its meaning. Until now.

The darkness of the *Gestalt* was all around him, seeping into the fabric of his existence, just as it had always done since the time of his birth. No, it had reached out to him before then, hadn't it? The *Gestalt* – Morlock's manifested purpose – had driven his parents to madness and tore him away before they might shape him. Caxton somehow managed to find a way back from the brink, and in time find his cast-adrift son, but by then the damage was done. This *place* had touched him in the womb and forever left its mark. So this was coming home, then, returning like the prodigal son to the source of his true making.

Once, this place had been an office. Now it was a cave, deep and dark, a sullen portal that no longer quite inhabited this framework of existence. Deep within that darkness, Morlock lurked like a singularity hidden by its cowl of pulverised matter.

For the moment, Adam just stared into the Abyss.

And the Abyss stared into him.

"So this is Pandora's box," Laura whispered. "Even I can feel it. He's through there, isn't he?"

He nodded, not taking his eyes from the double doors just visible and begging to be thrown open. The darkness clotted around the entrance was like a scab formed over a gash in reality, but the scab was broken and the dark essence oozed through the breach.

"Ladies first," he said, trying to mask his reluctance.

She snorted, "As if! In *Terapolis?* You go first!"

"Somehow, I just knew you'd say that."

"Stop complaining. I'm letting you play the hero, aren't I?"

With a sigh of the condemned, he stepped towards the shrouded doorway. He gripped Marla's gun and raised it with more readiness than he felt. After that, he took a deep breath and tried the door. It refused to budge. Frustrated, he grunted and pulled again. The door was locked.

"No way!"

Laura clucked her tongue and pushed him aside. She gave him a quick withering glance as she raised her own weapon, then she *pushed* the door. It swung open. Shadow spilled out. She vanished inside. Adam followed, dreading what they'd find.

On the other side there was nothing. It was just a gloomy office, barely lit by shimmering moonlight streaming in through the oblique window behind an ebony desk. *Terapolis* dominated the view beyond the glass; the dark monoliths blazed in a glittering bio-luminescent starscape.

Fear overcame any fascination for this new perspective on the city, and a quick glance took in the points of light reflecting from indistinct portraits lining the walls, the huddled shadow that was a high-backed leather chair to one side of the desk, the gloom clinging thick to the corners.

In the furthest corner beyond the desk, he saw a skull floating in mid air, contours of bone phosphorescing to highlight the orbits. The dark eye sockets stared intense and pulled at Adam's awareness with an eerily knowing gaze.

"This is a dead end! Where is he?"

He turned to follow the skull's gaze. Laura lowered the gun and ran a hand through her hair. Her eyes flashed with an unspoken accusation. The books shuffled audibly in the bag. Behind her, the door swung gently on its hinges, causing the shadows to move.

"He came this way. *I know!*"

"So where did he go?"

A shadow tore away from the wall and lunged at Laura. She turned towards the silhouette, the gun rising to defend, but a massive arm materialised to deliver a sideswipe blow that sent her spinning. The gun bounced into the shadows, and Laura stumbled to the floor.

Adam was caught off guard, frozen in the moment between fight and flight. This was no fat man with a frightened face, easily discarded from the path. Revealed by a shaft of ashen light, the creature glared with eyes the colour of curdled pus, an animal roar of pure bloodlust throbbed from its throat.

Laura looked up, face stricken with a livid mark that glared in the moonlight. Adam raised the gun and tried to take aim through the shakes, but then the creature reached out and pulled her from the floor. She shrieked a combination of rage and fear and tried to turn round in the beast's hold. Her arms and legs thrashed as she tried to find a body to kick and punch.

"Help me!"

There was no clear shot. At least not one he dared to try. In the light of the moon and the city, the struggling figures were a blur of motion, a tableau of grotesque silhouettes and images.

"Adam!"

The creature threw her to the ground then reached down as she tried to crawl clear. It reached for the rucksack on Laura's back, but she managed to roll over and lash out. Fists pummelled the creature's face. Her boot caught it between the legs; Adam felt his eyes water in reaction but the creature didn't even grunt. It was implacable. Fists slapped and punched in a struggle to subdue Laura, but her frenzied resistance made it hard for this man-thing to get a firm hold on its prey.

"Don't just! Stand there! Get it! Off me!"

There was only one thing for it. He wasted more seconds fumbling with the safety, then he swivelled the gun round and gripped it tight around the barrel. Two strides and he was in the fray, arm raised high, a bellowing roar of pure terror rushing from his lungs. The gun came down heavy and hard on the creature's scalp. The shock of impact rushed up his arm and almost took all the feeling from his fingers, but he held onto the weapon and struck again.

Every impact hurt him more than this nightmare, for all the effect it appeared to have. The creature was oblivious. Laura was pinned down by the monster's bulk. One meaty fist gripped her throat and held her tight, the other reached for the strap on her shoulder. Laura's fists alternated between punching the face and trying to prise the fingers open. Still, the thing ignored him.

Then the creature lashed out. Adam didn't see the blow coming. A fist smashed into his chest and sent him flying. Marla's gun span away in to the empty shadows. He sailed through the air until he landed with a heavy thump across the office. Pain shrieked from his rump all the way up his spine. His head cracked against a slender and metallic object. It wobbled behind his back and dropped something between his outstretched legs.

The skull stared up from his crotch. The shaded eyes seemed suggestive, as if attempting to beseech him from the other side of oblivion. Laura shrieked a piercing plea, her struggles weakening, as the creature began to strip the rucksack clear.

There was nothing else but the skull's invitation. He gripped the cranium and leapt to his feet. The skull wasn't heavy, but it added bite to his fists. Old bone and bone-hard muscle crashed together with a hollow pop. The skull's bonded lower jaw broke in two and leapt clear. Adam struck again, bludgeoning the creature's head for all he was worth. At the same time he kicked the thing in the back and side, then reached out with his free hand to grip its hair and try to pull its head up.

The creature turned to glare, exposing its face. Teeth bit deep into the flesh and tore strips away. An eye ruptured and sprayed yellow slime. The creature bellowed in every sign of pain, but glowing fluid and thrashing tendrils spilled from the wounds to try to grab Adam's arm. Revolted by their damp touch, he pulled clear before they might bind his wrist, and smacked the skull into the ruined orbit, chopping and mashing the writhing mess.

Laura's throat was free. She gasped and rasped a string of obscenities. Some strength returned to her struggles. She punched at the creature's head, but she was still pinned. Adam continued his work with the skull. Hammering endlessly. The creature tried to fend of the blows, losing strips of flesh from its powerful arms.

"Maaasssssttteeerrrr!"

The skull was his only focus now. Battering his foe until it lost its hold on Laura. She grabbed the rucksack's strap then shuffled clear of its brute presence. Once free, she lunged in, joining Adam with her boots. The creature's bellows took on a desperate quality. Adam began to sense victory.

And then the skull shattered in his grip.

Bone scattered everywhere. A tooth remained embedded in the creature's scarred cheek. After a fatal pause, Adam dropped what was left of the brain pan and clenched his fists. The creature leapt back to attack. A powerful arm shoved Laura away, then its full weight collided with Adam. He felt his back slam onto the desk; one hand splashed into a *simulacomm* plinth before he slid over the other side and tumbled in a heap beneath the window.

No time to curse or even catch a breath. The desk rattled with a loud thump of boots landing on its surface. He looked up see the creature standing there, looming over, ready to reach out with those powerful hands and nightmare tendrils. Adam braced himself to move. A glint of light winked from Marla's gun. He slipped to the side, reached for it and rolled under the desk. Despite the moment, he was impressed with himself as he crawled towards the far side of the room. There he turned and crouched back against the wall.

The creature growled. Tensed to leap. Fear did the rest.

A bullet exploded from the barrel. The creature's silhouette flicked off balance. Matter exploded from its shoulder. The bullet ended its journey embedded in the window's thick glass. More shots. Adam pulled the trigger relentlessly, barely bothering to aim. His wrist and forearm ached from the pulverising recoil. The creature's rage was overpowered by Marla's legacy. Golden shells whirled, smoking, through the air. Severed tentacles blasted from its torso and stuck to the glass. Globules of pungent phosphorescence spattered over the cracked window. The creature staggered ungainly, burbling in outrage.

One more bullet punched into the creature's nose and smashed through the back of its skull. The head flicked back with neck-breaking violence. Adam's finger kept pumping the trigger, but the gun only clicked empty. The creature overbalanced, arms gyrating in a futile attempt to prevent gravity from taking charge, then the bulky shoulders slammed against the glass. For a moment the window held, until the cracks expanded wildly and the glass caved outwards. The beast bellowed as it plunged into the depths of empty air.

Adam let the gun fall from his grip and hunched himself up against the caterwauling barrage. The wind blasted triumphant through the office, ripping portraits from the walls to smash them on the floor.

"Was that... *him?*" Laura's stricken face gaped weary and forlorn as she crawled over and slumped beside him.

"Don't you know? You shot him!"

"I didn't see him clearly. He was just a blurred glow."

"Oh. Then, no, that wasn't Morlock. I don't know who... or *what* that was."

"Shit. I thought. I hoped..." She slumped dejected. The wind howled. Laura looked around the empty room. "All this way. *All this...*"

They both turned their heads against the next blast of wind, an intimacy Adam had long missed. The memories of the moment were interrupted as the skull's metal pedestal toppled with a harsh sound. The doors slammed shut with a heart-rending bang. The walls boomed, hollow. Part of it gave way and swung inwards until the wind tore it back with a slap and then pushed it open again with another loud bang, as if trying to tear it from the hinges.

It wasn't quite dark beyond that opening. A faint, threatening light spilled out with the darkness. Wearily, he nudged Laura.

"*Okay*. So that's where he's hiding. Can we go home now?"

THE flesh had endured enough and it told him so when he tried to move, but the spirit knew it had no choice, so Adam's muscles were forced to flex. Laura shifted with him, the two of them untangling, for what he hoped was the last stage of this insane mission.

Not quite hand in hand, he and Laura approached the opening. Unarmed now, they were both naked before the dark and he didn't like the feeling. For all the good it would do them, he still felt the need for the cold comfort of a little hot lead.

"Wait," he said, then he stooped to use eyes and fingertips to search for Laura's lost weapon. It must be here somewhere. His fingers brushed hard metal. There it was. He was about to pick it up when Laura stopped him.

"Forget it," she said, "we don't need it now. It's no use in *there*."

He was about to argue, but then he just nodded. It was time to trust Laura and what ever *Incunabulan* secrets she knew.

"Let's go," she added, turning to face the door.

"Home?" If only.

"Later."

Adam shrugged. Sighed. She was right. "Ready then?"

"Not any more, but let's do it anyway."

That was the Laura he knew. Prepared to take on the world. This wasn't him, but he was doing it anyway; standing tall in the face of adversity, facing terrors, shaking his fist at the infinite and daring it to blink. One day he might be impressed with himself. Just not right now. Survive it first, let it become memory, then he'd savour the edited highlights from a safe distance.

Adam pushed the slapping door inwards. The wind provided an extra nudge as they stepped through. An eerie glow beckoned them on.

The same malignancy he'd sensed outside the office was washing over them. The darkness. The awareness contained within it. Call it Mind, call it Spirit, call it Soul, call it whatever, but Morlock's dark radiance immersed the fabric of their physical and spiritual existence. He was lurking beyond this tunnel, waiting, even while the particles of his essence permeated their skin and bone and blood. Even the very air they breathed. He was a dark thread interwoven with the intricate tapestry of the cosmos.

With one last heavy step he breached the cloying event horizon and reached the other side. Laura emerged beside him, breathing heavily with barely suppressed fear. A sharp pain of understanding barked behind his ear as if to confirm what his eyes perceived.

He knew this place. He had indeed been here before.

UNDER the grip of such thick shadow, the place closed in around them with a crushing claustrophobia, yet some ancient instinct sensed the vast cavern hidden from sight. The air reeked of *Terapolis*, concentrated and purified. The rank odours of damp mould, of stagnant earth, of old rotted meat, mingled with a musky tang.

Before them, an avenue of pestilent light beckoned. An aisle sliced through the night by sentinel rows of swollen, distended sacs that emanated pungent phosphorescence.

They illuminated the fragile metal hanging over a dark abyss. Seeing all this, Adam half-expected to come across a battered armchair in a sombre representation of his abandoned life. He knew better than to accept the invitation this time, but it was too late to turn back.

"I hope you know *what* we're doing," he said.

"A pretty good idea. I hope you know *where* we're going."

He glanced down the lighted aisle. "Pretty much, not that it's difficult."

By the time they were half way, the light was strong enough to show something of what lurked in the gloom on either side. Adam tried not to look, but it was there, a ghostly ghastly impression in the peripheral vision. A spaghetti tangle of damp flesh and endlessly branching tendrils slowly vanished into the gloom. The gruesome matter made him think of some segment of cortex, magnified to gigantic proportions. The brain of living *Terapolis* was pulsing and firing and feeding all around them. The massive coils and bundles of tangled fibre sprawled through the fabric of the world, ramifying smaller and smaller until its tiniest filaments found their purpose enmeshed in the synaptic web of human existence.

"I know this place," he blurted. "I know what it is. I've been here before."

"What? Nobody's –"

"I have. *I know it.*"

"How? When?"

"The *Gestalt.* The last time I tripped. Other times, too, I think. This place, it's always there if you choose to look. The truth of the place doesn't hide from us. *We* hide from the knowledge. We're inside it now. Inside Morlock."

"That's not possible. We haven't Gacked. We can't Gack."

He winced at a memory. "He told me once, we can enter it for a time without all the paraphernalia he grants us. I think… that's it. We enter him as he entered us. Somehow, we're supposed to… *I don't know.* My head is starting to throb. It's like I'm remembering some things, but not all of it. I just don't understand what all of this has to do with books."

"Books and the *Gestalt* don't mix. Remember?"

"So…" He frowned. There was something tickling his mind, but he couldn't dislodge the thought behind it.

"I don't understand half of what Caxton told me. I just know there's not enough books to stop this spreading and absorbing us all. But if we bring books to the right place…"

"Here."

"Somewhere in here. Find that place and we can end it. All of it."

"And then how do we get out?"

"Maybe we don't."

"We have to! I mean…"

"Got a date have you? Bit late for that."

"A man has to live in hope. Caxton wouldn't have brought me in for this if he didn't think we were going to make it."

Laura stopped suddenly and grabbed his arm. He winced against the tight grip as she pulled him to a halt. Her face, as far as he could tell in the alien light, was pale.

"No! Adam, he wanted you out of it. He wanted you kept out of harm's way. Neither one of us is supposed to be here. He was the one…"

"Cax planned to be here until I got him killed. Is that it?"

"Yes! No! I don't mean it like that. I mean…"

"That you decided to finish Caxton's work and babysit me at the same time. Well, it's a bit late for that. Or would you like me to turn back? It's easy for you now. Just follow the lighted walkways. You don't need me anymore."

"No! Wait! *Don't leave me!*"

The unexpected tone stopped him cold. She was shaking. *Physically shaking.* Suddenly, she was exposed to him, showing everything once hidden behind her tough façade. The insight punched him harder than Laura's fists could, and they packed some impact.

"I can't do this without you. I'm scared," she added. Tears spilled from her eyes. The final submission. He reached out and put his arms around her. For the first time since they'd split up, she let him.

"It's okay," he said, softly, "I'm scared too. I'm not going anywhere. Not until we've put him back in his place."

She made a half-laugh, half-sobbing sound, then she said: "Okay." She pushed him away, not forcefully as she might have done before. "I'm okay."

Adam let her brush him off, but enjoyed it as she kept hold of his hands. Hope bloomed. Maybe the two of them had a chance to work it out, later, in the life beyond this murk. Laura took a deep breath. She tried a smile, but it wasn't quite there yet.

"If you tell *anyone*…"

"Hey! I'm not as dumb as I look!"

"I know. So now you know, I'm not as tough as I look either."

"Tough enough."

This time the smile made it through her troubled expression. She squeezed his hand and then let go. The Laura he knew was back and he was glad of it, because *he* couldn't do this alone either.

"Come on, then," he said. "Let's do it."

THE lighted walkways took them onwards; they were no less unsettling than all the dark corridors that had come before. They turned left and right, heading inexorably to some unknown centre, until Adam began to feel like a rat in a maze.

Things rustled beyond the catwalk on either side but also – more alarmingly – above and below. Whatever was out there, it stayed on the far side of the light. Occasionally something strayed near enough to give some hint of form. Enough to set the imagination to work until he perceived a forest filled with alien *Geistmasques* and cabled claspers seeking to tear an opening into his mind.

"Why don't they come and kill us?"

"Books," she said simply. "So stay close to me."

"Like those things that had me before."

"That's right. I guess that's why we got this far. Now do you realise why Morlock hates books?"

"Beginning to get the idea. But what about that thing in the office?"

"Still think you've got an open invitation to see the boss?"

"Well, I–"

"You might be right. That thing seemed to be after the books more than me, but do you really want to put it to the test?"

"I'll stay close."

"Thought you might. Just don't get so close you cramp my style."

"As if I would!"

SOON, they came to another junction where a walkway cut across the path. The way ahead was as dark as the path to their left. The sacs dangled like empty shrouds, the rows disappearing into the gloom. Light beckoned them to the right, the glow pulsing to the rhythm of the heavy fluid gurgling through veins and vessels that linked the grotesque reservoirs.

Obedient to the guidance, they turned into the path. They stopped on the meniscus formed where the putrescent light ebbed into shadow and knew they'd found it.

THIS was the end of the world; the place where the light came to die, and didn't the *Incunabula* like to boast about books – they *were* the light and the life. The thought disturbed Adam. He sidled closer to Laura, suddenly feeling exposed and vulnerable; a sacrificial lamb blessed with foresight.

"This is the place," he whispered.

"You're sure, this time?"

He nodded. "Absolutely."

The sound of liquid gurgled an interruption overhead. Something else fluttered with a leathery ripple. Then a sibilant hiss lingered like ice poured in the ears, until it melted into words that seemed to come from everywhere and nowhere.

Cometh the hour, cometh the man and so it cometh to this… The words became a true voice, projected from within the clot of darkness. *"Face to face with my persecutors at last, but what is this? No mob of peasants wielding burning brands and agricultural tools? No priests and their tiresome incantations? Only a waif and a stray… such is to be my epitaph? Oh no, I think that will not do."*

Adam nudged Laura, "Whatever you're here to do, *now* might be a good time."

She nodded, hesitated, then turned to face him with an expression of dismay. "I don't know… Bring the books. That's what it said… it must be written somewhere…"

She fumbled inside her jacket. He stared in disbelieving horror. "What? We come this far and you don't even know?"

"Cax is meant to be here! He knew what to do, he didn't need it written down!"

"I don't *fucking* believe this!"

The darkness chuckled. *"Pity them, for they know not what they do. Caxton's script will not avail you now. Do you hear that; your quest for misplaced redemption was the death of you! Now it will perish your foundlings."*

The darkness erupted with a wet slurp. The catwalk shivered underfoot. All of a sudden the dark grotto didn't seem so empty. Adam edged backwards from the worrying presence, trying to catch Laura's attention and pull her back from the brink, but she was engrossed in Caxton's lapsed memory.

She turned towards him with an uncharacteristic, mad grin, just as the shadows lunged. "I—"

Laura fell backwards, parted from the manuscript, which slumped, dejected onto the metal grille. The catwalk shook with her impact, just as something heavy slammed into Adam's body.

Morlock's face glowed moonlight, emphasising dark eyes that gazed down into the depths of Adam's soul to grant some twisted interpretation of solace. Thin fingers were steel struts around his neck, squeezing hard even as they propelled him against the railing until his back bent over with shrieking agony.

"Relax, Adam, this will not take long, I promise. You might have joined us in *MorTek*, worked for the greater purpose, become something more than the tangled sum of your progenitors. Alas, you chose to disregard all the meaning and purpose you desired, the useful life you might have found before Completion."

The words were a conversational fly-buzz in his ears. Even the siren cry of pain was becoming muffled. Adam tried to prise the death grip from his throat, but his hands were now remote-controlled by a blind operator. Heat burned his face. The dull thud of his heart pounded his lungs flat. His tongue protruded from his mouth in a desperate attempt to taste a little air.

"Instead, you chose the fruitless path of a dead father and an abandoned cause. So now you must join the Lost Ones in their vigil. Join them and await Completion in the dreary emptiness of the Abyss. It will not be for long. I give you my word."

The gargling, gurgling sounds that escaped his throat were no kind of reply, but even mental speech was slurring. Thoughts were drowning in a liquefying mind. Far away, a powerful wind was rushing nearer, carrying a multitude of welcoming voices. Morlock's face appeared distant, seen through the eyeholes of a mask, even that slipping away as his mind began to disengage.

"*Pandora's* putting you back in the *box!*"

As suddenly as it began, the ordeal was over. Adam gratefully sucked in a deluge of air as the shout pulled him back into his body.

Laura was a fury of motion, beautiful to behold, the rucksack swinging wild and heavy. Each blow smashed the weight of words into Morlock's body, his arms tried to parry the blows, but she was too frenzied to be deflected. He staggered and fell back. His face was twisted in agonised rage. A final blow to the back of the head sent him sprawling onto the catwalk.

It gave Laura the chance to stay the bag's motion and in one fluid movement she ripped open the fastening and upended the bag. Adam was together enough to admire the choreography of her assault, but the scattering of the books bewildered him. They tumbled out of the bag and cascaded in a paper avalanche. Many struck Morlock's head and back before they slithered onto the metal floor around his body, but there was method there; careful adjustments that sent the books falling more or less where Laura wanted them, until they formed a rough perimeter. Some of the books, fallen open, began to flutter their pages, as if caught by a breeze.

Just as the last book fell, Morlock lashed out with his fist, then drew it back as if he'd reached through flame toward his target. The blow caught Laura hard in the stomach and threw her back. She crashed against the metal railing. For a horrible moment, Adam thought she was going to topple over the edge, but she bounced back and landed hard on the grille. She tried to rise, then slumped in a winded heap, her lower jaw dropping open as she gasped for air.

Morlock turned to assess his paper prison. When his eyes focused on Adam, he let out a slow hiss. Adam flinched against a resumption of his murderous attack, but Morlock only began to scrabble carefully on all fours, as if the books were the bars of an iron cage. When his fingers brushed against a tattered volume, there was a sharp crack and a stink of ozone. Morlock flinched, as if it was an *electrified* iron cage.

So, they'd come all this way to imprison the man in a literary circle. Adam wished he'd paid more attention to Caxton's talk back in better days, because he failed to understand what this was meant to achieve. He was beginning to doubt that Laura even knew exactly what was meant to happen, as if she was making it up as she went along.

"Adam! The ring, it's incomplete!" She pointed desperate towards the circle.

He saw the gap at the same time as their prisoner. Morlock was quicker to understand. The gap was just wide enough for him to squeeze through. He began to shuffle around towards the breach in the barrier.

"Close it! *Hurry!*"

So, he got to save the day after all, but he still felt a twinge of regret. There was nothing else to use. The movement took only a couple of heartbeats, but it felt slow and measured as he scooped up Caxton's manuscript and leapt. His feet made contact with Morlock's back and sent him sprawling again, even as Adam used the contact to propel himself to the far side of the ring. There, he landed heavily and his feet slipped out from under him. The metal slapped hard into his side, but he rolled with the pain and came up with the manuscript outstretched, ready to seal the prison.

Adam froze, the manuscript held out like some talisman, barring the way but not quite closing the breach. Morlock stared at him with the intensity of a vulture awaiting dinner. They faced each other over Caxton's last words in a silent conflict of wills; one that even now Adam felt sure he was going to lose as he stared at the *thing* that was Morlock buried deep in the pit behind those twin pupils.

Morlock gave the manuscript a brief glance then he smiled slowly, his expression again one of infallible calm.

"Check mate," he said softly, "*interesting.*"

Adam found he could not tear his gaze away from Morlock's face. The eyes held him. The sense of *knowing* gripped him with a morbid curiosity. He wanted to know what happened next. The books fluttered their pages. From beyond their inner circle, Laura's desperation tried to urge him back into her world.

"Close it! Close the gap!"

"Behold," Morlock whispered, "I am become the De-stroyer of Worlds. Is that what you are, Adam, is that what you wish to achieve? So be it. But are you aware of the price you will pay for this moment? There are always consequences, equal and opposite reactions counter-balancing every action. It is the cause and effect of equilibrium to which this universe wishes to return."

"Don't listen to him! Just do it!"

"Are you sure you want to listen to her? Caxton left your education sadly lacking. Your partner, she knows or suspects at least, but still she tells you nothing, as if your ignorance will prove a shield. I truly pity you Adam, for the grief you must inevitably endure. You are damned – and you don't even know it. Only I can save you."

Morlock's eyes were drilling into his soul, twisting his perception until he felt dizzy; he didn't want the man in his head anymore. He'd done enough of the *Gestalt*. "You're full of shit," he managed to say. Then louder: "You wrecked my life. Now it's my turn!"

"No, Adam, I made you. Caxton was my hammer. Marla my forge. You my tool. Now, let me pass and I shall make you Complete at last. I shall ease your pain. Indeed, you will never need to face it. The choice is yours. I have faith in your judgement. Trust me, as I trust you, and choose to change the world!"

"For God's sake, Adam, don't just lie there!"

"You wanted this. Now it's yours!"

Adam thrust the manuscript forward and closed the breach. With that mundane act he performed something profound. He re-ignited an ancient ember. He saw it glint in Morlock's eyes, a shimmer in the eternal darkness that slowly caught like a spark in bone-dry tinder.

"*Take it!*"

"Very well," Morlock said. "I accept your gift. I can wait. Take heart, my boy, there is still hope. We shall meet again. I will grant you salvation. As it was in the beginning, so shall it be at the end…"

Morlock reached out and gripped the manuscript. He hadn't expected that; surprised, Adam failed to relinquish his hold on the old paper. Just as, perhaps, Morlock was refusing to relinquish his hold on him. Deadlocked together, unable to pull back from the brink, they were doomed to share the same fate.

And here it came. The books came alive. Their pages fluttered wildly as if caught in a curious breeze. Voices began to murmur, rising to a confusing babble of a ghostly symposium, as if every dead author represented in the ring was reading their work for the final time.

Beyond the circle, the mysterious inhabitants of the cavern rustled in a frenzy. Startled and lamenting cries howled against the words. The catwalk began to shake. An eerie light arose all around, somehow reflecting off the pages to bathe Morlock in a shimmering aura. The books began to smoke and curl until they began to ignite.

Still Morlock stared. Adam couldn't move his fingers, even though he felt the heat of fire crawling closer. The eyes were swallowing him, pulling him in like a swimmer about to drown in a whirlpool. The shimmering sparks of glitter whirled like cream in coffee, orbiting swirls around his dark irises and even darker pupils, each a vortex pulling his mind into the depths of Morlock's abyss.

"Adam! Let go! Let go – or go with him!"

Morlock smiled slowly. His body crumpled inwards, shivering as his flesh resisted a slow implosion. Hairline cracks drew insane etchings across his features. Light peered out as the fissures opened up. Within the light, fluid darkness spilled and coiled like something trapped in liquid amber. With nowhere else to go, it was slowly drawn back into the broken shell.

"Until the next time," Morlock rasped. Then he closed his eyes. The body completed its implosion. Released from the enigmatic paralysis, Adam fought the strange gravitational pull and threw himself backwards just as the flames ignited Caxton's manuscript. Tongues of fire scorched his fingers before they raced up Morlock's shrivelled arm and began to consume his flesh.

Cloth and skin broke apart in a cascade of burning fragments, mimicking the death of books in the library long ago. Flesh burned and charred and blew apart into fragments, digested by the fire. Unleashed from its physical shell, a dark man-shaped silhouette writhed against the encapsulating light.

The fire began to gutter and die, but the unnatural glow was rising through the cavern, revealing and searing its hidden secrets. The shadow lost shape as its ethereal substance was sucked into the twin portals that had once been eyes. These two tiny balls of shadow lingered in the centre of the diminished books, slowly collapsing into points that wrenched at the human mind.

They were the last things Adam perceived, before consciousness vanished in a burst of light so intense it might have been the birth of the universe. Or, perhaps, merely a rebirth. There was, in that immeasurable instant, no awareness that might have formulated the equation, let alone pondered the solution. So it was in the beginning…

Until, as it was in the end after aeons uncharted, a spark ignited the fire of cognition. The universe awoke, and began to know itself.

SOFT radiance, as warm and refreshing as the morning sun, finally coaxed Adam back to face existence. There was a gap in his memory, something missing where his thoughts probed, like a chasm in a tooth that had ceased to hurt, but the light was calling him to forget the emptiness.

When Adam opened his eyes, he saw its source float above him; a shaft of misty light penetrating, far from where he lay on the catwalk. It took him a while to realise what it was. A rent in the cavern's distant *archiderm* had opened to let the new day peer into the remains of this dark domain.

The tower's structural flesh appeared to be mummified and fossil hardened. As he slowly cast his eyes around the world's expanded horizons, he saw that there were more cracks in the shell of *MorTek Prime*. The light let in was able to join forces with a few strategic utility lamps burning to illuminate the interior.

The turgid shadows were banished, revealing empty space as vast as the tower's girth and upper levels. Only a few pools of darkness remained, lifeless compared to the kind that had smothered the place before. These lingered, sullen, where the light failed to reach, with all the apparent resentment of old men remembering lost vigour.

Now he saw the tangled maze of metal suspended from the walls' inner surfaces. A wild scaffold of catwalks and ladders and flimsy staircases of metal struts, all joined into a multileveled web of steel like an insane arachnid's trap. The tangled growths seen on the way to meet their maker were gone. Incinerated, or something, to leave this skeleton bare. Only a few clumps of flesh remained, congealed and dead like the walls.

Below the catwalk, there were angular structures lurking in the depths. After a while, he realised they were the remains of buildings: structures from the Old World, the upper floors and war-shattered pinnacles of dead skyscrapers, ingested by *Terapolis* as it rose to glory. Broken walls abutted and jutted from mounds of shrivelled flesh, like broken teeth in the mouth of a corpse.

Adam stared at the scene in silent amazement for a long time, wondering what forgotten story was buried down there, until the catwalk wobbled and he heard Laura cough.

"I need a shower," she muttered.

Adam rolled over and sat up in a cloud of dust. Now he realised why the light appeared misty; it was fine ash lingering in the air. Both he and Laura were smothered in it.

"That's all it took?" he asked. "A few books!"

"Books have power. Caxton knew that. More than most."

He stared in disbelief at the dwindling pile of ash that had been Morlock's last stand. The irregular heap was dribbling slowly through the gaps in the catwalk to rain on the dead city below. Eventually, there'd be no trace *he* ever existed.

"So, he's dead then. It's really all over?"

"No, not dead, just not here. He's back where he started, waiting, but for you and me it's over."

"So where is he, then?"

Laura smiled. "I don't know, 'cos I'm not a priest or a philosopher, nor am I a cosmologist or a quantum physicist. I don't understand it all myself. Let's just be glad he's gone."

Adam nodded, then turned back to stare at the pile, as if he expected the last-minute resurrection of the bad guy he'd read in books past. "I don't think I will *ever* understand this."

"Don't try. Just understand this: you had to do it; there was no other choice. The alternative was worse. Whatever else happens, remember that!"

He frowned at the response. "Sure. Whatever. Can I go home now?"

"Yes. Let's get out of here."

She climbed to her feet in a flurry of ash. Adam prepared to follow suit, then he noticed something odd about the remains huddled within the legacy of the sacrificial books. An angular edge peered through the ash. Curious, he crawled forwards and reached out to brush it clear. Beneath it, there was a book. A survivor. Now that was odd. The cover was seared beyond legibility, but the type on the yellowed pages within was clear.

The pages felt crisp as he flicked through to the beginning of the story, a delightful sensation and a soothing noise that reminisced of fond moments with literature. When he reached the beginning, his eyes scanned the text. He frowned at the words dancing in his consciousness.

"What the?"

CAXTON was late.

A shadow darkened the page. An ashen hand gripped his and made him close the book. He looked around to find Laura's face tantalisingly close. "Not this one," she said. "*Never* this one."

Epilogue
Last Word & Testament

THERE were times, assembling these pages, when I felt like Victor Frankenstein; forever delving through old writings in search of forbidden knowledge and dark mysteries.

And then, once I found my secrets, to reach out for the cadavers of lost lives and assemble the disparate body parts into one unified whole.

Like my fictional predecessor, the knowledge almost cost me my mind; it certainly cost me my morality, my humanity, my innocence.

And like dear Victor, it will undoubtedly cost me my life. For like him, a monster stalks me.

Frankenstein's creation, however, was imbued with the possibilities of his mother Mary, for she composed him as a being capable of great virtue as much as ghastly deed. It was the neglect of the father creator, Victor, which chose the creature's path. As I learned too late in life, the promise of woman's life-giving spirit was corrupted by the world of men—and by the sins of the father.

It cost Victor everything.

And so too does my monster. For should I fail, then He will take all that is left. The books I have spent not enough of my life to protect. My wider family that is the Incunabula, and further still my entire species.

Yes, in my own way I am Victor Frankenstein, blind in my arrogance to shape the world, deceived by my own desire to render the world a better place. Hounded by the demons both of my making and those not.

And how close I came to being the Monster; bent to a twisted master's will.

There—however twisted and tortured to render them fit for my convocation—my similarities with Mademoiselle Shelley end.

Such is life. So much for fiction.

For I am Caxton. Man and—aspirant—Writer.

I have lived in a time when it is difficult to be either, though not impossible. Now my time is nearing its end. So, our journey together along the path of words reaches its conclusion.

I must remain here. You must go on, to whatever rewards and adventures lie beyond the horizons of my trusted typewriter.

With these words I hope I have armed you for the journey that lies ahead. Your eyes are opened, I trust, and you are prepared to meet your destination. I hope the fields are green there, the skies bright, and the nights clear so that you might gaze in wonder and inspiration at the stars.

Much as our forefathers once did.

After all, we are all living in the gutter, but some of us are looking up at those stars.

Ah! Oscar. For the life in the gutter.

We have fallen since then.

We dwell in the sewer, with precious few grates that might open our eyes to the heavens. Of necessity, for we must hide, and be ever ready to flee.

Now I must ask myself, do you sit and hide in the deep dark places, or do you know the peace of lighted spaces to browse calmly and at leisure?

I know not the answer, for as much as my words suggest, I cannot see what is to come. So, I must have faith. And I must have hope.

That you have emerged from the shadows.

That so, I leave with a warning.

I beg you—heed my words. I speak to you now from the heart of darkness: for I have wandered in its midst and learned its secrets.

Be wary of the dark places.

Pay heed to the shadows.

The darkness waits, as it did aeons ago.

It waits for our weakness, for our folly. Yes, my reader, look up and glance over your shoulder as we near the end. For that which lurks within the shadows beyond the light of lamps still watches.

He is out there. He is coming.

Silas Morlock _lives_.

"The virtue of much literature is that it is dangerous and may do you extreme harm."
John Mortimer

"Language is a virus from outer space."
William S Burroughs

"Words are the most powerful drug used by Mankind."
Rudyard Kipling

"Writing a book is a horrible exhausting struggle, like a long bout of some painful illness."
George Orwell

"A room without books is like a body without a soul."
Cicero

Lexicon

AQUAVEIN: A tough network of tubes that use muscular peristalsis to shunt clean water around the city.

ARCHIDERM: A general term used to indicate the tough integument that covers the architectural surfaces of the city. Consists of a hard hide heavy in collagen and chitin that protects an underlying support matrix for germative and support tissues.

BASELINE: Ground level.

CARRYPOD: Literally a 'pod' for carrying items. These ranges in size from those for carrying personal items, through to larger varieties capable of conveying people or freight.

CHROMOSPORE: Tiny packets of pigment assembled from the raw matter of a *simulacomm* that spread through the animate to provide appropriate colour and hues.

DERM-RAT: A colloquial expression for residents of the city's lower levels. Typically, it refers to youth gangs and itinerant wanders through the city's night life.

DISINCORPORATION: Heavy and prolonged use of the *Gestalt* can exert harmful effects on human physiology, disincorporation being the most severe mode of mortality. Used with care, the *Gestalt* can provide hours of safe existential transcendence. Users are considered responsible enough to police their own tolerance limits, however there are always those who for whatever reason see fit to push the bounds. *MorTek* cannot be held accountable for the irresponsible behaviour of a minority of its consumers.

FOLIO PLAGUES: The name given to a syndrome of contagious agents discovered to be lurking in stockpiled books and journals. Contemporary sources believed the agents to be a legacy of the war, although conspiracy theories abounded to say otherwise. The resulting epidemics so sourced to paper quickly resulted in the medium's timely obsolescence in favour of digital delivery systems. However, with the advent of the forerunner of the *Gestalt* all but a tiny minority had abandoned the concept of books and related material.

GACKING: Using the *Gestalt* or any subordinate technology accessed as a temporary substitute.

GEISTMASQUE: A device worn on the face to blanket the primary senses, but also to safely couple the active components with the client's sub-cranial implant.

GEIST-TEK: Any technology relating to and including the *Gestalt*. Commonly shortened to 'G-Tek'.

GESTALT LAG: *Gestalt* users frequently suffer from the 'lag' especially after prolonged exposure. They are typically slow-witted, clumsy, uncoordinated reflecting their mental disorientation and physical exhaustion, as well as re-adjustment to a four-dimensional frame of existence.

GESTALT NODE: See G-Spot.

GESTALT, THE: The Miracle of MorTek, Morlock's Gift, this esoteric technology has been called many things since its inception, but its fundamental nature has ever remained a mystery. That it grants release from worldly woes is beyond doubt, proven by its position at the heart of human fulfilment. In time, it promises to unleash humanity's deepest, most cherished desire. For some, that is believed to be eternal nirvana; for others, the ascendance of the species to a god-like existence beyond the physical plane.

GORSEDD: The *Incunabula's* Ruling Council. The word is from the Welsh language and means 'throne'. It was originally used in reference to a meeting of bards and druids prior to the annual *eisteddfod*.

G-SPOT: In *Terapolitan* street parlance, this is a reference to a *Gestalt* Node, a facility for accessing the *Gestalt*.

G-TEK: 'Geist-Tek' refers to any technology relating to and including the *Gestalt*.

HABITAT: Personal living space for a *Terapolitan*. In Old World terms an apartment. Entire towers, or those sections of towers given over to residential purposes, are called habitentiaries.

HABITENTIARY: Space is at a premium even in a city such as *Terapolis*. Residents live in blocks of apartments called habitats. The terminology applied to these tower blocks is a habitentiary.

INCUNABULITE: A member of the *Incunabula*.

INTER-REGIS: The prime minister in the Interregnum, the city's governing body. It began existence as a temporary executive committee superseding former national governments as *Terapolis* absorbed the geographic and political entities that had gone before, but in the world of the *Gestalt* has come to linger.

NECROLYSER: Located in the sub-terrestrial entrails of the city's towers and buildings, necrolysers are giant stomachs – part of the structure's organic infrastructure – that digest and recycle waste material and refuse. Commonly, in a city as crowded as *Terapolis*, they are also used to process the remains of the dead. The digested material provides nourishment for the living architecture, as well as basic nutritional material for the habitat residents, via nutrient glands.

PEDEDERM: A thick integument of keratin and chitin enriched tissue, generated from the underlying dermal fabric of the city. The growth provides pedestrian traction for the inhabitants of *Terapolis*. It is similar in nature to the *archidermis*.

SIMULACOMM: A by-product of *Geist-Tek* research. A communications device utilising an esoteric non-atomic material.

SKIN SALOON: A bar or club, where patrons might go to encounter and potentially acquire a casual sex partner. An old world equivalent is 'meat market'.

TUBE WORM: The city's mass-transit system.

Lightning Source UK Ltd.
Milton Keynes UK
UKOW04f2329010817
306502UK00001B/162/P